TOXIC

D0974929

VICKI V. LUCAS

 Fiction *on* *Fire*

Acknowledgments

Life is filled with adventures, though none as unexpected as writing this book. To my wonderful family – Brian, Deidre, Amelia, Tessa, Jesse, Sherry, Carissa, Colin, Candace, Mom and Dad – I love you much and am so blessed to have you in my life. Thank you, Mom, for the countless hours editing and brainstorming with me. Colin Sauskojus, thank you for your map drawing skills and for not laughing hysterically at what I drew. Jolene Burd, thank you for drawing up endless ideas of the cover for me and saving me from nightmares! To my husband, Cade, this would not have been finished if you hadn't been there to pick me up through the down times and celebrate in the up times. Thank you for your edits, advice, and for never letting me quit. I find myself without enough words to tell you how much I love you. Finally, all praise and glory is for God, the giver of life, love, purpose, joy and hope.

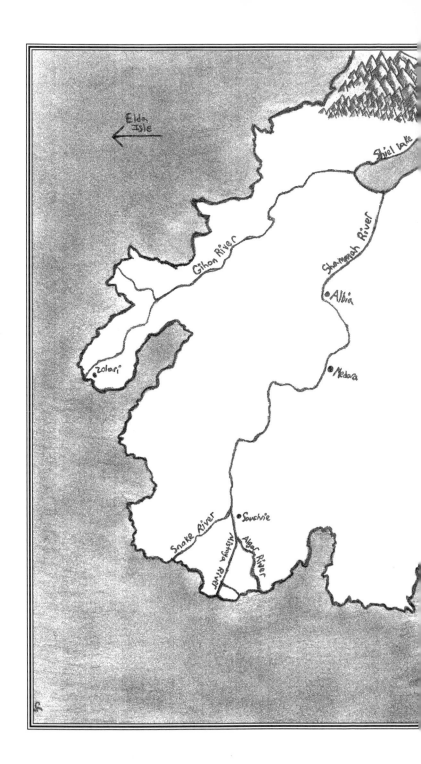

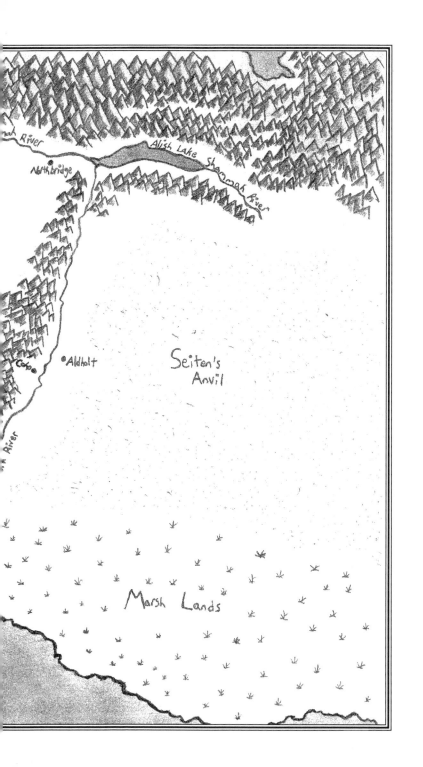

Contents

Shadows
The Night Race ∾ 9
And the Winner Is ∾ 14
Truth and Consequence ∾ 17
Ridiculous Rocks ∾ 26
An Irresistible Invitation ∾ 34

Promises
Should've Brought a Treat ∾ 46
Ups and Downs ∾ 52
Too Bad for Willie ∾ 56
A Walk in the Dark ∾ 60

Tears
The End of the Race ∾ 70
Time for a Tumble ∾ 75
Let's Get Off ∾ 80
A Straight Limb ∾ 85
Swing and Hit ∾ 89

Traps
Kidnapped ∾ 100
Friends and Foes ∾ 108
Packing Priorities ∾ 115
Fish and Rabbits ∾ 121

Changes
Bagboys and Cooks ∾ 134
Gentle Milk Cows ∾ 145
Visit Your Sister ∾ 151
Uncut Gems ∾ 159

Allies

Alone ∾ 169
Dirty Hands ∾ 175
Miracles or Luck ∾ 186
Impossible Deeds ∾ 191
Hidden Secrets ∾ 201

Failures

Spells and Prayers ∾ 216
Oh, Nuts ∾ 224
Man Up ∾ 233
Great Help ∾ 241

Feats

Paper to the Wind ∾ 252
Raspberry Juice ∾ 259
The Best and Worst Day ∾ 264
No Backing Down ∾ 272
Buckets of Rain ∾ 280

Defeats

One with the Unwanteds ∾ 329
Saving the Day ∾ 334
Hopes Fall ∾ 339
Through Doors ∾ 343
Wishes Come True ∾ 349
One Bloody Sword ∾ 355
A Few Inches Too Short ∾ 363
The Way Out ∾ 372
Out of the Frying Pan ∾ 381
This is For ∾ 391
Chosen ∾ 398

Petitions

Unanswered Questions ∾ 291
Shimmering Rocks ∾ 299
Pies in an Oven ∾ 303
It Takes Two ∾ 307
Reasons for Tears ∾ 312
Dreams Come True ∾ 318

SHADOWS

"You can only come to the morning through the shadows."
~J.R.R. TOLKIEN

The wind stirred restlessly through the mountains, roaming far from its home. Ignoring the instruction of the Ancients, the young wind, whose name was Foehn, journeyed to the city nestled in the foothills.

Eager to play, Foehn tugged at people's clothes and tousled the hair of a boy pushing a wheelchair. But the boy just smoothed down his hair, and the people pulled their cloaks closer. Turning their backs, they hustled home and locked him out in the dark. Foehn had never felt sadness or loneliness before. Now those feelings consumed him.

Foehn journeyed until he saw universities dotting the countryside. He entered one quiet bedroom and flipped through pages of a book that belonged to a boy who was studying, but the boy calmly turned the pages back and closed the window. Blocked from the room, the little dry wind heaved a deep sigh and turned to look elsewhere for a friend.

Continuing on, Foehn traveled farther away from home and found musicians playing lively songs. Hope rose like the golden sun in the morning. He joined the dance while a young girl sang a song of heroes. The wind whirled merrily around until the people

moved their party inside a lovely house. Shut out in
the dark, he turned away and resumed his journey.

Foehn moved across the country. His heart sank
into the bowels of dejection like a boulder chucked
heedlessly into the deep ocean. He wondered why
people shunned him. In the mountains of home, the
trees always danced with him. But home was far away,
and he didn't know how to return. He kept looking
for someone, someone who would be a friend.

And then he reached the coast.

There Foehn met up with one of his own kind.
But this new wind caused Foehn to quake. The coastal
wind whipped the ocean with such great force that
Foehn watched from behind some trees. Frothy and
foamy in their protest, the waves reached up into the
blackened sky.

A piece of wood rose and fell with the waves as
it washed up onto the beach. A man, looking half
dead, was draped over the board. Foehn jumped back
in terror when the man raised his head. The man
grabbed a handful of sand. Like magic, the brutal
wind ceased.

"Land." He doubled over in a fit of coughing.

The man stumbled to the trees and gazed up at
the sky as the moon tentatively peeked through the
scattering clouds. Foehn leaned closer to catch a
glimpse of him.

"They said it couldn't be done." His laughter
sounded harsh as it rang through the air, gaining
strength. "I did it, and now the power…so much
power at my fingertips."

He strode through the darkness to an oak tree. He tore a branch off and dug it into his skin. The blood spilled to the dirt as the moon shone down on him. Foehn gasped, now able to see that the man's whole body was covered with bruises and cuts.

The man spoke again. "By full moon's light, take this sacrifice and spread good health. Send energies far and near to heal all that I hold dear. So must it be." He let his blood drain to the earth as he repeated the words three times. His dark eyes glowed red as the dirt hungrily drank up the blood.

Foehn stared as the man trembled suddenly like his whole body were a tender leaf in a vicious wind. The cuts and bruises began to heal, leaving him whole and unscarred.

The man laughed with triumph. "No one will withstand me. All will bow at my feet."

He gazed back across the ocean. "For your gift of magnificent power, my Master, I vow to reclaim this land in honor of you."

Foehn was both terrified and awestruck. He circled above this strange man. When the man began walking, he followed from a distance.

CHAPTER ONE

The Night Race

They say evil lurks in the mountains. They say that if the rivers and cliffs don't kill you, the monsters will. They say there is only one difference between the brave and the stupid.

The brave die a little bit slower...

Kai knew what they said of the mountains. And he knew about the monsters because they were right behind him.

As he raced deeper into the lonely peaks, the tales of the old women sitting in the marketplace haunted him. *You should have listened*, they mocked. *Now you'll die.* He'd laughed at them, but they had been telling the truth: the monsters were real, and they terrified him more than anything he'd known in his sixteen years.

He raced through the darkness up the mountains and paused, clutching his side, gasping for air. He didn't hear any thudding footsteps. Maybe he'd lost them. He waited. The trees surrounding him hid the night sky. Only the sound of rain and his breathing filled the air.

A branch broke behind him. He held his breath. *It's just a deer.* But deep inside, he knew it wasn't. Leaves crunched as loud as thunder. *Something's right behind me.*

The moon darted behind clouds, and he bolted. The shadows lengthened, engulfing him. When the clouds parted, the light of the moon revealed cliffs that led up to towering snowy peaks. The hairs on the back of his neck rose as a distant cry echoed through the peaks. That wasn't a wolf. All the wolves had been killed in the Great Wars. Something more evil roamed the Razors. He turned in a slow circle, following the ragged line of the mountains along the horizon, and then strode to the edge of the cliff.

Northbridge filled the valley below him with hundreds of lights from the houses and inns twinkling like stars. River Shammah, the great river which flowed through Eltiria, curled like a ribbon through the valley. Gazing north, he saw throngs of people hustling over the Great Bridge to the Temple of All to celebrate the Festival of the New Moon. *Fools. The priests can't help you.* They hadn't helped Shona. But no matter how many people died at the Temple, people kept coming to Zoria for help. Maybe it was Her beauty, maybe it was Her power. Maybe they didn't have any other hope.

Thunder rolled and rain spattered on the bushes. A twig snapped in the trees to his right. He crouched in the shadows. Running only attracted predators. And normally he'd rather eat dinner then be dinner. Hiding was better than running.

Lightning flashed. The light fell onto two large figures so close to Kai that he felt like they'd swallow him into darkness. He leaped back with a cry of fear. They stood as still as rocks, their faces lost in their hoods. As thunder rolled, the giant axe in the hands of the creature on the right sparked in the fading light.

"Come with us, little one." The voice slid out of the shadows. "The Master desires you."

Kai wasn't sure what that meant, but it sounded like a bunch of horse manure. He should know. He shoveled the stuff all day.

"We won't kill you," the second one hissed. "But we have ways to make you come, Kai."

"How d... do you know m ... my name?" Kai stumbled over his words.

"Kai Teschner, the son of Tadd Teschner, the great jockey crippled in a racing accident." The first *thing* replied in a dull tone. "You spend your days shoveling out stalls where your Father was once revered."

Kai drew in a sharp breath. He glanced down at the city. One pure beam of light across the valley caught his eye. Alone, on the hillside, the light burned brighter than the others. *Adoyni's shrine. But that shrine was deserted. How can it be lit up like that?* Kai glared at the light. He had prayed and believed, and Adoyni hadn't bothered to help. *Some love.*

The second monster kept talking in a raspy voice. "If you don't come with us, your little sister won't die of her disease like she's about to. No, we'll kill her ourselves."

Kai took a step toward them. "I'm not going with you, and I'm not going to let you touch my family!"

The second monster lowered his hood as a burst of lightning illuminated it. The face, towering over Kai, had pale white skin flaking off in chunks. It looked like moldy cheese, the kind that was white with all the holes in it. But this cheese had been forgotten about for years. Out of two holes, amber eyes glared down at him.

Thunder rolled as the sky lit up again. In front of the creature was Shona. She looked even smaller next to the large creature. Her hazel eyes were wide with fright, her chestnut hair dark in the rain. The axe blade was poised at her throat. Everything went dark.

"Please, Kai," his sister pleaded. Her voice cut him deeper than any axe. "Please, help me. You said you would take care of me. Only you can rescue me."

"Shona! But...you... died." Kai felt the anger drain away as shock took over.

"Kai, do what they say." Shona's voice floated out of the darkness. "Please, rescue me."

"I can't, Shona." Kai's voice broke. "Rhiana's sick. Mom needs help getting money. I can't just leave them."

The lightning flashed again, lingering in the sky. Shona stood with her hand outstretched to Kai. The axe dug deeper into her neck, leaving a red streak on her pale skin. Blood slid down her neck as the axe dropped away. Before Kai could move, her eyes went blank, and she fell to the ground.

Kai yelled. He fell to his knees and crawled to Shona's body as the blood mixed with dirt. Twice he had seen her die. Twice he had failed to save her. Her lifeless hand still reached for him in the mud. He grasped it and held her tight as he fought back the sobs. He had lost one sister twice. He wasn't going to lose another. He'd save Rhiana if he had to fight through these two monsters.

He got to his feet, covered in mud and Shona's blood, and faced the monsters, shaking with rage and grief. He wanted to rip their throats out. But not today. He had to save Rhiana first. Reluctantly, he turned away from Shona and ran deep into the Razors - the very mountains that offered no help, only the promise of horrors.

CHAPTER TWO

And the Winner Is...

Kai rushed up the steep mountains. The rain blinded him as it fell in solid sheets, so violent that it dulled his senses. Pain stabbed his side. He gasped as he forced himself to run faster. Boulders replaced the trees as he climbed higher. He slipped and stumbled on the wet rocks, scraping his hands.

Stones tumbled behind him, and he urged his tired legs to keep moving. He had to escape this nightmare. He staggered as the rain hammered down on him. The lightning flashed, making it impossible to see in the complete darkness that followed. Kai took a step forward, and his foot found nothing but air.

Oh, yeah. That's just great.

He waved his arms wildly in various directions, but he tumbled down the cliff. There was a moment of silence as he hurtled down. He crashed on an overhang of rock and groaned as his body spun and slipped off the edge.

Tree branches smacked his face and rocks gouged his back. Yelling, he madly grabbed at anything to stop his descent. A branch slipped through his hand. Grasping desperately, he grabbed it and held on while his body came to an abrupt stop.

"Ah, ha!" he cried in triumph, his arms feeling like they were jerked out of their sockets. He tried to pull himself up, but his hands slid downwards.

"No, no." His hands cramped with the weight of his body, and his arms screamed with pain. He wiggled to find a foothold, but his squirming caused him to slip another inch.

"Please, no." He wasn't sure who he was talking to, but he didn't care. His grip loosened. In a mad panic, he forced his fingers to tighten around the branch, but it was no good. He plummeted downward as he yelled.

He slammed into the ground and rolled to his back. His whole body ached, but he'd never been so happy to be alive. He'd gotten away from them. He was safe. *Was Shona really alive, or was I just seeing things?* He sobered. *Was she alive all this time only to die now?* He shook his head. He had watched when the priests tried to heal her. He had watched as life left her, as her hand had lost its grip on his.

He sat up slowly, wincing as the blood raced to his head. The clouds parted, and moonlight shone on the cliff. Kai gazed up the rock face. He'd fallen over forty feet. Trees were scattered throughout the sheer rock wall, growing out of stone. *No one will believe me when I tell them about this! What a fall! There's no way those* things *could get down that!*

He stood, feeling the aches over his body. The moon broke out from behind the clouds. Standing right in front of him was one of the monsters. *Seeker!* The name from the fables leaped into his mind as he saw a scaly arm reaching for him. *The servants of the Evil One.*

The moon went behind a cloud, and the night was as dark as the insides of a panther. He jumped away from the monster only to land beside the second Seeker. Kai's eyes were drawn into amber eyes peering down at him.

"We always acquire that which we seek," it grunted.

Kai's feet pinned to the ground. "Leave me alone." He could see a scaly, three-fingered hand reaching for him moving in slow motion.

Only three inches away.

Run! He tensed, ready to bolt.

The hand moved closer. Two inches.

"Don't even think of it," the first Seeker warned. "No one has ever escaped."

Kai remembered Shona with the angry red streak across her throat. He was trapped. He couldn't fight them. He couldn't outrun them.

I've lost. The words circled in his mind. *I've lost. I've lost.*

But he didn't want to lose.

His mind screamed orders to run, but he was trapped like a rabbit. He stared at the scaly hand coming nearer.

Then it tightly gripped his shoulder.

CHAPTER THREE

Truth and Consequence

The forest hushed as the rays of the sun slipped through the branches with the budding leaves. The dust in the air looked like solid pillars of light. Lizzy slid between them in the darkness of the trees. A shadow beneath a giant oak moved. Something was there.

Lizzy took one careful step forward as the branches stirred. She raised her sling and aimed. A bird started to chirp in celebration of the warm weather as she squinted through the rays to see the dim shape. She let the strap go and heard a swish and then a thud. A deer burst out of the trees, unharmed. She watched it scurry through the trees.

"Zoria's blood!" She shot another stone at a leaf high up in a tree. The leaf shuddered and fell to the ground. She stared at it with disgust. *Why is it that I can hit anything I want when it's a leaf or a stick? And yet I miss any* real *target I aim at?*

A branch moved deep in the shadows. She squinted into the darkness. A snap of a branch cracked, loud in the silence. *Another deer's in there!* She drew out a flat rock from the pouch on her belt. It slipped and fell. She bent down, reaching for the stone, her heart beating loud in her ears as she strained for it.

The pounding of her heart disappeared as her head began to buzz.

Peace, daughter. I mean no harm.

Fear inched up her spine, leaving an icy chill. Rica had tormented her for years of strange creatures that could overcome thoughts and control a person to do whatever it wanted. She groped for the rock. The buzzing started again.

I will not hurt you. I am a friend.

She ignored the words. *Yeah, right, you're my friend. Up until the time comes to eat me!*

A chuckle filled her head. *I prefer grass or a special treat of apples.*

Her hands stopped. *It can read my thoughts!* She hunched down like a mouse hiding from a hawk. The trees swayed as if something large was walking through them. She gripped her sling as the branches parted. A white horse's head appeared. The small ears were pricked forward. A long white forelock covered the dark eyes that gleamed behind it.

Lizzy screamed and dashed through the trees until she could see the gates of Albia. She stopped running by the River Shammah. She didn't even notice the stench of the water as she gasped. *What was that about? Was that horse a monster, or was it trying to escape, too?* She took a deep breath.

She saw the sun dropping to the horizon. *Dinner! I'm in trouble!* Mother didn't allow the fear of death to affect her strict schedule. Dashing through the large stone gates, she slowed when she reached the market. The crowd who came to be cured of their illnesses had grown so large that she could barely walk through. Soldiers with long swords at their hips pushed people aside as they patrolled for troublemakers. They sauntered around, watching for anyone starting a protest. Last week the crowd had rioted over the price of water. They marched on the king's palace, and one girl was killed when the soldiers responded. Now all protests were illegal.

Someone had painted "Free water for all" on a wall of a booth selling clean water. She didn't quite understand why they were fighting. Everyone needed water. It wasn't a privilege for the rich. She sighed and stepped around a man lying in the gutter with a bucket out for aid.

The sign by his feet read, "Wife dead. Two children sick. No money. Please help."

Everyone passed by without a second glance. She fingered the money in her pocket. Her coin could help him, but Mother said to buy a dress. She stood there while the press of the crowd swirled around her. *Who cares about a dumb dress?* She threw her remaining coins in his bucket.

Lizzy marched deeper into the market, trying to ignore the other sick people. She loved it here, normally. But there weren't any fresh strawberries from northern Edgemont, or fish from Maruba in the south, or pastries with the delightful scent of *tsambi* anymore.

The vegetables for sale were brown and sickly, and the last of the meat looked bad. There was water, though. For now. Crowds clustered around the booths advertising clean water from Maruba. *In a few weeks, the whole world will have no water to drink. Will the Chancellor actually save us?* She fought back the panic that rose.

She pushed through the crowds until she was home. Mother's carriage was in front of their large white house. She passed the decorative columns, went through the dark oak door, and collided into Mother in the hall. The look on her face reminded Lizzy of a cat staring down a dog in its territory.

"Where have you been?" Mother snapped. Her long black hair was pulled back in a tight bun. Her voice, so rich and tender when she sang, was as tight as strings on a guitar.

"Shopping." Lizzy's heart sank. She hadn't seen Mother this angry since Dad left.

"And just *what* did you buy?" Mother shot back. "I see no dress in your hands."

Lizzy slowly pulled her new green and white sling out of her pocket. "I don't see why I have to buy a formal dress when we're all going to die."

Mother looked at the sling like it was poison and snatched it away from Lizzy. "We are not going to die, although you may soon wish to. For now, go to your room and clean up."

Lizzy began to protest. "But…"

Mother interrupted, her tone as sharp as a stagecoach driver's whip. "For once in your life, be the kind of daughter I always wanted."

Lizzy felt like she'd been slapped. She knew Mother was consistently disappointed with her, but she had never said it out loud. The words beat like a loud bass drum pounding out the wrong rhythm. She ran up the stairs and into her bedroom without a word.

Dad couldn't wait to get away from here, and Mother hates me. She sat by the window and gazed out over Albia. *If only I could go back five years when everyone was happy, when we told stories that made everyone laugh, and sang, and danced.* But those times were past, and now she heard Mother's awful words echoing in her mind, a bad song that you cannot forget. *Be the kind of daughter I always wanted.*

Mother opened the door slowly. She took two steps toward Lizzy and stopped like she was repulsed to come closer. "I can't take your disrespect anymore."

"It was just one day in the woods," Lizzy defended herself. "I don't see why that's such a horrible thing."

"I'm tired of your disobedience. You will still go with Rica to Northbridge." Mother scowled at her. "But once Chancellor Belial has purified the water, you will return here."

"But you said we could stay with Dad for a while," Lizzy protested but stopped when Mother lifted her hand up as a command to be silent. Lizzy stomped to her bed and flopped down.

Mother continued. "When you come back, you will act like a civilized person. I will tame this gypsy wildness of yours that your Father gave you. Your musical abilities aren't good enough, and you're not pretty enough for plays, but I'll find something you can do by the time you return."

Lizzy bit back her angry words.

"Clean up for dinner. We don't want to look at you like this." Mother didn't wait to hear anything Lizzy had to say as she left the room.

Lizzy punched her pillow, knowing that Mother would hear her if she screamed. She gulped back the tears and went to the gilded mirror. No wonder she wasn't the daughter Mother wanted. Her long auburn hair was sticking up all over the place. Her eyes were red, and her face was streaked with dirt and tears. *If I were prettier, she'd love me better.* She washed her face, combed the tangles out of her hair, and went to the dining room.

Rica was standing beside the big brick fireplace. He was watching the servants bring the food. One maid risked a glance at him, and he glared at her. The girl dropped the bread on the table. Lizzy saw her hands shaking as the maid hastened to brush off the tablecloth. *What's he so angry about?*

Rica frowned at her. "We've been waiting for you."

She saw the terrified maid scurry back to the safety of the kitchen. "Why'd you do that? You didn't have to scare her."

"Just look at you! Fifteen years old, and you're giving your older brother lessons in manners.

Manners for servants, no less!" Rica sighed. "She's just a servant. It's not like she has feelings. I'd be surprised if she still remembers her scare."

She opened her mouth to protest, but Mother waltzed in like she was on stage. She greeted Rica with a big smile and swept him to the table without a glance at Lizzy.

"You must be starving, Rica," Mother said, passing the meat to him. "I know you were busy getting ready for the trip."

Lizzy knew he was upset. He didn't normally frighten servants for nothing. *It must be because he doesn't want to leave his precious girlfriend. He probably loves her more than me.* His next words confirmed her suspicions.

"Mother, I know you are trying to look after us, but I'm not comfortable leaving Gwyneth. I want to stay and make sure she is okay." Rica handed her the beef.

"She's not your wife yet," Mother replied. "Her father is one of the wealthiest bankers in Albia. I'm sure he can take care of her."

"Why do we even have to go?" The words burst out of Lizzy's mouth before she could stop them. "Die here or die there. What's the difference?"

"We've been over this," Mother sighed angrily. "Chancellor Belial told me personally that he will be purifying the water at Northbridge. The water will be clean there first, giving Rica a better chance of survival. The topic is closed."

Lizzy glared at the potatoes on her plate. *She didn't say anything about me surviving. I bet she wants me to die. Then she wouldn't have to worry about me causing any more problems.*

Rica took a drink of his water and set down his goblet. "I had a weird thing happen at the temple today."

Lizzy glanced up from her food. *Religion.* Only Gwyneth could get him to do anything religious. He'd do the stupidest things for that girl. Rica had told her to take care of herself because no god or goddess cared about her, and now he was following Gwyneth right into the temple he used to scoff.

"A priest started asking about our family. He wanted to know if we were related to The Slayers. Do you know?" Rica asked.

"The Slayers?" Mother laughed. "The three warriors who defeated Seiten? They're just stories to entertain children."

Rica shifted back in his chair. "It was just so weird because he was so insistent. I was a little afraid of what he might do."

"You, afraid of something?" Lizzy risked Mother's attention because Rica was never scared of anything.

"Well, not scared." Rica winked at her. "Not like you that time we saw…"

"Maybe he saw you singing about the Slayers once," Mother cast an exasperated look at Lizzy. "Lizabeth, you need to go through your suitcases and sort out only what you need for a few weeks. Then go to bed."

"But I'm not finished eating," Lizzy said before she could stop herself.

"You would've had more time if you hadn't disobeyed me today. Do what you are told."

Lizzy pushed her chair back and dashed to the room. *Why is she always so mean to me? I can't make her love me no matter what I do.* She threw clothes from her bag to the bed. Angry tears streaked down her cheeks, and she wiped them away impatiently. She plopped down in the middle of the floor. *Maybe if I brought her some purified water, she'd love me for saving her life. That's what I'll do. I'll save her life, and then she'll always love me.*

CHAPTER FOUR

Ridiculous Rocks

The scaly hand of the Seeker drew closer, the claws on the three fingers reaching to him. Kai knew he was trapped. "No, please, no," he whimpered.

The Seeker grabbed him and shook his shoulder. "Kai, wake up. I don't feel good."

He blinked. The small hand on his shoulder had five fingers. Rhiana's voice cut through the storm. He sat up and hit his head on the roof above his bed. Rain splattered on the window.

"What are you doing?" He didn't mean to snap, but his heart was still beating fast.

"I don't feel good, and I heard you talking in your sleep. What were you dreaming about?"

She stood at the edge of his bed. Her white nightgown made her look thinner and bleached her skin even more. Her hair, normally the warm color of the nuts in the market, was brittle and thin. She trembled from the exertion of standing. *She does not look like Shona did before she died.* Kai refused to admit that Rhiana was dying of the very same disease. He got up and plopped her on the bed.

"I dreamt Shona was still alive," he said. "But then there were monsters chasing me."

Rhiana snuggled down and giggled. "You're still scared of monsters." She sobered. "I'm just scared of dying."

Kai picked up his breeches off the floor. "I already told you. I'm not letting you die, so stop talking about it. You're going to be fine. Now close your eyes."

Rhiana pulled the covers over her head. "Did she talk to you?"

Kai pulled his shirt over his head before answering. *What do I tell her? That I saw Shona die?* "Yeah," he said, running his hands through his hair. "She said to tell you to stop asking so many questions and to stop touching her stuff."

"Liar!" Rhiana screeched as he scooped her up. "She would never say such things."

"She would, too." Kai made his way to Rhiana's room. She was lighter than a pillow. He swallowed down panic as he realized how fast she was fading away. "You two were always arguing."

Rhiana sighed. "She wouldn't answer all of my questions."

"Not even Adoyni could answer all your questions." Kai laughed as he kicked her bedroom door open. Shona's presence in the room made him wince. He could still hear her voice from his dream. *I didn't save her.* He placed Rhiana on her bed carefully. It felt like the slightest bump would break her in two. As she pulled the blue quilt up, a glint of light around her neck sparked.

"Why are you wearing that crystal?" Kai asked. "Mom said she'd throw it out if it didn't help Shona."

Rhiana put her hand over the necklace protectively. "It's pretty, and Mom said it might make me feel better. I think it is working."

He raised his eyebrows. "Well, it certainly made Shona better." It was sarcastic, but he couldn't stop himself. All he wanted to do was to throw that dumb crystal away.

Rhiana's eyes filled with tears, making him feel like dirt. Kai bit back his irritation. *How in the world does she go from laughing to crying so fast?* The crystal glittered in the sunlight again. He ran his fingers through his hair. *Why does this bother me so much?*

"Sorry, Rhiana," he apologized. "Just take it off, okay? It's not good for you."

Rhiana's eyes grew dark. "It was blessed by the Goddess. Nothing else can help me."

"It's a rock." His irritation slipped into his words. "How can a rock heal you?"

"You don't understand," Rhiana cried out. Tears streamed down her face. "You want me to die, and you don't care. Just get out of my room!"

Kai stomped to the door. "I do care! That's why I want you to take it off!"

A pillow flew past him and hit the wall with such force that Kai turned back. Her hair was messed up, but her dark eyes flashed with rage. She looked like a wild animal ready to kill.

"Rhiana, I do care," he repeated softer. "I would do anything to make you better."

She blinked and began to tremble. Shivers racked her body as she lay down. He went back to the bed and pulled the quilt up, ignoring the crystal that she still held in her hand.

When he finished, she reached her free hand out of the covers and squeezed his hand. "You have to save me, Kai. I'm afraid of the Temple. If I go there, I'll die. It won't be easy for you. But there's a way. Just like in the stories. You won't believe it, but you got to do it. Promise me you'll do it." Her words came in loud gasps. "Promise I don't have to go to the Temple. Please."

"Everything will be all right. I'll make sure you don't die. Now get some rest." He freed his hand and tiptoed to the door. When he closed the door, he caught a glimpse of her. She had a slight smile even though her eyes were closed.

He leaned against the wall in the hallway and groaned. *What in all of Eltiria can I do for her?* The smell of bacon frying made his stomach grumble with hunger. He made his way down the rickety stairs and entered the kitchen. Dad was at the old scarred wooden table. *I'd be taller than him if he could stand. Why don't I look like either of them?* Mom said he was a throwback from some tall ancestor with golden brown hair and blue eyes, but he knew she was just trying to make him feel better.

Dad grunted *good morning* but did not look at him. As Kai settled into a chair, he wondered what it would be like to have a real conversation with Dad. Mom smiled and served up scrambled eggs and bacon as he sat down.

"Rhiana's not coming down," he said. "She's worse today."

"I'll take her up some eggs in a bit," Mom said. She placed some toast on the table and ran a hand over Shona's empty chair, as if a simple caress could bring Shona back or soothe her raw grief.

Kai paused, waiting for the prayer before eating, but no one mentioned it. He gave up waiting and dug into the eggs and bacon.

Dad glanced up from his plate. "I want you to bring home some pure water from the stables, Kai. Don't forget."

Kai glanced at Mom. *Hasn't she told him that there's not much water left?* Mom glared at him with a look that would fry the eggs on the table if they weren't already cooked. He was sure it was starting to burn the toast.

She answered before Kai could swallow his eggs. "He won't be able to get it. The owners are paying such high prices for it that they are watching every drop."

So she hasn't told him. Why is she hiding the truth from him? We only have a few weeks left. Kai shifted in his seat.

"Well, I can't grow vegetables without it. And we can't afford to buy more water." Dad's voice rose in anger. "All he needs to do is bring back a bucket."

Kai finished his milk. "It'd probably be easier to steal a horse and squeeze the water out. Did you know that Maruba is almost out of water?"

"Kaison Alaric Teschner! You shouldn't spread rumors!" Mom scowled at him.

Dad frowned. "Why wouldn't you tell me? Do you think I'm too crippled to handle it?"

"You have enough to worry about. I didn't want to burden you more," Mom defended.

"Well, I sure wouldn't be worrying about how we're going to eat if I knew we're going to die in a few weeks," Dad replied angrily. There was a long pause, and then he sighed. "The Chancellor is a great man, but there are too many problems for just one man to solve. Did you know Jesh next to me hasn't come to his booth for two days? His stuff is right there on the table. It's like he just disappeared. What's weird is that no one's stealing it." He shrugged. "Maybe it's cursed."

Mom put her fork on the table. "Chancellor Belial will fix the river on the first day of spring. He's even coming here to do it, so we don't have to worry. Then he'll take care of everything else."

"Why is Rhiana wearing that crystal?" Kai changed the subject. "It didn't help Shona."

"It's been blessed by Zoria," Mom sighed. "It helped a lady I work with."

"It's a stupid stone!" Kai couldn't stop. "How's a rock supposed to take away diseases? This is why we can't pay the rent. I'm going to have to get a second job to pay for a healer for Rhiana, and you're spending all the money on ridiculous rocks!"

Dad cleared his throat. "Kai, it's time for you to go to work now."

"I guess it is. Someone around here has to make all the money. Maybe I'll earn enough today for you to buy a pebble that will make us rich." Kai slammed the chair into the table. "Have a great day wasting money while I'm working."

He banged the door shut and trotted through the narrow streets of Northbridge, dodging the puddles. The sun was trying to peek out from the clouds, but Kai knew it didn't have a chance. The clouds intensified his black mood. He detested living in the middle of the city, especially now that it was flooded with people going to the Temple to be healed.

He sighed. He didn't mean to yell at Mom. *Why doesn't something go right for once?* As he turned the corner onto the main road, the din from the crowds made his head spin. He hated everything about the city, the noise, the garbage, the tightness of the narrow streets, the buildings made with stone and thatched roofs.

The only good thing was that horses were everywhere, from the names of the inns, to the decorations on the lamp pools. Booths lined both sides where the merchants sold souvenirs of small statues of famous horses and jockeys. Kai scanned one table to see if Dad's image was there, but it wasn't.

He picked up a statue and pictured his face on it. Seeing the merchant approaching, he put the figure back and wondered if they had statues of stable boys. Maybe he could start a new fad. Tables lined with images of men carrying shovels and pushing wheelbarrows. Signs that said, "New statue! Kai Teschner. None like him before!"

He snorted as the table lit up with weak sunshine. Glancing up at the eastern hills, he groaned. The sun had risen higher than the mountains. "I'm dead!" He darted down the road. He hadn't told Mom, but if Timo caught him coming in late again, he'd lose his job. *Dad may be in a wheelchair, but he'd still find a way to kill me.* He ran even faster.

CHAPTER FIVE

An Irresistible Invitation

Taryn stared out the window as Mischa prattled about ancient battles. *Why is Father making me study? No one else is.* The street below his window looked like all of Albia was taking a holiday. And why not? With death looming at the door, it seemed worthless to do anything productive.

Mischa's voice droned on like the battles he was describing. Taryn tried to pay attention, but the people in the street kept his attention. The crowds parted. Taryn caught a flash of red hair against a blue dress. *Teacher Nephesus!* She was carrying papers as she hurried down the street. As she passed the front door of Taryn's house, a paper slipped from her hands, drifted on the breeze, and landed on his lawn.

"Wait!" Taryn cried out. Mischa looked up from the book he was reading out loud. Taryn leaped to his feet. "I'll be back!"

He dashed down the stairs and out the door. A white parchment was lying on the grass. He picked it up, but Teacher Nephesus was nowhere to be seen.

"Stars above!" Taryn exclaimed. "Where'd she go?"

He pushed through the press of the crowd and saw a flash of red turning the corner. He ducked around the group of women chatting on the side of the road and jogged to the corner.

"Teacher Nephesus!" Taryn shouted. "Wait up!"

Nighthawk Nephesus stopped and turned, shifting her papers and books to her other hand. Taryn trotted up to her.

"You dropped this," he panted. "By my house."

"Why, thank you," she smiled, her brown eyes lighting up with delight. "Taryn, right? Taryn Wallick?"

"Yes, Teach…I mean, ma'am," he stuttered. Although he had taken classes in the Temple with her, he'd never talked to her before.

He never realized that she was so short. She came to his shoulders, but her poise and dignity made Taryn feel small. Her copper hair was streaked with touches of gray that made her look wise. The blue dress was lined with silver embroidery down the sleeves and at the hem small blue shoes poked out. There was a silver belt around her waist with a large key hanging on it. Her brown eyes shone with the intelligence and wisdom of her years as a great seer.

She smiled up at him. "Just call me Nighthawk, Taryn. There's no need for titles between friends. Now let's see what I dropped."

She called me *a friend!* His heart thudded in his ears as he felt his face getting hot. Like an idiot, he realized he was still holding her paper.

"Here," he stammered. "I saw you drop it."

She glanced at the paper. A smile of triumph grew over her face. "Oh, this is just a pamphlet." She paused and then held it out for him. "You should keep it. I would love to see you at this event."

With trembling hands, he took the pamphlet back. Big bold words were splashed across the front. *Explore Your Hidden Power!* There was going to be a conference in three days in Northbridge. Four days of meetings at the Temple of All with classes like Finding Your True Name, Discovering the Hidden Secrets of the Stars, and Tapping into Your Power.

"You should come," Nighthawk said. "After the classes, Chancellor Belial and I are going to pick the best student to help us purify the river. If you find your true name, you could be the one."

Taryn felt a surge of excitement shoot through him. Looking at the pamphlet, he knew two things: Nighthawk Nephesus would help him find his true name, and with it, he would purify the river and become the greatest seer in history.

Nighthawk lightly touched his hand. "Taryn, your special talents are needed. Don't let your father stand in front of your destiny. I'll see you in Northbridge."

She slipped away in the crowd before he could say anything. He stared after her with the pamphlet still in his hands.

"What are you doing in the middle of the street?"

The words broke his thoughts, and he jumped with surprise. Father was standing beside him, glaring at him like he'd done something wrong.

"Look!" Taryn held out the pamphlet. "I just talked to Nighthawk Nephesus! Can you believe that? She gave me this. She said they need me to go to Northbridge."

Father took the paper with a disgusted look on his face. Noting the suspicion in Father's hazel eyes, Taryn started to think this might not go the way he'd planned. He'd failed to calculate Father's distaste of religion. He only believed in the math equations that he taught every day at the university.

"Hidden power? Astrology?" The words sounded silly when Father read it out loud. "You weren't going to pursue this anymore. You said that you couldn't even find your true self."

"True name," Taryn corrected, folding his arms over his chest. "I just needed more time. The Goddess doesn't work in time frames like we do. At the Temple of All in Northbridge, I'll be able to access it."

"True self, true name, it's all the same thing." Father took off his glasses. "You had one semester to amuse yourself. It's over, and now you're behind in your studies."

"I don't care about those studies, Pater." His childish name for Father slipped out before he could stop it. "This is more important than math equations." He knew as soon as those words popped out that they were a bad choice.

"It's frivolous. You would have a more beneficial career if you chose something like medicine or law." Pater started toward the house. "All of this foolishness is from your mother. She was always fixated on religion. It is something you must surmount, and I'll do everything within my power to guarantee you do."

"But being a seer is my destiny." Taryn's words tripped over each other in their hurry to get out of his mouth.

"You're sixteen. What do you know of destiny?" Pater snorted. "You are not going to squander your life away. Put this rubbish out of your mind."

With a totally careless manner, Father crumbled the pamphlet into a ball and stuffed it in his pocket. Taryn bit back a cry of anger as he saw it being treated like garbage.

Taryn followed Father to the house. He realized that although they may look alike with their matching hazel eyes and blonde hair, they would never think alike. And they would never agree about his future. Father didn't say a word to him until they closed the front door.

"I lack the time to peruse your report. Tell Mischa..." Father held up a hand. "I'll write it out for you. You don't have the mental capacity to remember with that poppycock in your head."

Taryn was standing close enough to see what his father wrote. "Taryn needs to be propelled into deeper studies of law and focus heavily on medicine. I expect to see improvement in all his studies by this time next week." He signed it and handed it to Taryn.

"I study all day as it is," Taryn protested.

"You study your astrology books." Pater put on his spectacles, a sure sign that their conversation was finished. "It's time to settle down to real life."

Taryn watched Father leave. *I want my pamphlet back!* But the door closed before he could say anything. He shoved his hands in his pockets. *He never understands!* His hand felt something in his pocket. He pulled out a ball of paper in his hand and carefully opened it. The pamphlet!

He laughed with triumph. *Of course the Goddess would return it to me!* Now he had to get to Northbridge and seize his destiny. Excitement tingled across his skin as he thought of the great things he would do with his power.

"I'll show you, Father. You'll see I'm a great seer!"

He carefully put it in the pocket by his heart. Ignoring the sitting room with its rich velvet curtains, he strode through the formal dining room. Kicking Pater's chair at the large oak table, he went into the deserted kitchen to make a snack. He made a sandwich, his fingers moving mechanically as he tried to sort out his problem. *How can I get Father to let me go to Northbridge?* Pouring water from a gilded glass pitcher, he watched the crystal clear liquid tumble into his glass. *How could something so natural cause such a horrible death?* They said over three thousand people had died in Hedgewoods. *What would happen when it reached Maruba?* He shook his head. *How did the king let this happen? How could no one notice our main river dying until it was too late?*

Taking his sandwich and glass of water with him, he slowly climbed the stairs that curled to the second floor where Mischa was waiting. At the top of the stairs, he paused, munching on his sandwich, and looked at the painting in the hallway. It was a picture of Mom and Father before he was born. Pater posed with his chin up in the air and a somber expression on his face.

It was Mom that drew Taryn's attention. She had long golden hair and a twinkle in her sea-green eyes. But it was not her hair or the color of her eyes that was so compelling. Her smile lit up her whole face and made him smile when he looked at it. The longing to know her piled up like homework on the first day of class.

She hadn't let Father steal her joy. It was there on her face. And then the perfect plan fell like a star from heaven. It was so good he was almost surprised by his genius. He gulped down the rest of the sandwich and threw the schoolroom door open. He tripped over his feet as he entered the room. "Mischa, you'll never believe it!"

Mischa put down his papers. "So, you're back?"

Taryn closed the door and winced as it slammed shut. "I saw Pater, and I told him how much I was enjoying the history lessons. He encouraged me to study more extensively in that area." He had purposely used the childish name for Father, thinking Mischa would think he had connected with Father.

"You're excited about history?" Mischa's gaze was one of those looks that made Taryn sweat, even if he knew the answer. "I thought you are only interested in the future."

"I was, but your stories of The Slayers are so fascinating. Pater suggested we go to Northbridge." Taryn laid his glasses on his desk.

Silence hung in the air. *Please let this work, Great Zoria.*

"I thought it was a good idea." Taryn almost believed his own lie. "I haven't ever traveled anywhere, and it would broaden my mind to travel."

Mischa smiled. "Broaden your mind? Didn't I say that when I forced you to read classic literature?"

"You did?" Taryn forced a smile, suddenly ashamed of deceiving his teacher. "Please, we could leave tomorrow."

Mischa tapped his chin, thinking. "You're right. It would be good for you to travel, and who can focus with all of the upheaval going on? I will take you."

"Really?" Taryn let his breath out in one large puff. He fell into a chair. "I'll study harder than ever when we return."

"Oh, I'm not worried about that," Mischa drawled. Taryn couldn't tell if he was being sarcastic or serious. Then he ordered Taryn to open his books, and it was back to law.

He had a hard time containing his glee, even as he turned to the section on *Dissertations Concerning Hiasuits.* The lie made him feel a bit uncomfortable, but he had a feeling that his real life, the one he had always been denied, was going to start tomorrow. He tried to brush aside the shadow of fear that grew in him. *Tonight I'll do it.* Tonight he would dedicate himself to Zoria. *Once I take my place at Nighthawk's side, I'll be able to control my life.*

But the feeling of dread remained.

PROMISES

"That which was promised must be performed."
~Unknown

Foehn circled high in the sky while he followed the man to Northbridge. From his vantage point, he could see all the way from the Razors to the southern sea. He studied the land with disgust. It was early spring, and yet the barren fields and brown rivers looked like winter. A stink rose from the ground, like the stench of death. The only place that looked alive was Sauchrie. But for how long? River Shammah flowed from the north, and the toxic water was slowly working its way farther south. Nothing would survive for much longer.

Foehn shuddered. Thousands had drunk the water and perished. Ghost towns littered the countryside where people had left or just died. Or disappeared. Numbers of people from the capital of Medora to the smallest village in the northern mountains had vanished. A great cry had gone up, asking the king to find these people. But Foehn knew that they would never be found. He knew what had happened to them. He trembled again.

The man entered Northbridge. People lined the streets glowing with hope as he stopped to talk to them. Foehn remembered the first words the man had spoken to him. How could he ever forget the joy and excitement they brought?

He had cautiously followed the man at a distance that night, curiosity slowly overpowering shyness. The days on the plains were cold, and the nights hinted of frost. Each night he put out his hands and called forth water and vegetables from the earth.

Foehn gained courage as the man continued his slow journey. On the fourth night, the cold attacked with a vengeance, determined to eradicate all summer heat. Barely clothed, the man shivered in the attack. Gently blowing through the field, Foehn crept forward. The man sat in a pentacle drawn in the dirt with his eyes closed and hands outstretched. His lips moved, but his voice was quiet. As clear as the morning birds, the words sang to his ears. The wind stopped moving and let the man's words roll over it like waves of the sea.

"Gentle wind. Please stir my coals. Bring life to the flames."

Foehn wanted to dance across the empty fields. This was the first time anyone had spoken to him. He was needed to stir the coals and help this man. The ancients said to flee from such requests, but this was such a simple thing that couldn't hurt to help. He could not turn his back on this appeal. Foehn blew on the coals. Fire leaped into the air.

The man dropped his hands and smiled. "Thank you."

Foehn felt a glow as warm as the fire crackling below. And the next morning came. When the man got up again, he asked Foehn to come and serve him. Foehn didn't hesitate. He vowed to never leave this man's side. And so the little wind followed him across the barren plains to the great capital past the golden gates and up into the halls of the palace of the king.

CHAPTER SIX

Should've Brought a Treat

Kai sprinted to the stables. The road led past the Temple of All as it left the city behind. The crowds grew larger as he approached the Temple. He glared at the cedar archways lined with ivy. The courtyard was filled with beautiful flowers and fountains of water. Everything about it emphasized life. Kai only saw death. Shona's body lying on the cobblestones sprung to his mind, and he pushed the people aside to get out of the throng.

Timo was serious when he had said that he would fire Kai for being late again. It wasn't that he didn't want to work. The work was not as good as being a jockey, but at least he was around horses. *Could I tell Timo about Deston...?* He shoved the thought aside. He would take care of his own problems and not run to Timo like a crybaby.

The road followed River Shammah out of the city toward the racing stables. The river had lost the bright blue color with the taint, and it flowed sullenly. It reeked like death, killing everything close to it. Kai shuddered as he thought of all the water in Eltiria poisoned. It had started only a year ago, with just one river poisoned, and now the whole world was on the brink of death. *Who would poison us? Or was it just an accident? And how come the king can't fix it?* But the question that was even harder to answer replaced all the others. *How long will we survive?* Mom believed that Chancellor Belial would fix the problem on the first day of spring, but Kai didn't believe in promises anymore. *The only thing I can be sure of is what I do.*

The road left the river and climbed steeper hills as it led closer to the mountains with their peaks still covered with snow. A large wooden sign announced the renowned Shalock Stables. Kai was always hopeful when he saw it. This was where Dad rode his way to fame. One day he would ride just like Dad did and lift his family out of despair. One day he would prove to the world he was his father's son. One day he would ride faster than the wind.

Kai dashed through the gates, dodging the preparations for the Opening Ceremonies of the Chelten Festival - the biggest event of Northbridge. There were two weeks of horse races over traditional tracks, cross country across open fields and deep into the mountains. From night races to bareback races, the horse that completed all races in the fastest time was crowned the Grand Champion. This year, Kai knew that Kedar was the horse to win. The owners were always generous when they won, and rewards were always given to everyone, even the stable boys. That extra money may save Rhiana, if she could hold on that long.

He slowed his step as he entered the largest barn in Shalock Stables. Stallions stretched their long necks over the gates to welcome him. The smell of horses and leather greeted him as he walked down the wide aisle lined with fifty stalls. *And some people think this stinks.* He took a deep breath, letting the aroma wash away the anger of the morning.

"Kai!" Timo burst out of the office. Normally calm, today he seemed frantic. His gray hair stood straight up. "Where have you been? Get Kedar and bring him here. Chancellor Belial wants to see him before he races. And make sure to mind your manners."

Kai grabbed the nearest lead rope and hustled to the stall, hope soaring. Chancellor Belial not only owned the best horses, he was the King's beloved advisor, even taking the place of the king's lost son. Kedar was waiting eagerly for him to bring his treats. Kedar's temper would match his black coat unless you had something sweet for him.

Kai felt his pockets but couldn't find the treats he normally kept. "Sorry, old boy," he said. "No time to get one. Later."

Kai stepped in the stall. Kedar snorted as if offended. Before he could hook the rope to his halter, the black horse shoved Kai into the wall with his large head.

"Ow! That hurt." He pushed on Kedar's big neck.

Kedar took a step away, holding his head high and rolling his eyes back. The one white snippet on his forehead showed as his long forelock fell away from his face.

"Now, relax," Kai continued in a calmer tone. "I know the storm's got you worried, and I didn't bring a treat, but if you come along nicely, I'll get you one afterwards."

Kedar heaved a big sigh and dropped his head. Kai smiled. *It's like he actually knows what I'm saying.* But he watched for more antics as he snapped the lead rope on the halter. Kedar hesitated as if to show that he still wasn't pleased and followed Kai to the office door.

Chancellor Belial strode into the aisle like he had all the power of a king. He was taller than Kai, but he looked like he'd never been out in the sun. His peppered hair slicked back and his dark eyes were highlighted with black eyeliner making his skin look even whiter.

Timo introduced him. "This is Tadd Teschner's son, Kai Teschner. I knew his father and I know him, and Kai has all the horse sense that his father had."

The Chancellor barely looked at Kai. "Does he now?" His voice was smooth as he walked around the horse. Kedar pawed at the cobblestones. "If he does, why does Kedar look like a wild horse? It looks like he hasn't been groomed for ages."

Kai glanced over Kedar. His dark coat was a little messy, but he wasn't dirty. "Sir, I groom him every day. Perhaps you don't know much about horses, but he just needs a light brushing."

Belial seemed to be aware of Kai for the first time. He gave Kai the same look that he had given Kedar. Kai felt like he was an animal being scrutinized, and a chill swept his body. He looked away, unable to meet Belial's steady stare. Kedar took advantage of Kai's distraction and reared. The rope burned as it pulled through his hands. Belial leaped back as the black hooves struck close to his face. Timo jumped past Kai to grab the rope.

"Are you trying to kill me?" Belial snapped.

Kedar pranced and snorted, shaking his big black head while Kai took the rope back from Timo and struggled to calm the wild horse. They circled as Kai attempted to soothe Kedar.

Timo apologized to Belial. "My lord, our deepest apologies. Horses are always more edgy when there is a storm coming. And I'd bet my last Flame Kedar knows there is a race today."

"That may be." Belial glared at Kai. "But that stable boy's no good. I don't want him anywhere around Kedar."

Kai froze, the horse forgotten. Kedar reared again. The jerk on the rope felt like his arm was going to be pulled out of his socket. Kai struggled to keep Kedar under control. *What's wrong with him?* He didn't have time to respond.

"But, sir," Timo protested. "Kai's the best we have when it comes to Kedar. No one else can get that stallion to do anything if he's not around."

"Find someone else," the Chancellor bit out. "Money's not an issue. Get that Deston kid that rode the last race for me. He's good with horses."

"Not as good as Kai, Chancellor," Timo pleaded. "Don't judge him because Kedar is a little jumpy today."

"I don't like him," Belial said with finality. "He reminds me too much of his father, and that's one reminder I don't need. Get rid of him. I don't want him around any of my horses."

Without waiting for a response, Belial swept out of the barn as regal as a king. Kai stopped fighting Kedar. Timo took the lead before the big black horse felt the slack in the rope.

"I'm sorry, kid," Timo said gruffly, his blue eyes darker without their usual twinkle. "We'll work something out."

"But he owns every horse you work with." Kai fought down the rising panic. "If I don't have a job, Rhiana…"

"Something will work out," Timo said a little louder. Kedar shied and snorted.

Not if Belial has anything to do with it. The thought lingered in the air, unsaid. Whatever Belial did prospered, so everyone imitated him. If he fired someone, no one hired that person. Kai knew of several jockeys that were now teaching little girls how to ride ponies because they had lost a race on one of Belial's horses.

"Here." Kai reached for Kedar's rope. "I'll put him up."

Timo sighed. "Not any more. I can't go against the Chancellor's orders."

Kai ran his hand through his hair and bit back his anger. "So that's it." He took a deep breath. *No more job. No more money. And when Kedar wins, I won't get that bonus. And there won't be any money for Rhiana.* He groaned and walked into the rain without another word.

CHAPTER SEVEN

Ups and Downs

Kai slumped against the barn. Dark clouds hung low in the sky, hiding the mountain peaks. Thunder rolled in the distance. He couldn't go home and tell them that he'd lost his job. He pictured Mom and Dad's disappointed faces and grimaced. *What are we going to do?* It was not fair. Everyone else his age was training in their chosen occupations. No one was burdened with all these troubles that he had no idea how to fix.

"So, your Dad can't stay on a horse, and you can't hold onto one."

Kai jumped, jolted out of his dark thoughts. Deston was leaning against the barn with four of his friends. The top of his head reached Kai's shoulder. His black hair was slicked back. Kai looked at his smug face and wondered how they'd ever been friends. "Leave me alone."

Deston ignored him. "Did you hear that Chancellor Belial personally requested my help? But, sadly, one man's loss is another's gain. Still, if you'd been better with horses, Belial may have liked you. Too bad you learned all about horses from your Dad." Deston watched Kai with an evil glint as his pals roared with laughter.

Kai's face burned, but he kept his clenched fists inside the pockets of his jacket. He wasn't giving Deston the satisfaction this time.

Deston kept talking. "My dad said if your dad had been paying attention, the accident would've never happened."

"The accident was your dad's fault! Dad's handicapped because of *him*. He's a sloppy jockey," Kai yelled.

Deston's pals stirred, and Kai stepped back. He wasn't afraid of Deston. The little shrimp would be easy to fight. But they always came in numbers. Today it was five against one. The last time they baited him left him with a broken rib.

"Is that what the crippled failure says?" Deston laughed. "Well, we'll let him think that."

Kai roared, unable to contain himself anymore. He grabbed Deston by the shirt and began shaking him. His arms, strong from shoveling, threw Deston around like a rag doll.

"Not...his...fault. Your dad...just...bad..." Deston gasped out between shakes.

Kai punched him in the mouth. Deston's head flew back, but he blocked Kai's next swing. Deston kneed him in the stomach. Kai doubled over with pain. He straightened and threw another blow. But Deston danced aside as Kai's fist swung wide. Deston walloped him in the nose. Kai blinked and staggered back against the barn. Deston clobbered him in the stomach. He crumpled to the ground.

Gasping for air, he panted. "This...isn't...over."

Deston looked down at him with disdain. "It was over when your Dad fell off his horse. All you're good for is shoveling horse manure." He walked into the barn without another glance.

One of Deston's friends kicked Kai in the back as he walked by. Kai fought to catch his breath as he lay in the mud. *Someday they'll be sorry. I'll make them pay.* He'd catch each of them alone and beat them to a pulp like they'd done to him so many times.

The wind gusted through the gates as the thunder rolled. From the ground, he saw a sign flap in the wind. He read the words. "*Opening Ceremonies! Don't miss the First Race. Grand Prize of 5,000 Flames.*"

Kai sat up, groaning, and scooted back to the shelter of the barn. He must've seen the tattered sign a thousand times. The black paint highlighted the word *Flames.* One of Chancellor Belial's recent acts was to issue gold coins with a flame stamped on it. They were worth twice the amount of the old coins with a scepter. *Five thousand Flames is more than Mom and I could make in a year! I could get a doctor for Rhiana. I could ...*

A plan sprang to his mind, something so clever he could hardly wait to do it. He grinned.

Deston's bullying finally did something good! And after the race, I'll teach him how to really beat up someone! He pushed back his hair out of his eyes. *This will solve everything in one swoop!*

He sprung to his feet, barely feeling the pain. He trotted out of the gates and headed toward the mountains. He had to stay away for a while before he could put his plan into motion. The road dipped into a hollow lined with trees, and a familiar fear from his dream crept down the back of his neck. It grew with every step he took. There was a strange movement in the trees, like a great shadow moving. He took a cautious step forward.

Run! The thought came unbidden into his mind. *Get out of there!*

Kai shook his head, but there remained a tingling like someone was in his head. The feeling grew, and he dashed back to the stables. He ducked through the crowds and found shelter in the hay. Something had been in the trees. *Could it be the monsters from my dream? But that's impossible!*

He had a strange feeling that someone else, not him, whispered those words in his head. They were not *his* thoughts - he was sure about that.

CHAPTER EIGHT

Too Bad for Willie

Kai hid until the first race was about to start. The rain was coming down hard, making the late afternoon dark. He grabbed a board he'd found in the hay and slipped through the crowds gathering around the starting line. The track left the stands and led through the foothills of the mountains over streams and through the forest until it circled back to the stands. He'd tramped over it many times, dreaming of racing it.

The rain soaked him to the bone as he crept to the jockeys' dressing room. Glancing in the window, he could see the preparations for the race. There was a dull roar of shouts, laughter and loud chatter. Memories sprung up of visiting Dad before races. He remembered the smell of the leather and the laughter. Dad, dressed in the colorful silks, set his helmet on Kai's head.

"Soon he'll be my biggest competition," Dad said. "He's already better than you."

The other jockeys roared in protest, but Dad just winked at him. Now, with the rain drenching him, he wondered if Dad or Deston was right. Well, he'd find out in a few minutes.

As he watched through the window, he saw Willie, Kedar's jockey, stretch and get up. He put a slicker on over his racing silks and walked outside. If Kai was right, he would head straight for the outhouse. Kai followed him silently in the shadows.

He was right. Willie went straight to the outhouse. When Willie closed the door, Kai made sure no one was around and jammed the piece of wood he'd been carrying against the door. It would be a long night for Willie in that stinky outhouse, but he'd be okay. He crept back to the dressing room.

Now to get on Kedar. When he returned to the dressing room, it was empty. His heart raced as he pulled the extra set of green and yellow silks on. They were short for him, but he pulled the high leather boots over them and picked up a quirt.

He walked to the paddock where Kedar was pacing while a groom tried to keep him still. The darkness increased as the storm blocked the light. Kai hesitated and put the helmet on his head with shaking hands. *All I have to do is walk to Kedar. We're late, and it's dark. They won't even look at me. Even a sack of potatoes like Deston could win on Kedar.*

He thought about praying. *But why?* Adoyni hadn't answered any of his prayers in a very long time. He wasn't wasting his time anymore waiting for Adoyni to do something. It was time to take matters into his hands. He took a deep breath and strode to Kedar.

"Just where have you been, Willie?" The trainer, wrapped in a slicker, didn't even glance at Kai. "We're late."

Kai grunted, afraid to say anything in case he was recognized. Kedar's ears pricked up at the sound of his voice and nickered. The groom lifted him up, and he was in the saddle.

"What've ya been eating?" The groom complained. "Keep it up, and they'll have to get a winch to lift you."

Kai ignored the comment as the trainer took the lead rope and started to the track. He gathered the reins nervously. *It worked! The rest will be easy!*

A flash of lightning cracked above as they made it to the track. He could hear old Avi calling out the horses' names and positions. Kai grinned.

"Here comes Sentinel Colors, number 3! He's ready to win! Behind him comes Kedar, perhaps the fastest horse here. Make your bets cuz this is goin' to be a race to beat all!"

Kai's heart pounded at the sound of Kedar's name. Waves of nerves flowed over him. These were veteran jockeys. As merry as they were in the dressing room, all friendship ended on the track, especially in the dark places far away from the stands and the judges.

They were at the gates. The stallions challenged each other as they were positioned. His heart pounded as he gripped the reins. This race would change his life forever. Five thousand flames to do what they needed. And owners would hire him when they saw him win.

Kedar reared as the trainer snapped off the lead rope. Kai struggled for control. Kedar stilled, alert for the trumpet to signal the beginning. He reached down and petted Kedar's neck.

"Good boy. Are you ready to fly? We have to win this one, so run hard, boy." Kai looked down the long line of fifteen stallions. The horses were quiet in their gates.

Without warning, the trumpet sounded.

CHAPTER NINE

A Walk in the Dark

Lizzy tossed and turned in her bed, still stinging from Mother's words. All the things she wanted to take to Northbridge were beside her door - one suitcase and her guitar.

Mother didn't want her as a daughter. Fine. She didn't want Mother, either. She didn't need her, and life would be much better without all the yelling. Maybe Dad would let her stay.

Sleep escaped like a note too high to be sung. The house became quiet, except for her thoughts. Lizzy rolled over again. *What did Mom do with my sling? It's probably in her desk. I'm not leaving without it!*

She crept to her door. It creaked as she pushed it open. She peered up and down the hallway. No one was in sight, so she slipped out of her room and down the stairs. *Watch that squeaky fifth step.* She arrived at the bottom of the stairs at Mother's office without a sound and sat behind the desk. *Where did she put it?*

She opened a drawer, but she couldn't see a thing. She felt her way to the plush curtains and pushed them open. The front lawn was bathed with moonlight, making the trees and flowers look like silver. The beams lit up the office as bright as day. She grinned.

Returning to the desk, she searched the drawers and lifted the contents into the light. She found financial records, files on students, and sheets of music, but no sling.

Lizzy heard the stairs creak and jumped. *Someone's coming down.* She slid open the last drawer. The steps came closer. There was only paper in the drawer. *What did Mother do with it?*

Her heart raced as the footsteps came steadily down the stairs and approached Mother's office door. She reached to the back and felt the sling. She grabbed it, closed the drawer, and hid under the desk. The steps stopped in the hallway. *Mother will kill me if she finds me here.* She held her breath. After a long moment, the footsteps moved away. She let out her breath. *That was close.*

She had to get back to her room. She rushed to the curtains to close them. But a movement caught her eye. Rica slipped off the porch, making his way to the trees by the street. She leaned forward as a shadow moved. Rica hesitated and then walked to it. The shadow towered over him several feet. It gestured angrily once, and Rica stepped back.

He's afraid of it! She felt the sling in her hands and dashed out the front door. She paused to pick up some stones from the flower bed. *I'll teach it to come around here and bother us.* She stayed in the shadows of the oak trees. The long grass muffled her steps as she approached Rica.

"I asked, and there is no relation," Rica said. "Please just leave us alone."

"My Master knows the truth even if you try to hide it." The second voice slipped out of the shadows. "It'll be better for you and your family if you come quietly."

"Just leave us alone. My family is not who you want."

The shadow shrugged. "That is not for me or you to decide."

Lizzy put a stone in her sling. *You're not going anywhere with my brother.* She began to swing. It would be a tricky shot with Rica between her and the *thing*.

"Just give me more time." Rica's voice jerked her attention back to him. "I'll find out the answers. I can search through the records in Northbridge. Just give me time."

"Northbridge?" The voice rasped across the grass. "Yes, I'll find you there."

The shadow pulled Rica close. Rica twisted and kicked, but the iron grip of it was too strong. It growled and threw Rica to the ground. Rica lunged to his feet, tripping as he scrambled away in his haste. When Lizzy searched the trees, the creature was gone. She lost her nerve and dashed into the house and up to her room.

But she could not sleep. A sense of evil, like a damp fog, crept through the walls of the house and into her heart. Something was down there, lurking nearby. She finally drifted into an uneasy slumber.

* * *

Taryn paced in his room between the bed and the window, aware of the irony of the situation. He normally spent the evenings hoping Pater would come home in time for dinner or at least poke his head in his bedroom to say a cheery good night. It rarely happened, and if it did, it was never cheery. But tonight he hoped Pater wouldn't come.

His pack was loaded with all he deemed necessary to live: a couple changes of clothes, money, some beef jerky, an apple, a flask of water, and three books.

Of all the decisions to make, he'd spent a fair amount of time agonizing over which books to take, but *The Complete Atlas of the Heavens* and *The Stars and What We Can Learn From Them* by Nighthawk Nephesus won. Not only were they the definitive work on astrology, he didn't have them autographed yet. He added them to *The Ultimate Book of Spells: Every Spell You'll Ever Require.* He wrapped them up in a sheet and placed them reverently in his pack.

The last thing to be placed in his bag was his crystal sphere. It had taken months of saving his allowance to afford it. It was a small one, the size of an apple, and it glittered like the stars in the sky. He'd used spells to fill it with power in case he needed anything from the Goddess while traveling. His coat was flung over the pack in a corner of the room. No one would notice it in all of the mess, his quiet disobedience to the perfection on the other side of the door.

In the other corner were the items for the dedication, camouflaged in shoes and books. He was ready. Now if only Pater would go to bed. Taryn flipped aimlessly through his books while his father's room grew quiet. It was late when he put on his glasses and gathered his things.

He tiptoed toward Pater's room, the note he'd written earlier gripped in his hand. Taryn placed the note against the door. He thought about what he had written once more.

Pater, the note read, *I'm sorry to sneak out like this. I know you said you didn't want me to go. I have to help Nighthawk Nephesus and meet my destiny. I told a lie to convince Mischa, so don't blame him. I'll be back in a couple of days, Taryn.*

Father would be furious, but if he succeeded, Pater would have to accept him for who he was. He turned and slammed into a table next to the stairs. He froze. The whole plan could be cancelled right here because of his clumsiness. He silently cursed his big feet. Nothing happened.

Taking a deep breath, Taryn felt his way around the table and crept down the creaky stairs. He hurried out the back door where there was a high fence and many trees. The trees were silver-lined with moonlight and the grass shimmered with early dew. He moved to the back where the foliage was the thickest.

Putting his pack by a tree, Taryn went to the center of the trees and knelt down in the moonlight. He laid a napkin on the ground in front of him and sprinkled some ash on top of it, then placed a white candle in the center. He hesitated before lighting it. This oath would bind him to Zoria forever. Only the truly passionate breathed these words. Zoria demanded complete obedience and was jealous of Her servants. Once these words were uttered, his life would be determined by what She wanted. Her punishment was death. He took a deep breath as he contemplated what he was about to do. The price was high, but the rewards were great. He pictured himself helping to cleanse the river. Glory and honor would be heaped upon him, and he would be revered.

Glancing around, he took off his shirt. He was going to do it. This was the life he wanted. Not something Father thought was good for him. He undressed and sat down close to the candle. Every sound broke his concentration. Everything inside of him screamed for him to put on his clothes.

He closed his eyes and forced himself to think of only his desire to know the Goddess more. Filling his mind with the thoughts of dedicating himself to Her, the rest of the world slowly slipped away. Taryn spread out his hands over the small flame, letting the purity of white candle and the flame come to him. He concentrated his thoughts on his goals.

Taryn breathed the words, "I am a child of Zoria, and I ask Her to accept me." He dipped his finger in the wax and anointed his forehead, tracing a pentagram. "Tonight I pledge my devotion to Zoria above all others. I will walk with Her and obey Her guidance. Let death come to me if I should ever depart from Her. As I will, so it shall be."

He snuffed out the candle with his fingers. The moon shone on him as he closed his eyes and felt energy well up inside of him. Zoria had heard and accepted. He could feel Her stirring in the leaves of the trees, in his blood. This success proved the rest of the journey would be filled with triumph. *What if She asks me to do something that I can't do or don't want to do?* Fear gripped him. He couldn't do this. He couldn't venture into the unknown. He put his clothes on and considered going back into the house. But if he went back, the world would die. He had to follow Nighthawk to Northbridge.

He picked up his pack and followed the street that led to the inn where he and Mischa would board the stagecoach. The street was empty and quiet, long shadows falling into his path. He'd never been out so late before. He trotted through the street, his footsteps echoing in the silence. His pack kept slipping as he tried to keep it close to guard against the pickpockets and thieves that might be around.

The sound of footsteps thudded behind him. He stopped in the shadows, his heart racing. They stopped when he did. Trying to walk quietly, he dashed to the next group of trees. The sound continued when he moved.

He abandoned stealth and ran as fast as he could to the inn. People lay in the streets, trying to sleep, while they waited for the morning to come. He huddled down between them and glanced back the way he had come.

"Great Goddess," he whispered. "Protect me from whatever demon that was."

Slowly his heart rate returned to normal, yet the scare he'd received only intensified. *What was out there, chasing me?* Something was out there, trying to stop him from going to Northbridge. Until he reached the Temple of All, he couldn't trust anyone. He cradled his head in his hands, despair creeping into his heart along with fear. *Who am I for such a burden? I don't want to be alone.*

"Help me, Zoria," he moaned. "Please help me."

TEARS

"If you have tears, prepare to shed them now."
~William Shakespeare

Foehn pushed the door open as the man he served
stepped into the Temple of All. The man paused in
the doorway while he pushed back his hood. Foehn
whipped around him, causing the candles to flutter.

The man entered the room. His dark eyes glowed
yellow, reflecting the Temple's candles. He had never
lost his pale skin, but now he wore rich robes of
purple and red. Golden rings inlayed with large jewels
hung heavily on his hands. The years in the palace
had given him many things – riches, influence of the
king, palatial houses, respect of many people. And yet
Foehn sometimes felt scared to be with him.

Like now. Foehn couldn't stop the shiver that
came, and one of the candles lost its glow. The man
whipped around and snapped. "Wind, be still."

Foehn forced his quakes to a bare shiver. He hated
this dark temple, no matter how often they traveled
to Northbridge. The strong incense made him want
to blow hard and cleanse the place with fresh air.

The man continued past the crowds to the deep
parts of the temple. Foehn quietly followed behind
like a whipped cur, stirring the gowns of the priests
and the clothes of the worshippers. The man slipped
through a secret door, moving swiftly in the hidden

hallways to where the shadows were the darkest. A large shape materialized. Yellow eyes glowed in the black, creating an eerie light. Foehn cowered in a corner.

"I have found the last of the three. Our search is now over." The man smiled, triumph on his face. "One is coming to the Temple on his own accord, the second will be picked up from a coach tomorrow, and you will bring the last one from the stables to me tonight during the storm. Do not hurt him. They will bow before me or die before the first day of spring. Either way I shall gain their power."

"What storm, master?" The shape in the shadow whispered.

"This storm." The man turned away from the shadow. "Wind, do my bidding. Stir up lightning and rain. Make all in its path hide from its fury."

Foehn shrunk further back. He didn't want to do this. He wanted to go see his home, the mountains on the edge of Northbridge. He was weary of obeying the man's every whim. He paused.

"Wind," the man commanded, his voice ringing with authority. "Bring a storm as I command now in the name of my master, Seiten. Go now and obey your Master."

Foehn had no choice. He whipped out of the temple, snuffing out candles and blowing papers around in his anger. The rain that fell was like tears from his eyes.

CHAPTER TEN

The End of the Race

Kedar surged ahead on the track before Kai heard the trumpet. Slammed back into his saddle, he clutched the reins and fought for his balance. *Idiot! Dad always said to grip the mane to stay on.* He settled back into the saddle with the reins tighter. Ahead on the track, two horses separated them from Sentinel Colors. But if Kedar was half the horse they said he was, they would catch up. He had to gain the lead where the track was the widest at the end of the stands. Traditionally, the horse that gained the lead here won the race. A gap between the two horses ahead of him opened.

"Now, big boy," he yelled. "Let's run."

Kedar leaped forward, his black mane slapping Kai in the face. He crouched low over Kedar's neck. The rain felt like little rocks hitting his face. They shot between the two horses and drew up beside Sentinel Colors.

Two hundred feet from the lead.

Kedar ran beside Sentinel Colors. Kai glanced over at Deston's father, Garrick. The same person who'd caused Dad's accident. He pulled on the reins. Maybe it'd be better to let Garrick go first. Maybe Sentinel Colors would slow, or he'd make a mistake. He pictured life in a wheelchair and tightened the reins. Kedar felt the pressure and shook his head in protest.

Garrick looked over his shoulder as Kai started to fall back. As the light of recognition swept his face, he grinned, certain in his triumph of taking The Gap. Kai stared at his back, thinking of Dad. Of the life he now had because of this man who was taking the lead and then the victory.

"Not this time," Kai whispered. "I've taken more than enough from him and Deston."

He loosened the reins. Kedar responded with fury as his energy was unleashed in the long strides. Kai shouted at Kedar, urging him to run faster. They drew up alongside Sentinel Colors.

One hundred and fifty feet.

Kai bent over the horse's neck, not using the whip. Kedar needed no urging. His long legs moved even faster in his anger at being held back. Garrick laid the quirt on Sentinel Colors as Kedar overtook him. Garrick yelled and pulled Sentinel Colors into Kedar's shoulder.

Kedar squealed and twisted. Kai was thrown to the side. He felt Kedar struggle to keep up his speed while staying on his feet. *I'm not going to fall off today!* He pushed himself against Kedar's neck and regained his seat.

Ninety feet.

Kedar forged ahead. By the time Kai had gathered up the reins, they were passing Garrick. Kai dodged as Garrick struck at him with his quirt.

He heard Sentinel Colors scream with pain as
Garrick switched the quirt to the horse.

Fifty feet.

Kai grinned back at Garrick as Sentinel Colors
fell into the background. Shock settled over
Garrick's face, and he stopped whipping his horse.

Thirty feet.

Kedar gave a final burst of speed, sweeping into
the narrow section of the track first. Kai joined
in the shouts from the crowd as he swept past the
stands. Pride swelled in his heart as he felt the beat
of Kedar's hooves under him. He was a champion -
fast, intelligent, strong.

"Good boy," he shouted. "Keep it up. We've got
three miles to go."

They settled into a nice rhythm, fast enough to
keep ahead of Sentinel Colors but easy enough not
to wear Kedar out too soon. Kai checked over his
shoulder every few minutes, but they were alone.

Even though it was late afternoon, the storm
had made it dark as night. The rain fell harder
than before, making the track slippery. The
lightning and thunder flashed and crashed above
him, but Kedar ran without any concern. He placed
every foot with caution in the slick mud. *They sure
knew what they were doing when they bred him.* Kai was
already picturing them running the final stretch to
victory.

Kedar raced around a corner. A bolt of
lightning struck in front of them. Kai caught a
glimpse of a fallen tree lying in their path before it

went dark again. He yanked on the reins to avoid the tree. Kedar twisted as he plunged over the massive trunk. There was a jolt, and Kai was flying through the air.

Kai landed on his shoulder and rolled to his knees. A sharp pain in his shoulder shot down his arm. He got slowly to his feet. He rubbed his shoulder and glanced around for Kedar. He was nowhere to be seen. *Dumb horse. He kept going.* Kai fought back the panic and anger that swept through him. If he didn't find Kedar soon, he'd lose the race.

There was a large shadow in the middle of the track. *No. It couldn't be...* He stumbled closer. Kedar was lying in the shadows. Gulping back a sob, he ran and fell to his knees. Kedar's knees were cut and bruised, his neck twisted in a funny way, but his eyes were open.

"Come on, big boy." He brushed Kedar's forelock out of his eyes. Kedar answered with a soft nicker. "Get up. We've got to finish this. We're not at the end of the race yet."

Kedar groaned but didn't move. Kai sat down in the mud and gathered Kedar's head in his lap. Tears mingled with the rain as he stroked Kedar one last time.

"I'm so sorry," he sobbed. "I'm so sorry."

Kedar closed his eyes and exhaled shallowly. He never moved again. Kai buried his head in the mane. He felt hot tears streak down his face but didn't care. All he cared about was Kedar.

"What have I done? Oh, what have I done?"

Time passed. Kai heard the sounds of hooves pounding in the mud and men shouting. *The other jockeys!* They'd see him and know he'd killed Kedar.

Grief gave way to panic. Carefully setting Kedar's head down, Kai smoothed his mane and petted his white snippet for the last time. Then, with a wrenching moan, Kai ran in the only direction he could.

He ran into the mountains.

CHAPTER ELEVEN

Time for a Tumble

The hill Kai was running up grew steeper as he left the race track far behind. The darkness grew deeper, but flashes of lightning revealed sparse trees and large rocks. Just when he thought that he couldn't run anymore, he reached a plateau that revealed Northbridge below him. He took off his helmet and threw it across the meadow.

He walked to the edge of the cliff, ignoring the rain, and peered down at the city. Torches from the stables were lit for the jockeys thundering down to the finish line. He could still feel the thrill of riding Kedar to victory. Then he remembered Kedar dead on the ground. Never again would Kedar nicker for a pet or beg for a treat. Never again would he run. He groaned. *Why wasn't I paying better attention?*

He stared at the lights below, despair filling his heart. His only chance was gone. He'd failed. He winced. Kedar was the most valuable horse Chancellor Belial owned. He couldn't even come close to paying for one of Kedar's hooves. He'd be forced to slavery, working until the debt was gone or he died. He ran his hands through his wet hair. *What am I going to do now? I can't go back.*

Kai heard a noise like a twig snapping under the weight of a foot. He glanced back at the trees.

Branches moved. *A Seeker!* Then he almost laughed. It was just a dream. Lightning flashed, and he saw a spark of metal. *Is that an axe?* There was a large shadow standing in the meadow.

Run.

The thought bounced through his head. It was the voice he'd heard before.

I can't outrun them! Kai argued with the voice in his head.

It's the only chance you have. They're going to kill you. Don't be a fool.

He blinked. *Don't be a fool? I'm having a conversation with a voice in my head, and it tells me that?* He stared at the shadows of the trees.

The voice returned in his head, now urgent. *Kai, listen. You must run. Run deep into the mountains.*

He didn't need another urging. He sprinted into the mountains. His riding silks tore as he twisted through the bushes. The lightning gave him a second where he could see rocks and very few trees. He followed the steep incline. He tripped and stumbled over the rocks, scraping his hands. The slope leveled out, and he paused to catch his breath. A rock tumbled down the hill behind him. He held his breath. *There's something right behind me.*

He waited. Nothing. Out of the darkness, a sound, like a foot hitting a rock, echoed. *They're coming.* Kai burst into a run, ignoring the ache in his lungs. His left foot slipped on a loose rock, and he fell to the ground. A searing pain shot through his ankle.

There was the noise of scrambling over the rocks behind him. He pulled himself to his feet and limped on. His ankle shrieked with pain with every step. After a few feet, his left ankle collapsed. He fought to regain his balance and then tumbled in the dirt and rolled downwards. Then the ground disappeared from under him, and he yelled as he dropped through the air. He rolled and tumbled down, his body twisting and turning. He fell faster, the darkness swallowing him.

He crashed into rock without slowing down. Sharp pain jolted through his right leg. He cried out with pain. A rock cut his face as he rolled, grabbing at tree roots and rocks, scraping his hands and knuckles. He slowed to a stop, perched on the edge of an overhang.

He inched closer to the cliff, letting the rain wash over him. He felt his leg. Waves of nausea rose in him, threatening to make him hurl. He pulled his hand away and laid back on the rock, unable to do anything but breathe. His hand, he noticed in a flash of lightning, was covered in blood. He raised his head to see bone sticking out of his pants.

Gritting his teeth, Kai tried to move his leg. Black spots appeared in his eyes. He closed his eyes, hoping that he wouldn't pass out. He let the rain hit his face. The sun had set, leaving the world in darkness. Kai had an image of Dad in a wheelchair. *Am I going to end up like that?* He fought back tears. He was not going to cry, not even where no one could see him.

He peered up at the cliff. *This was all my fault. I messed everything up. If I hadn't done anything, Kedar would still be alive. But now he's dead, and Mom won't have enough money to get Rhiana to a healer.* Anger began to boil in him. He was going to find a way out of this mess and somehow fix everything he had wrecked.

Kai felt bumps and grooves in the rock. He'd climbed worst places before. Pulling himself to his feet, he doubled over with the pain from his leg. He waited until the throbbing subsided and reached up for the first handhold. His leg shrieked with pain when it collided with the cliff.

His foot slipped, and he lost his grip. He landed on the overhang again. The jolt sent waves of pain up his leg. He rolled close to the cliff and groaned. Using the rocks, he pulled himself up to his feet and started again. He moved slower this time, taking his time to make sure of the holds before he trusted them. It was slow, and his arms burned with the strain, but he was close to the top.

He put some weight on his right leg to reach the next handhold. As he reached for the next handhold, his leg crumbled under the pain. He fell like a rock, surrounded by a weird feeling of emptiness.

Out of the darkness, he heard a noise beneath him. A loud *swoop, swoop.* It sounded like the wings of a bird, but it was slower, stronger. Looking down, he caught a glimpse of something white underneath him. Something was very near.

He heard a soft thudding sound. He grabbed for it and felt soft fur under his hands. He shifted until he could cling to the creature with his legs. He felt something like wings beneath him beat faster like they were rising through the air.

Something had rescued him. Something with wings. Something with a familiar scent. He knew it. He'd smelled it many times.

It was the smell of wet horse.

And then he blacked out.

CHAPTER TWELVE

Let's Get Off

Lizzy stood on the porch. Mother's face glowed as her long dark hair was swept back over her shoulders and her bright red gown matched the brilliant sunrise.

"I'll see you in a month," Mother said. "Don't get into trouble."

Lizzy hoped she wouldn't have to hug her. And then she hoped Mother would snatch her up in a big hug and beg her not to go. "Bye."

No hug. *Whatever.* She climbed into the carriage as the driver called to the horses. *She didn't say she loved me. Did she tell Rica she loved him? I'll bring her some purified water and then she'll say that she loves me every day.*

Rica didn't say anything as they rolled through the streets. They passed the town pole that proudly bore Zoria's flame. The Spring Celebration would be starting soon. At the inn, there were sick people everywhere. Most were just starting to get weak, the sickness showing in their tired gait, the brittle hair. A few were so close to dying that their skin was almost transparent. They climbed out when the horses stopped close to the waiting stagecoaches.

Tucking her bags closer to her, she glanced at her brother. She sighed and rolled her eyes. Once full of adventure, Rica had been her hero. Now he wore stuffy clothes and a stupid hat that was supposed to be, according to him, the height of fashion.

"Rica, why did Mother and Dad stop living together?" She didn't know what made her ask the question, but she had to know.

He stared off into the distance. She hated it when he ignored her. She opened her mouth to ask again. Rica snapped an answer. "Ask them. Come on, that's our stagecoach." He grabbed the bags and pushed through the crowd. She groaned as she picked up her guitar.

Rica looked back at her a few feet away. "Any time now."

Lizzy glared at him while she trotted to catch up. She remembered when they used to have great adventures, back when he was fun. Her long lashes blinked away the stinging tears. She wasn't going to let Rica see her cry. Hitching up her skirts, she climbed nimbly up the two steps and plopped down on the seat beside him.

"Happy?" She glared at him.

"Thrilled."

Knowing any word would spark an argument, she stared out the window at the chaos around the coach. "Oh, Zoria's blood," Lizzy swore. "I can't believe it! I think him and that older gentleman are coming on our coach."

Rica lifted his dark eyebrows at her language, but she didn't care. "The correct grammar is *he* and

the gentleman. The tall kid with the purple coat
and red hat?"

She nodded. "He was at Mother's last
performance. He spilled red juice all over my dress
and dashed off without an apology. It's his fault that
Mother's so mad at me."

"I don't think you can blame him for all that,"
Rica said drily. "You're extremely capable of
making Mother angry."

The guy in the purple coat saw her as he
entered the coach, and his face went white. *He can
start with an apology before I say anything.* Lizzy glared
at him.

The driver popped his head through the door
with a cross look on his face. "Folks, this is gonna
be a fast ride." His curly red hair bounced as he
talked. The few teeth he had left were as yellow as
a barn cat. She almost laughed, but his next words
killed the amusement in her.

"There's strange creatures on the road. Such
could kill ya' with a look, they says. Some says they
are demons. I seen some weird things out there
lately. Monsters with yellow eyes. Dead bodies lying
along the road with their arms and legs cut off.
Some were skinned." His bright blue eyes held a
certain kind of craziness.

Lizzy glanced at Rica, fear creeping up her
spine. He was as white as his frilly shirt. She'd never
seen him look so scared.

"I talked to the other drivers, and they made
it here from Northbridge just dandy," the driver

continued. "So we're gonna try for it. When we take a break, stay close to the coach and keep your business short. And if you need anything, don't bother asking, cuz' I ain't gonna stop."

The door slammed with a bang. Lizzy waited for someone to laugh at the joke. But they sat there, staring at the closed door.

The guy in the purple coat turned to his companion. "Mischa, those creatures he's talking about are just fables, right?"

"Evil exists, Taryn." Mischa looked out the window. "But if we keep on the right path, we'll be safe."

"I'm pretty sure this is the right path. I mean, it's leading to the Temple of All. It's got to be right," Taryn continued. "But we could still get off."

Lizzy wondered if he meant getting off the coach or the path.

The older man, Mischa, sighed. "Taryn, your father wouldn't have let you go if there were any problems."

Lizzy could see Taryn was upset. His hands shook as he took off his dark-framed glasses and rubbed his hazel eyes. The coach rocked as the driver climbed up to his seat. Taryn's words circled in her head. *We could still get off.* She wanted out. Now. There was still time.

"Rica?" He didn't seem to hear, so she tugged on his jacket. "We don't have to go."

"It'll be okay, Lizzy." Rica seemed distracted. "But if anyone asks you to go with them, don't do it. Don't believe that they're safe. Just run, okay?"

"What are you talking about?" Lizzy pulled back to look at him better. The monster from last night flashed in her mind. *Does that have something to do with this?*

"Just promise." His dark eyes were serious. "If they're coming for you, it's real bad."

"Okay, fine. I promise. I won't go with anyone." She was really confused now.

"Good. It'll be okay at the end." His words sounded hollow.

She wasn't sure if he was reassuring her or himself. The driver called to the horses, and the coach lurched. Everything in her cried out to get off. When she glanced at Taryn, she could see that they both knew this was a mistake. They were going to their deaths.

She could pray, but what good would that do? There was no one out there to hear her. Her heart drummed loudly in her ears, matching the rhythm of the horses' pounding hooves on the hard trail as they wound out of the city and into the low hills. The words echoed over and over in her ears.

Shadows, monsters, demons. Shadows, monsters, demons.

CHAPTER THIRTEEN

A Straight Limb

Taryn wasn't having a good day. He'd come prepared for a rough trip, but it was much worse than anything he had imagined. His list of "Things That Could Go Wrong" included being kicked by a horse, losing his books, and having Pater find him and haul him home.

Blood, murder, and evil monsters were *not* on the list.

As the stagecoach passed through Albia and made its way over the gentle hills, Taryn fretted about what the driver said about monsters, but he came to the realization that it simply wasn't possible. If there were such creatures out there, the news would have reached the king. Rumors said the king was very sick, but surely not so ill that he wouldn't send soldiers to take care of the problems.

Slowly the rocking of the coach put him to sleep. He woke up on the floor with a jerk. Everything was in a heap on top of him in a tangle of body parts, baskets, hats and luggage. He managed to untangle himself and lift the old woman back to the seat.

The coach lurched as the driver climbed down. He opened the door while spouting orders. "Lost a wheel. Everybody get out, but stay close. This place ain't safe. We're not far from Roj where we're gonna spend the night."

Taryn glanced around. They'd stopped in the middle of meadow. The mountains peeked over the treetops, looking down on the flowers and grass.

The driver returned with a few tools and impaled Taryn with a glare. "You! Fetch me the straightest limb you can find! I'm goin' to have to fix the axle. Hurry, now, lad!"

"Me?" Taryn was surprised to be singled out for this task. "I…I can't…"

"Come on," Rica laughed. "I'll help you find something we can use. Lizzy, let's go. We could use a walk."

Taryn barely suppressed a sigh as she joined them. *Why does she have to come?*

Rica nodded and messed up Lizzy's hair. "Fine. A walk will do us good."

Taryn bit back his angry words. *The only straight limb I want to find is my leg. And just what am I supposed to do when I find a stupid stick?* As if he spoke the words out loud, Rica shoved an axe into his hands. *Right. Of course. Chop it down.*

Mischa turned to Taryn. "You'll be all right. A little time in the woods won't kill you. You might even find out that you like it."

"There's not much of a chance that will happen," Taryn snorted. "Will you be okay?"

"I'll be fine. I'll be better when we can get out of here. Get going. You have work to do."

Taryn swallowed his dread and trotted into the forest after Rica and Lizzy. He stopped where the trees started to grow thick and looked back at Mischa grinning. *So, he finds this funny, does he? Well, I'll show him! I'll find the biggest stick in the whole darned woods. Then I'll bring it back. We'll see who laughs then!*

Rica stepped over a log. "There should be something close."

"Um…maybe you could do the chopping," he stammered. He admired the muscles on Rica's arms. "I haven't ever chopped anything…"

"Nothing to it, lad. Just swing and hit." Rica began whistling a song that Taryn thought was a bar tune as they made their way deeper into the forest. Lizzy moved silently through the woods in front of them, her red dress contrasting the greens and browns of the trees.

He couldn't help but look back the way they'd come. *What if we get lost?* Rica continued farther into the hills, craning his neck to look up into the trees. Taryn tripped over a log lying in his path and almost impaled himself with the dumb axe.

"Maybe we should go back and say that we can't find any," he suggested.

Rica only laughed as if it was all a great joke. He strode confidently up a hill, paused to scan the trees, and then continued down the other side. Taryn was seeing less and less humor in this situation. Fingering the axe, he followed slowly.

A crashing sound echoed through the trees. Jumping like a scared cat, he almost dropped the axe. "What was that?"

Rica didn't even bother to look back. "Nothing. It's just a …" Rica's voice died out as he stood still and raised his hand to signal to be quiet. They stood still for a second.

"Is it monsters?" Lizzy whispered.

Taryn stared through the darkening woods but didn't see anything. Then out of nowhere, they heard a scream. There was the sound of metal clashing. Once, twice. Then silence.

He turned to Rica. Rica stared back at him. Words were not necessary. *There's something out there.*

"Just swing and hit," Rica said, his black eyes serious. "Something's coming."

CHAPTER FOURTEEN

Swing and Hit

Taryn caught a flash of something silver in Rica's hand. Rica pulled Lizzy closer. "Take this," he said, wrapping her fingers around it. "It'll keep you safe. Gwyneth gave it to me. It's filled with mugwort."

"But you said this stuff was stupid." Lizzy tried to give it back.

"Listen to me for once!" Rica was almost yelling. "It'll protect you. Take it!"

"Fine." Lizzy stuffed it in her deep pocket of her red traveling dress, her green eyes sparking with anger.

A scream echoed through the woods, and Taryn felt goose bumps run down his arms. A tall creature wrapped in a long dark cloak silently stepped from the trees. Leather straps holding knives crisscrossed its chest. At its waist was a gigantic broadsword. The face was covered by a large hood. It swung a large axe as it leisurely approached them.

Rica didn't hesitate. He ran at the monster and leaped into the air. The axe swept over him as he punched it in the face and landed behind it. The *thing* roared in anger. Lizzy pulled out a sling, her face was white. The stone shot out of the sling and hit the axe with a loud ring.

Working up his courage, Taryn ran toward the monster, his own axe raised high. The creature turned to face him, its hood flying from its face as it turned to reveal skin pockmarked and cruddy. Taryn stared in horror, the attack forgotten. It charged like a wild bull, and in a wild moment, he swung his axe. The creature batted it aside like it was a twig and hit him on the chest. He crumbled to the ground, gasping for breath.

"Hey, ugly," Rica called out as the monster stood over Taryn. "Over here."

The *thing* snarled like a wild animal. Rica dodged it as the creature charged him. Growling in anger, it circled him. Rica grabbed a stick, smacking the brute on the chest, but the monster didn't seem to notice. Lizzy yelled, shooting another stone at it, but the stone flew wide.

The axe lay three feet away from Taryn. He rolled through the dirt and grasped it. The stick in Rica's hands broke. *You can't do this. You're not a warrior.* He ignored the doubt and snuck up behind the beast. He drew the axe back over his head, closed his eyes, and swung. His arms felt like they were being pulled out of his sockets as the axe arched. When he opened one eye, he saw that he missed completely.

"Toss it here! Taryn! Here!" Rica danced sideways and reached for the weapon.

Taryn ignored him. *Swing and hit.* He landed a blow on the monster's shoulder, but no blood gushed out of the wound. The creature bellowed with rage, its yellow eyes filled with hate, its mouth open and axe uplifted. It looked just like a picture in one of his books he'd read years ago. *A Seeker. But they only exist in stories!*

He swung again, but the sweat from his hands made the handle slippery. It flew out of his hands and into a tree. He ran to it and yanked hard, but it didn't move. The Seeker smacked Rica in the chest.

Rica flew backwards, tumbling, and landed against a tree. The Seeker leaped on Rica. Taryn heard the gasp of air leaving Rica as the huge body fell on him. Flipping Rica over, the brute began to tie his hands behind his back. Rica lifted his head and looked at Taryn, blood streaming down his face.

"Take Lizzy and run! Get out of here," he gasped out.

Taryn grabbed Lizzy's arm as they ran deeper into the woods.

* * *

Lizzy screamed as the Seeker threw Rica to the ground. Rica's voice sounded like he was far away. Taryn held her arm in a tight grip as he forced her to run.

"Remember what I said," Rica yelled.

The forest fell into deep silence. Rica screamed again like an animal being killed. His voice sent shivers down her spine. She fought Taryn's hand.

"Let me go!" She ordered. "He's dying!"

"You'll die too if you go back, and you know it!" Taryn retorted. "Keep quiet, or it'll come after us."

His warning made her quiet, but her thoughts raced as they hustled through the forest. The trees grew close together, casting shadows. She couldn't hear a thing, only the echo of Rica's cry. She cringed and closed her eyes, but the sight of him with the monster haunted her. She gripped her sling until it cut into her palm.

"Stop!" She shook Taryn's hand off her arm. "We have to go back!"

"Back?" Taryn stared at her, his brown eyes filled with shock. "Are you crazy? We'll die. We need to get help."

"If we don't go now, we won't know what happened to Rica." Lizzy glared at him. "And we need to save him."

"How are we going to do that? As far as I saw, you didn't hit anything with that sling of yours," Taryn snapped.

A wave of anger swept over her. "You're a coward." She dashed through the woods, not looking back. She heard Taryn following her. She slowed as she reached the meadow. On the other side, two Seekers held Rica by his arms, pulling him along at a fast pace. Rica's head was hanging down and his feet dragged through the dirt like he was dead.

He raised his head and glanced back at the meadow. Their eyes met across the long grass. In his dark eyes was despair, but when he saw her, he managed a weak grin. A Seeker yanked harder on his arm, and Rica looked away. Then he was gone.

Lizzy fell to the ground, her knees trembling too much to hold her. Her hand shook as she coiled the sling. She could rescue him. Then she saw the wreckage in the meadow and her hopes of saving Rica died.

Three of the horses were dead in their harness. The coach was torn to pieces. There were the mounds of clothes on the ground. It took her a minute to realize they were dead bodies. Taryn shoved her aside and dashed into the meadow.

* * *

Mischa! Taryn dashed into the meadow. Mischa was lying beside one of the horses, his cane broken beside him. Mischa's face was in the dirt, and his legs were twisted.

"Mischa, can you hear me?" He rolled the old man over, a wave of hopelessness sweeping through his body, leaving him cold. "Please, wake up."

The tutor's fine linen shirt was soaked in blood. There was a deep gash in his chest. Taryn tried to sop up the blood with Mischa's cloak.

Mischa opened his hazel eyes. "Taryn." The word was as faint as Mischa's heartbeat.

Taryn leaned closer. "Mischa, don't die."

Mischa gripped his hand and pulled Taryn closer. "Taryn, you need to know. Your mother. She's…n…n…" He paused to take a breath.

Taryn took Mischa's hand, seeing that his ring with a white dove was gone. *How would he know about Mom?* Mischa didn't become his tutor until he was ten. He leaned closer as Mischa continued.

"She's n…n…"

"Taryn!" Lizzy shouted, pointing to the far side of the meadow. "Something's out there. It was right there. We have to get out of here!"

Taryn felt Mischa's hand loosen from his and then it fell to the ground. He stared at Mischa's face. *In just a minute, he will open his eyes again.* But he never did. Taryn laid his head on the old man's shoulder. Tears flooded his eyes. His whole body shook as he cried.

"I'm so sorry." Lizzy was now at his side and put her hand on his arm.

"Why didn't you keep your mouth shut?" He pulled away. "He was trying to tell me something, and you interrupted him. And now I'll never know." He didn't wipe away his tears, and he didn't care if she saw them.

She stepped back. "You're not the only one to lose someone. I don't even know what happened to my brother." Tears welled up in her eyes.

Taryn turned back to Mischa. "Just go away."
Resting his head in his hands, he could not feel
anything. It was like the world stopped, and he was
in a mist.

Lizzy reached out and put her hand on his
shoulder. "I'm sorry."

The words were said softly like she really meant
it. Taryn still couldn't look at her.

"But we need to go."

*Good heavens! She's not apologizing about
interrupting Mischa. She doesn't even care. Doesn't she
even have the decency to say that she's sorry for taking
away his last words?*

Taryn didn't even look at her. "I'm not leaving
him. You go into the woods if you want."

"I saw something out there. It was circling the
meadow. If you stay here, it'll kill you. Is that what
you want?"

Taryn turned to her. She was standing there
with her sling in her hands, her dress soiled
with blood and mud. Tears streaked her cheeks.
Everything about her was just so infuriating. "What
I want is to hear Mischa's last words. What I want is
for him not to be dead. In fact, what I really want is
to be home where I didn't know you."

Lizzy took a step back, her eyes widening.
"You're a stuck up pig who doesn't even know when
to apologize like a civilized person. I'm not saying
I want you to go to the forest because I like you. I
just don't want to bury you."

Taryn sat back, his mouth hanging open. Lizzy huffed and stomped off toward the woods. He took his glasses off and rubbed his eyes. A stick in the woods behind him snapped. She was right. There *was* something out there. He started after her, but he looked down at his tutor. Carefully he pulled Mischa's fine warm cloak over the body.

"I'll be back. I'll find some way to make this right."

TRAPS

"As fish are caught in a cruel net, or birds are taken in a snare, so men are trapped by evil times…"
~ECCLESIASTES 9:12

Foehn halted near the main entrance to the Temple of All, trembling with exhaustion. He had brought a massive storm like Master ordered. Huffing furiously, he knocked over houses with tornadoes and damaged crops. The destruction made him sick as he surveyed his work. Foehn gathered his courage before entering the Temple. He was going to tell the man he was going home. Maybe there he could forget about all the misery he had seen.

The man was in the great hall talking with two Seekers. Between them was a young man on his knees with his hands tied behind his back and his head drooping down to his chest. Foehn felt a twinge of sympathy. The man lifted the head of the boy and gazed into his dark eyes. The boy struggled weakly and then succumbed to the unyielding stare.

"What's your name, boy?" The man asked, his eyes glinting with the candlelight.

"Rica." The boy tried to jerk his chin free. "What do you want with me?"

"You'll find out in good time." The man turned to the Seekers. "Take him downstairs and throw him

in a cell. Don't give him water or food. And make
sure no worshippers see you this time. I don't want to
have to deal with that again."

Foehn turned away when the Seekers began to
drag the boy to the secret places of the Temple. He
didn't want to be a part of this anymore.

"Where do you think you're going?" The man
snapped.

Foehn stopped.

"I know you're thinking about your home." The
man slammed the door shut. Foehn leaped back and
accidently snuffed out some candles. "You do not
have permission to go. What gives you the right to
leave just because you are homesick?"

The man's voice rose with authority and power.
Foehn sank back into the Temple as far as he could.
He'd seen the man's anger before, but he'd never
been on the receiving end. He trembled. The candles
were snuffed out, one by one. The man's eyes seemed
to glow brighter as the room darkened.

"I am your master," the man continued. "You will
obey me, and you will not slink off. Don't you think
that I could command you back? Do you really think
that there is a place on this world that you could go
where I can't order you to return? You will stay with
me and obey me. Do you understand?"

Foehn repeated the binding words for a second
time. It was the only way to soothe the anger. He
could not run, could not hide. His life was the

master's to command. When it was done, his master strode out of the room without a word. Foehn felt like he was in a prison cell.

He was trapped like a fox in a snare.

CHAPTER FIFTEEN

Kidnapped

Kai leaned over and touched Rhiana's pain-ridden face. But he jerked back when it changed into the face of a monster. He blinked several times and rubbed his eyes. *Another dream.* He felt the wind blowing on his face. *Where am I?*

There was a strong smell of horse and hair was stinging his face. Muscles rippled under his legs reminding him of riding Kedar. He pushed himself up to a sitting position. Wind blew his hair back from his face with a force that made him squint. The quiet motions on his legs made him think that he was riding, but there was no jolting, no sounds of hooves on the dirt - only a steady beat like a drum.

The clouds were highlighted with sunlight. *It can't be morning already.* But the sun grew steadily larger. In the growing light, he could see his hands were wrapped in a horse's mane. *Kedar!* He shook his head to clear the fog. *What will they say when they see what I've done?* Timo's sad eyes, Mom's anger, and Dad's disappointed face flashed through his mind. *I'll fix everything when my leg is better somehow. If it gets better.* The last thought made him feel sick. *If I get better.* Glancing down, he saw a long white mane wrapped around his fingers, and it matched the white horse he was riding. *White? But Kedar is black.*

As the sun rose taller than the mountains, the clouds looked like they were on fire. He squinted in the light. Mountain peaks poked out of the clouds, but he was looking *down* on the peaks. He could see the streams grow into rivers that led to the valleys. The rocks and cliffs were illuminated by the rays, shining from the night's rain. He had never seen anything so beautiful. He stared at them, captivated, until they started to tilt.

His stomach lurched as he fell against the horse's neck. He peered through the mane. At first, he couldn't recognize what he was seeing. He should be seeing dirt and rocks. But one of the things he thought was a rock moved. As he stared, he saw it wasn't a rock. It was a cloud. He was looking at the ground like an eagle.

"Mother of a mare!" Kai gripped tightly with his knees. "I'm flying!"

The morning rays shone over the mountains, chasing the last of the darkness away. Now he could see long wings, slowly beating a steady rhythm, creating the slight rocking. The horse turned its head to glance back at Kai, regarding him with dark eyes.

An Archippos? Kai gasped. Archippos were in the old stories, flying with the heroes on their backs to win battles. Kai laughed. *Flying! On an Archippos!* He raised his arms as he let out a yell of excitement. The horse dipped its wings again, and Kai saw the ground below him. The thrill slowly disappeared, replaced with fear of falling. He clung to the white horse.

Welcome back to the world of the living! I thought you were going to sleep all day.

The words pierced through his brain. He ignored them and laughed again. This was better than riding a horse. The jolts were replaced by ripples of the wings through the back of the Archippos, and the wings made a deep pounding sound as they pushed the air smoothly. He laughed again. He could see Deston's jealous face as he rode in…no, *flew* over the racetrack. People would pay for rides. *What did the stories say about Archippi? Don't I need something to control it?*

The horse's ears laid flat against its head crossly. *That's enough, young man. You can stop thinking of me as a horse and call me Eladar instead. You will* not *be selling rides on me, so put those thoughts from your head before I drop you.*

Kai stared at the back of the horse's head. *Is it* talking *to me?* "You've got to be kidding! You can understand me!" He grinned. "That will make this easier. I need your help."

The horse turned its head and looked at him. There was a hint of humor in the dark eyes. *You mean to say that you want more help from me? I've saved you from falling to your death. I've healed your leg. And now you want more?*

"You haven't healed my leg," Kai replied and then realized that he hadn't felt any pain in his leg.

He touched the place on his leg where he felt the bone poking through the skin last night. No pain. He pulled back the bloody silks to look. No cuts, no scrapes, just wonderful healthy skin. Kai quickly felt his nose. It wasn't bashed in or broken.

"Horse nuggets!" He lifted his leg and wiggled it around. The movement made him lose his balance, and he grabbed at the mane. "And here I thought I'd ruined it all! But instead, look at what I have done." He let out a yell of triumph. "I've fixed everything. All my problems are over. When we get to Northbridge, the first thing we'll do is heal Rhiana. And then we'll go over the stables and…"

We are not going to Northbridge. Eladar's voice was stern. *We are headed south where we will meet some others who will help you purify the river.*

Kai snorted. "Yeah, and pigs fly, too. Even Chancellor Belial says he can only hope to fix the river. I've got to get back. And you're coming to help me with everything."

Belial put the poison in, it will be no problem for him to take it out. He's just saying that to remove suspicion. Eladar sighed. *The last thing we want is for him to succeed.*

"Oh, yeah. We like living with tainted water." Kai said sarcastically as he glared at the white neck with disgust. "I hope he succeeds."

If he cleanses it, his power will increase and make him almost invincible. Eladar never stopped flying south. *He would be one step closer to taking over the kingdom. Once he achieves the throne, there will be no stopping his*

true plans for Eltiria. You have been chosen to cleanse the
water before he does.

"I have been *kidnapped,* you mean," Kai yelled.
"You snatched me, and you are forcing me to go
somewhere I don't want to go! I don't want to be
chosen. I'm very grateful to you for saving and
healing me, but I really need to get back."

Do you really think you can fix your problems?

Kai paused. They'd tried praying to Adoyni
for Shona, and they'd taken her to the Temple.
Neither helped. Even if he got home, what *was*
he going to do for Rhiana? He'd be seized and
taken to Belial if he showed up in Northbridge. He
shuddered when he thought of what Belial would
do to him for killing Kedar.

Kai ran his hands through his hair. "Adoyni has
done nothing for me. Besides, I'm just a stable boy.
Why would you want me?"

*You haven't come to your full potential yet. And don't
forget about the Seekers. They never give up and can track
a fish through the ocean. They'll find you.*

The thought of those things chasing him
relentlessly sent shivers up his spine. He wanted
to go home. He wanted to see Mom and mess up
Rhiana's hair. He wanted to talk to Dad. But he was
trapped as neatly as a raccoon.

Eladar broke out of his glide with a tilt to the
left. *Rhiana may be saved. No one can know the future.
Hope is not lost. When you surrender, miracles happen.*

Kai snorted. *Surrender?* "Doesn't look like I have
much of a choice, do I?"

Not much. Not unless you want to jump! Eladar sounded cheerful as he moved faster through the clouds. *Now let's see if you can ride.* The clouds fell away as Eladar dove to the ground. Kai clung to the white mane and yelled as they plunged headfirst toward the ground, gliding down the cliff like a hawk streaking out of the sky for its prey. Eladar's wings were tucked up against his body. The ground was coming toward them fast.

Kai's legs, strong from riding horses, trembled as he held on. Eladar pulled up and began a steady beat. Each thrust of the wings took them higher and higher. Kai's shout was now filled with the sheer thrill of being alive. He slipped to the left as Eladar tilted and grasped at the mane to get a better seat.

If you would stop pulling on my mane, this would be more pleasant. Eladar's words cut through his panic. *I thought you could ride.*

The horse's great wings beat evenly as they rose up through the air. Kai watched the trees grow smaller and smaller as each push took them higher. His head spun.

"I can ride anything with four legs." His voice shook a bit.

Eladar didn't even bother to answer. He shot straight up into the air. Kai slipped onto Eladar's rump. Yelling, Kai grabbed for the mane, but it was out of his reach. His legs dangled in the air until

Eladar leveled out again. Kai pulled himself back
to a sitting position and tightened his grip with his
knees.

*Are you okay back there? It seems like you slipped a
little.*

"You're getting some sick sort of amusement
out of this, aren't you?" Kai glared at the back of
Eladar's head, trying to shove down the anger that
was growing inside of him.

You could be enjoying this, too, if you'd learn to stay on.

Eladar twisted to the left. Kai hugged Eladar's
neck as he corkscrewed up into the air. The ground
spun and blurred with the sky as Eladar weaved in
and out of the clouds. The mane whipped his face
as he buried his face in it. His arms burned and
started to slip. He wanted to beg Eladar to stop, but
he gritted his teeth and hung on. Eladar stopped
spinning.

*Well, you can ride. But you ride like a sack of
potatoes. At least we have something to work with.*

"If you would give me a warning," Kai retorted
angrily. "Then maybe I could stay on better."

*In battle, I may not have the time to warn you. You
have to be ready for anything.*

"Who said anything about battle?"

Always expect to be attacked, and perhaps you'll live.

"Well, this just keeps getting better and better."
Kai snapped, still stinging from Eladar's criticism of
his riding skills.

Eladar began a series of drills. But Kai still had time to wonder if Eladar was taking him away from where he should be going. The worry grew as Northbridge dropped farther and farther behind them.

CHAPTER SIXTEEN

Friends and Foes

Lizzy stood still in the trees at the edge of the meadow. If it was a Seeker, she could follow it to Rica and find a way to rescue him. *He should've kept his box. He needs it more than I do now.* The silver box he'd given her was in her pocket, protecting her. Her heart was beating so loud she was sure Taryn could hear it. She pulled out her sling and put a stone in the pouch. *I can hit it this time.* There was a pounding sound, like a large bird.

Taryn stood behind her, breathing heavily. The red hat was gone, and his blonde hair was flattened against his head. His hands were covered with Mischa's blood, and his fine purple coat was covered with dirt. She felt bad for him, even if he still hadn't apologized.

She saw something with white wings descend into the meadow. For a moment, she thought it had legs like a horse and almost laughed. As it drew nearer, she gasped. It was a large white horse with giant wings. *An Archippos!* Was everything from the old songs coming true?

She felt the wind on her face as it landed in the meadow, its back legs reaching the ground first. It folded its wings as someone slid off its back. He moved like he'd been riding for a long time. The songs told of men of great valor riding Archippi with giant swords, slaying all their enemies. But this rider was her age, and his torn clothes were filthy, covered with muck and torn almost to shreds. Maybe he was the horse's servant. He pushed back his golden blonde hair, and his eyes glinted blue in the sunlight.

Lizzy and Taryn, you can come out now.

The thought bounced in her mind. *Is the horse talking?* She stepped forward.

"What are you doing?" Taryn hissed. "You don't know if he's a friend or foe."

She ignored him. Taryn held back before following her. She studied the Archippos. He was one of the largest horses she'd seen, but it was his beauty that took her breath away. His delicate head, with a forelock hiding dark eyes, was set on a strong neck that sloped gently to a wide chest and a strong broad back. The wings looked soft and powerful at the same time. She could barely tear her eyes away from him. *Could this be the horse I saw in the forest?*

"What in all heavens now?" Taryn stopped behind her. "Is this really an Archippos?

The guy stood beside the horse's head, barely noticing them. "Eladar, why are we wasting our time here?"

Hush, Kai. The voice reminded her of Dad's voice with its confidence. *Lizzy and Taryn, I'm sorry I didn't get here soon enough to stop the attack. Seekers haven't attacked in broad daylight for many years. I thought you would be safe until tonight.* The Archippos shook his head in an apologetic manner.

Lizzy thought she was dreaming. *It* is *the horse from the forest!* The voice sounded deeper than any man's voice she had ever heard.

"How do you know our names?" Taryn must be hearing the words, too. He was staring at the horse with his mouth hanging open.

I've been watching for you for many years, waiting for the time to come when you were needed. That time is here.

When the horse uttered those words, Lizzy felt a stirring in her heart, something she'd never felt before. It wasn't fear, although there was a hint of that. It wasn't excitement, even though his words made her forget the events of the day. It was like she was summoned. But she didn't know who called.

"It was you, wasn't it, sir?" She realized in a flash. "You were in the forest yesterday."

Yes, I was. The horse lowered his head, and his mane rippled gracefully.

She resisted the urge to run to Eladar and pat its soft nose. Dignity seemed to radiate from him, and so she hesitated. Before she could ask, he started talking again.

But the time for questions is not now. You must follow me to safety. Seekers travel in packs of four. There is a good chance that one may be near. Eladar turned to the stagecoach. *But there are a few things that need to be done first.*

Lizzy paused. Rica said not to go with anyone. *Did he mean something as beautiful as Eladar?* She

watched Eladar walk away and felt as lost as she did
before he came.

*What would Mom say if she knew what's happening
to us?* She had the funny feeling she knew exactly
what Mom would say. *They should've taken you and rid
us of all our problems.* She came to a decision. She'd
go with Eladar tonight and then leave at the first
light to rescue Rica. She fingered the silver box and
hoped it would keep her safe.

* * *

Taryn couldn't look away from the wings
on Eladar. *Seekers? An Archippos?* He barely
remembered the fables he read when he was a
child, but he knew Eladar was a servant of Adoyni.
He watched the white horse, barely containing the
shivers that ran up and down his back from being
so close to such a deluded creature.

Kai turned in a circle and let out a low whistle.
"What happened here?"

Taryn glanced at Kai, wondering who he was.
He certainly was a laborer. It made him feel dirty
just looking at Kai. He refused to answer and
watched Eladar.

Lizzy finally answered, her green eyes sober.
"We were attacked. Everyone was killed. They took
my brother. I don't know if he's still alive."

"Would you look at that?" Taryn broke in,
unable to keep his astonishment quiet.

The large Archippos stopped beside the dead driver. He sniffed the hand of the body and snorted. Eladar tapped the ground twice with his hoof. The ground trembled and began to move. As the dirt shifted, the body sunk into a hole until it disappeared from sight. The earth continued to move, covering the body. The dirt settled, heaped in a mound and grass grew over it again.

Taryn couldn't believe it. Here was power. He knew that all great seers had sources of power, like crystals, that they could store power in until they needed it. He could tap into Eladar's abilities and find his true name if he had that kind of power behind him. Maybe Nighthawk Nephesus meant him to find this Archippos and bring him to the Temple of All.

Eladar buried all the bodies and then turned to them. *Taryn, say goodbye while we gather the supplies for the journey.*

"What journey?" Lizzy hesitated. "Look, I can't go with someone I don't know."

"With them?" Kai broke in. "How's a girl and a city boy going to help us? They'll just slow us down!"

"Who do you think you are to talk like that?" Taryn shot Kai an angry glance. "You need to show proper respect and speak only when your betters address you."

"My betters? You think you are better than me?" Kai's face flushed. "You need to realize that your fancy clothes don't make you a better person…just more stupid."

Taryn gasped. *This ignorant drudge dare call me stupid!* "You'll take that back or I'll…"

Children, this is not the time to be fighting with each other. Did not you understand what I said? The Seekers may return to this place. Do you want to face one again? Hurry now.

Taryn found himself halfway across the meadow to Mischa's grave before he realized what had just happened. He had obeyed without even thinking. *The thing must have used his magic on me.* He'd have to watch it closer if he was going to gain the upper hand. The thought of Adoyni's power touching him made him queasy.

Taryn sat down beside the grave. Mischa's lifeless body flashed across his mind, and he flinched. *What did he say? 'Your mother is…n…n…' What was he saying? Never? Nobody?*

His stomach turned at the thought of the death he had led Mischa into. It was *his* fault he'd died. *How can I ever go home and explain to Pater what I've done?* He sighed. *Who'd believe me? Seekers from the legends of old, and a horse that flies and talks in your mind? Pater will lock me up in the crazy house, saying I'm like Mom.*

He felt the pamphlet in his pocket and grimaced. *The Law of Intent. Whatever is done by you will be returned three-fold. I led Mischa to his death. What will happen to me? What's three times worse than this?*

He looked back at the grave. "I'm really sorry. I thought I was making things better by going to

Northbridge. I didn't mean for you to die. Thanks for being my friend." He wiped the tears away and walked over to the others.

CHAPTER SEVENTEEN

Packing Priorities

Kai followed Eladar and Lizzy to the coach seething with anger. *Eladar took me hostage for this! Those two are the most irritating stuck up prigs I've ever met!* He heard a chuckle from Eladar in his head, and it only added to his frustration. *I can't even think in privacy!*

Lizzy pulled her hair out of her face, tying it into a ponytail, and began to dig through the bags. "We're not going to be able to carry all this stuff. Just the water alone is too heavy."

"We'll take the horse." Kai pointed to the large brown horse that was twisted in the leather. "We can't leave her like this."

He stepped over to the horse, talking in a quiet tone. The horse pricked up her ears and nickered. He took a moment to rub the horse's neck. The horse trembled but stood quietly as Kai unharnessed her, keeping a steady stream of chatter while he attached a long rope to her halter.

"Better, Minnie?" Kai asked as he staked her to graze.

Lizzy snorted, "Great name."

"Minnie? Sounds like a mouse," Taryn said as he walked up. He turned to Eladar. "Where are we going? Northbridge?"

The last place you're going is Northbridge.
Eladar was eating grass while he talked. *It's too
dangerous.*

"But I have to go there. That's where my future
lays. I need to go find my true name to have the
power to heal the river," Taryn explained.

The only response was a long snort. Obviously
Eladar didn't think much about finding true
names.

Kai turned to Eladar. "Maybe we should go back
if that's where they want to go, too. Rhiana's going
to die because we're rescuing strangers. I mean, I
feel bad for them, but this isn't helping my family."

"*Your* family?" Lizzy was shorter than Kai by
a foot, but that didn't stop her green eyes from
glaring at him. "What about my family? My brother
was kidnapped by Seekers. Even if we find the
King's Guards, who's going to believe me? I'll tell
you. No one! I don't know about your problems,
but they can't be much worse than that. It's my
family that needs the help."

"My little sister is dying," Kai snapped
back. "Stallion's straws! If I don't get back to
Northbridge, that disease from the water will kill
her, just like it killed my big sister, and I'm not
going to let that happen!"

*That's enough bickering, unless you want to wait
here for the Seekers. Finish packing up. We need to leave
quickly.* Eladar's voice held little patience.

They stared at each other until Lizzy huffed and
turned away. Kai searched the bags until he found

some breeches and a tan shirt with long sleeves. He slipped into the woods and changed. He held up the silks for a minute. They were torn and tattered from his race through the woods. Blood streaked down where his leg was broken. *Why won't Eladar heal Rhiana?*

Balling up the silks, he went back to the meadow. Lizzy was standing in the middle of a number of bags. Her long red hair looked more blonde in the sunlight. He might like her, if she would control her temper.

"Look." Lizzy pointed beside the pile of bags. "I found those in the coach. I think the driver had one, but I don't know who owned the second one."

There were two swords in the grass. The first one was shorter, fastened to a black hilt. But it was the second sword that caught his eye. The hilt was deep silver with a small blue gem in the center. Pulling the sword free of the scabbard, Kai grinned. Even he knew this sword was far better than the ones he saw the soldiers carry around. The silver blade glistened in the sunlight as he waved the sword around, feeling its weight and balance.

"Wow." He felt the sharp edge of the sword.

"It's too heavy for me," Lizzy smiled an apology. "I'll take the smaller one. We have to carry the food. With the barrels of water, I don't know how much more Minnie can carry. I've made a stack of things to take over there." Lizzy gestured to a large pile beside Taryn.

Kai inspected it and held up a guitar. "Wait a minute. This isn't something that we need. Why's this in here?"

"Put it down," Lizzy snapped. "It's going with us whether you like it or not."

Taryn looked up, showing interest for the first time. "Did you get my books?"

"Books? A guitar? Are you two crazy?" Kai couldn't believe what he was hearing. With all this junk, they'd be moving slower than a turtle. "We need to take only important things."

Taryn stood up and crossed his arms. "My books are important. If you could read, you would know that."

"I'm not leaving my guitar. And who do you think you are? I don't remember anyone making you the boss." Lizzy glared at him over the suitcases.

"Bring them." Kai was feeling trapped between them. "Wood burns. When we get cold, your guitar will be great firewood." Taryn snickered as Lizzy gasped. Kai continued, "And paper's great for starting a fire."

Taryn turned red, his brown eyes filled with anger. "If you dare touch my books, I'll...I'll..."

"What? You'll hit me?" Kai laughed at the thought of Taryn attacking him.

Children! Eladar's voice cut through the argument. Kai wanted to protest that he was not a child, but Eladar didn't give him a chance.

Perhaps the seriousness of our predicament hasn't hit you yet. We're going to get nowhere if you keep squabbling like this.

No one said anything for a minute.

"Fine then." Kai ran his hands through his hair in frustration. "But they're the last thing I load. Food and water goes first."

Taryn pawed through the pile of bags. He placed his three books on top of the guitar and kept a knapsack with him. Both of them ignored Kai. The pile had barrels of water, a small hatchet, and a small pile of gold coins. He fingered them, wishing that they weren't the old coins with the scepter of Adoyni on them. The Flames Belial issued would buy them much more than these old things. He shook his head when he saw the meager pile of food.

"We're going to have to ration our food," Kai said. "We might have enough for a couple of days."

"Might?" Taryn looked panicked. "What'll we do after that?"

"Hunt," Lizzy said. "But we'll have to go easy on the water."

Taryn looked down at his stomach. "But I'm already hungry."

"Get used to it." Lizzy was offering no sympathy.

Kai didn't think there was any way to get it all on Minnie. But then Lizzy came over and with an adjustment here and there, suddenly there was room for the guitar and the books. *How'd she learn to pack like that?* She stood, hands on her hips, with her eyebrows raised like he was supposed to kiss her feet for getting it all on Minnie.

Taryn got to his feet when he saw they were finished. He poked at three cloaks on the ground with his toe. "You forgot to load these. If they're going."

"We're wearing them," Lizzy explained. "We need to carry everything we can to save room on Minnie."

"I'm not wearing that." Taryn looked disgusted. "They're scratchy and ugly. Look at how plain they are."

"Plain but warm," Kai snapped. *Mom would give her right hand to have something this warm for Dad.* "Feel how thick it is. That keeps out the cold. No one's forcing you to take it, but you won't be getting mine when you're freezing to death."

Taryn finally put it on. He grimaced every time it touched his skin. Kai ran his hands through his hair. *This is a disaster. I'll never make it with these two. I hope she can at least cook.*

"Let's go," he said. He picked up his sword, feeling a bit out of place.

Eladar twitched his tail as he regarded them for a minute. *This way.* He turned and led the way east as Lizzy and Taryn followed him. Kai grabbed Minnie's lead rope and clucked softly.

Turning at the edge of the meadow, Kai saw the burnt coach and the graves. He had the feeling that they were all going to end up in a grave just like those people. The thought sent shivers through his body, and he followed with a heavy heart.

CHAPTER EIGHTEEN

Fish and Rabbits

Lizzy followed Eladar, anger pounding through her with every beat of her heart. She even forgot to look down the road one more time to see if Rica was returning. All she could think about was how Kai threatened to burn her guitar. *Just who does this country bumpkin think he is?* She amused herself with thinking about his things she would burn. Since he didn't have anything with him, she'd start with his feet. Maybe his hands.

Eladar turned and looked at her. If he were human, she was sure that one eyebrow would be raised and the dark eyes would hold a warning with a slight twinkle. *He knows what I'm thinking.* She blushed. *I've got to control my thoughts better!*

It wasn't like she would do any of that. Kai just made her so mad. Well, she'd show both of them. She'd walk faster and farther than them. She'd even fight better. *Why can I hit everything perfectly when I practice, but when it really matters, I can't hit anything?* The shadows grew longer with the approaching night, and she glanced around nervously, wondering if another Seeker was stalking them.

Taryn called out. "Hold up." He ran over to a tree. There hung the axe he had thrown right before Rica was captured.

Taryn tugged on it, but it didn't budge. He braced against the tree and pulled with his foot against the tree. It didn't even shift. Nothing worked. He stepped back to catch his breath. Kai went up and beside him and pulled. It slid out of the tree as easily as a hot knife through butter. Lizzy couldn't help giggling, even with the horrors of the day. Kai gave him the axe with his eyebrows raised, his blue eyes twinkling. He opened his mouth to say something, but then merely shrugged and slapped Taryn on the shoulder. Taryn stumbled. Lizzy bit her lip to keep from laughing. Whoever he was in Albia, he certainly wasn't a woodsman.

"Eladar," Taryn spoke up. "Can we all hear you at once?"

I can speak to just one of you or all of you if I wish. It's like shouting or whispering for you. Eladar twitched his ears.

Taryn pushed ahead of Lizzy to get closer to Eladar. Lizzy glared at Taryn's back.

"Where are we going?" Kai strode faster to get closer to Eladar. Minnie followed behind him. Lizzy found herself at the back of the line. She scowled at both of the boys.

You must journey until you find a way to stop the poison in River Shammah before it kills the whole world. Adoyni will guide and help you, and I promise to do all that I can.

"Adoyni?" Taryn spat out the word like it was poison. "He doesn't exist. Zoria, the Goddess, is the ruler of the world. One only has to look to at nature to see Her handiwork. Doctors, scientists, seers, everyone of importance have looked for a cure. It can only be done through Zoria."

"Why us?" Lizzy asked. "Why do the Seekers want us? Why do *we* have to stop the poison?"

Each one of you is directly related to The Slayers. As you might remember from the stories, The Slayers promised that they and their descendants would fight the evil as long as it was needed. Belial knows this and rightfully fears you. He'll stop at nothing to kill you.

"But that's impossible. The Slayers are just from the stories." Kai looked at the wings and shook his head. "I know that you are too, but they were just regular people."

They were regular people with a strong belief in Adoyni. He gave them the power to imprison Seiten on Elda Isle, and they brought peace after years of war and hate.

"I heard my mother say that we weren't related to them. Rica, my brother, was asking about them last night," Lizzy argued.

"I can't imagine Pater being related to any heroes," Taryn interrupted. "The only thing he rescues is math questions answered incorrectly."

The trees began to thin out as they climbed steeper hills. Lizzy missed the shelter of the brush where it was easier to hide. But Eladar didn't seem to mind as he strode ahead of them. She swallowed. Soon they would be in the open where anything could see them.

Your parents have no idea who their ancestors were. The bloodline was hidden to protect them until the time came. Even the Wise Ones in Merrihaven had to search many years to find you. We have reason to believe that Belial has actually survived a journey to Elda Isle and consulted with Seiten.

"Don't listen to him," Taryn said, his hazel eyes serious. "No seer would attempt to contact Seiten, if he exists. Belial is wise and kind, and has done more than the King, who claims to worship Adoyni, ever did before he got sick. Belial gave us a better money system and built countless schools."

Yes, he has done those things. But the poor can no longer afford to buy the supplies they need because they have only the Scepters. And the schools are only for those that worship Zoria. Thousands are turned away from learning for staying faithful to Adoyni. The motive behind Belial's actions is foul. He desired power to rule and to wipe out Adoyni. The Goddess is just a cover for Seiten. And you were walking straight into their trap. They didn't know you were on that coach. They're at the Temple of All waiting for you to walk willingly through the doors.

"That's not true," Taryn said, his voice rising. "It's a special event of classes for the Goddess. Nighthawk Nephesus told me about that. They wouldn't think about killing me."

Did you hear of anyone else going to the classes? Did you find the information in your temple? Was anyone else talking about it? Did anyone else, besides you, know about this event?

Taryn was quiet, his jaw clenched. "I don't know," he finally said. "But I know I'm supposed to heal the river at the Temple of All."

"What about me?" Lizzy asked. "They took Rica, not me."

They must've thought Rica would be the one, perhaps looking for a male descendent. Eladar's voice grew softer. *My child, I fear for Rica when they discover he's not the one they want.*

But why…?" Kai began, but Eladar's voice cut through his thoughts.

Quiet! Eladar froze, his ears pricked to the east. They obeyed without question, even Taryn. Lizzy was afraid to breathe. Fear crept up her spine when she thought of the Seekers. Eladar gazed into the trees behind them for a long time. The birds hushed as the forest grew darker.

I hear something beyond what your ears can hear. Head south to the dip in those two hills. And move quietly. I'll be back as soon as I can.

"I could come," Kai spoke up.

Eladar shook his head. *Stay with the others and keep them safe.* He took off at a run, spreading his wings, and leapt into the air, leaving them alone. Lizzy stared after him until he disappeared over the treetops. They started walking again.

Taryn finally broke the silence. "He's put some sort of enchantment on us. Look at how we're so willing to believe him and do what he says."

"What if he's right?" Kai asked. "What if they are waiting to kill you? Do you really think the second greatest seer is dying for you to join them? Stop being an idiot."

"Don't you dare call me an idiot," Taryn yelled, his face red with anger. "He's not right. He's a servant of Adoyni. No one worships Adoyni anymore because He doesn't care about us. All those prayers, all those pointless services, are wasted. If He does hear, He doesn't care. The Goddess hears and cares. Belial and Nighthawk have done good. I'm not listening to any servant of Adoyni." Taryn spat out the last words like they were poison.

No one had anything to say in reply. They walked on, lost in their own thoughts. The sun began to set, its beams filtering through the trees. Rica's voice echoed in her head.

Lizzy stopped walking. "Well, I can't help him with the whole river thing. If what he says is true, then Rica's going to need me. They'll kill him if it's me they're looking for."

Both of the boys stopped and turned to stare at her like she'd just spoken in gibberish.

"What do you think you are going to do?" Kai asked. "You're not a seer or a warrior. You're just a girl."

"I don't know." Lizzy felt tears rising and fought them back, but her voice shook. "But I have to try."

"I guess that just leaves you, then," Taryn turned to Kai. "You can go with Eladar."

"I don't think so," Kai snorted. "He said that the three of us were needed, and if you don't come, then there's no way to heal Rhiana. You're coming with me."

"Why do you think you're the boss?" Lizzy snapped. "My brother has been kidnapped by monsters, and you have the audacity to tell me that I have to follow you. What makes your sister better than my brother? Someone who has sense should lead us, and I'm obviously the only one around here who has any. I say we go back and rescue Rica."

Taryn snorted. "You? You're just the daughter of an entertainer. She's very good, but your family will never rise out of the level of servants, living on the good will of the aristocrats. If you want a leader, I accept. Apparently I'm the only one here with any sort of decent education, and my family has noble blood."

"Are you calling my family servants?" Lizzy said in a very low tone.

"What if Eladar's right?" Kai ignored her question. "You didn't answer that. If you go to the Temple of All, what if they kill you? Are you willing to risk that? And Lizzy, what good is it to try to save your brother if you are killed before you do it? What if the only way to help our families is to purify the water before Belial does it?"

"But how in the universe are you going to fix the river?" Taryn pointed to the sky. "Seers have studied the stars for the answer and haven't found a thing. Why are you so special? The only way to access enough power to heal it is at the Temple of All."

Kai's question kept circling through Lizzy's mind. *What if he's right?* She knew she didn't have a chance to rescue Rica. "I don't know. I don't want to die, and I don't want Rica to die." The words seemed to tear the very breath away from her. "But I've got to do something for him."

"Eladar is *not* right." Taryn continued to protest. "Nighthawk dropped a pamphlet in my lawn. That's when she invited me to the classes. Maybe she sensed my power. Maybe the pamphlet was searching for the one who was strong enough to help them, and she found me."

"Maybe the pamphlet was searching for the one who is related to The Slayers, and you went running happily into her trap," Kai emphasized his words with a jab of his finger.

Taryn put a hand on his pants pocket as if protecting something. Lizzy thought she heard the crackle of paper. His face lost all color as he considered what Kai had said.

"Maybe. But I still say all this Adoyni stuff is a lie." Taryn paused, his face white, and sighed. "But the stupid horse has scared me about the Temple. If he's right…"

Kai turned and walked south, not waiting to hear the rest of what Taryn was going to say. "Let's save the river then, and get it over with as fast as possible so that we can get back and take care of our problems."

"Great," Lizzy said with little enthusiasm. "Eladar had better be right about this, or I'll take it out of his hide."

"We're trapped." Taryn groaned. "Caught like a fish in a net. Trapped like a rabbit. And you know what always happens to that rabbit? It gets killed by the first thing to come along."

CHANGES

*"There is nothing wrong with change,
if it is in the right direction."*
~Winston Churchill

Foehn waited for the Master outside his palace in
Northbridge. Long lines of sick people filled the street
to the palace, for they'd heard that the Master was
in town. It was rumored that one touch of his robe
would heal the deadly disease from the water.

But Foehn knew the truth. While the Master was
the most powerful seer in the land, he didn't use his
power for good like Foehn once thought. He only
helped when there was a profit. The last person the
Master healed was a small boy around the age of five.
His father was one of the richest men in the land,
until he paid the price for healing. Now the man
was poor with a healthy son, and the Master was the
richest man in the world. Foehn wasn't shocked when
people didn't see the evil. It had taken him years to
see that the Master only desired power and money.

The crowds parted. Foehn saw Nighthawk
Nephesus hustle up to the golden gates that kept the
crowd away from the palace. Her red hair was covered
with a black cloak. They stretched their hands out
to her, begging for a healing. She swept past them
without a glance.

The master's steward ran out and unlocked the gates with a large golden key while the soldiers stepped forward to block the crowd from rushing the palace. Nighthawk slipped through the gates without a glance at the steward or soldiers. The crowd roared with disapproval when they saw that she passed them by, and they rushed the gates. The soldiers pulled out their swords and advanced on the people. They retreated at the threat and settled down to wait for the Master to appear.

Foehn followed Nighthawk into the palace. Her long black cloak streamed out behind her as she strode up the steps. Throwing the cloak to a servant, she smoothed down her rich velvet blue skirts and straightened her red hair.

She followed the servant to the library. He opened the door and bowed as she entered. Foehn crept carefully through the door as it closed behind her, his presence betrayed only by the briefest ripple in a page of a book. Neither the Master nor Nighthawk noticed.

"What news?" The Master shut his book with a slam but didn't rise.

Nighthawk curtsied before him. "My lord, I've tested him as all the others."

Belial stood and poured two glasses of wine from a silver pitcher. "The results, Nighthawk. Now."

Nighthawk hesitated. Her brown eyes reflected the candle light. Foehn saw fear in them. "He's not the one. He's a descendant, but he has none of the power you seek."

The Master held the two goblets in his hands. With a roar of anger, he threw them against the stone wall. They crashed and spun to the floor, red wine spilling from them like blood from a dead body.

"You said he was the one!" he roared. Nighthawk took a step back. "You lied!"

"I said his family was." Her words came fast. "Perhaps he has a sibling. The Seekers may have passed over them, especially if he is the elder."

The Master glared at her. Foehn saw sparks on his fingertips, a sign of his uncontrollable rage. He wrapped his fingers around her throat, and she flinched as the sparks burnt her skin. "If you're lying to me, I'll kill you without a thought."

Nighthawk struggled to breathe as his fingers squeezed. "Master, I would never lie to you. Your goals are my goals. I live to serve you."

The Master held her in his grip for a minute longer and shoved her back. She stumbled a few steps, holding her throat. He ignored her while he poured wine into another goblet and strode to the fireplace. He sipped the wine as he stared at the fire.

"Go question him." He ordered, his voice rising with anger. "Find out where his siblings are. Torture him if you must, but do not kill him. He could be used as bait. But find the one with the power. I need

all three of them. I will have their power." Belial
screamed out the last words.

"As you command, my lord." Nighthawk curtsied
deeply.

As she opened the door, the Master said quietly,
"You'd better find that sibling, or you'll regret it. In
what little life you might have left."

Foehn followed Nighthawk out of the library and
into the streets. The good man Foehn thought he
followed had deceived him. And now changes were
on the horizon. Changes that would bring only pain
and destruction.

CHAPTER NINETEEN

Bagboys and Cooks

Kai walked in silence to the dip in the hills. *A rabbit in a snare.* It described him better than Taryn knew. The troubles surrounding his family had trapped him into a life he never wanted. *Eladar had better be telling the truth, and these two better pull their own to fix the river.* If Rhiana died, he would never forgive Eladar for kidnapping him and dumping him with these two city folks.

Lizzy and Taryn were quiet as they walked. *For once.* They made it to the dip between the two hills where Eladar was waiting for them in the trees.

He nickered a welcome. *On the top of this hill is a safe place where we can rest tonight.*

Taryn panted behind them as Eladar led the way up the steep slope. The trees gave way to rock and sparse grass, and the wind still had a bite from winter. When Kai reached the top, he could see the meadow, the coach just a small dot. Eladar paused on the top, the wind blowing his mane back and forelock out of his eyes.

"Oh, good. No shelter. No place to hide. This just keeps getting better." Taryn said between gasps of air when he caught up. "Looks like a great place to be caught."

A flat plateau stretched out in front of them with a few boulders dotting the landscape. The wind rustled through the long grass still brown from the winter. If the Seekers found them here, there would be nowhere to hide. Two large stones, taller than his head, stood directly in front of them, not ten feet away. *Did Eladar lead us into a trap?*

Lizzy squinted and tilted her head. "I see something...like a castle or part of a castle."

Eladar approached the two large stones. They were smooth sided, like they'd been quarried, and they stood alone on the plateau as if someone had placed them there. Kai couldn't imagine anyone being big enough to move such giant rocks. Eladar placed his hoof on one. Kai heard Lizzy gasp as an object shimmered in front of them. It snapped into view, and a large stone tower stood in the center of the hill. Eladar moved back from the boulders.

Welcome to Heniah, a refuge of many Archippi and their riders for many years. After we enter, the shield will descend again and protect us for a short while.

"If this place will hide us, why can't we stay here forever?" Lizzy asked as they made their way to the tower. "You could bring us food and stuff."

I wish it were that easy, but the Seekers would eventually find you. They are creatures of magic and would eventually realize that this place is not all that it seems to be.

Kai examined the stone tower as they drew close. It was taller than two houses stacked on top of each other and had windows encircling

it, making it possible for a person to see in all
directions. There was one large wooden door with
an iron handle in front of them. He lifted the latch,
but as he pulled on the handle, the door stuck. He
wiggled the latch and pulled as hard as he could.
The door refused to open.

"Open, you stupid door," he growled and pulled
again. The door groaned and creaked, but it gave
way, opening to reveal a large room. There was
a tall stone table down the middle of the room,
stretching through the length of the tower. The
wooden chairs were built to fit the table, but they
had foot rests on them so that whoever sat on them
wouldn't have to dangle their feet. *It's designed to be
comfortable for both Archippi and people.* Kai grinned
as he pictured the table full of Archippi standing
at the table and people sitting on the big chairs. To
the left was a pot for cooking with a wood box filled
with kindling. Stairs circled the tower on the right.

"Lizzy, start a fire," he ordered. "Taryn, come
with me and help unload Minnie."

"Why me?" Lizzy snapped. "Because I'm a girl?
I'm not doing it, and you can't make me."

"Help you unload?" Taryn snorted, sounding
much like Eladar. "I think not. You're not my boss."

"Someone has to do it," he protested.

Taryn looked him up and down, taking in the
dirty hands and face. "Well, you look the most
qualified."

Kai felt his face grow hot as he tried to think of
something to say when he saw Eladar twitching an

ear. He swallowed the rage as he stomped outside. *No one, not even Eladar cares about my problems. I'm just a bagboy for this stupid trip.* He fumed as he unloaded Minnie and tethered her where the grass was the thickest.

The night air grew colder by the minute. He reluctantly joined the group. Taryn had flung off his cloak and was trying to clean the blood off his shirt, while Lizzy was busy combing her sorrel colored hair. There was no fire and no food cooking.

"You've got to be kidding," Kai groaned. No one acknowledged his presence. He took some of the wood from the box and threw it into the fire pit with as much force as he could. Eladar blew on the wood until embers appeared under the wood, blazing into a fire. Taryn gasped. Lizzy laughed and ran to Eladar's side.

"That was amazing," she said shyly. She put her hand on his neck as she stared at the fire.

Eladar chuckled. *A handy trick when everything is wet, and there's no tinder box. Now, daughter, do you think you could warm up some food for dinner?*

"But of course." Lizzy grinned and placed some cold chicken on a pan.

Kai flopped onto a chair, feeling his anger return. *Why wouldn't she cook when I told her to? Well, at least she* can *cook. Maybe this won't be so bad after all.*

"How are you doing all of this?" Taryn asked. "Fire spells, invisibility spells. What is your power source?"

Eladar moved to the table. *Adoyni gives his children abilities when we surrender to His guidance. He uses us to accomplish His purposes.*

"Abilities? You mean powers, right?" Taryn learned forward. "What else can you do?"

Kai watched the chicken warm up. "He healed my leg. The bone was sticking through the skin, but it's fine now."

"Really?" He took his glasses off and leaned closer to Eladar. "Can you teach me?"

I can teach you in a sense. I can teach you about Adoyni. As you grow in Him, He may use you to do great things. But, there's a big difference between what you think of as magic and living your life open to His will.

Taryn stopped asking questions. Maybe all the talk of Adoyni stopped him, or maybe it was the chicken Lizzy handed out. Kai didn't care. At least he had stopped talking.

"Does Merrihaven really exist?" Kai asked around his chicken. *Well, if she calls this cooking, she sure has a lot to learn.*

Of course it does. Eladar shook his head as he laughed. *We have to live somewhere.*

"We? There's more of you?" Taryn finished up his chicken. "Can they do magic like you?"

Kai sighed. All Taryn wanted to talk about was magic. *How is all of this supposed to save the world? Or Rhiana? If we had to join up with someone, why couldn't it have been warriors?*

Patience, Kai. Eladar's voice broke through his thoughts, and Kai wondered how much he'd heard. *They're just like you. Not up to their full potential yet.*

He ran his hands through his hair. He wanted to know what was happening at home. He shoved his thoughts to a place where Eladar couldn't hear. *Are they okay? What am I doing?*

"What happened?" Kai interrupted another question about magic. "Why did you all go to Merrihaven and never come back until now?"

Eladar sighed. *In the time of the Slayers, Archippi and people lived together. However, after the war, people began to drift away from Adoyni. Knowing change was coming, we settled in Merrihaven. After some time, Amhar, the grandfather of King Adric, ordered the Archippi to leave and never come back. When some of the Archippi resisted, the king ordered his soldiers to kill any Archippi on sight. Although we could've fought back, we chose to leave. We wait until the king commands us back.*

"But if you had stayed, maybe this would've never happened," Lizzy spoke up. Her green eyes were dark as the light grew dimmer. "Aren't the Archippi supposed to keep us safe?"

Yes, Lizzy, they are. But our own safety from evil lies in you. Your faith in Adoyni gives us a shield against the evil. Without that, we are easily killed and wounded. Belial knows this and has worked hard to position himself where he can do the most damage to us. With King Adric's health declining and his son gone, Belial has wormed his way close to the king's heart. If he fixes the water, the people will clamor to his side to worship him. Then when the king dies, it will be easy for him to take the throne, becoming a god king. As more follow him, we are limited in what we can do.

Taryn sat at the table, his hazel eyes smoldering with anger as Eladar mentioned Belial. But he kept quiet, chewing on his lip like he was thinking hard. The conversation died as they pondered what Eladar said.

Kai followed Lizzy up the stairs and found a room with two beds in it. Lizzy slipped into the second room. Kai tried not to roll his eyes as Taryn inspected each speck of dust, muttering about fleas the whole time. Kai gave up and rolled his eyes when Taryn was sure to notice. Taryn glared at him and checked the pillow. Nothing was said as Taryn gingerly crawled between the sheets and lay stiff as a board. Kai pulled his blanket over him without a thought or care.

Thoughts tumbled in his head. He lay awake, wondering about what Eladar had said. With no heir and extended family, everyone assumed Belial would take the throne. It'd never bothered him before, but after meeting Belial, Kai wasn't so sure about Belial being king. He remembered the angry words and stare Belial had given him. A king should not be possessed of such rage. Despite his weariness, sleep wouldn't come. He listened to Taryn's snores for a long time before drifting into an uneasy slumber.

* * *

The next morning, Lizzy helped Kai pack up Minnie after breakfast, and they followed Eladar across the plateau. She made sure her silver box was still in her pocket. She was tired. Every time she closed her eyes last night, she saw Rica being hauled off. She traced the heart with the circle of roses on the silver box for reassurance. *How can an herb protect me against a Seeker? But Rica believed it.* She knew he was rarely wrong, so she was going to keep it close.

Eladar walked in front of her, his steps graceful as he moved around the rocks that littered the ground. His white coat shimmered in the sunlight, making him look like a star on the earth.

Eladar? She called out in her mind, hoping he would hear her.

Eladar flicked an ear back but kept walking. *Yes, Lizzy?*

I'm scared. Tears threatened to build. She turned her face into the wind, determined not to let the guys see her cry.

Eladar laughed quietly. *As you should be. Seasoned warriors would hesitate to do what you are doing. But remember courage is not the absence of fear. Courage is moving forward when you have every reason to go back.*

I keep thinking about Rica. The wind blew her hair over her face, and she brushed it back.

Eladar gave no inclination that they were talking. *Don't lose hope. We don't yet know what will happen.*

Tears came to her eyes and she blinked them away angrily. *It's so hard to believe that I'm the one they want. No one ever wants me. Rica is the one that everyone loves. I'm just...* She stopped talking. She didn't really know what she was. *Useless.*

There is One who loves you more than you can ever imagine. You were created by Adoyni, just so He could talk to you. And you can do more than you ever dreamed. And if you'll let Him, He'll use you for great deeds. Eladar blew through his nose softly. *And everyone messes things up once in a while. Don't dwell on that too much.*

"*Everyone? Even you?*" Lizzy looked over at the horse.

Even me. Eladar chuckled. *Although I don't like to admit it.*

Kai spoke up, "How come we are going south?"

Lizzy glanced up. He was right, and she hadn't even noticed. Eladar stopped at the drop off. Standing on the ridge, Lizzy caught her breath and gazed across a beautiful valley stretched out before them. On the other side, it sloped up into mountains peaked with snow.

What I heard last night surprised me. The enemy is moving faster than I had imagined. It wasn't a Seeker like we thought. It was a scout for an army. I followed it back to this valley. There's an army of Unwanteds down there, the first for many years.

"Unwanteds?" Taryn exclaimed, his brown eyes wide behind his glasses. "They don't exist because there is no heaven or hell."

"Everyone knows Archippi don't exist, either," Kai reminded him. "And yet here one is. Maybe everything from the stories exists."

Almost everything.

Eladar's answer sent chills through Lizzy. There were a lot of evil creatures in the stories. She kept quiet, knowing her voice would shake if she spoke, and she didn't want them to know she was scared. The songs said the Unwanteds were rejected by Adoyni, and neither heaven nor hell would allow them to enter. They were left to wander the world where powerful sorcerers could command them. In her nightmares, she always dreamt that she was turning into one, her skin turning gray and her eyes turning completely black.

See those fires in the north. That's where they are gathered. They turned and saw smoke rising through the air. The air was thick with it. *This valley is full of them. I wanted to put some distance between them before we cross the valley. If we move quietly and if they are not patrolling, we might be able to pass by without being noticed.*

"What if we're attacked?" Lizzy asked before she could stop herself. The last word squeaked a bit.

If we're attacked, Adoyni will protect us. See the bottom of the mountains? Eladar nodded toward the mountains on the other side of the valley. *There is a river there. The Unwanted only cross water when they are forced by a master. I haven't sensed anyone close with such power, so I'm assuming their orders are to wait for him. We have to get across the river before they see us. Don't worry, children, Adoyni will protect us.*

Lizzy fought the tears that rose to her eyes. They were facing the horrors from the legends with Adoyni as their only defense. It was like walking up to a mountain lion pretending to have a sword in your hand.

"Can't we just go around?" Taryn asked. "We could miss the valley completely."

It will take several days to do that, and we don't have that much time. We have to fix the river before the first day of spring.

She slipped the box Rica gave her out of her pocket and held it tightly in her right hand for further protection. It was all she had left now. Lizzy followed Eladar, watching the tower disappear. When it vanished from sight, she knew safety would also be gone.

CHAPTER TWENTY

Gentle Milk Cows

Taryn followed Lizzy down the hill. He wondered how Eladar could be so delusional. He wasn't going to believe anything the horse said. Belial and Nighthawk were good people, doing good things, and he wasn't going to change his mind until he saw anything different. And he certainly wasn't going to believe that the Unwanteds existed until he saw one. He felt his pocket and heard the reassuring crackle of the pamphlet.

And for the first time in his life, he would rather *not* know something. He felt the crystal sphere in his bag on his back. *If anything jumps out, I'll show them what I can do.* Thank the stars he'd loaded the sphere with as much power as it could hold. If they were attacked, he knew one spell to defend himself. It should have enough power for that.

They went into the forest. The trees grew close, making the air oppressive. As the sun rose above them, the heat made it worse. They walked for hours through the shadows with no sounds other than their feet.

A figure stepped out in front of Eladar and stood still. Taryn thought nothing was more frightening than a Seeker, but this creature made his blood turn to ice. It was a human. Almost. It was barely clothed and had long dirty black hair hanging to his waist. The hair, matted and caked with mud, fell over its face. The transparent skin showed every vein and artery racing over the body.

It began to call to the others with a high pitched scream. Taryn felt goose bumps rise on his arms. His hands trembled as he gripped the axe. He wanted to run away from the thing but didn't know where would be safe. Eladar reared and spread out his wings as he flew at the Unwanted. Before it could react, Eladar struck it in the head with his front hoof. Taryn closed his eyes as it sunk to the ground, its head caved in. Taryn looked away from Eladar's hoof red with blood, and all hopes of taking the Archippos to the Temple of All to use as a source of power vanished. As nice as the horse seemed, he was a warrior at heart.

"Y...you killed him!" Lizzy exclaimed, her face ashen. "How could you do something like that?"

Eladar didn't respond. Instead, his eyes were pricked toward the woods north of them. They froze, listening to the silence. Taryn couldn't hear a thing. Four more Unwanted rushed out of the forest. Taryn stared at the once humans running at them with swords and branches. One Unwanted, an older woman, raced at Eladar with a stick. Kai leaped to the center of the path, holding the sword awkwardly like a young child holding a pencil.

Taryn took a step forward and gripped the axe tighter. If Kai could fight, so could he. He swallowed. He held the axe ready to swing. It pulled at his muscles, making them burn as he waited. He shifted positions as the axe slipped in his sweaty hands.

He caught a glimpse of Lizzy. She was aiming at an Unwanted rushing her. It was yelling as it swung a large branch. She released the strap of the sling, and a small rock shot out, faster than he could see. The creature came to a stumbling stop and looked at its weapon that had exploded in its hands. It tossed the limb away and rushed at Lizzy. She screamed and fumbled for another rock. Taryn yelled and ran toward her, but the Unwanted was almost on her, ready to tear her apart with its bare hands.

Light flashed, and Taryn caught a glimpse of lightning coming from Eladar. It streaked across the opening and struck the Unwanted in the back. It screamed as it exploded. After he blinked, he saw Lizzy trembling and staring at the pieces of the Unwanted in front of her. He swallowed, wanting to throw up, and heard Kai yelling.

Kai was facing a younger Unwanted. He was holding his ground, dancing around and slashing at it. The Unwanted snarled and lunged at Kai. He stepped back, stumbled on a rock, and fell.

"Do something!" Kai was rolling in the dirt, not able to get to his feet, barely avoiding the creature's furious stabbing.

Lizzy searched for another rock while Taryn ran up and swung his axe. He missed, but Kai gained his feet while Taryn distracted it. Out of the corner of his eye, he saw Lizzy grab a rock and put it in her sling.

Kai yelled in pain and clutched his arm. "Ow!"

Lizzy stood behind Kai with a hand over her face. "I'm sorry," she said, horror filled her eyes. "I didn't mean to hit you."

"I should hope not," Kai snapped. "Watch what you're doing. That stung!"

The Unwanted charged Taryn. He swung at it and missed. It kept coming, swinging its sword. A flash of white streaked in front of him. Taryn saw Eladar's hooves in front of his face, and the Unwanted dropped to the ground. When the dust cleared, Taryn saw that its head was caved in like a smashed melon. He looked away quickly and desperately hoped that he wouldn't throw up. Kai and Lizzy would never let him forget it if he did.

Kai poked the one by him with his toe. "I guess they exist."

Lizzy's face was white, but giggled with what Taryn thought was panic in her laugh. "Or they did." She didn't glance at any of the bodies.

The two of them exchanged a glance and smiled weakly. Taryn felt a stab of jealousy. If only he had used a spell. Then they would like him.

Eladar glanced at them. *Is everyone okay? Let's keep going. The river is still far away.*

Kai walked to where Minnie stood trembling. Taryn was shocked when Kai shoved the rope in his face. Taryn took it tentatively. *What am I supposed to do with this?*

"Here's something you can do." Kai slapped him on the shoulder with a grin, but his eyes held no warmth.

Taryn looked away. "That's a servant's job, and I'm not a servant."

"Don't worry," Kai ignored him. "She's as gentle as a milk cow."

A milk cow is gentle? Taryn guessed he was supposed to know that.

Eladar led again, speaking as he walked. *Stealth will have to be forgotten now. I'm afraid the others heard the sounds of our fight. We must go as fast as we can.*

They moved off at a fast lope. Taryn started walking. After three steps, he was jerked to a stop. Looking back, he saw Minnie deeply involved in a patch of grass. *She didn't do this for Kai.* He pulled a couple of times, but Minnie just flicked an ear.

Taryn started to panic. They weren't waiting for him, and the stupid horse wouldn't move. He was going to be left here to be killed. He tugged again, but Minnie ignored him. A short whistle pierced through the air. Minnie jerked her head up and trotted down the path. He had to run to catch up.

Taryn looked up to see Kai watching him with a mocking smile. *They'll treat me with respect when they see what power I have. I'll show them next time we're attacked.* Fear gripped him. He didn't want to face anything like that again. But as long as he followed Eladar, he was sure there would be more danger. At the first opportunity, he'd leave Eladar. He'd head to Northbridge and find peace in the Great Temple. And a hot bath. And a table full of food. A warm glow spread through his body. He'd take the first chance he got.

CHAPTER TWENTY-ONE

Visit Your Sister

Lizzy marched behind Eladar with her sling ready. *Not that I could hit them if they were right in front of me! What's wrong with me?* She shot a stone at a leaf high in the trees and watched it float to the ground. *Why can't I hit anything when it really matters?*

They hiked for hours, and her legs ached with each step. The ground grew steeper until they reached the top of the hill. The setting sun reflected on a small river in front of them. Lizzy could see the familiar brown of the poison in the water, and the stench made her want to gag.

"What are we going to do? We can't go through that," Taryn exclaimed. "It'll poison us."

You'll ride on me.

"But what about Minnie?" Kai asked. "You can't fly her over, can you?"

No. I'll take you over first and give her a longing to join you. She'll pick the shallowest place to cross. If you use some of the pure water to wash her off when she gets to you, she should be fine. He started to say more, but cries of the Unwanted interrupted him. They were hidden by the trees, but they sounded close.

"I guess we don't have much of a choice," Kai said as he jumped on Eladar's back.

Eladar spread his wings and broke into a run. As he picked up speed, he began to beat his wings. Lizzy gasped as he rose into the air and across the river.

She grinned at Taryn. "Have you ever seen anything more beautiful?"

"Beautiful? Him? Terrifying is more like it." Taryn looked more sick than impressed.

Taryn, let Minnie go. Eladar landed to let Kai slip off and glided back to them.

Minnie trotted down the hill to the river. She jogged downstream before plunging in. Lizzy held her breath. If Minnie decided to take a dip, all of their supplies would be useless. Minnie paused when the water was up to her belly and then continued to Kai. He took her lead rope and liberally washed her legs and belly with pure water. Lizzy frowned. *At this rate, we'll run out of water tonight!*

Eladar landed beside him, the air from his wings blowing her hair back. *Taryn's next.* Eladar twitched his ears.

"Is this absolutely necessary?" Taryn's face was white. "I've never ridden a horse."

I am not *a horse.* Eladar knelt down. *Mount up, Taryn. Time is short.*

Taryn awkwardly got his leg over Eladar's back. When Eladar stood up, Taryn yelped and wrapped his fingers in Eladar's mane.

"Don't go very high, okay?" His voice cracked.

Eladar chuckled. He opened his wings, gently rising in the air. Taryn slipped to the side and clung onto Eladar's neck over the river. Eladar wasn't even touching the ground when Taryn slid off and fell to the ground beside Kai. Lizzy could see Kai's grin from across the river. As Eladar made his way over the river for her, the yells of the Unwanted were louder. He quickly landed. *Let's go. They're closing the distance.*

She shoved her sling in her pocket as he knelt down. Her heart pounded when she thought of *flying.* The skirt of her red dress tangled with her legs as she jumped astride him. But as she settled on his back, her heart slowed, her fears faded as he broke into a run.

She took a deep breath, feeling like she had done this all her life. She didn't even bother to hold onto the mane. Eladar lifted into the air, and she squealed with delight as he rose higher. She watched the trees grow smaller as they circled over the river.

Eladar's laughter rolled through her. *We should do some scouting. Are you up to it?*

"Oh, yes, a thousand times, yes!"

Kai, go upstream. You will find a cave. It's easy to miss from the river, so make sure you follow the tree line. Lizzy and I are going to take a look at our situation.

Lizzy watched the ground as Eladar flew. It was amazing to see things from the view of birds. She saw the trail they had followed through the valley and tried to find the hill they had stood on. Eladar circled around and went upstream.

There's the cave where we'll meet Kai and Taryn. But let's look farther up and see if we can find a path through these mountains. The wings continued their beat as the wind blew her hair back. They continued up the river. The mountains were tall with ragged, steep cliffs. *See that trail? That should take us straight through the mountains. See that tree by the river? That's where we turn into the mountains. Remember that. You're the best woodsman of all three.*

But she wasn't the best of anything. She didn't say anything as Eladar turned and flew back to the cave. She felt a wave of sadness when Eladar landed not far from where Kai and Taryn had stopped for the night outside the cave.

Minnie stretched her nose out to Lizzy, and she gave her a quick pat. Taryn, exhausted from the steep hike, dropped the lead rope for Minnie as he fell to the ground. Kai groaned as he unloaded Minnie. Lizzy got out the water and found the last boiled eggs and the last three apples. They moved inside the cave, settling down on the soft sand. Eladar stood in the opening.

We'll stop here for the night, but no fire. We are still too close to that valley.

"What are they?" Kai asked Eladar. "Those Unwanted. Are they people?"

They were, but very little human remains. The name is false. They are wanted, but they chose to turn their back to Adoyni, and Seiten has used his power to create them into a walking dead. Once the disease takes hold, they turn quickly.

"What do you mean *the disease?* You're not saying this disease from the water does this to people." Kai whipped around to face him.

Some die. Some live. If you can call that living.

"If you have so much power, why don't you just take care of everything? We don't know how to fight or anything." Lizzy flopped down with some of the chicken.

You have special abilities, given by Adoyni. With these, you have great power. I can't be in your world for long. The evil weakens me. Eladar took a bite of grass. *Before the evil didn't saturate the air and the water. The enemy is growing stronger, feeding off death and fear.*

"And just how are we supposed to purify the river?" Kai's voice sounded angry.

There's a prophecy that says one day three descendants of The Slayers will save the world by journeying to the Slayers' graves east of Aldholt to a crescent shaped canyon. They will find a stone that gives life. From this, they will find a gift from Adoyni that will heal the river.

Silence filled the cave.

"That's the dumbest prophecy I've ever heard," Taryn blurted out. "I mean, usually they at least rhyme. And there's an obvious way to tell who the prophecy is about, like they're born under a new moon. Not only that, but the directions are specific. A crescent shaped canyon? That could take years to find! A stone that gives life? It's asinine. It's worse than that. It's suicide. No one in their right mind goes out to save the world like this. And, the prophesy says the three people have to be related to The Slayers. Do you know if you are?" Taryn glanced at her and Kai. They shook their heads at the same time. "So why should we believe him?"

You must believe in Adoyni, not me. Eladar flicked an ear back. *Through Him, you receive the power to do what's needed.*

Taryn sat back. "And all he has to say later is that we didn't believe enough. I'm not throwing my life away for such an inane prophecy. Ever since Eladar came along, we've followed him like a lost dog. I need to go to Northbridge to meet Nighthawk Nephesus. I'm leaving in the morning." Taryn laid back on the rock.

"It says it has to be three people. If you don't come, then it won't work," Kai pointed out, his blue eyes growing hard with anger. "And my sister will die."

Lizzy watched them. She had a funny feeling this wasn't going well.

Taryn closed his eyes. "Your sister's probably already an Unwanted. Maybe she's down there in the valley. You could go say hi."

With a roar, Kai launched himself at Taryn. Taryn curled up in a ball. Kai punched him in the jaw. Lizzy jumped to Taryn's rescue and grabbed Kai's arm, but he pushed her back.

"Keep your nose where it belongs for once!" He ordered.

Children! Eladar's voice was stronger. It echoed through her head until she had to sit down. Kai grabbed his head and sat back. Taryn just groaned louder. *Nothing will be accomplished if you don't learn to work together. You're so concerned about your own feelings and problems you don't see that by working together, you can solve all your problems. You're acting like selfish children, and it's going to destroy the world. You must stand firm together.*

Lizzy glared at the two of them. Kai was covered with dirt, his eyes filled with rage, trying to hide the agony he kept hidden. Taryn was rubbing his jaw, equally angry and stubborn. She shook her head. She couldn't imagine them ever agreeing on something, much less liking each other.

Taryn rubbed his jaw. "I was on my way to make my life better, to do what I've always wanted to do. I want to go back."

Lizzy shoved her hair behind her shoulder. "But if we can just do what he says, then we can go home."

"Home to what?" Kai threw a stone across the cave. "Another dead sister?"

Lizzy didn't have an answer as she stared at the dark night outside the cave. When she got back home, she'd rescue Rica, and then Mother and Dad would be so happy they'd get back together, and Mother would love her.

"If we finish this thing, we can get back to our real life?" Taryn asked.

"If you survive." Kai looked over at Taryn.

Taryn returned Kai's look. "We're going to die."

"Probably." Kai started grinning. Lizzy had no idea what was so funny, but it didn't seem like they were going to tell her.

"Great. Wouldn't miss it for the world." Taryn grabbed a second piece of chicken out of defiance from the basket in front of Lizzy and began eating like it was his last meal. Kai chuckled and followed his lead.

Lizzy shook her head in confusion. *They're friends now?*

She would never understand boys.

CHAPTER TWENTY-TWO

Uncut Gems

That night Kai tossed and turned for a long time. He got up and tiptoed to the edge of the cave to get a better look at the stars.

Can't sleep? Eladar asked.

"No," he whispered. "They don't seem to have a problem, but I can't stop thinking about everything you said. Rhiana's going to die, and we can't protect ourselves against the Seekers and the Unwanted."

You have a start on the enemy. It's become a race, and it's possible you'll win this one. As for Rhiana, all you can do is surrender to Adoyni. He cares about her more than you do.

Kai sighed. He wanted something to be easy. Someone to give him a potion that guaranteed instant health and wealth. "But how can I believe that? You'd probably say that He cared for Shona just as much. He sat there, and let her die, when He could've done something."

We can't see the way things will work out in the end. We see the pain today, and it's hard to look ahead and see the joy tomorrow. That doesn't mean it's not there, waiting for us.

"I think you should find the prince or someone more skilled," he said quietly. "I'm just a stable boy."

No, you're an uncut gem, like a diamond. Eladar's
voice was filled with warmth. *An untrained eye would
pass by and never see its value. But a craftsman will stop
in a field of stones for that one small rock. With some
cutting and polishing, that pebble will outshine all the
others. You are that stone, and you are in the process of
being cut and polished. It will take time and it might
hurt, but you will be a prince. You'll outshine all the
others.*

Kai gulped, not knowing what to say. Eladar's
voice rang with such confidence he had to believe
him. And yet the doubts returned. He didn't even
really know how to hold a sword.

*However, we've got to keep you alive until you are
polished.* Eladar laughed. *Now, let's talk about Seekers
and the Unwanted.*

Eladar talked long into the night. Kai listened as
well as he could, but the voice seemed to put him
to sleep and his eyes drooped. Eladar sent him off
for a few hours of sleep before dawn.

He stumbled back to where Taryn and Lizzy
were snoring, lost in their dreams. Rhiana
appeared in front of him as he closed his eyes.
He missed his family so much it ached, so he did
something he had never really done before. He
prayed from his heart.

*Adoyni, I know I haven't talked to you or paid You
any attention for a long time. But if You could, please
watch over Rhiana for me while I do this? Keep her alive
until I can find some way to cure her.*

And with that, he fell asleep.

The next morning he woke up with an ache in his neck from sleeping on the ground. As he groaned, his dream came back to him. He had dreamt of Shona running through the field, and he was chasing her. She was laughing as she sprinted across the grass. When he caught up to her and grabbed her arm, she whirled around. Her eyes were like the Unwanted. Black. Lifeless. She fell to the ground, and when he brushed her hair away from her face, he saw that she was Rhiana.

He rubbed his eyes, trying to wipe the dream out of his head, and joined the others. They were quiet as they started upstream by the time the sun had risen over the mountains.

They hadn't gone far when suddenly Eladar stopped abruptly. Ten Unwanteds circled them. Kai drew his sword while Taryn and Lizzy moved closer together. Eladar stood in front of them with his ears laid back against his head. The Unwanteds parted as a Seeker strolled into the meadow. Eladar reared at the sight of the Seeker and struck out with his front hooves. Taryn and Lizzy moved closer to Kai. He gripped his sword until the hilt cut into his palm.

Eladar reared. *Stand down, vile creature. These humans are under my protection.*

Kai studied the Seeker with horror. The brute was abnormally tall but rippled with muscles like the wrestlers he'd seen in the town square. Its skin was as white as snow but spotted with holes like it was being eating away. Under its long dark cloak, it wore a breastplate made of chainmail. In its hands

was a giant axe. It grinned, revealing jagged teeth.
The yellow eyes bore down on Eladar.

"It's been a long time since I've killed an
Archippos." The Seeker swung his axe around. "I
thought we chased you cowards out of here."

Eladar pawed the ground. *My master is stronger
than yours and this is still His world. And by His
command, I order you to leave now.*

"Is it? No one cares about Him anymore," the
Seeker mocked. "Those three are mine."

Kai swallowed. He could still feel the fear from his
dream. He could still see the hand approaching his
shoulder. *I won't go with them. I won't go to their Master.*
He was sick of being hunted, sick of running. And
he wanted to go home and see his family. Eladar had
no right to kidnap him and throw him into more
problems. Fear disappeared as rage grew.

*A remnant remains to fight, and it is enough. Don't
you remember that it only took one man to destroy an
army? You will not touch these three.* Eladar stood
quietly.

"Maybe not while you're alive," the Seeker
sneered. "But you're not going to be alive much
longer."

The Seeker lunged at Eladar, axe swinging
in a wide arc. Eladar reared and charged. Lizzy
screamed. The Unwanted rushed at them. Taryn
pulled something out of his bag and uncovered
a crystal stone. He closed his eyes and began to
mumble words.

Kai shook his head. *That's not going to help much unless he chucks it at one of them.*

Lizzy aimed at a charging Unwanted. A rock whizzed by Kai's face. He winced and turned to Lizzy. She swore and took out another stone. He shook his head. *Taryn's axe and Lizzy's aim will do more damage, if they actually hit something.* He wanted to yell at them to stop fooling around, but the words died as an Unwanted ran straight at him. Its gray hair flew out of its face to reveal a man. His eyes were vacant like black holes, and he carried a big stick. He roared, his decayed teeth showing.

Kai gritted his teeth. Waves of fury swept over him in a tempest shaking the limbs of a tree. He blocked the attack with his sword. The clash of the two weapons jarred him, making him wonder if his teeth were going to fall out. He thrust at the creature's head, twisted the blade at the last moment, and slashed its stomach.

The Unwanted jumped aside, stumbling into a second one behind it. Kai rushed them, slashing madly. Dodging the stick, he moved closer and stabbed at them. He could hear Taryn's voice rise as he continued his recitation. *What's he going to do? Talk them to death?* Eladar squealed as he attacked, and Lizzy shrieked. He didn't have time to look, but it was good to hear that they were still alive.

Pushed back, Kai swung wildly with his sword, blocking the stick. His breath came in gasps, and sweat ran down his face and into his eyes. Yelling in anger, he stabbed at the creature. The

sword pierced through the Unwanted's chest.
As he pulled his sword free, the creature fell to
the ground dead. Kai gagged, but the second
Unwanted stepped forward, weaving its sword with
skill. Kai took a deep breath and lunged at it.

He overreached. Off balance, he fell to his
knees. The Unwanted slashed quickly. A stone flew
through the air and hit the blade, knocking it away.
Kai caught a glimpse of Lizzy putting another stone
in her sling. He jumped to his feet and blocked
at the last moment. They strained against each
other, locked in a fierce battle of strength. His arms
trembled as the force of the Unwanted overcame
him.

His sword snapped, unable to bear the pressure.
Kai fell against the Unwanted as the blade split in
two. The Unwanted knocked him into the dirt.
Gasping from the weight of the Unwanted landing
on him, he tried to tear its hands from his throat.
Its strong fingers gripped tighter, crushing his
throat. Kicking wildly and tearing at the monster's
fingers, Kai saw black spots in front of his eyes. He
took a ragged breath.

As the spots covered his eyes, he saw a large
rock streak toward him. It hit the Unwanted in the
head with as much force as a kick from a young
horse. The fingers around Kai's throat loosened as
the Unwanted jerked back. Blood splattered as he
shoved the creature off.

*Where'd that rock come from? It was too big for
Lizzie's sling.* The Unwanted lay in front of him. He

rolled to his stomach, holding his throat, taking deep breaths of sweet air. He saw the face of the Unwanted and wanted to throw up. He had been a person. Someone's brother, son.

Three Unwanteds circled them warily. Eladar was still fighting the Seeker, his white coat was streaked with blood. *How did we kill them all? Surely Lizzy and Taryn didn't do that!*

An Unwanted charged Lizzy. Three rocks around Eladar rose off the ground and hurtled toward them. Yelling, the Unwanteds saw the stones coming and sprinted for the trees, but the rocks followed them until they found their mark, killing them as they ran.

So that's where the rock had come from. Eladar's helping us while fighting that Seeker at the same time.

The Seeker evaded Eladar's hooves. It spun on its heel and brought the axe up for the kill. The axe sliced his neck open from side to side.

Red covered white as Eladar screamed in pain.

"No!" Kai cried as he lurched toward him.

A bolt of lightning streaked across the distance and hit the Seeker. Screaming in agony, it fell to the ground, its body smoldering. Kai sprinted toward Eladar. Lizzy cried out, but her scream seemed like she was far away.

Kai's feet felt like lead as he tried to cover the distance to the fallen horse. Eladar sank to the ground, his wings spread out. His head dropped, and he lay like he was dead.

ALLIES

*"If we are together, nothing is impossible.
If we are divided, all will fail.*
~Winston Churchill

Foehn was wandering the streets of Northbridge, trying to catch a glimpse of the mountains when he felt the Master's tug. He considered ignoring it, but after witnessing the Master's anger at Nighthawk, his favorite servant, Foehn wasn't brave enough to rebel.

The Master was sitting on a black horse outside his palace. Nighthawk stood beside him. The horse reared and pranced as the Master held it back.

"The second one should be arriving for his classes to find his true name tonight," the Master smirked. His previous anger seemed to be forgotten with the news of the other sibling. "That pamphlet was a nice touch of yours in Albia."

Nighthawk beamed. "I'll be waiting for him."

"Once he arrives, bring him and Rica to the fortress. Do not linger, for I shall want both of them there when I arrive. By the way, is Rica well enough to travel?" The stallion pawed the ground impatiently.

"Yes, my lord. I didn't have to hurt him much," Nighthawk leered. Her brown eyes sparked with pleasure. "He'll survive."

"Good," the Master said. "We don't have long before the first day of spring. Come quickly."

Nighthawk curtsied as the Master wheeled the stallion toward the gates. The horse whinnied wildly, frantic to run. The Master snapped one word to Foehn as he released the reins. "Come."

Obediently, Foehn followed behind the horse. The Master threw gold coins at the crowd while he raced past. The crowd cheered with joy as they scrambled to find one.

They headed south. When the houses and farms disappeared in the distance, three Seekers joined them. They rode no horse, for none was large enough to carry them. Yet their long strides matched the pace, and they moved quickly over the fields.

The Master acknowledged them with a nod. "Where's the last one?"

"Our brother was killed, my lord," the nearest one spoke. "We know not how."

The Master scowled. "Things are getting out of control."

They journeyed until they came to a small meadow. There were graves surrounding a stagecoach. It looked like robbers had attacked and thrown the contents of the baggage around the meadow.

The Master slipped off his horse and paced around, looking at the tracks.

"Three people. Two horses," he said. "It has to be all of them together, but how did the third one get here? One of the horses could be an Archippos."

The Master turned on his heel and walked to one of the footsteps. Kneeling down, he placed his hand on it and whispered something. Then he closed his eyes for a minute.

Standing up, the Master turned to the Seekers. "They're heading east, just like I thought they would. Follow them and bring them back to me alive. Use the army of Unwanteds if you need to."

"Yes, Master." The three Seekers repeated in chorus.

The Master reached into one of his pockets and pulled out a black stone with flecks of silver through it. It looked like the night sky. "Take this." The Master handed it to the largest Seeker, Refkell. The round stone, the size of a large apple, looked tiny in his giant hand. "When you capture them, rub the stone and say *Reveal*. I'll hear your call and give you further instructions. I will join you as soon as I can."

"I hear and obey, Master." Refkell put the stone in his cloak. Without a word, the three of them sprinted for the woods and were lost in the shadows.

"As for you, my reluctant servant," the Master turned to Foehn. "Blow the Three into a trap until the Seekers can reach them. Then return to me."

Foehn obeyed, knowing he had no choice.

CHAPTER TWENTY-THREE

Alone

Lizzy stumbled as Kai pushed by her and knelt beside Eladar. She stared at Eladar's motionless body lying in the dust. Crimson blood flowed down Eladar's white neck. His wings were covered with dust. She choked back a sob and moved closer. There were rugged cuts on his sides, but the gash in his neck gushed with blood. Taryn followed her, his steps more reluctant than hers.

Kai looked up. "He's breathing."

She took a deep breath and ran forward to kneel beside him. Not sure what to do, she stroked his mane. "Please don't die. We need you."

Eladar took a deep breath and opened his eyes. *I'm not going to die. Not yet, anyways.* He lay in the dirt for a while. The bleeding eased, and his breath came more evenly. *Back up. I'm standing up.*

They obeyed without a word. Eladar rolled to his stomach, gathered his wings, and then rose. His legs wobbled as he found his balance. The cuts over his body began to heal.

"Look at that!" Taryn said. "By the Goddess! He's healing himself."

Most of the cuts disappeared except for the one across his neck. It stayed there, an angry red gash on a sea of white. Blood oozed out of it. He stood with his front legs spread apart like he was trying to find his balance.

No, Taryn. That's where you're wrong. Adoyni is the One who heals. Eladar's voice sounded quieter, weaker than Lizzy had heard before. *Are you three okay?*

"We're fine," Kai said. "But we'd better get moving. We can't run into another group."

I agree. Lizzy, take them to the trail and follow it higher. You're not safe until you're further away, so go fast.

Lizzy tore her eyes away from the ugly red gash on Eladar's neck. "Why didn't that cut heal?"

Eladar flicked an ear. *The evil in this world is too much for me. My shields cannot protect me anymore. I must get to Merrihaven for it to heal. I'll return to you.*

Lizzy wanted to cry. *We can't protect ourselves.* She felt tears in her eyes and gripped her silver box tightly.

Go fast. This has become a race, and you must run hard. I will return as soon as I can. If you have to fight, remember to stand firm. Kai, you must lead them, but listen to them as well. Your success lies in your trust in each other and in Adoyni. Taryn and Lizzy, heed what he says like you would obey me.

Obey Kai? Why him? She forgot her questions as she glanced over at her companions. Taryn looked as out of place as a librarian on a dance floor, with his frilly shirt and expensive pants. Kai ignored her glance, focusing on Eladar. His eyes glinted

bright blue in the sun as he soaked in everything
the Archippos was saying. He looked nothing like a
hero she ever imagined. He was a common laborer
with his scruffy appearance. He didn't even have a
sword anymore. The only knightly thing about him
was the hilt in his hand. But the sword was broken.
Just like their chances of making it out alive.

*How can we stand firm together? The only thing we're
firm about is our dislike for each other.* But she didn't
voice her doubts. The time for questions had past.

"Hurry back," Kai said. "And thanks. I think."

Wow. Great words from our leader. Lizzy couldn't
stop the thought from popping in her head.
Thankfully, she was able to keep her mouth shut.

"Be safe," Taryn echoed. "And make sure to
return to teach me about that stuff you do."

Lizzy rolled her eyes. *Boys.* Glancing up to
Eladar, she tried to say something, but her eyes
filled with tears, and she couldn't speak.

*Do not fear, Lizzy. Trust in Adoyni, and He will be
your savior. Not I. Soon you will have your family.*

She nodded. "Thanks. Hurry back."

There was more that she wanted to say, but
Eladar spread his wings and lifted himself slowly
into the air. He circled over their heads, his final
words bouncing through her head like a marching
band. They stood there as each beat of his wings
took him farther away. Her tears spilled onto her
cheeks as he grew smaller. Soon he was a speck on
the horizon, and then he was gone.

They were alone.

* * *

Kai gripped the hilt of his broken sword tightly as Eladar rose in the air. It gouged into his fingers, but he kept his hold. He wanted to call him back, to beg him to stay with them. He wanted Eladar to protect them.

He glanced over at the others. Taryn's jaw was clenched and his knuckles were white as he held a book tightly to his chest. But as Kai looked closer, he realized that it wasn't anger. It was fear. Lizzy was fighting back tears as she stared at the horizon. Her hair, a dark red in the morning light, was pulled back in a ponytail, and her face was covered with dirt. With tears threatening to fall, Kai wanted to do something to make her anger rage or smile flash. Anything but to see her sad. *How am I supposed to lead them? I'm just a stable boy. I don't even know where to go.*

He swallowed. This next step would be the biggest one of his life. He thought about what Eladar had said. Go east, purify the river, and save Rhiana. Nothing else mattered. He would find a way to work with Lizzy and Taryn to get this done. And he would make sure they hightailed it to the canyon and back.

He threw the ruined sword away in frustration and took a deep breath. It felt like he was jumping off a cliff. He tried not to think about what would happen when he hit the bottom.

"Well, let's go." He started down off the ridge, following a dim trail. He didn't look back, but he could hear Lizzy's quiet footsteps and Minnie's hoof beats in the dirt. He heard a quiet thud and then an "Ouch!" and knew that Taryn followed.

After a few minutes, Lizzy spoke up. "Here. Up here is where the trail is. I saw it yesterday when I was on Eladar."

Kai wanted to make a joke about girls getting lost, but he saw Lizzy's sadness in her green eyes and saw the doubt that filled her. He shook his head. He thought she was not too bad, sort of pretty and braver than most guys, but right now she looked vulnerable. He gestured for her to lead and saw a delighted smile fill her face.

She darted up the trail. It wound through the boulders and trees through a narrow canyon that led up the mountains. They reached the crest of the hill and looked east. The land spread out before them, forsaken and lonely. The rolling hills rose higher and higher to a rugged mountain range. The mountains were bigger than anything Kai had ever seen, piercing the sky with their jagged peaks.

Taryn whistled. "Let me guess, that's east, right? We get to go over that."

"That's east," Kai said. "We're crossing those mountains."

"Or facing *them*." Lizzy pointed back the way they had come. Down below in the valley they'd just crossed, smoke rose above the trees. They could almost smell it. "That's the army Eladar was talking about. They're closing in."

The thought of the large army filled Kai with dread. He had a strong urge to grab Minnie's lead rope and run until he dropped. He could see the Unwanteds down by the fires, planning their attack and sharpening their swords. They had to go *now*.

"Then we'd better keep moving." Kai grabbed Minnie's lead rope. "If they catch up to us, we're dead or something worse. And so are our families. We have to outrun them."

Lizzy and Taryn had a look on their faces like they were trying not to ask a question. *And what then?* That was what he wanted to ask, too. The question hung in the air, but no one dared say it out loud. They started east.

Kai thought it was rather ironic that he was in another race. Only this time, he wasn't racing for money. He was racing for his life. He knew this time he had to win.

But he didn't know if he could.

CHAPTER TWENTY-FOUR

Dirty Hands

Lizzy led the way up the trail. They walked, stopping briefly for rest before continuing on. No one had breath for talking, which was just fine for Lizzy. She didn't have anything to say. Watching Eladar leave gave her a sick feeling in her stomach. *He'll be back soon. He's got to.*

They stopped in the shadows of the peaks as it was getting dark. There was barely light to unload Minnie. The next morning she took in the view. The valley they'd crossed yesterday was small in the distance. She stretched and stumbled to the small fire where Kai was warming up the last of the chicken. Taryn was reading a book, too engrossed to say good morning. His lips were moving with the words. She flopped down beside him. "*The Ultimate Book of Spells: Every Spell You'll Ever Require.* What are you reading about?"

"Spells." Taryn muttered, not even looking up from the book.

Lizzy sighed with frustration. "What kind of spells?"

"Anything you want. To take away warts, to make someone fall in love with you, to make you more attractive. This book has it all. I'm memorizing a few for when we're attacked."

Kai snorted. "Is that what you were trying to do yesterday? Cast spells? That Unwanted would've split you in two if I hadn't helped."

"I wasn't prepared," Taryn shot back, his hazel eyes dark with anger. "But I won't be surprised next time. I'll blast them with lightning just like Eladar did."

"I'll have to see that to believe it," Kai scoffed and threw some water on the fire. "Come on, we're losing daylight."

Lizzy was drawn to the book. On every page was a picture showing the magic working. The pictures showed ugly people turning into beautiful people and lonely people finding love.

"Hello?" Kai's voice shattered her thoughts. "Let's get going, people."

Lizzy ignored him and nudged Taryn to turn the page.

Taryn tapped the page showing how to weaken your enemies. "There may be answers in this book. It may have a way to fix the river without this nonsense of trying to find crescent shaped canyons."

"I doubt it." Kai used his foot to spread out the embers of the fire.

"Who do you think you are?" Taryn asked, giving Lizzy the book and standing up. "You know nothing about the Goddess. You probably don't even know how to read."

"Take that back," Kai said in a very low tone. "Or your jaw might regret it."

Taryn towered over Kai with an angry look on his face. Lizzy knew that Kai was struggling to keep his rage from exploding. It didn't take much for him to blow. *They're going to start fighting again!* She needed to stop them, but nothing came to mind other than to scream at them to stop being dumb boys.

"I'm getting very tired of Adoyni worshippers telling me what to do," Taryn sneered. "All of you are a bunch of deluded, outdated dupes."

Kai ordered, "Put your book up, and get going."

"Save it for the Unwanteds!" Lizzy snapped the book shut and stood between them. "Can we just do this and go home?"

"You think you have all the answers in those books," Kai said, ignoring her. "That you know everything. But you don't know a thing that matters."

"At least I know the truth from lies," Taryn replied. "I know enough not to be deceived. You wouldn't even give the Goddess a chance. Where was Adoyni when your sister died?"

"We took her to the Temple, and she died. So what good is your Goddess?" Kai grabbed a bag and threw it in Minnie's direction. "Your priests said it was too late."

"It probably was if you wasted time with this Adoyni garbage. The Goddess knows who truly believes in her." Taryn opened his book. "See, it says right here, *If one who has worshipped another god*

*has not declared allegiance to Me, I will not hear their
prayers."*

"You think I really care about allegiances?"
Kai's anger flamed. "She let my sister die. Eladar's
the only one to give me a way of helping Rhiana.
Keep your religion stuff to yourself and don't
slow me down. You and Lizzy have been dragging
your feet the last two days. Now get moving before
those Unwanteds come, and we lose any chance we
have!"

Lizzy felt her face burn. She knew the urgency.
Rica's life depended on them finishing quickly.
But the book looked so interesting, she couldn't
resist it. Without saying a word, she went to help.
Taryn stayed where he was, his arms folded over his
chest. *It's time for him to do his share of the work around
here.*

She turned to him. "Come on, Taryn. You need
to learn this."

"I don't think so." He sat down and opened the
book. "I don't get my hands dirty, and I don't load
horses. That's not what I am called to do."

"You think you're going to sit around while we do
all the work?" Lizzy wasn't going to take his snobby
behavior anymore. "I don't think so. You'll load
Minnie, you'll cook, and you'll get your hands dirty."

Taryn opened his mouth to protest. She put
her hands on her hips and glared at him. His face
turned bright red, but he followed her to Minnie
and did what she told him to. She noticed that Kai

no longer looked angry. In fact, it seemed like he
was trying not to grin. Taryn grunted and strained
under the weight of the bags but got them on and
tied to Lizzy's approval. It took twice the amount
of time, but even Kai didn't seem to mind. Minnie
groaned and huffed as much as Taryn did, clearly
not enjoying the way he tossed the bags on her, but
she stood with her nose buried in Kai's chest while
he scratched her ears.

* * *

Taryn watched as Kai climbed a tree, his daily
routine for the last two days. He'd scan the sky for
a sign of Eladar. When that turned up empty, he'd
search for the Unwanted army behind them. He
always saw them.

Taryn sat down on a stump and sighed. All
he wanted to do was turn around and go to the
Temple of All and solve the mystery of Mischa's
words. *Maybe Nighthawk Nephesus will help me figure
out what Mischa was trying to say. Your mother is
n…n…*

Taryn sat straight up, ignoring Minnie as she
jumped. *N…n… Mom is Nighthawk Nephesus! That's
why Father is always commenting about Mom talking
about religion. I bet he kicked her out of the house. That's
why I'm so gifted! It all makes sense!*

He found it hard to sit still. His mind was
whirling. *She must've changed her appearance, so Father*

wouldn't know who she was. I wonder how Mischa found out. He grinned. *Now I have to get back there and tell her who I am! She'll welcome me with open arms.* He pictured their joyful reunion. She'd take him around the Temple, introducing him as her son. *When I get there, I'll be treated like a prince.*

Right now he was being treated like a servant. Or worse. Lizzy was making him do all the work. He loaded and unloaded Minnie while she watched with her arms folded. She inspected his work, tightening a strap here, adjusting a bag there. But he had noticed today that she didn't have to correct much. She didn't say anything, but he knew that he was getting better. The strangest thing was that he was actually proud of himself.

His stomach rumbled as he thought about food. They only ate a little bit, which came nowhere near satisfying his hunger. Lizzy thought they had enough for two more days, if they ate lightly. His mouth watered at the thought of the juicy steaks, freshly sliced bread and delicious apple tarts at home.

The tree shook as Kai reached the top. There was silence for a second. Kai yelped and scrambled down the tree as fast as he could. Pine needles fell as he jumped to the ground. "Run!" He grabbed Minnie's rope. "Come on," he shouted as he ran closer to the peaks.

"What in the universe?" Taryn refused to move a step without knowing what was going on. "What did you see?"

Kai paused and looked back, his face white. "The Unwanteds. They're right behind us."

"What?" Lizzy cried. "How in the world? We had a lead on them. Are you sure?"

Kai glared at her. "Of course I'm sure. They must not have slept like we did. Now would you get moving? They'll be here in a few minutes. We've got to get over those peaks somehow."

Taryn hardly comprehended what was happening. He followed Kai's gesture and examined the peaks. Sheer rocks led to the top. Piles of boulders were scattered around them at the bottom of the steep cliffs. There was no way up. Not unless they were amazing climbers with ample rope and an abundance of time.

"It's going to rain." Lizzy glanced at the storm clouds building in the north. "Looks like it's going to be a good one."

"Great." Taryn put all the sarcasm in his voice that he possibly could. "So on top of starving to death, we're going to drown."

"I've never heard of anyone drowning from a thunderstorm," Lizzy said.

Kai shook his head. "Are you *even* listening? In a few minutes, we'll be captured."

Taryn glanced at Lizzy. Yesterday she'd abruptly announced that skirts were dumb, grabbed some clothes from a pack, and disappeared into the woods. When she came back, she had on dark brown breeches, soft leather boots and a green shirt. Since then she moved as quietly as a cat.

More than once, she'd snuck up behind him. She claimed that she wasn't trying to scare him, but he wasn't convinced.

"We didn't last very long, did we?" Lizzy asked with a sick look on her face. "Without Eladar, I mean."

"Eladar? He's probably the one leading them to us," Taryn snorted.

Kai ignored Taryn. "We'll last longer if you start running, like I've told you to."

"But where are we going?" Taryn pointed to the rocks. "There's no way over that."

"They haven't caught me until they have me tied up, and even then I will fight," Kai said.

Taryn stood up. "With what? A stick? That army will catch up with us while we're playing mountaineers."

"Maybe and maybe not." Kai started trotting down the trail.

The sun was setting as the shadows began to lengthen, making weird shapes with the large boulders. Taryn thought he saw the monsters, leering at them beneath the trees, in every shadow. The wind picked up as they got closer to the mountain. They reached the top of a hill, and the wind hit him in the face and almost knocked him over.

Lizzy's hair hid her face, blowing it wildly around. Frantically she gathered it into a knot. "Where'd this wind come from?"

"There's a canyon over there," Kai said, pulling his cloak around him. "If we go that way, the wind will be behind us. I bet that canyon will take us to the top."

Taryn followed, leading Minnie. They turned their backs to the wind and made their way to the canyon. The wind died away as they entered a gorge that led closer to the mountain. It was lined with high rock walls and trees. They jogged farther down until the cliffs were suffocating him. *This is a death trap.*

His heart pounded as they went deeper in the canyon. The pathway led to a dead end. The cliff in front of them rose straight above their heads. They craned their necks to see the top. At the base of the cliff, a jumble of rocks lay at their feet. Kai jumped up on a boulder, then like a monkey, he climbed to a higher one. He got stuck and tried to find another handhold.

Falling back to the ground, he panted. "Huh. It's tougher than it looks."

"I hear something." Taryn stared into the shadows behind them. The sound of marching feet echoed down the canyon. "They're here! What're we going to do?"

Taryn's knees felt like wet noodles. The glimmer of torches approaching shone through the trees. Sweat beaded his forehead. He turned to Kai. "We've been following you around the last two days, and now you've messed it up. We're trapped."

Kai continued to stare up at the rock wall.

"Are you even listening to me?" Taryn raised his voice to jolt him to the present.

"No, I'm not." Kai said. "I am trying to figure a way out instead of crying like a baby. Lizzy, what do you think? Take off at that crack and head right? Do you think that would work?"

She stared at the place where Kai was pointing. "I don't know. It smoothes out as you go higher. I wish we had a longer rope."

"And some spikes to anchor with." Kai nodded. "It'd be no problem if we had those."

Taryn paced in the small space below the cliff. "All you can do is wish for rope."

"At least I'm doing something!" Kai whipped around, his anger at full blaze. "You're just making it so we can't think. Why don't you do something useful like putting your great brains to work on how to get out of here?"

"If you had listened to my great brains earlier, we wouldn't be in this mess. But, no, you had to go this way." Taryn wasn't backing down this time.

Kai glanced down the canyon. "We have to do something. We can't run, we can't get up that mountain. I guess there's prayer."

"Prayer!" Lizzy screeched. "That's your answer?"

Kai shrugged, "It's worth a shot." Kai closed his eyes, his lips moving.

Lizzy pulled out her sword as Taryn pushed up his glasses and turned to face the Unwanteds. *Why aren't they coming? What are they waiting for?* He backed against the cliff. Its jagged stones cut into his skin. *Is there a spell that would take out hundreds of Unwanteds?* But before he could do anything else, he saw them at the mouth of canyon, their weapons glinting in the setting sun. Taryn's heart fell to his shoes and his mouth went dry. *We're going to die.*

CHAPTER TWENTY-FIVE

Miracles or Luck

Lizzy heard the footsteps of the approaching army pound an ugly rhythm. *It can't end like this.* She looked to the sky with hopes that Eladar would appear and whisk them away, but the sky was filled with clouds. There was no sight of him anywhere. She groaned as she watched the storm clouds approach. The wind whipped into a fury as the rain began to fall. It pelted her face as she watched the mist settling across the mouth of the canyon. The entrance disappeared in the grayness. They were hidden.

"Look!" She pointed to the trail. The mist was as thick as fog. It muffled the sounds of the army to the faintest whisper. "Those Unwanteds can't see us! What a coincidence."

Kai chuckled. "I think I'd call it a miracle. What do you think, Taryn? Think Adoyni has power now?" He smacked Taryn on the shoulder with a twinkle in his blue eyes.

"I'd call it lucky," Taryn drawled as he rubbed his shoulder. He sounded unimpressed, but he stared at the mist. "Eventually they'll find where we are. We're still stuck."

"Then let's find a way out of here," Kai said. He climbed up the way he had suggested earlier, but it smoothed out. He dropped down and examined the cliff again.

"Maybe you should pray again," Taryn commented as he perched on a rock. "We're not going to have much longer until they figure things out."

"Maybe I will," Kai snapped. His good mood seemed to be quickly disappearing with Taryn's pessimism. "Or throw you to the Unwanteds."

"Is this the way you treat your friends?" A voice, rich and full like a song, said behind Lizzy.

She shrieked and whipped around while reaching for her sling. A man stood in the rocks close enough to touch. He was tall with a dark hood covering most of his face. She could see the hilt of a sword hung out of his cloak, ready for him to draw.

"Where'd you come from?" Kai challenged. "Think twice about attacking. We're trained to use our weapons."

The man's laugh was deep. "A kitten has claws, but one need not fear them. As for what I want, I'm here to show you the way out of this canyon." The stranger's laugh rang out again. "You were too focused on that army to watch your back. If I were an enemy, I could have slit your throats before you knew I was there. You should be glad that I'm a friend." He climbed up past several boulders before looking back. "Maybe I should be clearer. You can stay here and get captured by the Unwanteds, or you can follow me to safety."

"Be on your guard. We don't have much of a choice right now." Kai ordered quietly. "Lizzy, give me your sword."

"But what will I use?" Lizzy protested in a whisper.

"Your sling. You're bound to hit something with it sometime. This might be a good time to start." Kai reached for the sword.

Lizzy slid the sword out of the scabbard reluctantly. "Just don't break this one, too."

Kai glared at her as he snatched the blade out of her hand. "Let's go."

Lizzy watched as Taryn grabbed Minnie's rope and scrambled up the boulders, eager to escape the horde behind them. Minnie leaped from one boulder to the next, balancing as carefully as a mountain goat. Lizzy glanced at Kai. Worry filled his blue eyes, but he nodded for her to go first. The strange man stood silently, waiting for them beside a rock that was the size of a small house. Lizzy stared nervously at the cliff, wondering if another rock would split from the cliff and come rolling down.

"Get moving," Kai grunted behind her.

The angry response on the tip of her tongue died as she moved forward. Taryn and Minnie were gone. In the second it took for her to study the rocks above them, they had disappeared. *Did that man use some sort of magic on them?* She rushed to where he had been standing. She heard Kai scramble up the rocks behind her. She approached

the giant slab of rock, but there weren't any sign
of them. Her heart fell. *How could we have lost them?*
Kai looked as confused as she felt.

"Where'd they go?" Kai asked. "They were right
here and then…"

Lizzy grabbed his arm. "Look!"

There was a small space between the cliff and
the boulder. Enough space to fit a horse through.
She squeezed into the small path and felt the
rocks surround her. The rocks seemed to press
down on her. Darkness grew as she groped further
back, masking any sign of Taryn or Minnie. The
mountain around her suffocated all light. She
sensed the path turning right, but it never grew
wider. Remembering the box from Rica, she
slipped her hand in her pocket and held it tightly.

After what seemed a lifetime, Lizzy could
see her hands in front of her as she felt the way
forward with hesitant steps. The darkness lifted.
Then suddenly the cave ended and she blinked in
the setting sun.

The hidden tunnel had led under the tall
peaks to the other side of the mountains. The
storm remained on the other side. They stood on
a plateau that opened up to the east. She stared at
the open plains that stretched forever. There were
no lights or fires as far as she could see. Around
her, there were trees with trunks that glistened blue
and silver. Low green bushes and yellow flowers
grew among the rocks. The air was fresh and clean,
mixed with the sweetest smell from the flowers. The

last of the sun lit the snow on the peaks. The clouds darkened to a dark pink as the sun set. *This has to be the prettiest place I've ever seen.*

Taryn and Minnie were in front of her next to the stranger, staring over the plains. No one moved or said a word until Kai joined them. The man drew his sword.

"I've been looking for you three."

CHAPTER TWENTY-SIX

Impossible Deeds

The ease of the stranger's movements told Kai this man was used to fighting. His heart was pounding as he bit his lip. He wasn't going to let this man hurt them, but he didn't have much of a chance. He could almost feel Deston's fist slamming into him again. He couldn't stand up to a shrimp like him. *How am I going to fight this warrior?* He gripped the hilt tighter.

"I knew it!" Taryn exclaimed. "He brought us here to kill us. We should've stayed in the canyon."

"Would you ever shut up?" Kai snapped, never taking his eyes off the sword pointed at his chest. "For once why don't you stop blabbing all your thoughts out loud?"

"Does it matter?" Taryn yelled back. "I know you have illusions of grandeur, but you're not a hero, even though you've ridden an Archippos. You can't purify the river. You're just a dumb stable boy." Taryn gasped as he realized how much he had revealed.

Kai gripped his sword tighter. He might have had a chance if Taryn hadn't shouted all their secrets out. *If I survive this, I'll wring Taryn's little neck. If this stranger is an enemy, he'll kill me without a thought.*

"Shut up!" Lizzy hissed.

The man laughed without any humor. "Have I got work to do!" He lowered his gray hood to reveal blue eyes like the laughing waters of a mountain river in spring. They seemed to see through Kai's defenses. His face, burnished bronze by hours in the sun, was framed by long hair that was silvery blonde and was tied back out of his face with braids.

Kai couldn't imagine this man indoors. He was part of the shadows and tall like the trees. But he knew he had no hope of him being slow. He moved like a mountain lion stalking its prey. His trousers and tunic were an earthy brown, making him almost invisible.

Kai relaxed. This was not a Seeker. "Who are you?"

"You may call me Alyn, Kai." He took off his gray cloak, revealing two daggers strapped to his back, and hung the cloak on a nearby branch.

Now. When his back is turned. Kai moved forward, pulling out Lizzy's sword, but something made him wait. *But it's the only chance I've got. But how did he know my name?* Alyn turned and caught Kai's eye. He lifted one eyebrow with a one-sided grin. The smile didn't reach his eyes. Kai felt his face going hot. It was like Alyn knew exactly knew what he was thinking.

Lizzy grinned, recognition flashing in her eyes. "You're a Sentinel, aren't you? The songs still talk of your people patrolling the world for evil. I didn't think you existed."

"Yes, I am. And my people have searched for weapons from the Slayers for many years, for the enemy would stop at nothing to keep you from having them. Many died to keep them safe until you were ready for them. When Eladar told us the time had come, I was selected to bring them to you." Alyn grinned, this time with warmth, and reached into the branches of a tree close by. He pulled out a bundle that was the color of the trees. It looked heavy and awkward in its shape.

"For you, Lizzy." He handed her a long package wrapped in soft deer hide.

She laid the package on the ground and unwrapped it, revealing an elaborately carved piece of wood that was shorter and thicker than an arrow. On one end, it was thicker with a notch on it. Beside it lay a number of long spears, but they were too thin. They looked more like a long arrow with an arrowhead at the tip of it, but they were almost as tall as she was.

"You are looking at a norsaq," Alyn explained. "A weapon almost forgotten, but a powerful one. The short thick part holds the darts in place. You use it like you are throwing a ball. Just a snap of your wrist." He waved at a tree a couple hundred feet away. "It can pierce the strongest of metal, too. Your ancestor could hit an apple from a great distance and brought down many enemies before they could reach a sword's blade. Be careful not to lose the darts, though. They possess the power to cut through the vilest evil to bring new life."

Lizzy picked up the norsaq and set a dart against the hook on it. She held it in place with her thumb and finger. "But I can't hit anything, not with my sling, not when it matters." Her voice was low, like she didn't want Taryn or him to hear.

"You have a kind, good heart and wish to hurt no one. There is something to be proud of, not ashamed." Alyn's voice lost all mockery. "But evil exists, and you have to stand firm against it. Remember that those who attack you desire the death of you and your loved ones. Then clear your mind. Think of nothing else but what your target is. Your aim will be true."

"Thanks," Lizzy said softly. She looked around at the trees. "See that knot on the tree to the far left?"

Kai squinted. He could hardly see anything that far. He nodded as she drew the norsaq back. There was a pause as she steadied her grip. She turned to face the tree sideways with her right arm raised. She stepped into the throw, moving her weight forward. She snapped her wrist as the dart flexed. It flew out of her hand, wobbling as it propelled toward the tree. It slammed into the knot with a thud. All three of them gasped as Lizzy hooted and ran to collect the dart.

Taryn's curiosity overtook his politeness. He stepped forward as Alyn handed out a shield. Taryn laughed as he slid it onto his arm. It was shaped in a triangle. Inlaid on the silver was a picture of a brilliant sun etched in gold. The beams reached to the corners of the shield.

"It bears the symbol of Adoyni's light, breaking the spell of darkness and how His light spreads to the darkest corners," Alyn explained. "It will keep you safe when all else fails."

Taryn couldn't stop looking at the shield with a silly grin on his face. "It's what I needed. Something to hide behind when I do my spells."

A dark shadow fell over Alyn's face but disappeared before Kai was certain he saw it. Alyn reached into the bundle a third time. Kai's heart beat twice as fast as he realized he was next. He pulled out a sword and handed it to Kai. He accepted it with a laugh of surprise.

Alyn presented him the sword, hilt first, with a slight bow. "For you, young warrior."

The hilt was as bright red as a fire. He took the sword from Alyn hesitantly, half-expecting to feel heat on his fingers as they tightened. The guard gleamed bright silver, and lines of fire ran down the scabbard.

"I've never seen anything so beautiful," Kai said. *It's a sword for a warrior.* He pulled it free of the scabbard and noticed the etching spelled a word. He turned the blade and looked closer. "Surrender? What's that suppose to mean?"

"Your ancestor had that word etched into the blade after the Final Battle," Alyn folded up the sack. "For him, it summed up his life."

"But why surrender? Why not victory?" Kai tried to keep back the angry words, and he swallowed hard against the sharp disappointment. The blade was ruined. He couldn't even begin to imagine pulling it out in front of an enemy. Alyn regarded him with a stony expression. "Thank you. It's better than nothing."

"It's time for lessons." Alyn drew his sword. "If you're going to carry a weapon, you're going to be expected to use it."

Alyn swung his sword in Taryn's direction. "You, too. The axe and sword are more similar than you think."

"Me?" Taryn stuttered.

"That's an axe in your hands, is it not?" Alyn's voice sounded dangerously low, like he wasn't used to people questioning him.

Taryn looked at the axe in his hands like he had never seen it before. "Y...Yes, it is." Taryn gained some of his courage back. "But I'm a seer, not a soldier."

Alyn's laugh rang through the trees. "That's a good one. You're not a seer. Eladar wouldn't have been able to fly with you if you were."

"You know Eladar?" Taryn asked quickly, his face red with anger. "He's the one who led that army to us! You're just another creature of Adoyni's, probably trying to stop us from purifying the river!"

"Enough!" Alyn roared. They jumped away from him as his cry echoed through the trees. "You should be very careful with your accusations, Taryn. Now to your mark."

His words rang with authority. No one thought of questioning him again. They rushed to form a line. Kai made sure to stand far away from the axe. The last thing he wanted was to be hit by Taryn. Lizzy waved her sword around with great enthusiasm until Alyn glared at her. He examined each of their grips and made them place their feet in a careful way. When he was satisfied, he stepped back and grunted.

"It will have to do for now." And then he sighed.

Kai felt a flash of anger. *Have to do? I'm doing everything he told me. Anyways, how will any of this help me block an attack?* He remembered how clearly Alyn seemed to know what he was thinking and tried to hide his irate thoughts.

The shadows lengthened as Alyn taught them how to hold the sword, thrust, and block. They practiced until their arms hurt and their legs felt like collapsing. No matter what they did, Alyn just shook his head in disappointment. Kai grew angrier by the moment and pushed himself harder than he thought possible, determined for one sign of praise. Alyn didn't seem to notice.

Alyn showed them ways to disarm their opponent with a flick of the wrist, making the sword dance and fly through the air. Lizzy giggled through her sweat when Kai's sword went flying. *She's actually enjoying this!* Kai's anger turned to a slow burn when Alyn complimented Lizzy on her skill. She beamed with a giant smile and bowed to

Alyn, her sword flourishing. *Show off! I'll show Alyn
what I can do!*

Kai brushed the sweat out of his eyes when Alyn
nodded. Taryn sank to the ground with a grateful
groan. Lizzy lowered her sword and panted, sweat
soaking her shirt. Kai put his hands on his knees,
taking deep breaths and hiding his temper. Alyn
still hadn't said anything good about him. Even
Taryn had gotten praised after he had almost taken
off Kai's head.

"Now for drills." Alyn nudged Taryn with his
boot. "On your feet, seer. The enemy won't give you
time for rest."

Lizzy groaned in agony, and Kai wanted to join
her, but he wasn't going to complain. He'd prove
that he was tough. Alyn led them through a series
of drills and made them repeat them until they
could do them without hesitating.

Finally, Alyn stopped them. "If you practice
every night and stay ahead of the Seekers, you
might survive."

Kai held back his angry words. *Might survive?* He
wanted to fall down and gasp for air, but he wasn't
going to with Alyn watching. Alyn hadn't even
broken into a sweat. Kai refused to wipe his face
dry. He wasn't going to admit how much he was
struggling.

"Kai," Alyn called. "It's just you and me now."

Kai fought back the waves of weariness. *Why
can't I rest like Taryn and Lizzy? This isn't fair.* The

tiredness washed away as he gripped his sword tighter. Alyn had a grin on his face like he knew exactly what Kai was thinking. Rage flashed before Kai and he charged, yelling as he ran. Alyn waited. Kai swung with all the strength he had left. Alyn ducked under Kai's sword and whacked Kai across his back with the flat of the sword. It stung as he lurched to a stop.

Kai faced Alyn and tried to catch his breath. His fury made it difficult to think. He couldn't beat Alyn in strength or speed. *What else do I have?* Alyn attacked. The sword was a blur of silver as Kai blocked it. He had to back away to avoid being hit. He spun on his heel and struck Alyn.

Swords clashed. Kai felt a surge of triumph. He shoved with everything he had, pushing Alyn down. His eyes stung from the sweat running into his eyes. Alyn faltered, overcome by Kai's strength. Kai leaned in harder, certain of victory. As quick as a fish leaping from the water, Alyn pulled back and spun, smacking Kai on the back. Kai fell to the ground with a yelp of pain and lay panting.

"Giving up?" Alyn mocked. "Is that all it takes to beat you?"

Exhaustion disappeared as anger flooded through Kai. He gripped his sword and pushed himself up. The aches disappeared as he let the rage ripple through him. Alyn grinned mockingly. Kai didn't even bother to answer him. He charged with a yell. Alyn brought up his sword leisurely, ready to block and strike, like he wasn't bothered at all by Kai's threat. *Does he really think I'm that bad that he can move so slowly?* Kai pushed down the thought. *He'll see when he's lying in the dirt.* He twisted his sword and jerked. Alyn's sword went flying through the air. Kai stormed forward, pushing Alyn over. Alyn landed on his back. Kai stood over him with his sword at Alyn's throat.

"Well, this kitten has claws," Alyn chuckled. He pushed away Kai's sword and stood up, brushing off his clothes. "Well done, Kai. It took some goading, but it finally came out."

Kai noticed Lizzy and Taryn were standing at the edge of the meadow with their mouths open and eyes wide with surprise. *Does everyone think I'm that useless?* He turned back to Alyn, never moving his sword. "Why'd you do it?"

Alyn blinked. "Do what?"

"Why did you move so slowly? Did you think I couldn't do anything even when you leave yourself wide open?" Kai yelled. "Why are you wasting your time on me if you think I'm not good enough?"

The long shadows hid Alyn's face as he picked up his sword and put it in his scabbard. He returned to Kai and laid a hand on his shoulder.

"I didn't slow down," he said quietly. "Only four warriors have disarmed me. There's no way an apprentice should have been able to. Come. We must talk."

CHAPTER TWENTY-SEVEN

Hidden Secrets

Kai followed Alyn into the trees. Lizzy and Taryn followed closely behind. No one spoke. Kai's hands still trembled with the remnants of battle fury. Sweat soaked his shirt, cooling him in the night breeze. Alyn led them to a small meadow. In the center of the grass were embers glowing under a pot. He stirred them to a small fire and lifted the lid of the pot. The smell of soup filled the area.

"Food," Taryn whispered. "Hot, yummy food." He sniffed again.

They quickly unloaded Minnie and tethered her in the long grass. Kai's stomach growled in anticipation. He passed one bowl to Lizzy and took the second one. He hadn't smelled anything that good since the last dinner Mom made him. He grimaced, remembering his last angry words to her.

He forgot his regrets when he took his first bite. There was some kind of meat in it and vegetables he had never seen before. He gulped it down and refilled his dish again, noting Alyn's grin. For the first time in a long while, his stomach was content.

Kai glanced at Lizzy taking another helping. "You could learn a thing or two from Alyn."

"What are you talking about?" Lizzy asked.

"This is far better food than anything you've made." He took another bite of the soup, savoring it as it slid down his throat. "You can't expect Taryn or me to do the cooking." He stretched his legs and groaned happily.

"Because of that sexist comment, I'm not doing any cooking. So if you like to eat, then you'll find out that cooking is man's work, too." Lizzy's words were getting sharper. "I'm not here to feed you. I can track and hunt far better than either of you. Get used to cooking if you want to eat."

"I am. I mean, I will." Kai didn't know what the right answer was, but he knew he had to keep the laughter from escaping.

"Eladar said you were, what was the word, amusing," Alyn grinned.

"You know Eladar?" Taryn said, gazing longingly at the pot, and then helped himself to a fourth bowl.

Alyn nodded. "It might be better to say that Eladar knows me. He contacted me to be on the lookout for you."

Kai looked up from his empty bowl. "How's that possible? Eladar would've mentioned you to us before he left."

"When you know what to listen for, you can hear him from a great distance. You'll find out, Kai. It's your inheritance, along with your skill with a sword. No novice can disarm me. Yet you did, and judging by the way you first held a sword, you haven't had any training. Your ability comes from Adoyni. It will grow as you allow Him to have control of your life. Yet, you only began to access your ability when you were enraged. You must learn to control your anger, for it is very dangerous uncontrolled. Learn to let Adoyni guide you and your sword instead of your rage."

Kai shifted to hide his embarrassment and wondered if what Alyn was saying was true. He did hear Eladar's voice telling him to run from the Seekers. Eladar must have been far away at that time, maybe even in Albia.

Alyn pointed behind him. "My instructions were to point you in the right direction. You see that path through the trees there? Follow that to the plains. Then go straight east to Aldholt. If you go quickly, you may beat that army."

"Won't you be coming with us?" Kai asked.

"There are other deeds to be done, some as important as your task," Alyn said, lost in thought. "I am needed elsewhere. There are few left to patrol the wild lands. This is the first time for many years I've journeyed so close to any town."

"Do you know what stone gives life?" Lizzy asked.

"Only what the prophesy says. I hope it's enough to cleanse the river. With the number of Unwanteds rapidly growing, we may have already lost the battle. Surely you of all people must grasp the implication of the contaminated water."

Kai shook his head and glanced at the others. They looked just as confused as he felt. *Does everyone know more about our lives than we do?* He stuffed down the irritation.

Alyn poked the fire with a stick. "The longer the water poisons people, the more people believe that Adoyni is evil. If many more turn from Him, the shields of the Archippos will be so severely weakened that it won't be safe to enter our world anymore. We'll lose one of our most powerful allies."

"Why are we always falling in with Adoyni believers?" Taryn still held the bowl in his hands. "Why can't you face the fact that the Goddess gives us more power and more freedom."

"And do you really know what you want or need?" Alyn questioned back. "I'm not saying the Goddess doesn't have power, but you'll find that power lonely and empty, and She will enslave you. The crystals that everyone is so fond of are a direct channel to Seiten." Alyn's eyes were dark in the firelight. "Anyone who wears one is a target for death."

Kai remembered the crystal hanging around Rhiana's neck. *Why didn't I throw it away when I had the chance?* He rubbed his forehead and rested his elbows on his knees.

"I know of many people who were healed through the crystals," Taryn spoke up. "They say it cures all sorts of diseases, heals crippled people, and fixes every kind of ailment."

"Have you seen these healings with your own eyes? The power of the Goddess is as filthy as the river." Alyn stirred the fire. "And don't forget that Adoyni gives power to those who ask."

Conversation died out after this. The others settled down quickly, snores rising from their blankets, but Kai couldn't sleep. *Is Alyn right? Or Taryn?* He slipped away from the fire and walked to the cliff. He could leave and go back to Northbridge. Then he'd rip that crystal off Rhiana and throw it down the deepest hole he could find. *But is it too late? Is she already dead?*

Alyn's words echoed in his head. *If Zoria is causing this disease, why would her priests save Rhiana?* He stared up at the stars twinkling brightly in the night sky. *Does Adoyni have power? Where was He when Shona died?*

His anger rose as he thought about how he had prayed for Shona to get better. He could still feel the aching in his knees and smell the musty stink from her blankets as he pressed his head against her bed. He remembered watching her fade away in front of his eyes, despite his pleas to Adoyni every day, every night, every minute.

"You didn't hear my prayers then," he said. "Or You heard them and couldn't do a thing about it. Why should I pray now?"

He thought back to those long days by her bed. One night replayed in his head. He was in Shona's room, telling her about his first day at the stables. Timo had sent him to clean stalls when Deston appeared with his friends. Already embarrassed, Deston's taunts pushed him over the edge. He had fought, but they ganged up on him and beat him until he laid still. He lied to Timo, saying that he had tripped to explain the cuts and bruises. Shona was the only one he told the truth to. She listened without saying a word.

Then she tried to sit up. "I'll beat them up for you. I'm going to get better. Look what Mom gave me." She held a crystal on a chain around her neck with a weak grin. "This was blessed by the Temple seers. I'll be okay in a little while."

The crystal grew into one of the stars on the horizon. He groaned. *Adoyni didn't ignore us. We turned our backs on Him.* They'd stopped praying, and Mom only talked about herbs, crystals, and potions that would heal Shona. After walking away from Him, would Adoyni still care for him? They said that His love was never ending, and a lot of crazy things had been happening lately. *Why not give this a shot?* He closed his eyes and took a deep breath.

"Um, hello, Adoyni," he whispered. "How have you been?" He cleared his throat. *That had to be the dumbest start to a prayer ever.* "I'm sorry I haven't talked to You. But I need your help. I'm really worried about Rhiana. Could You take care of her while I do this? Please heal her. Thank you."

He opened his eyes. He wanted a sign, like a thunderclap to show that Adoyni heard. The night was still. He yawned and stumbled back to the fire. He didn't remember falling asleep.

But when he woke, he knew what he was going to do. He was going to trust Adoyni, take up his sword, and put an end to this disease.

* * *

Taryn was lonely when he woke up. He wasn't going to admit it out loud, but it was the truth. Alyn was gone, taking his pot of soup with him. They'd packed up and begun down the path. His books in Minnie's packs were waiting for him, but they were just books, as much as he loved them. Maybe there was something with this Adoyni thing. *Or maybe I'm hanging around too many of His freaks.*

Lizzy and Kai chattered in front of him. There was something different about Kai today. He walked with more confidence, like the sword really belonged to him. He seemed a lot happier than Taryn was. *Is Adoyni making him like that?* Kai said something, and Lizzy burst out laughing. Taryn felt an ache tear through him. He never had friends like that. Lizzy looked back at him, her green eyes were dancing with laughter.

"Get up here and tell us about you," she laughed. "I've heard all I can about racing, horses, and the proper poop scooping methods. You have to be more interesting than that!"

Kai swatted her on the arm, and she yelled. Taryn joined them, answering all of Lizzy's questions. She'd make a good examiner. She wiggled everything personal out of him. Except his belief that Nighthawk Nephesus was his mother.

They walked into a glade lined with willow trees. Flowers led up to an altar made from red stones and lined with gold. It sparkled as the sun's rays hit it. Behind the altar was a wall taller than Taryn. It circled half the meadow. There were carvings on the wall of Archippi flying. It showed three people riding them, carrying swords, bows and arrows, and spears.

"The Shadow Slayers," Lizzy breathed. "Look! That picture is of the song *Riding to Battle.* Mother sang it just before we left Albia. But there are pictures here that haven't been written into song. I could write them. I wonder what Mother would think of that!"

Taryn looked at the pictures telling the stories of Adoyni's work. He had heard Mischa tell some, but now it seemed more real. Seiten wanted to rule the world, so he raised an army of humans and monsters. The Archippi tried to stop him. The war raged for years, leaving the land stripped and wasted. Over time, Seiten and his army of Seekers and Unwanteds began to prevail. As time passed, there were only ten Archippi and five people left to fight the enemy while Seiten had amassed an army of thousands.

The wall told of a man named Lesu, who joined the small remnant of warriors preparing for the last battle against Seiten. He healed their wounds, fed them, and comforted them. After they fell into a deep sleep, he left them to engage the enemy alone. They woke to the sounds of swords clashing. Rushing to the top of a hill, they saw Lesu battling hundreds of Unwanteds and Seekers. Before they could go to his rescue, he was overcome and taken to Seiten. Under his orders, Lesu was hacked into pieces on a rock. They left him there for all to see his defeat.

The soldiers who had been with Lesu fled in fear. As Taryn moved farther down the wall, he smiled. When dawn came the next day, Seiten watched hopelessly as Lesu's body melted into the sun's rays and became whole again. The prophecy of the Divine Prince, who would perish to save his people and live again, had come true. Seiten's hold was broken.

The pictures showed Lesu returning. Gathering them together, he gave them great powers to battle Seiten. In the years to come, three of these warriors came to be known as the Shadow Slayers. When Lesu returned to His Father, he left the Slayers in command of the kingdom.

Taryn stared at the wall. *Why would Lesu do that? Why leave His Father in the first place, knowing the torture he would go through? They say it's love. Love for the people then and now.* Taryn returned to the pictures of Lesu being killed.

Kai knelt in front of the altar. A few days ago, Taryn would have mocked Kai severely for being deluded, but now he was envious of the peace Kai had. *Are Eladar and Alyn right?*

Kai placed his hands on the altar as he stood up. The top twisted and slid back. He jumped. "Gelding's gold!"

Taryn grinned. *He has no idea how to swear!* "What's going on?"

"There's a secret compartment." Kai's voice was muffled as he stuck his head into the hole. "There's something in the back."

"Is it alive?" Taryn peered over Kai's shoulder.

"I don't know. You're taller. Can you reach back and grab it?" Kai said.

"I'm not grabbing anything until I know what it is. Are you insane?"

Kai gave Taryn an exasperated look. "Come on, Taryn. I can touch it, but I can't grab it. It's not going to hurt you. It feels like leather."

"Leather means dead animals. I'm not pulling out a dead animal that's been in there for years." Taryn folded him arms against his chest.

Kai glared at Taryn and tried again, groaning as he did. He backed up and pulled out something bound in leather.

"It's a book!" Taryn exclaimed and snatched it out of Kai's hands.

"Oh, so now you'll touch it," Kai said dryly.

Lizzy stood on her toes to see over Kai's shoulder. "What is it?"

"A book. Only there doesn't seem to be any words." Taryn flipped through the pages. It was bound with a dark leather cover. The cream pages were gold lined. Every page was blank.

"That's dumb." Lizzy reached for the book. She pulled it toward her, but Taryn didn't let go. He kept leafing through the pages. She pulled it a little harder. "Let me see."

Taryn tried to shake her off. "Wait. I'm looking at it."

"Hey, be careful with it. It was there for a reason. I haven't even seen it yet." Kai grabbed the book. "You're acting like children. Look! There's something there."

They peered at the book. A word slowly appeared.

"B…it starts with a B." Kai tilted his head to read.

"And that's a L." Lizzy squinted. "Look. B….L… there's a V."

"Believe!" Taryn shouted. "It says *believe.*"

Kai let go of the book, and the word disappeared. "It's so faint that it's hard to tell. Why would someone put a book in a hidden compartment in a forgotten altar? And the only word in it is *believe.* That doesn't make any sense. Well, put it back. There's no use taking it."

"We can't just put it back. There's a reason why you found it. It has a secret. I can figure it out." Taryn clutched the book.

"It's a book without words." Kai said like that ended the argument. "We don't need it."

"How do you know?" Taryn shot back. "You may be glad I kept it one day."

"Fine." Kai slid the lid of the altar shut. "You carry it. I don't understand why you would want a book that doesn't even have words."

"It had *one* word." Lizzy giggled.

Taryn carefully put it with his other books on Minnie. There was something mysterious about this book, and he wasn't going to leave it behind until he figured it out. As they left the meadow, he looked back, the altar in the sunshine. *I hope Alyn and Eladar are right. I hope Adoyni does exist and is what they say He is.*

The thought shocked him, and he shoved it down before he thought about it anymore. He'd better watch it, or he'd lose his focus before he got to the Temple of All.

FAILURES

"Success builds character,
Failure reveals it."
~Dave Checkett

Foehn returned to the army where Refkell, the leader of the Seekers, was waiting. He shivered when he thought of the certain wrath.

Refkell began yelling as soon as he felt Foehn approach, his amber eyes glowing with anger. "Only an idiot like you would push them into a canyon where they could escape. Stay here while I contact the Master. I'm certain he'll have words for you." He reached into his cloak and took out a dark ball. He rubbed the dark ball and said, "Reveal."

The ball instantly shimmered. The white specks in the ball grew, connected, and overtook the black. The Master's face appeared, and Foehn drew back in surprise.

"So you have them," the Master said.

Refkell bowed to the ball. "My lord, I have not obtained them yet. They escaped into the canyons and somehow made it over the mountains before we could reach them."

There was silence. The Master's voice came again, low with anger. "It's obvious that they are no longer able to be turned for my goals. They must die. I'll join you and put an end to them. Foehn, find them and slow them down."

"Yes, Master. We eagerly await your presence." Refkell bowed again.

"You shouldn't," the Master sneered. "For you shall feel my wrath when I arrive."

The image faded as Refkell held his bow. When it was gone, he turned to Foehn. "Hope that the Master takes his anger out on you, for if he doesn't, I'll make you pay twofold for every ounce of pain I receive. Now go."

Foehn blew over the army of Unwanteds, a sea of humans reduced to beasts. Whatever Refkell ordered, they would do without hesitation. Will and reason had vanished with their souls. They huddled down to the ground as he passed over them. Foehn felt a wave of pity for them and a surge of fear that he was being forced into the same fate.

He headed for the mountains and meandered through the crags and peaks, trying to forget the loneliness and despair that filled him. He came to a small meadow. In the center of the glade was a small altar. Behind the altar rose a wall with pictures of people on it. Here was peace. Love. This was what he had begun searching for, so long ago.

Fear crept back into his thoughts. Anguish filled his being. He knew what the Master would do if he tried to leave again. He had tried to leave and failed. Now he must pay the price of his oath. If he could.

He left the meadow behind, not looking at the altar or the wall of heroes. He had his chance for happiness. Now he was paying for his stupidity. He roamed the mountains, his failures weighing him down, and wondered if there was any end to his misery.

CHAPTER TWENTY-EIGHT

Spells and Prayers

Two days! Kai snorted to himself with disgust. *And what has been done?* Two long days where they marched until their muscles ached. Two days of doing without much food. Two days of thirst while the buckets of water on Minnie grew lighter. *Nothing! We're getting nowhere!* Kai forced each foot forward. All he wanted to do was to run home. But once he got home, he didn't know what he'd do. He stepped around a jumble of rocks and remembered what Eladar said. *An uncut gem?* He snorted. *More like an old lump of coal.*

Is everyone at home okay? He couldn't bear it if Mom had to take his place as a servant. The peace that had flowed into him by the altar was gone. He had no way to fix these problems. *I can't let them down again.*

When they stopped for the night, Kai built a small fire to warm up some meat. There were only four pieces of bread and a bit of the beef left. But worse, their water was almost gone, and even up here, the small streams were tainted.

He wandered around the campsite, unable to sit down. He shook his head at Lizzy and Taryn. *You would think we were traveling for fun.* Lizzy's hair was neatly brushed for the first time, and she was playing her guitar and singing. Taryn's red hat was off, his blonde hair was sticking up, and he had his nose stuck in a book. Kai didn't know if he should laugh or scream.

He dumped the wood on the ground. He couldn't stop thinking about Rhiana. He was not going to let another sister die. He missed Shona more every day. *Was Alyn right about the crystals? Could Rhiana end up an Unwanted?*

"Do you think they are?" Kai asked, the words popping out with any thought. Lizzy stopped playing, her green eyes regarding him like he had lost his mind. "The Unwanteds, I mean. Do you think that heaven and hell both refused to let them come in?"

Taryn closed his book. "Aren't Adoyni and Lesu supposed to love everyone? How could they not want them if that is true?"

"I don't think they are," Lizzy answered. "Zoria's temples make me feel weird. I don't like them. But, that meadow made me feel happy and…good. Maybe the people ignored Adoyni and didn't want to know Him."

Before he could answer, the wind arose from the north, bringing a downpour of rain. The tops of the trees bent over as dirt flew through the air. The fire let out a puff of smoke as the rain quenched it. Lizzy threw the guitar in its case to protect it. Taryn grabbed his books and placed them under his shirt, using his body to shield them from the rain. Kai snatched the food and threw it in the basket. He heard Lizzy yelling.

"Save the water!" Lizzy shouted. "It's clean water!"

We could drink it! He pulled out the food with a surge of triumph and held up the basket. *We'll have water.* The rain eased and slowed. The violent downpour turned to a few drips. There was enough water for a swallow. The rain stopped. The meat was soggy, the bread ruined. And only a little water collected. Kai kicked the basket as hard as he could. It hit a tree and rolled toward Minnie, who shied away from it. Taryn placed his books on the driest spot around and gathered some wood.

"You're more of a city boy than I thought," Kai said, his teeth clenched with anger. "You need *dry* wood to start a fire."

"We can try." Taryn was soaked, his purple coat streaking the white shirt underneath.

Kai ran his hands through his hair. Taryn and Lizzy were already shivering in the cold. He sat down by Lizzy. It was going to be a long, cold night.

"I'm glad we have these cloaks," Taryn said as he placed a few more sticks on top of each other. "I can't imagine how much colder it would be without them."

Kai raised an eyebrow and glanced over to see if Taryn was joking. He was dead serious. Kai wanted desperately to mention that he'd refused to wear them at the stagecoach. "I knew we'd burn your books before this was over."

Taryn looked at him like he'd suggested chopping an arm off. "I'm *not* burning books."

Kai held his hands up in the air. "I must not be as smart as you because I don't know how to start a fire out of wet wood."

Taryn ignored him and flipped the book open to a page. He mumbled some more words. Lizzy crept closer to Taryn. They watched the sticks, but no flame ignited. Taryn mumbled some more and stopped.

Lizzy touched the wood. "Ow! It's hot!" She put her finger in her mouth.

Flames leaped up, the water from the wood sizzling as the fire grew larger. Taryn sat back and laughed. "I did it! Look at what I did!"

Kai stared at the fire. He should be jumping for joy, but all he could think was that Taryn was right. Zoria had given Taryn power. Adoyni had never answered Kai's prayers like that. Maybe he was praying to the wrong god.

* * *

Rhiana sat up in bed. "Kai!" Her stomach heaved, so she lay back in bed and pulled the sheets up. *Why am I cold and sweating at the same time?* She rolled on her side and looked at the one window in her room.

Sadness grew as she thought about last week when the racing officials came. She sat at the top of the stairs as they accused Kai of killing a race horse.

And when Mom came to wake him up, Kai wasn't
in his room. The men said the Council was going
to decide if Mother should become an indented
servant, or something like that. Dad yelled at them
to get out and to keep their grubby hands off his
wife. When they were gone, Mom started crying.
Rhiana stumbled down the stairs and into Mom's
arms.

Dad rolled over in his wheelchair and
awkwardly patted them. "Everything will be okay."

"He wouldn't leave us!" Rhiana stiffened. "He
wouldn't!"

Mom's eyes were red from crying. "But he did.
Now the Council may decide that I may have to
take his place. If I do, I will have to go and pay off
his debt."

"We don't know what will happen," Dad said
angrily. "We'll see what the Council decides.
Perhaps I'll have a talk with that Belial fellow and
explain our situation."

But that night, after Mom had tucked her
into bed and gone back downstairs, she snuck
back to the top of the stairs as Mom washed the
dishes.

"I saw Timo today," Dad was saying. "He's
going to talk with people about standing up to
the Council. I guess most of the men think you
shouldn't have pay Kai's debt."

Timo? Rhiana muffled a yawn. *Was that the man
who put me on that stallion once and said I was a better
rider than Dad?*

Dishes rattled as Mom spoke. "Chancellor Belial isn't a forgiving man, especially when it comes to money. He's furious and is looking to get back some of the money he lost."

Dad snorted. "He has more money than the king."

"What are you going to do if I have to go?" Mom sounded like she was going to cry again. "How will you survive?"

There was a long pause, and then Dad cleared his throat. "You don't worry about that. We'll make it somehow. If Kai ever returns, I'll beat him senseless. What was he thinking, pulling a stunt like that?"

Rhiana felt a sneeze coming and rushed to her room before she was discovered. She lay down on her bed and clutched the crystal. She was so confused, but now she was angry. Kai promised her that she wouldn't have to go to the Temple. She didn't know what was happening because she was too tired to walk to the top of the stairs. It even hurt when Mom picked her up.

Sharp pains pounded through her head like it was going to split in two. Sweat poured down her body in tiny rivers, and she fought back the urge to throw up. She called for Mom, but her voice squeaked. She couldn't even sit up. She started to cry. *I don't want to die.*

And then the pain started to go away, her stomach settled. As it disappeared, she stopped crying. She felt like someone was there holding her as she drifted off to sleep. She woke up feeling much better. Mom took her down to see Dad at breakfast. When Mom carried her back to her room, she laughed at her cat curled up on the bed. But when Mom left and the door was shut, the blackness of the room seeped into her heart. She could only think of Kai.

You could pray.

The thought sprung to her mind. That was something they hadn't done since Shona died. *Who should I pray to?* The crystal burned around her neck. *Zoria! But I need a spell.* She knew Mom had supplies for spells downstairs. *Should I use a white or red candle?*

She swung her legs over the edge of the bed, but a wave of dizziness hit her, and she laid back into bed. *I can't make it downstairs.* She'd failed Kai. Tears streamed down her face as she let go of the crystal and wiped them from her face with her drenched pillow.

There's Adoyni.

He didn't need any spells. She remembered the times they had gotten on their knees around Shona's bed and prayed. They never used candles.

She closed her eyes and folded her hands. *Adoyni, I'm sorry I'm not on my knees, but I'm very sick, and I don't want to die. Could you help me? Also, my brother is in a lot of trouble. Could You take care of him? I miss him so much, and we need him to help us. We need lots of help, Adoyni. Please. I know You can do it. Thank you.*

She wiped off her face and rolled over, her eyes quickly closing as she fell into a deep sleep.

CHAPTER TWENTY-NINE

Oh, Nuts

Taryn was going to throw up. He could feel the bile in his stomach coming up his throat. And he hadn't even taken one bite yet.

Gazing at the pale blue sky that was fading to darkness, he was thankful that the weather had improved from yesterday. After the fire had sparked into life, the rain returned. They'd endured a continuous downpour that made everything wet and brought a chill that seeped past his cloak and into his bones.

Kai had suggested stopping early to dry out their things. As soon as Minnie was settled, Lizzy and Kai left to hunt. Taryn was lost in studying magic when they returned with a squirrel. Lizzy had thrown down her norsaq with great disgust, saying it was worthless. She had tried her norsaq and her sling numerous times, but it was Kai who killed the squirrel. She flopped down on her cloak in a giant fit of despair, saying that she never hit anything. Kai didn't say much, but his face was white as he skinned and cooked the poor rodent.

Now the squirrel was sitting on his plate, a blackened lump of meat. Kai was already half done with his portion.

"You have to eat," Lizzy said. "Think about something else and take a bite. It's not that bad when you get past the thought of it."

Taryn picked the meat up. He pictured a nice steak, a proper one from a cow, but his stomach didn't believe him. He put it back down on his plate and glanced around the camp to avoid looking at it. Lizzy's guitar was drying in the sun, even though she announced in a great deal of depression that it was ruined forever.

"Yeah, and think about what we're going to do for water." Lizzy's words jolted him out of his thoughts. "How long can a person go without anything to drink?"

"Don't know. Maybe three or four days." Kai glanced at Taryn with a wicked gleam in his blue eyes. "Are you going to eat that or squirrel it away for later?" Kai burst out laughing at his stupid joke.

"Funny," Taryn said sarcastically. He took a deep breath, thought about a piece of steak, and took a bite of the meat. Grimacing, he forced himself to chew and swallow.

"Tomorrow we could try some grubs," Lizzy joined in. "I've heard they're delicious."

Grubs? Just what are those? Taryn wasn't about to ask. "Don't the stories always have the people drinking dew off plants? Does that really work?"

"I have no idea. It'd have to be a lot of plants." Kai ran his hands through his hair.

Taryn took a deep breath and popped the last bite in his mouth. An image of a squirrel emerged in his brain, and he gagged. It took all his self-will to swallow.

"Hey, what about your spells, Taryn? Don't you have something in your books about purifying water?" Lizzy inspected her guitar. She strummed once. It didn't sound too bad. She got an annoyed look on her face and started fidgeting with the pegs.

"That's not a good idea," Kai said.

"It's better than dying of dehydration." Taryn grabbed his books.

"I don't think we should get Zoria involved. Maybe we could pray to Adoyni," Kai suggested.

"You really need to stop with this Adoyni stuff." Taryn flopped down on the ground and pulled out *The Ultimate Book of Spells.* "You can get in a lot of trouble talking about a false god."

"He's not false," Kai shot back.

"Didn't you pray to Him when Shona was dying? And didn't she die? Where was He when that happened?" Taryn flipped through the book, keeping his fingers in different sections. "When you're dying of thirst, you'll change your mind." Taryn dropped all the saved places in the book and pointed to one section. "This might work. Lizzy, get a bucket of water. There's not much hope to get any mugwort. What could we substitute?"

Lizzy froze. "What did you say?"

"Mugwort." Taryn noticed she had a strange look on her face. "What's wrong?"

She pulled out a silver box. "Remember Rica giving this to me? It has mugwort in it. He said it would keep me safe. Maybe it was meant for this."

"It seems like this was destined to be." Taryn took some of the herb out and handed it back to her. "Now, can you find something with the color of lavender on it?"

"I'll look." She rummaged through the bags until she found a small strip of lavender on Minnie's blanket. Then she grabbed the bucket and skipped to the stream.

Taryn felt a surge of excitement. He'd never experimented with many spells, always waiting for the right moment. Now he would purify some water to drink, proving his abilities.

"I really don't think you should do this." Kai's voice broke through his concentration. "Besides, haven't the seers tried all of this already? What makes you different?"

Taryn shoved down his anger. "For one, they tried it on the whole river which probably overextended their power. And secondly, it's my calling to purify the river. Why don't you take your negative energy away from here? I don't need you infecting me with it."

"Whatever. Call me when it doesn't work." Kai stalked off.

Taryn took a deep breath. His fingers brushed against the book with no words. He yelped and pulled back his hand. It felt like his fingers were burned. He picked it up carefully as it continued to tingle. The pages held no words. He was about to put it down when a word briefly appeared on the page. He squinted.

"Flee?" He stared at the word as it faded. "Flee what? Why won't you just show all the words at once like a normal book?"

He tossed it on the sheet and picked up the *Ultimate Book of Spells*. But his mind kept going back to the one word: Flee. *Is it a warning that I shouldn't do this spell?* Lizzy ran up and put the bucket beside him. The smell from the water reached his nose, and the stench made him want to vomit. He could taste that poor little squirrel in his throat.

"What's wrong?" Lizzy sat down, confidence shining in her green eyes.

Taryn hesitated and then decided to tell her. "I picked up that book. It burned my fingers. Then I saw another word. It said flee."

"Well, that's appropriate. Isn't that what we are doing, fleeing from that army?" Lizzy picked up the book and flipped through it. It didn't seem to hurt her at all. "Where's Kai?"

Fleeing from the army! Why didn't I think of that? But he still couldn't shake the feeling of dread as he pulled the bucket closer. "He didn't want to be part of this."

"Wait until he gets thirsty. Let's do this!" Lizzy was bouncing with excitement.

He placed the bucket in front of him. Adding some salt and a pinch of mugwort, he dropped in the lavender cloth. He read the words, concentrating on the energy around him. "Mother Earth, I ask thee to cleanse this water. What was done was done. Be it now undone."

Lizzy peered over the bucket, holding her nose. He stared at the water. Nothing changed. It was as brown as dirt, and it smelled like there was a dead animal in it. He picked up the bucket and sloshed it around. Nothing changed. He waited a minute and then stomped to the trees and threw the tainted water on the ground. The grass withered as the poisoned water hit it. He threw the pail back at the campfire. Minnie jumped and snorted like it was a dangerous animal.

Lizzy watched him, confused. "I thought you said it would work."

"Well, it didn't," he snapped. He was so angry that he didn't even care about the tears springing up in her eyes. "Maybe I don't have enough faith in myself. Maybe it was Kai with his negative energy. Maybe Zoria's a lie. All I know is that in a couple of days, we'll be dead."

He spun around, tripped on a rock, and stomped away. *Even if I could get to the Temple of All, I wouldn't be able to do anything if I can't fix a stupid bucket of water. And Nighthawk…I mean, Mom…will never want me around.*

The trees opened up to reveal a cliff that dropped sharply down to the foothills below. The sheer emptiness of the land matched the hopelessness in his heart. Kai was sitting on a rock with his feet dangling over the edge.

Kai didn't look up as Taryn joined him. "Didn't think it would work."

Taryn inched to the edge. He tried to hang his feet over like Kai but ended up sideways with an arm curled around a large boulder for support. "Really? I didn't pick up on that at all," he said drily. "How'd you know?"

"Guess I'm smarter than you." Kai grinned. "Are you as attached to gophers as you are to squirrels?"

"What? No. Why?" Taryn asked, confused by the subject change.

"They'll probably be next on the menu." Kai gave him an evil grin.

Taryn groaned. "What else do you think we'll find?"

"I don't know," Kai sighed. "I've been watching for a sign of people out there, but it's quieter than a cemetery. We'd better find some water, though. If we don't, we're going to die."

* * *

Lizzy pulled out the silver box and ran her thumb over it. Tears stung her eyes. She blinked as they overflowed and ran down her cheeks. She stared at the books in front of her, the book of spells teasing her with hope. She picked up the wordless book. A tear splashed on it, and she wiped it away. *What are we going to do? Will no one help us?*

She opened the book. No words. She felt the crushing weight of disappointment as she flipped through the pages. And then her eye caught something. She turned back a page. Dark words filled the page. "Do not fear." But she was so scared. Scared that Rica would die and she would die. Tears splashed on the page as she read the words again.

The tightness in her chest eased, and her tears dried as she read the words.

"Adoyni, I'm Lizzy. I really liked how I felt in Your shrine. If I believe in You, would You help me feel that way again?"

She closed her eyes and waited for the feelings to return. She waited for a minute longer and glanced back down at the book, but the words were gone. "Stupid book!" She slammed the book shut. She marched through the woods and saw the guys sitting at the edge of the cliff. "Where have you been?"

"Just looking at where we're going next. If that army is around, they'll catch up soon. We'll have to move even faster than we have been." Kai stood up. "Let's get some sleep."

Lizzy started to follow them back to camp and stopped when her hand grazed the silver box. *Maybe Kai's right about Adoyni. It's rather silly to think that an herb could do anything. But a God like Adoyni might be strong enough to help me.* It sat in her hand, shining in the last rays of the sun. *It's so pretty.* She ran a finger over it. *Why would Adoyni care about*

*me? Even Mother doesn't like me. A God surely wouldn't
bother with someone as insufficient as me.*

She slid the silver container back to her pocket.
She couldn't part with the last thing Rica had given
her. But she was tired of feeling lonely, and she
longed to be loved. She was sick of being scared,
and lost, and alone. A silver box with some herbs
didn't seem to be helping. Her fingers tightened
on it. *Alyn said that the crystals from the Goddess were
killing people. Could this thing be evil?* She almost
laughed. *How could something like this cause any harm?*

Before she could think anymore, she whipped
the box out and over the cliff. She heard it hit the
rocks below once, twice, and then silence. She
stood there, frightened by what she had done.
Rica's going to kill me, if he gets the chance. The setting
sun cast long shadows over the prairie, but it no
longer looked lonely. Instead, there was a quiet
beauty as the sun sank. The wind blew her hair over
her face. As she tossed it back over her shoulder,
she saw black shadows nestled in the grass. She
squinted in the sun.

"Kai! Taryn! Come back!" She shouted. "Look!
There's a town!"

CHAPTER THIRTY

Man Up

Kai eyed the town in the morning sun. The handful of buildings was as quiet as an empty barn. No smoke, no sign of movement. He was suddenly glad that they'd decided to wait until the sun came up to investigate the town.

"What are you waiting for?" Taryn pushed Kai forward. His energy had increased with the hope of civilization.

It's awfully quiet. Kai had an unsettling feeling that something wasn't quite right. *No one's moving around.*

Lizzy and Taryn trotted along with grins. Kai tried to think positively. *So what if the town looks deserted? Maybe they're hiding from us!* He focused on a nice steak with some fresh bread. He'd wash it down with water. Lots and lots of water.

They approached and hesitated. The gates were open but barely hanging on the hinges. Dirt piled up in front of them like they hadn't been used for a long time. Kai peered over Taryn's shoulder to see corpses in the street. Men fallen on the ground, not to move again, with parcels beside them. Women holding children. There was a young man reaching out to a young girl. He shuddered. They looked like his age.

But there wasn't any blood. *What killed them?* Dust covered the bodies, making their skin white. One old woman sat in her chair in front of a house with a cup in her hand. *Water! They were poisoned!* Kai's stomach heaved as the wind stirred up the stench.

"What in all of the stars happened?" Taryn pinched his nose. "Did the water kill them?"

"I think so." Kai handed Minnie's rope to Lizzy. "But we've got to go in. Our water's all gone, and we need food and supplies, and Minnie needs grain," Kai said.

"I can't go in there," Lizzy's voice shook. "I just can't. I don't want to see a bunch of dead people."

"You're not going. You'll stay here with Minnie and watch for the army. If you see them, holler. Come on, Taryn, let's do this." Kai slapped him on the shoulder and drew his sword.

"Why me? Why not her?" Taryn rubbed his shoulder like Kai had hurt him.

"Because she's the girl," Kai snapped. "Man up."

"Man up? What's that suppose to mean? I'm all for equality of women, so I'll stay here." Taryn refused to take a step closer to the town.

"I can't carry everything and be on the lookout. If that disease creates Unwanteds, there might be some of them in there. Move it." Kai pointed to the town.

Taryn's face turned white, but he gripped his axe. He unfastened the shield Alyn had given him and put it on his arm. Kai pulled his shirt over his nose and led the way into the town.

"Be careful," Lizzy said as they walked through the gates. Kai shuddered. Death permeated this place, soaking into every nook and cranny. *Can it seep into us and kill us, too?* It was colder inside the gates. A dank smell reached his nose, like stale water and dead bodies.

Kai shivered and walked forward.

* * *

Taryn followed Kai through the gates. The cold seeped through his clothes and sank into his bones. But this wasn't the cold he felt at night. This was death. His heart was pounding heavily. He clutched the axe with dread. He didn't want to test what Alyn had shown him. Not even on a tree.

Kai stopped a few feet inside the gates, and Taryn edged closer to him. Kai's eyes flicked from the bodies to the vacant buildings. He lowered his shirt from his nose. "Look, I don't like this either, but we have to do it. So, let's just get it done, okay?"

"Don't worry. I manned up," Taryn said, proud he used slang for the first time in his life. *Father would kill me if he heard me say that.*

Kai grinned weakly. "That's the general store, and the stables are next to it. We'll go to the store for food and water. Then we'll get some grain."

The building Kai pointed to was across the street and down three buildings. The windows were broken, and the door was half open. A body was blocking the door from closing. The sign over the building had been worn off, but you could see the letters *ore* on the end. He swallowed. *Why isn't it closer to the gates?*

Kai studied the street, his blue eyes dark in the shadows. "Watch for Unwanteds. Don't count on everyone being dead. They may be pretending until we get close. Be as quiet as you can. Stand firm." He raised his sword.

Taryn shifted his grip on the axe. "Stand firm."

They moved slowly. The stench threatened to gag him, so he copied Kai and pulled his shirt over his nose. *Why did I agree to do this? I'm not a hero. I just want to go home.* He never imagined that he'd wish to go home. In fact, studying law didn't seem like such a horrid thing anymore. Anything would be better than this. The wind blew a hat across the street in front of them. Taryn swung his axe wildly and almost hit Kai in the shoulder.

Kai glared at Taryn. "Maybe you should walk beside me, not behind me."

"Sorry. I thought it was an Unwanted," Taryn whispered.

Taryn crept alongside Kai as they moved down the street. *This is all a mistake. That stupid horse had better be right about the river. If I can cleanse the river, maybe Zoria will show me favor. Maybe Nighthawk… Mom…will want me around.*

The stores and houses along the street were so run down that they looked like they'd fall over with the first puff of wind. The glass in the windows was broken and lying on the ground. Some of the houses were burnt. The town pole stood in the center of the street. Strangely, Zoria's flame on top of it was still burning. *How does that work if there's no one to tend to it?*

Taryn jumped when Kai's foot hit the boardwalk. Kai poked the body on the threshold with his sword, but it didn't move. He slipped over it and through the door. Taryn followed, not daring to look down. The store was covered with a thick dust. There were stacks of faded clothes across from the shelves of groceries.

"You get us some warmer clothes," Kai whispered. "Anything that will protect us from the rain. Nothing fancy. I'll see if there's any food or water left."

"Okay, be careful." Taryn didn't want to split up, but it was the quickest way out of here.

Kai disappeared behind the rows of beans, rice, and other goods. Taryn found the clothes. Putting down his axe, he began sorting through them. The dust tickled his nose, and he sneezed. He heard Kai jump, and something crashed to the floor.

"Was that you?" Kai peered over the counter.

"Yeah. Sorry." Taryn hissed back.

"You scared the wits out of me," Kai frowned. The air between them was full of dust, dotting the sunlight that streamed through the dirty windows.

"What wits you have, you mean," Taryn chuckled.

"Nice." Kai grinned and disappeared behind the counter again.

The next thing Taryn picked up was a green dress. He put it aside. He found a couple of rain slickers. He paused and looked back at the dress. It was Lizzy's favorite color, and it was small, like her. *Would it be wrong to take it? We should only take what we need.*

"Are you done?" Kai broke through his thoughts.

"Yeah." *We're taking other stuff. Besides, who around here is going to use it?* He snatched up the dress. "Let's go."

It was much harder to hold his axe and the clothes at the same time. When he got to the door, he saw that Kai struggled to keep his sword ready and hang onto an armful of dry food. Taryn saw he had some beans, and there were two water bags on his back.

"I think this water is okay. That's all there was. We'll have to get some saddle bags at the stables to carry all this." Kai rubbed dirt away from the window and looked out. "Let's go."

Awkwardly carrying their weapons and goods, they made their way outside. They stepped around two more bodies and paused outside the open doorway to the stables. The doors hung on one hinge. They exchanged a glance. Inside, the reek was worse. Taryn blinked and peered through the gloom. As his eyes adjusted, he saw that Kai had his shirt over his nose again.

"Smells like something died," Kai commented.

"You think? Grab what we need and let's get out of here." Taryn set his axe down and took the food from Kai.

"Open the door more. We need air." Kai headed deeper in the blackness.

Taryn kicked the door open. Sunlight streamed in as he took a deep breath of fresh air. The town was deathly quiet. He tried to see Lizzy standing by the gates, but she wasn't there. Kai was banging around in the back of the stable. Taryn heard a clatter of things hitting the ground. "Saddle Suds!"

Taryn grinned. *That's a new swear word!* "Hey, Kai, I can't see Lizzy."

There was no answer for a minute. Taryn swung around to check on Kai.

"There's dead horses back here," Kai shouted. Clanging came from the back like he was throwing things around. "At least four. I found some saddle bags, but I'm still looking for grain. It reeks so bad I think I'm going to throw up."

Obviously Kai hadn't heard what he said about Lizzy. He peered out the door. *Where did she go?* They wouldn't have heard her when they were in the store if something had attacked her. He went out to the street. The gates were empty. Both Minnie and Lizzy were gone. He stepped out farther. Kai was still banging around in the back of the stable. He took a few steps down the street. *She's gone. Where did she go?*

He walked down the street, dropping the clothes as he broke into a sprint. He could see around the posts. There was no sign of her at all. He was halfway down the street when Kai started screaming from the stables between the pounding of steel. The clashing grew louder amidst his yells.

Then the inaudible shouts changed to words. "Taryn! There's one of them in here! Taryn! Help!"

He whirled around. Kai was still yelling as he ran to the stable. But before he entered it, the shouting and the clattering stopped. The town sank into silence as death became the victor once again.

CHAPTER THIRTY-ONE

Great Help

Lizzy watched Kai and Taryn enter the town. *Why'd I throw the box away?* She could've given it to them or kept herself safe. She was torn between running after them into that death town and staying to face the unknown alone. Minnie was frantically chowing down on grass. *She looks half dead.* Lizzy stroked her neck. The sound of her teeth tearing up the grass was a welcome change to the silence. *I hate waiting.* She saw Taryn's books on the side of the packs. She untied the books and sat down on the road.

"Let's see what he has, Minnie." Her voice sounded empty in the silence. "This is *The Stars and What We Can Learn From Them* by Nighthawk Nephesus. What do you think, Minnie? Think Taryn has a bit of crush on this Nephesus?"

A thought streaked across her mind. "Listen to this, Minnie. Mischa was trying to tell Taryn something before he died, and he said, 'Your mother is n…n…'. He used the 'n' twice. Nighthawk Nephesus. I wonder if she's Taryn's mom. Don't say anything to him, though. We wouldn't want to get his hopes up. Or trampled if he has a crush on her."

She giggled, but Minnie just flicked an ear. Lizzy took that as a promise to be quiet. *The Ultimate Book of Spells* lay in front of her. It made her want to do something powerful no one else could do. She picked it up carefully and opened the first page.

There were hundreds of spells. Spells to make you smarter, make someone fall in love, make them fall out of love, make you taller, shorter, skinnier, happier. Everything a person could ever want to do or be was in here. The pictures made her smile when she looked at them.

"Hey, Minnie," she laughed. "Do you want a smaller nose? I could do that." Lizzy turned back to the book, thinking about what she'd just said. *I could do this.* She could change her hair color. She could make her voice better. *What if I was better than Mother and everyone came to see me?* She pictured singing on stage with hundreds of people gathered to hear her while Mother watched. She lingered on that spell. She'd sing wherever she wanted, even at the palace. Mother's fame would end like a candle snuffed out. *I'll do that one later. When we get home.*

She saw another spell that called to her. *Beauty Spell.* The picture showed a girl with dull reddish hair. There was no smile on her plain face. On the other side of the page was the same girl. You could tell because the green eyes were the same. But now she had hair that shone like the summer sun. Lizzy gasped at how beautiful she was.

"That could be me, Minnie. I'd be prettier than all the girls in Albia. With this and a new voice, Mother would love me." She stared at the picture. *This would give me everything I need. With Rica back, my voice and beauty would draw Mom and Dad together. We'll be happy again.*

"I'll do it," she said. "I deserve it." But she hesitated. "I'll do it when all this is over." She flipped the pages.

Bravery Spell.

She was so tired of being scared. Ever since she got on that coach, she'd been terrified. *I'm not going to be scared anymore.* The pictures showed a girl sitting on the ground, alone and trembling. On the opposite side, the girl was standing strong with a sword in her hand. Her face was in the sunshine as she faced a massive army.

"I'm doing it." She ran her fingers over the steps. There were some words to say, but she needed a few things. Her finger stopped on the first ingredient. "Water," she snapped. "Why does everything in this world need water?"

She glared at the book. She had everything else on the list. The water flask only had a couple of swallows, and if she used it, they wouldn't have any to drink.

"It's no good being brave if you're dead." She slammed the book shut. Minnie jumped. "I'll just have to find more water."

She tied the books back on Minnie and took her lead rope. Minnie balked for a minute and looked toward the gate.

"Come on." Lizzy gave a sharp tug on the rope. "They'll be fine."

Surely there was a creek going into the town with clean water. She left the gates behind without a thought of Kai or Taryn.

* * *

Kai shuffled to the back of the stables, trying not to breathe in the stink. He kept his sword out and tried to make out dim shapes. He saw rows of harnesses and breathed a sigh of relief. The saddlebags would be here. He groped around until he found two. He threw them over his shoulder.

He heard a rustling behind him. Footsteps came closer.

"Taryn?" he whispered. "Is that you?"

There was no answer, but the footsteps stopped. He gripped his sword and shifted the saddlebags. *Probably just my imagination.* He fumbled around in the dark before finding the barrels of grain. He put down his sword and took one of saddlebags. As he pulled it over his shoulder, he heard the sound of metal scraping on metal. He froze.

"Is that you, Taryn?" he hissed when he didn't hear anything else. "Stop fooling around."

Taryn never answered. *Where'd he go?* Kai felt a flash of anger. *He was supposed to be here.* There were no more sounds, so he filled the saddlebags with grain, his back to the door.

When he heaved the bag to his shoulder, he saw an Unwanted launch toward him, but before he could react, it slammed into him, knocking him into the harnesses hanging on the wall. The bags slid off his shoulder as he struggled free and groped to find his sword.

Light flashed in the darkness, and Kai saw a hammer speeding toward him. He ducked and felt a sharp pain as it grazed the top of his head. He yelled with pain, swinging his fist, but his arm was caught in the straps of leather.

He shouted, "Taryn! There's one of them in here! Taryn!"

The Unwanted charged, and Kai twisted to dodge it. He wrestled with the straps and dropped to the floor. The creature smashed into the harnesses, trying to find him. Kai leaped at its legs and wrestled it to the ground. The Unwanted fell onto its back and roared in anger, striking the empty air with its hammer. Kai found his sword and stood up.

The Unwanted gained its feet. *Can it see better than I can? Where's Taryn? Did this Unwanted kill him, too?* Kai fought back anger as he realized he was going to have to kill this beast alone. He thrust, but it dodged the blade.

Kai circled it warily. If he could get to the saddlebags, then he could slip back to where the light was better. He stepped closer to the bags, gauging the distance. Then he heard the Unwanted step toward him. He sliced sideways with his sword.

The blade jerked in his hand like he'd hit something solid. He put all his weight into the blade. The Unwanted fell into some shelves and lay still. The silence was eerie. He listened for any movement, but the stable was strangely silent. *Surely Taryn can't be dead.* He picked up the saddlebags, never turning his back to the dead Unwanted, and kept both hands on the sword. A floor board squeaked like someone stepped on it.

He knew it was another Unwanted coming in the door. He shifted the bags up onto his shoulder. He was going to kill this one before it had a chance to attack him. He stepped closer to the door and swung.

* * *

Taryn rushed into the stable. *Where'd I put my axe?* He remembered setting it down, but it was so dark he couldn't see anything. He crawled on the ground, grasping for the axe. He snatched up something cold. In the light from the door, he saw that he was holding an arm of a dead person. He dropped it and slid over something hard.

He grimaced. *Please don't let it be another dead body.* He curled his fingers around it and felt the familiar feel of a wooden handle. He took a deep breath and turned to go deeper into the dark stables. The reek seemed worse than before.

He took a step and then paused. *Where's Kai?*
I should've heard him rustling around. The stable is
as quiet as a grave. Taryn shivered. He didn't like
that comparison at all. There was a quiet footstep
from the back. Taryn slid to the wall, his heart was
pounding so loud that he could barely hear the
next footstep. *Here it comes.* He wanted to scream
for help. The footsteps came closer. *I can't do this!*
I'm not brave. Please, someone, help me. The thought of
his crystal flashed through his mind, but he had left
it on Minnie's back. Zoria couldn't help him now.

What about Adoyni? The thought leaped through
his mind. *He might help. It's worth a try. Adoyni, if You*
exist, can You help me? I don't want to die, and I can't do
this alone.

He heard the next footstep and pulled his axe
back, ready to swing. He took a deep breath. *One...*
two...three... He swung.

"It's me! Stop!" Kai dodged the axe and
scrambled out to the sunshine, saddlebags and
grain flying through the air. Taryn tried to stop, but
the axe embedded itself in the door.

Taryn stared at Kai. "I thought you were an
Unwanted."

"I thought *you* were one." Kai lay on the
boardwalk, catching his breath. His sword was
bloody. "Where in all the blazes did you go?"

"Lizzy isn't at the gates anymore. I went to
check on her." Taryn stepped out of the stables.
"What happened?"

"An Unwanted attacked me." Kai sat up. "It's dead."

"Good. Let's get out of here and find Lizzy." Taryn wanted out of there. Now.

They walked to the gates. For some reason, Taryn didn't feel so worried. He felt like they could handle anything, even the Unwanteds. Kai marched beside him with a sour look on his face. *He's probably mad I left him at the stables. But he did fine.* They stomped through the gates and looked around. Lizzy was nowhere to be seen.

Kai pointed to the west. "That's the army! Horses' hooves! Where did she go? Now we've lost the jump we had, and she's gone." He sprinted down the wall. "Lizzy!" He waited a few seconds and then yelled again. There was no answer. "Come on! I don't want to get separated again."

They rounded the corner of the wall. Minnie was standing with her ears pricked like she was waiting for them. Behind her was a dried up creek bed surrounded by dead vegetation.

"What in good heavens is going on?" Taryn gripped his axe. They walked closer to the creek bed. Lizzy sat covered in the dirt, a bewildered expression on her face.

"What in all the blazes are you doing?" Kai yelled.

Lizzy stared at them. "Water. I need water."

"We have water, you idiot. What do you think we were doing? Sightseeing?" Kai was yelling. "Now get out of there. Thanks to you, that army is on our heels. Both of you have been a great help today. We're going to fail, and when we do, everyone will die, thanks to you!"

Kai grabbed Minnie's rope. She jumped from him, afraid of his anger, but he ignored her and started loading the saddle bags on her. Lizzy looked dazed, like she was coming out of a trance.

She glanced at Kai as she climbed out of the ditch. "What got his panties in a twist?"

"I saw you were missing, so I went to check on you. Then Kai was attacked by an Unwanted while I was gone. He didn't take that so well," Taryn said.

"Oops," Lizzy giggled. "But he's okay, right? Why isn't he happy?"

"I don't know." Taryn started laughing, too. It was either laugh or cry. *We'd better stop. I don't think Kai would get the joke.* That thought sent him on another round of giggles. He choked out his thoughts to Lizzy, who started laughing all over again.

As soon as they could control themselves, they got a drink, strapped on their packs, and started out. He realized that Kai was right about one thing. That army was close, and they had lost their lead. The thought chased all the laughter out of him, and Kai still wasn't talking to either of them. They turned their backs to the army and trudged into the night without a word.

FEATS

---

*"Some of the world's greatest feats were accomplished
by people not smart enough to know they were impossible."*
~DOUG LARSON

Foehn turned onto the grasslands and swept east.
He spotted the three people making their way across
the prairie. They were talking and laughing. The large
sorrel horse followed behind. The sight filled him with
jealousy, so he swooped down and blew off the hat
of the blonde boy. The girl laughed as the hat spun
through the air.

The boy ran after the hat and picked it up. Grinning
at the girl, he threw it up in the air. The wind caught it
again and tossed it high before dropping it back to the
ground. The girl said something which made the two
boys laugh as they retrieved the hat.

Foehn felt a wave of loneliness. They were so
happy, so free. He knew that they were the enemy, but
he didn't see why the Master wanted to destroy them
so badly. He blew on them harder, but the girl only
spread her arms to the wind, her long red hair flying
behind her. She spun and twirled before collapsing on
the ground, laughing as she fell. Foehn watched her.
What did she find so funny? He hadn't meant to make
her laugh.

He whirled away and left them behind. But no matter how fast he blew, he couldn't erase the sound of the girl's laughter, so free and happy, in his ears. He suppressed the thought that it might be the last time the girl laughed. Once the Master arrived, they would be caught and killed.

The Master knew everything. He knew where they were going, how they would get there, where they would find water and food. The three could not outrace or outsmart him.

And the Master was not in a forgiving mood. Once he had talked about keeping the three alive, using their power to do his will, but now he only spoke of their death. They had developed too much of their abilities without his guidance. He was going to kill them and steal their power.

No. The three had no chance of survival. They would soon be dead, for the Master was coming.

And with him came death.

CHAPTER THIRTY-TWO

Paper to the Wind

Kai yawned while he waited for Taryn and Lizzy to catch up. In the pale moonlight, they looked as tired as he felt. Lizzy struggled to keep up. Her red hair was pulled back in a braid, but strands had fallen out, and every so often she'd push them out of her face.

Minnie followed Lizzy with her head low and her mane tangled and matted with dirt. They didn't bother with the lead rope anymore. There was nowhere she could go, and her complete devotion kept her close.

Taryn came behind Minnie. His head drooped, and he stumbled with exhaustion. He complained all the time, but he stayed with them, step by step. His purple coat was now brown, and his red hat was bent from where he'd slept on it in a desperate attempt to have a pillow.

They had been walking as fast and as long as they could, but it didn't matter where or how fast they went. The army gained on them every day. No matter how hard they pushed, it was closer every time Kai looked back. And there was no possible way they could keep up the pace. His feet ached. Lizzy and Taryn were exhausted, and their supplies were almost gone. They were going to lose.

"Let's stop for the night," Kai said.

The only response was groans of approval. Minnie snorted like she understood. Kai ignored his aching muscles and took the packs off her. She shook in approval. They settled with their cloaks tucked tightly around them against the chilly wind. The foothills looked lonely at night as the moonlight made the grass shimmer silver.

"How'd they know?" Kai asked. "How did that army know where we were? They were coming straight for us like they knew our location."

"They could be tracking us, except that they came around the mountains and wouldn't have crossed our tracks." Lizzy shook her head. "Can you track with magic?"

"Did either of you take something from those Unwanteds?" Taryn asked. They shook their heads. "There's a way to locate a person if they have a prepared item. They carry it around thinking it's just a coin or a trinket, but the person who set a spell on it can follow them."

Kai dug the toe of his boot into the dirt. *There has to be a way. They can't be that lucky to just find us in the hills like that.* "Has anyone given you anything on the trip?"

"Rica gave me that box, but I threw it away after we tried to purify the water." Lizzy looked embarrassed. "Rica's going to kill me when he finds out."

Taryn reached his hand into his shirt pocket and pulled out a carefully folded piece of paper. His face was white in the moonlight and his fingers shook a bit. "Nighthawk Nephesus gave this to me that day before I left."

"Could a piece of paper work for that?" Lizzy asked.

"Paper's a good way of tracking a person with magic. But this isn't what you're looking for." Taryn unfolded it and stroked it lightly.

"Why not?" Kai wanted to tear the paper out of his hand and shred it to pieces.

"Because it's from Nighthawk." Taryn looked at Kai like he was incredibly dumb. "She'd never be involved with this. Besides, she wanted me to go to Northbridge. She said she needed me to help purify the river."

Kai ran his hands through his hair and tried to keep his temper from erupting. *If we only knew days ago!* "Taryn, Nighthawk Nephesus is a servant of Belial, who's trying to kill us."

"That's impossible!" Taryn's fingers curled around the pamphlet. "She'd never do that."

"Why not?" Kai roared, unable to keep his rage back. "Just because she does magic?"

"She's my mom!" Taryn roared back.

Kai froze, shocked by Taryn's reaction. He never shouted. He whined, he pouted, he complained, he grumbled, but Kai could not remember him once shouting. Lizzy sat in her cloak watching both of them with her mouth open. Kai looked at her, but even she was speechless.

"I think." Taryn glanced down at the paper. "I don't know for sure, but I think that's what Mischa was trying to tell me right before he died."

Kai noticed that Taryn was no longer paying any attention to the paper. He snatched the pamphlet out of Taryn's hand before Taryn knew what was happening. Kai tore it up, dodging Taryn's grasp, and threw it into the wind.

"Mother or not, that army is tracking us somehow, and I'm not taking the risk. You can get a new souvenir when this is all over." Kai wasn't going to take any more chances than was necessary, and he was sick of running. *A jockey tired of running!* The thought made him laugh.

"Laugh, you half-wit stable boy!" Taryn yelled.

"Say what you want." Kai wrapped up in his cloak. "But you'll thank me when you survive."

"No, I won't," Taryn snapped. "Because I'm never talking to you again."

That would be a relief. Kai ignored Taryn. If that piece of paper betrayed them to the army, he was glad it was gone. If it wasn't, well then, he'd probably have to do some serious apologizing. But he had to be right. *Nephesus is a servant of Belial. Belial is bad, so she must be, too. Right?*

Kai thought of something else. "And you are going to stop trying to do magic. Every time you do, something worse happens. You started a fire, but then it rained for a day. You tried to fix the water, and that led us straight to a town filled with Unwanteds. No more magic."

Taryn hurled more insults at Kai. It almost made Kai smile. Deston used to follow him around and provoke him into a fight. As the years passed, it took longer for the insults to accumulate enough for Kai to start swinging. Taryn had nothing on Deston. Seeing that Kai wasn't going to respond, Taryn picked up his cloak and retreated to the other side of Lizzy. With a great sigh, he flopped to the ground and was quiet.

Kai listened to Lizzy snore. After a while, Taryn began a horrible duet with her. But Kai couldn't sleep. *Did I do the right thing? Where are we going to get food or water? If we make it to the river, how are we going to be able to purify it?*

He slid his sword from the scabbard. It glittered in the moonlight as he traced the word *Surrender* with his finger. *Why would someone ruin the blade by etching this word in it? Surrender is the last thing I'm going to do.*

He got up and flipped through the pages of the book with no words in it, but the pages were blank. He ran his hands through his hair. *What are we going to do, Adoyni?* Words appeared on the page like stars appearing as the day ends.

"Be strong and courageous…for the Lord your God will be with you wherever you go." The words filled him with strength. *Trust Adoyni. That's all I have to do.* He fell asleep, sprawled across the baggage, until the sun woke him up. When he looked, the words were gone.

The next day, as he shuffled along in the hot sun, he thought about those words. *If Adoyni really is with us, then we can do anything.* Hope made him stride a little faster while the others struggled to keep up. He slowed down and suggested lunch.

Lizzy stumbled up. "There's only some beans left. Maybe enough for us to have a few bites. You didn't get all that much from the town."

"What do you suggest we do?" Kai snapped. "Go back? Ask that army for food?"

Taryn stared off in the distance. "Eladar set us up. He whisks us off to the wilderness closer to the army, and then suddenly he has to go away and doesn't return."

"By Zoria's blood, are you saying we can't trust him?" Lizzy sounded angry.

"Why should we? We don't know a thing about him," Taryn said. "I'm just saying it looks awfully suspicious."

Kai shifted. Taryn's words sounded a lot like some of the doubts he had. Eladar seemed to give answers that created more questions. "Yeah, but why not just take us?"

"That I haven't figured out yet," Taryn admitted. "Maybe it would've been too hard for him to carry us to his master. Maybe he was trying to slow us down until the Seekers came. We haven't seen any stone that gives life, either."

"That's just hogwash," Lizzy snapped. "Eladar was kind and beautiful. He wouldn't do such a thing."

"That's just my point. He seemed so wonderful that he deceived us all and sent us happily on the wrong track," Taryn retorted. "And don't all the stories say that Seiten is very beautiful?"

"Well, whatever it is, let's be on the lookout for a trap," Kai said. "The faster we get this done, the faster we can help Rhiana."

"What about Rica?" Lizzy glared at Kai.

Taryn stretched out on the ground. "I don't care about either of them. I'm heading for the Temple of All."

"Don't care? How could you not care?" Kai was shocked at Taryn's indifference. "They're our family."

Lizzy glared at them. "Well, obviously both of you are only thinking of yourselves."

"Rica's probably dead, but we could still help Rhiana," Kai snapped.

"Everyone, including us, is going to be dead soon," Taryn said very calmly.

"Shut up!" Kai and Lizzy said at the same time. Kai found it slightly interesting that he could agree with her about something.

They walked east without talking. There was no way to guess how far they'd come because there was nothing but grass. The wind whipped through his hair and burned his face. It made each step a struggle. He was ready to fall down and never get up again when Lizzy stopped in front of him. He ran into her, but she pushed him away and pointed.

"Look! Another town!"

CHAPTER THIRTY-THREE

Raspberry Juice

Lizzy was furious. *How could they say such things about Eladar? Anyone could see that he didn't mean us any harm.* She stomped on, fuming. *I won't help them with their problems. Why should I care about Rhiana?* But she didn't want Rhiana to die just because her brother was a jerk.

Seeing the town made her forget all her anger. When she saw smoke rising out of the buildings and people moving around, she felt like dancing. She could feel the bath water warming her toes. She imagined pork chops and salad with fresh tomatoes. And, oh, the joy of lying in bed with soft sheets, warm blankets, and a real pillow. The guys must have felt the same way because they started jogging. For the first time, Taryn pushed ahead. The promise of food ahead made him walk faster than certain death behind them.

"Just think, we'll have a hot supper," Kai grinned. "And all the water we want."

Lizzy smiled. *A normal night!* "What about the army? Will it catch up with us?"

Taryn and Kai just shrugged. They were too focused on food to care. But the thought persisted. *Those Seekers know we need food and water.* Fear grew until it overtook all thoughts of food or a bed. *What if we're walking into a trap?*

Finally, she couldn't keep her mouth shut. "Maybe we shouldn't go there."

Taryn and Kai were walking ahead of her. When she spoke, they looked at her like she was crazy.

"I mean, we should just think about it," she stammered. "You were talking about traps."

"I was talking about mystical creatures that appear out of nowhere," Kai said like she was a child. "Not from towns."

"And baths," Taryn scratched his head. "There's food in front of us. Why don't you stop delaying and walk for a change?"

"Me?" Lizzy's temper flared. "Aren't you always the last one? We have to wait for you to catch up all of the time, and you accuse me of walking slow!"

Taryn took a step toward her. "Not only that, but you are rude and self-centered. All you care about is your precious brother. You can't even wait for a dying man to utter his last breath before you start screeching about how we need to go rescue *your* brother."

"You think I'm rude?" Lizzy yelled. "Look in a mirror! You're the one who threw raspberry juice on my dress and didn't even apologize. Someone who wasn't rude would've stayed to clean it up or at least said they were sorry."

"What are you talking about?" Kai had a puzzled look on his face. "We've never had raspberry juice."

Taryn glared at her like she was an insect. "You're the one who couldn't wait two seconds for Mischa to say his last words. A polite person would've waited for a second. I guess that's what you can expect from traveling entertainers. They never learn the niceties of society."

"I didn't apologize to you because you didn't apologize about my dress," she lashed out. "Obviously, the niceties of society haven't attached themselves to you yet, because I know better than you. It must hurt your precious pride that someone like me is better than you."

Taryn blinked, then stepped forward, his face red, his hazel eyes cold behind his glasses. "The day you are better than me is the day I sprout wings and fly away."

She clenched her fists, trying not to tear his eyes out. "You'd better start sprouting because that day is here."

"What in all the horses' herds is going on?" Kai stepped in between them.

"And, you! I'm sick of your swearing!" Lizzy shouted. "Why don't you swear like a normal person?"

"What's wrong with it?" Kai blinked, shock replacing his bewilderment.

She turned to him. "It's dumb. No one says things like donkey dung. It just makes everyone remember that all you do is shovel manure."

Kai held up his hands. "Look! I don't know what's going on, but if we keep it up, we won't make it in time for dinner. You both need to apologize. Taryn, you go first. Then we can get some hot food."

Taryn's mouth opened and closed a few times. "Why do I have to go first?"

Kai sighed. "You two are acting like children. From what I heard, you spilled that juice first."

"Fine," Taryn bit out. "I'm sorry I spilled juice on your precious dress."

"That wasn't an apology," Lizzy protested. "It was sarcastic."

"Now you apologize for interrupting Mischa." Kai ignored her protests.

If that's how we apologize around here, I can do it, too. She made her voice as sarcastic as she could. "I'm sorry for telling you that you were about to be killed."

"Everyone happy?" Kai took Lizzy by the arm and pushed her forward. "Let's go. It's getting late."

Lizzy shook off his hand and stormed forward. *Why do guys always take each other's side? If they want to go into this stupid town, then fine. But when they get captured by the Seekers, it's not my fault. I warned them.*

She fumed over Taryn's words. His words about being travelling entertainers stung. It brought back memories of people chasing them out of town, accusing them of having loose morals and stealing property.

No one talked as they marched quickly to the town. As the sun sank over the prairie, they approached the wall and the heavy gates. There was no one outside the high wooden walls of the town, but the wind carried a smell of wood burning and food cooking.

Kai attached Minnie's lead rope. "Let's find an inn."

Lizzy lingered behind. She didn't know why, but something didn't feel right. It felt as dead as that first town they'd found. "Guys, wait a minute," she called.

They turned and looked at her. Even Minnie looked at her like she was crazy. She swallowed her fear and thought of a hot bath. *I'm just imagining things.*

"Never mind. Let's go."

CHAPTER THIRTY-FOUR

The Best and Worst Day

Taryn wanted to dance through the streets. *We found a town!* He was sure he'd kiss the first person who offered him something to eat. If it was a good meal, he might even forgive Kai.

The town was so small that he saw the whole place in three steps. The town pole in the center of the street proclaimed its allegiance to Zoria with its sacred flame on the top. The figures on it were of farmers and a few shopkeepers.

He panicked. "There isn't an innkeeper here. What are we going to do?"

"There's always an inn," Lizzy said from behind him. "Even if it's not on the pole."

"But what if there's not?" Taryn's voice cracked. "I've gotta eat. And how are we going to pay for it? And for supplies?"

"We have the coin from the stagecoach," Kai reminded him as he headed down the street. "We'll have to use that."

Taryn knew he'd die without food and a bath. *There'd better be an inn.* They passed the general store. The third building had a large sign. *Buckwheat Inn.* Taryn started grinning, and he didn't care if he looked like a fool. Food was almost in his grasp. *Praise the Goddess!*

A young boy rushed out of the inn and up to Taryn. "Stable your horse for you, sir?"

Taryn stared at the boy. He was the filthiest person Taryn had ever seen. Around the dirt, he had the tan skin and dark hair of the plains people. He grinned up at them with excitement.

Kai started to grin but managed to keep a straight face. "Let us get our things first."

Taryn jumped as Kai slapped his shoulder. Rubbing the burn, Taryn helped Lizzy and Kai remove the guitar, the books, and the pile of clothes they'd acquired.

Kai handed the boy Minnie's lead rope and patted her on the neck. "Take good care of her. She's had a hard journey."

"Yes, sir. I will, sir." The boy nodded his head. "I'll groom her and give her some grain."

They watched him lead Minnie away. She turned to look back at them like she didn't want to leave but obediently followed the boy. They picked up their belongings and walked into the inn, blinking as their eyes adjusted to the dark room. Rickety tables circled a large stone fireplace. The smell of food wafted from the kitchen. Taryn's stomach rumbled hopefully. They stopped at a small desk as an older woman in a brown dress with a white apron tied around her waist regarded them. Her gray hair was tied back in a bun.

"Will you be wanting a room?" Puzzlement spread across her face as she looked at them.

Taryn realized they weren't the normal travelers. Normal travelers wouldn't be in this part of the country, covered with dirt and blood, carrying weapons, and they wouldn't be so young.

"Yes, two rooms, please," Lizzy stepped out from behind Kai.

"Of course." The lady reached for a key and then hesitated. "What brings you here?"

Lizzy smiled sweetly and adjusted her grip on her guitar. "I'm doing my apprenticeship as an entertainer, and my teachers assigned me to this region. These two are my guards. It's not safe to travel alone anymore, you know."

Kai stood up a little straighter and put his hand on his sword. Taryn wanted to roll his eyes, but he was impressed with Lizzy's quick thinking.

"It's not safe to do much anymore. An entertainer, eh?" The woman was buying everything Lizzy said. "It's been a long time since we've heard music. You play a few songs after dinner tonight, and you can have your meals for free."

If there was anything better than food, it was *free* food. Taryn forced himself not to scream an acceptance.

Lizzy shook her head. "I think we'll just pay for the food. I'm exhausted from our trip."

Taryn struggled to keep quiet. *I'll kill her. How in the universe could she turn down free food?*

The woman looked disappointed. "Well, if that's what you want…"

"Throw in our rooms and baths for free, and she'll play," Kai jumped in. Lizzy glared at him. "You'll get money from drinks and food if word gets around."

The woman paused. "Alright, it's a deal."

She introduced herself as Mrs. Morhan and escorted them to the rooms upstairs. The room she gave to him and Kai was plain but clean. She bustled off to warm their bath water as he stretched out on the bed, moaning in sheer delight.

Suddenly Lizzy threw the door to their room open and stormed in. She headed straight for Kai. "How dare you sell me like that!" she blazed.

Kai looked like a trapped wild animal. "What did I do?"

"You are making me sing," she snapped. "You could've at least asked if I wanted to do this." Lizzy fell onto Taryn's bed and crossed her arms. Taryn wished she'd chosen somewhere else. He'd been on the receiving end of her anger today, and he didn't want to get involved.

"I thought that's what you did," Kai said. "Didn't you say you loved traveling with your parents, performing in different towns?"

Lizzy looked at the floor. After a second, she spoke while staring at the floor. "It's what they did. I've never performed much. I'm not good."

"But this is a good thing." Kai tried to cheer her up. "We got this all for free. We can buy a lot of supplies now."

"I know." Lizzy looked like she was going to her death. "But I don't have anything to wear. My skirt is filthy. And I'm not pretty, and every singer's supposed to be pretty."

Taryn started to laugh. They stared at him as he reached into the bags on the floor. "I can solve that problem. I found this. I thought it might fit you." He pulled out the green dress. It was wrinkled from being stuffed in the bag, but he thought it was in pretty good shape. "And you are pretty. Well, not right now but when you're cleaned up, you look nice."

She started to grin and fingered the dress. "Taryn, I believe that is the nicest thing I've ever heard you say. It's a beautiful dress. Thanks."

Kai laughed. "I've heard you sing, and you have a nice voice. Someone who has faced Unwanteds shouldn't be scared of a few people. I'm going to check on Minnie while the water heats up."

Lizzy followed Kai out the door, and Taryn fluffed his pillow for a nap. He couldn't remember when he had felt so happy or content.

This is going to be the best night of my life!

* * *

Lizzy carried the dress back to her room and sat on the window sill. The bed was covered with an old red quilt and one pillow. A worn red rug covered the scuffed floor.

She wanted to kill Kai for saying she would sing. Her heart was already racing. She looked out the window to distract herself. Kai was walking to the stables, talking to that boy who'd taken Minnie. The boy was listening intently and nodding. Kai gave him something from his pocket, and the boy sped off down the street.

She watched the boy run down the dirty streets and into the general store. From her vantage point, the town had seen too many winters. There were twenty buildings if you counted the houses. *How do you survive out here?* There must be farmers on the prairie, but she couldn't imagine such a lonely life.

She glanced down at the dress. *I'll never figure guys out.* She wanted to kill Taryn and Kai, and then they did something that made everything better, and she wanted to hug them. *Why can't they just be like girls?*

She stood up. The dress was badly wrinkled. It was a dark green, like the color of the pine trees in winter, trimmed with white lace. The sleeves were long with delicate stitching down them. She wasn't one for dresses, but she had to admit it was beautiful.

She turned and glanced in the mirror. "Oh, for Zoria's love!" Her face was streaked with dirt and tears. But her hair was worse. It had leaves, twigs, and something white, stuck in it. "Gross!" She took it out of the braid and tried to straighten the tangles. "Ow!"

I'm going to ask Taryn for that Beauty Spell. I need something more than water. She took a step toward the door as someone knocked on the door. "Come in," she called.

Mrs. Morhan opened the door. "The water's ready. Oh, how pretty your dress is!"

Lizzy smiled, "Yes, it is. Mother gave it to me before I left. She said it would be perfect no matter where I sang." The lie came easily. "It's awfully wrinkled. I don't know what to do."

"You get yourself prettied up," Mrs. Morhan smiled. "I'll get these wrinkles right out. Don't you worry about a thing. I'm just so excited to hear some songs. It's been a long time since anyone visited Aldholt. It feels like we've been forgotten."

"Thank you, Mrs. Morhan." She felt horrid for all the lies. "You're awfully nice. I do appreciate your kindness."

"Go enjoy your bath," Mrs. Morhan took the dress and closed the door.

Lizzy turned back to the mirror. She pulled out a few more twigs from her hair and stared at her reflection. *I look horrible.* Mother always said that a singer needed two things. A nice voice and a pretty face. Lizzy knew that she wasn't pretty. But Mother knew more about music than anyone she knew, even more than Dad, and she said Lizzy didn't have a good voice, either. She couldn't look in the mirror anymore and sat down on her bed.

She knew without a doubt that she was going to mess everything up, and word would spread all over Eltiria that she was a terrible singer.

I can't do this. This is going to be the worst night of my life.

CHAPTER THIRTY-FIVE

No Backing Down

Kai slid into the hot bath water, feeling his aches melt away. He leaned his head back and breathed in the steam. This was a huge luxury with the shortage of pure water, and he was going to enjoy every minute of it.

The boy, Jehan, told him that half of the people had died before they figured out it was the water making people sick. Mrs. Morhan took him in when his parents died. *How many people have suffered grief?* He was going to find whoever poisoned the river and strangle him with his bare hands. The villagers paid the priest of Zoria at the next town to bring them water. *Are the priests using the tainted water to profit themselves? I bet they charge a huge amount.*

Kai shifted in the tub. Listening to Jehan prattle on had reminded him of Rhiana. She could talk a saddle off a horse. He suddenly felt guilty. Here he was lounging in a bath tub, dreaming about supper, and she was dying. *Adoyni, please keep her safe until I return. And be with Lizzy tonight. Oh, by the way, thanks for the inn.*

He dried off and pulled on brown breeches and a blue shirt. He found Taryn reclining on his bed, reading a book, his glasses on the floor. He was now wearing tan pants with a red shirt.

"Dinner time yet?" Taryn asked without looking up from his book.

Kai grinned. "Let's check. I hope it's as good as it smells. Bring your axe. You want to look like a guard."

They walked into the hallway as Lizzy came out of her room. The green dress highlighted her eyes, and her long auburn hair was loose around her shoulders. They stared at her, food forgotten for a minute. She *was* pretty. He'd never seen her like this before.

"Wow!" Kai finally said. "You look great, Lizard-Breath."

She blushed. "Really?"

"Yeah, you do," Taryn stammered.

"As good-looking as that roast I smell cooking downstairs!" Kai laughed and led the way down to the kitchen. There lay the loveliest sight he'd ever seen. The table was filled with corn, fresh bread, roast beef, and a huge bowl of gravy next to a heaping pile of mashed potatoes. The aroma from the food made his mouth water. Taryn sat down and began filling his plate.

"Wait!" Kai said. After all they'd been through, this had to be done right. "Let's pray."

He held out his hands. Lizzy timidly took his, and Taryn finally broke down and took his other hand. Lizzy looked confused. *Has she never prayed?*

"Close your eyes," he said. Lizzy obeyed, but Taryn kept his on the food. Kai tried to remember how Dad prayed long ago. "Adoyni, thank you for leading us to this inn. Thanks for the food and pure water to drink. Bless all we do, and keep our families safe. Amen."

His voice cracked when he thought of his family. *Where are they? Are they healthy?* He missed them in so many ways. Lizzy patted his arm like she understood. Taryn never even noticed. As soon as Kai uttered *Amen*, he was digging into the potatoes. Kai and Lizzy laughed.

"You better dig in," Kai winked. "Before he eats it all."

And so they ate. Lizzy commented she wouldn't be able to sing with her stomach so full as she took another helping of the roast beef. Mrs. Morhan checked on them, smiling as she refilled the bowls.

"Reminds me of my son." She patted Taryn on the shoulder. "He used to eat like you!"

Taryn looked up at her. "This has to be the best meal I've ever had in my entire life."

"Oh, now tell the truth," Mrs. Morhan giggled. But Kai could tell she was eating up the compliments. She made sure to put a little extra meat on Taryn's plate. When they had all they could, Mrs. Morhan pulled an apple pie out of the oven. They groaned in chorus.

"There's always room for dessert." Mrs. Morhan grinned. "My grandpa always said that it slides through the cracks."

"Three cheers for Mrs. Morhan's grandpa." Taryn raised his glass of water. "I have some cracks that need filled."

"Yeah, in your brain," Lizzy shot back. They all burst out laughing.

They found some way to squish the pie down and moved into the great room. Several people sat around the room talking. Lizzy got out her guitar. She stepped over to the fireplace where Taryn had claimed a table and was opening his books.

"I can't do this," she whispered. "I ate too much. I won't be able to sing."

The people at the tables looked like they were fighting a losing battle. Grief was hanging on them like cobwebs in a deserted barn. It was like they had forgotten how to smile, if they ever knew at all.

"Lizzy, look around," he said. "These people are so desperate for something good to happen they won't care about a couple of wrong notes. When you get up there, you'll make them forget about their worries. That's what they'll remember. Not a few mistakes."

Lizzy stared at him like she was seeing something new. And then she did something she had never done before. She squeezed him tightly and whispered, "Thanks."

With that, she slipped up onto the stage and sat down on the stool. Taryn looked up from his books. "What in the Zoria's name did you say?"

"I'm not sure," Kai sat down. "I wish I knew, though."

Lizzy strummed her first chord. Her voice shook as she began, but after the first chorus on the first song, her nerves seemed to disappear. When she began the second song, the crowd had grown to twenty people, and Kai thought she was singing better. By the fourth song, the crowd was about thirty-five people, and she was giving the performance of her life.

The people clapped and sang along with her, shouting out requests when she asked for one. Her face was flushed, but it made her look even prettier as she bent over her guitar. Some got up to dance. Mrs. Morhan was running around, sweat pouring down her face, trying to keep everyone's drinks filled. She came over to Kai and Taryn.

"It's been years since we've been this happy," she beamed, watching Lizzy. "Adoyni bless her and you two. You've been sent by Him, that's for sure."

She whisked off to fill more drinks as Kai wondered at her words. Taryn glanced at him and went back to his book. Kai was surprised that he was looking at the wordless book.

"Do you see anything?" Kai leaned closer, shouting over Lizzy and the crowd.

"There's something here on this page," Taryn pointed. "I think it says *Rest*. See?"

"Kind of." Kai squinted. He saw lines on the page. He tried to adjust the book to see better. As his hand touched the book, more words grew darker.

"Come to me, you who are weary, and I'll give you rest," Taryn read out loud.

"What does that mean? Who are we supposed to go to?" Kai let go of the book. The words disappeared.

"Whoa! Where'd the words go?" Taryn picked up the book. "Put your hand back on it."

Kai took the book from Taryn. When his hand touched the book, the words reappeared as dark as they were before.

"It's you," Taryn exclaimed. "You make the words appear."

Taryn let go of the book. The words disappeared. "By all the stars in the heavens," Taryn breathed. "It's not you. It's us. When we touch the book together, the words appear. I wonder what we'd see with Lizzy."

There was no way they were going to find out now. She'd started a rousing tune that had everyone dancing. She looked the happiest they'd ever seen her. Kai felt someone tugging on his sleeve and turned to see Jehan standing behind him, his hat now off and his dark curls sticking up in every direction.

"Hey, there," Kai said. "Having fun?"

Jehan grinned, his brown eyes twinkling, and nodded. "She's the most wonderful person on earth." He stopped smiling. "This weird guy I've never seen before asked about you."

"What did he look like?" Kai asked. Uneasiness crept into his heart. "Did you see his face?"

Jehan shook his head. "No, he was covered in a big black cloak. But he was very tall, taller than Minnie. And his voice was weird. He kind of scared me. I didn't think anyone was around, but he slipped out of the shadows."

Kai knew now. *A Seeker. They found us.* He groaned at his stupidity. Lizzy was right. He was too focused on food to stop and think. He glanced around. *What are we going to do?*

"I said I hadn't seen anyone," Jehan continued. "And he asked what was going on. I said there was a wedding. I didn't even see him leave. He just kind of disappeared into the shadows."

Kai ran his hands through his hair in frustration. *He's still here. We walked into trap. It's the first place anyone would go to if they were traveling this way. There's no way I'm letting the Seekers kill these people.*

He grabbed Taryn's arm. "Listen, you get Lizzy to the stables. Just say she needs a break. Don't tell her anything. They've found us. We've got to get out of here."

Taryn tensed. He nodded and swallowed nervously, his face pale in the firelight.

Kai turned to Jehan. "You did great, kid. Now do two more things for me. Bring our things to the stables. Then, wait a while and tell Mrs. Morhan thank you for us. Tell her that we don't want to go, but we have to. Give her this." He placed a few of the gold coins in Jehan's hands. "Tell her that if she doesn't need it, give it to someone who does. Can you do this?"

Jehan nodded again, his eyes filling with tears. "Are you leaving already?"

"Yes, kiddo." Kai squatted down to his level. "I'm sorry. I really am. Keep it our secret for a little while, okay?"

Jehan nodded, and Kai gave him a hug. It felt like he was hugging Rhiana, and he choked back tears. He gave Jehan one last smile and slipped through the crowd to the door. He paused for a second. Lizzy was on her feet singing, the stool long forgotten. Everyone was clapping and dancing. Sadness swept over him. *Protect them, Adoyni. Keep these people safe.*

He stepped out into the night and closed the door to the inn. The lights and noise dimmed as he made his way to the stables. He slid the sword free of its scabbard. He moved in the shadows quietly and smoothly. He knew it was out there. And he knew it had come for them.

And this time he wasn't backing down without a fight.

CHAPTER THIRTY-SIX

Buckets of Rain

Taryn pulled Lizzy off the stage and scooped up her guitar case. They ducked into the kitchen. He glanced out the window, but all he saw was blackness. *Somewhere out there, death waits.* "We're leaving. Now."

Lizzy held back. "Why? Where are we going? Why now?"

"Like we have time for all of your incessant questions," he said sarcastically. "Come on. Kai's waiting."

He ignored her sputtering as he pulled her by the arm and led the way into the darkness as he took one last sniff of the lingering aroma of food. A small light flickered from the barn. When they entered, Kai was waiting by the door with his sword in his hand.

"Wasn't sure if it was you or the Seekers," Kai whispered. "Lizzy, there's some clothes for you in that stall. I'm sure glad I sent Jehan to get us some supplies earlier."

"Would someone tell me what's going on?" Lizzy waited for a second while they loaded the guitar on Minnie.

Taryn paused. He wasn't going to tell her that she had been right when she said that they shouldn't come to the town. Seeing her look of satisfaction and hearing her say that she told them so was more than he could bear. He saw Kai looking at him, and Taryn quickly shook his head.

Kai paused. "We don't have time for questions. Get moving."

Lizzy stood still for a minute. Her face flushed from anger, then she dashed to the stall. She came out dressed in brown pants and a light brown shirt. She hung the green dress with the bridles, her hand lingering on it. "You could have at least picked something with color," she complained as she pulled a darker brown cloak around her shoulders and pulled her auburn hair loose. "I feel like a dead tree."

"You look like one, too," Kai grinned.

Lizzy stuck her tongue at him as she pulled her hair into a ponytail. "What's going on? Where are we going? What are we doing?"

Kai sobered. "We need to stop being so predictable. We'll go south all night and turn east when the sun rises."

Taryn placed his axe on his shoulder and took Minnie's rope. "If I see that Seeker, I'm going to let it know how I feel about missing sleeping in a real bed."

Kai slapped him in the shoulder, but it didn't sting as much. "That's the spirit."

Taryn felt the heavy weight of his sphere on his back and shifted his bag closer. Kai led with his sword ready. Taryn followed as Lizzy trailed behind.

They walked out of the barn and into the night. The wind had picked up, and rain drops hit his face. *Great. Just what we need.* He pulled up the hood of his cloak. *Man, I love this cloak.*

A door clanged and someone laughed. They jumped. He focused on Kai's dark cloak as he moved through the shadows. Only an occasional flap of the cloak or light glinting off the sword gave him away. When they made it to the gates, Taryn heaved a big sigh of relief. *We're going to make it.* They stopped and looked back. Laughter streamed out of the inn. Taryn turned to face the dark prairie where the wind was bringing lightning and torrential rain.

"Kai," he gulped. "Behind you."

The shadow moved closer as Kai waited. Taryn squinted in the dark. It didn't move like the Seeker had. It didn't even look much like a Seeker. It wasn't much taller than Kai. The shadow stopped.

"Put your sword up, Kai," a voice said. "You're not going to attack me."

Kai lowered his sword. "Chancellor Belial?"

Taryn let out his breath that he'd been holding. *Finally. With Belial here, he'll set everything right.*

"All three of you together." Belial ignored Kai's question. "Off on a noble quest. How inspiring. How like the Archippi to set you up." Laughter filled with triumph rumbled in the darkness.

There was a movement in the shadows of the gates. A Seeker moved to stand in the light with his axe in his hands. Taryn felt his joy wash out of him.

"What do you mean?" Kai's voice sounded hollow.

"You didn't really believe the stories it told, did you?" Belial sounded shocked. "You aren't related to any mythical ancestors. That's a lie the Archippi have been using for years to deceive innocent young people. The king banished them from this world because of their refusal to quit such nonsense."

"I don't believe you," Lizzy said weakly. Her voice, before so sweet and joyful, sounded brittle and harsh. "Eladar wouldn't lie to us."

"But he led you into the wilderness, far from your families and far from where you could actually do good," Belial said. "While you've been wandering through all of these hardships, we've begun to solve the mystery of that horrible disease. We could've used your help. He's done a great wrong and will answer for it one day."

"But the Seekers?" Kai questioned. His sword was pointed to the ground, and he didn't seem to notice the rain running down his face. "They were trying to kill us."

Taryn felt like his brain was in a fog. He could remember the fear that surrounded the Seekers. There was a second one to his right, but Taryn didn't feel any fear. Just waves of tiredness swept over him. *We were a bit hasty to believe everything the Archippos said. What was his name? Why can't I remember?* He really didn't care anymore what that winged creature was called. He stopped trying.

"The Seekers?" Belial laughed gently. "My servants wouldn't kill you. They were trying to bring you to me so that you could have the honor in purifying the river. They never chased you in the woods, Kai. That was the meddling Archippos. My servants found the stagecoach after it was attacked. And Rica is comfortably waiting for you in my palace. It was all just a misunderstanding. And now I must get you to Northbridge."

Taryn sighed deeply. *All a misunderstanding. So silly of us to be running from the one who wants to help us. Finally we'll be going to the right place.* The torches from the town flickered on Belial's face.

"Mother," Taryn remembered unexpectedly. "Is my mother waiting for me to join her?"

"Your mother," Belial's voice was sharp and piercing. "How do you know about her?"

Taryn blinked. *How* do *I know?* He glanced at the others for help. Lizzy stared at Belial with a stupid grin on her face. Kai stood with his mouth hanging open, his eyes never blinking. *What's wrong with them?* "I...I don't know. Nighthawk Nephesus told me, I guess." It was getting harder to think.

"Nighthawk told you?" Belial answered like Taryn was a little child. "Well, it seems like we all have our little secrets. Come now. There are warm beds and plenty of good food waiting for you."

He gestured for them to join him. Kai weakly nodded and took a stumbling step forward. Taryn watched Kai and Lizzy obediently move closer to

Belial. He hung back, trying to clear his thoughts, but the effort seemed to overwhelm him.

Belial's voice cut through the fog. "Taryn. We're waiting for you."

He took a step forward. A huge weight lifted off his chest. It felt much better not to think. It was much easier to do as he was told. He shifted the pack on his back and meekly took a step toward Belial. His hand felt a book. *That's probably the book we found in…in that place.* He shook his head. *In Adoyni's meadow.* The fog lifted with Adoyni's name. Belial was watching Kai and didn't notice that Taryn was suddenly alert.

"Kai, put your sword down," Belial commanded.

In the light from the torches, Taryn saw something cold flash over Belial's face. His dark eyes filled with hate. Kai nodded dumbly and clumsily dropped the sword in the mud. *Kai's never clumsy! Belial's enchanting us!*

Taryn shook his head. *Why would he?* Belial was the chief seer of the Goddess, and the Goddess was good. Maybe being around the Archippos so long had deluded him into believing the lies it told. He had to decide who was evil. He had dedicated himself to the Goddess, could he now turn his back on Her? Was She evil? *Show me a sign. Show me the truth.*

Belial reached out his left hand to Lizzy and the light caught a ring on his hand. On it was inscribed a white dove. Taryn had seen it before on Mischa's finger. Mischa's words rang through his head.

"It's a symbol of the joy that has been given to me," Mischa said. Taryn knew he was wearing it when they were on the coach, but it wasn't on his hand when he died. And then Taryn knew the truth. *Oh, Adoyni. I've been so wrong. I'm sorry. Help us now!*

"Liar," Taryn breathed out. Kai and Lizzy didn't seem to hear him. "You are a liar! Eladar was telling the truth. I see it now where once I was blind. I shall be blind no more!"

He lunged forward to pick up Kai's sword. As his hand closed on the hilt, he heard a roaring like the rushing of a mighty river. He forced Minnie's rope in Lizzy's outstretched hand. Spinning, he yanked Kai away from Belial. The roaring grew louder in his head as the rain came harder and faster. He could see Belial's lips moving, but his voice sounded like it was far away. Kai and Lizzy struggled to push past Taryn, but he shoved them behind him.

The Seekers leaped forward. Their axes glinted in the torches. *Adoyni, I can't handle this on my own, we need Your help.* The downpour increased as the Seekers moved in slow motion. The sound of the river grew louder, drowning Belial's commands. The drops of rain grew larger until they blended into each other. Taryn's last sight was of Belial. His face was flushed with anger as he screamed.

"I'll find you. I'll track you down, and I'll kill you!"

Then water fell onto Taryn like a giant bathtub had been overturned on them. Kai and Lizzy fell away as he started swimming. But he didn't even know which way was up. He thrashed around. His lungs began to burn as he struggled to find air.

PETITIONS

Let petitions and praises shape your worries into prayers,
letting God know your concerns.
~PHILIPPIANS 4:6

Foehn watched in amazement as the three fought
the master. The one with glasses had conquered the
fog that Foehn had seen successfully work on so many
other people, including the king. And then the rain
poured harder than he'd ever seen before and a flood
came from nowhere, washing them away. He wondered
if this Adoyni had done something miraculous because
when the storm eased, the three were nowhere to be
found.

"Foehn, find Nighthawk," the Master ordered.
His voice was quiet and low, but it was filled
with rage. "She should be somewhere between
Northbridge and the stronghold with the prisoners.
Tell her what happened. She must get there quickly.
Once you have delivered the message, return
to me."

Foehn flew high up in the clouds, the ground
slipping by swiftly until he saw with horror that
the poisoned water had reached Sauchrie. It
wouldn't be long until it reached the coast and all
pure water would be gone. He descended when

he found Nighthawk with the prisoners and the
army of Unwanteds. The smell of dirty Unwanteds
overpowered his senses as he approached.

Foehn steeled himself and approached Nighthawk.
The prisoners stirred as he came closer. He was surprised
to see that she had acquired even more hostages. There
were close to a hundred women, children, and men.
He hated seeing people chained like animals. He hated
smelling the body odors and the fear that saturated
them. He passed the rows of people when one young
man caught his eye. Foehn thought his name was Rica.
He was staring at Nighthawk with a look of adoration
like a young boy with his first love. Unlike the others,
he was freshly washed and, although his clothes had
bloodstains, Foehn couldn't see any injuries. Foehn
wondered why he looked like he was dead.

He entered the tent where Nighthawk was lounging
on a bed covered with the thick velvet blanket. She was
reading a book of spells.

"And what brings you here, Foehn?" She snapped
the book shut. "Where's Belial?"

Foehn imparted his message, watching Nighthawk's
amazement grow.

Nighthawk laughed cruelly. "Tell Belial I shall deliver
the prisoners as quickly as I can. Go now, slave. Your
Master has need of you."

Foehn's oath forced him to obey Belial and
Nighthawk. He fled south, terrified of what he'd find

when he returned to Belial. Terrified of what he would be made to do. If he ever found the source of the three's power, he would ask to be saved from this cruel Master.

CHAPTER THIRTY-SEVEN

Unanswered Questions

Lizzy gasped as the water surrounded her, the cold feeling like a slap in the face. She choked as she felt the ground disappear from under her feet. The water swirled around her, dragging her deeper. She fought against it, desperate for air, but it kept pulling her down.

The water spun her until she didn't know which direction was up. Her lungs burned for air. She stopped struggling, overwhelmed by the pain. Pain in her lungs. Pain in her heart. She wanted to hear Mother say *I love you.* She never found out why Dad left. *Oh, Adoyni, I just wanted to be loved.* Black appeared before her eyes as the pressure in her lungs burned hotter.

She panicked and thrashed around violently as the urge to breathe overcame every thought. She was vaguely aware of the water draining away as she dropped to the ground. She fell down, coughing and choking, and breathed in sweet air. She heard Kai and Taryn beside her.

Anger crept over the panic she was feeling. "If I'm going to be pulled around, pushed down, shushed up, and ignored, at least give me the courtesy of telling me first." Her voice rose, making her cough again from the strain.

Kai pushed himself up to a sitting position but let his head hang as he breathed heavily. "If I knew, I'd be the first to tell you."

"But what happened? Why'd you pull me off the stage?" Lizzy blinked as her head spun. "Where are we?"

In the east, the sun was rising. Its rays touched the tops of the trees that grew on the hills surrounding them. Minnie stood in front of them, eating grass, thoroughly drenched.

"I think the better question is *when* are we?" Kai rolled to his feet. "It shouldn't be dawn already. Are you okay, Minnie? I bet that scared you."

Lizzy glared at Kai. *He's more concerned about that dumb horse than answering me.* "Perhaps you could care more about people instead of dumb animals for once and check on us."

Kai gave her a confused look. "She's an animal that doesn't understand what happened."

"I'm a person, and I don't understand what happened!" Lizzy found herself screaming. "I don't know why or how I almost drowned to death in the middle of dry land. And I don't know where I am! Or *when* I am!"

"I know what happened." Taryn's voice was quiet, but it cut like a knife. He was lying on the ground. "I prayed to Adoyni, and He washed us away to here. Somehow. Wherever here is. Belial almost enchanted us so that he could take us to Northbridge and kill us."

A bird chirped while they stared at Taryn. He sat up, pushing his glasses up his nose.

"Taryn," Kai said slowly. "That's pretty much what's been happening for all week. Remember Eladar saying that Belial wanted to kill us?"

"I know." Taryn stared at the ground. "But I didn't believe. But I saw Belial use his voice to trap you, and I saw Mischa's ring on his hand. He was wearing it as a reminder of what he'd done. Then I knew Eladar was right."

"So, you're saying you believe in Adoyni now?" Lizzy asked, feeling slightly sorry for Taryn. He looked droopy and sad.

Taryn didn't seem to hear her. "I prayed to Him in that deserted town. But I didn't want to believe that Belial was evil because that would mean my mom is, too."

"So, Nighthawk Nephesus is your mother," Lizzy summarized. "How do you know?"

"Well, the good thing is that you'll give up on that magic junk," Kai said as he straightened Minnie's mane. "It was bad for us. Every time you use it, something bad happens. It's like you're trying to be your own god, and how can you know what's best?"

Taryn looked up for the first time. "I thought I did know best, but I was walking straight to my death. You might just be right."

"I am once in a while." Kai grinned. "Now look. I know *when* we are and *where* we are. You city folks surely know it's dawn by the sun coming up, and look up there on top of the hill."

In the trees were three statues made of gray stone. Each one of them held a weapon while one pointed east, its hand missing several fingers. Even from the distance, they looked fierce and noble.

"The Slayers," Lizzy gasped. "How did we get here?"

Kai sighed. "You two can sit here all day and ask questions. I'm going up that hill to take a closer look at those statues while I eat some breakfast."

He took Minnie's rope and left without seeing if they followed. Lizzy stood up, still dizzy. *Not one of my questions was answered. And now it's off for food. After they feed their mouths, they'll forget what I asked.* Lizzy's stomach growled. Food did sound good. She followed Kai up the hill and examined the statues. *I wonder which one I'm related to.*

"So we have to cross that?" Taryn asked, looking east. "Does it even end?"

Lizzy followed his glance. The hill dropped off in a steep incline lined with rocks and boulders. At the bottom was a desert filled with nothing but black sand. *I don't think anything, not even the smallest plant, ever lived down there. Parts of it even look like ash.* Heat waves were rising as the sun heated the desolate land. The black sand stretched as far as she could see.

But Lizzy knew the stories as well as the guys did. They were looking at Seiten's Anvil. Some songs called it the Spit, saying that this was where he spit in defiance to Adoyni. They said that to enter the desert was to taunt Seiten and death itself. No one had ever crossed it and lived to tell the tale. She sighed. *It has to end. What if it just leads to the end of the world, and we just find piles of dead bones of others who tried to cross it?*

"I'm sure it ends somewhere." Kai didn't sound convincing.

"Yeah, when you're dead," Taryn retorted.

No one had anything to say to that as Kai started a small fire to warm up the bread and hash Jehan had bought them. Lizzy chewed on the bread, thinking of Mrs. Morhan's bread. This piece tasted like she was eating a tree branch.

Lizzy thought she'd try again to get some questions answered. "What are we going to do about Belial? He's trying to kill the world, and he's the favorite of the king, now that the prince is gone. Who's going to believe he's the reason everyone's dying?"

Kai ran his hand through his hair. "I killed one of Belial's horses. Kedar was really valuable. He may have my family as indentured servants. I've got to get back to them."

"And do what?" Taryn asked. "Politely ask him to free them? What's that going to accomplish? We've got to keep going and purify that river. I know," Taryn grinned. "It doesn't sound like me. But if you think about it logically, he'll kill us if we go back. Let's weaken his power. Then we can deal with him easier."

"So it all revolves around the river," Kai said, glancing at Lizzy. "Once we take care of that, we can go back to help our families."

Taryn grinned. "And I can use the power at the Temple of All to stand against him."

Lizzy interrupted Kai. "Wait a minute. You're going to help me get Rica back?"

They stared at her like she was speaking gibberish. Kai looked back at Taryn. "How are you going to use the Temple? You know it's evil." Kai said.

"I've had it with you two!" Lizzy screamed. "You keep ignoring my questions and changing the subject. Minnie's had more questions answered than I have! Well, no more! You will answer one of my questions. Are you going to help me get Rica back?"

"Donkey dumplings!" Kai exclaimed. He jumped to his feet, pushed past Lizzy, and pointed slightly behind them in the west. "Look at that."

On the horizon was a streak of black that was slowly moving toward them. The sunlight glinted off metal. *Unwanteds!* The thought filled her with fear. The army moved at a steady pace.

Lizzy groaned. "Do you think Belial is with them?"

"Eladar would say that all we can do is surrender to His will and let Him work through us." Taryn stared at the approaching horde.

"Surrendering isn't going to do anything, except allow that army to win," Kai said slowly. "Adoyni needs to have a better plan than that."

Lizzy's questions died as she watched the army come closer. Only one question mattered now. *Will we survive?* She squeezed her eyes shut, but she could see the Unwanteds getting close enough to touch her. She repressed the shivers.

* * *

Kai felt Seiten's Anvil fill his heart, leaving it empty and dead. One legend said that it was once a great plain, lush with grass and wildlife. Until the final battle was fought here. Very few survived that day. Seiten scoured the land, turning the sand black, mixed with ash. The quietness overwhelmed him with despair.

He laid out their options. "We have to make a decision. We can go around the desert, but it will slow us down, and we'll run into that army." He paused and took a breath. "Or we could go through the desert." Both Lizzy and Taryn started to protest. He held his hands up. "I know. No one has ever made it across. So, what do you think? Go through or around?"

Neither of them spoke. He sighed. *Oh, Adoyni, give me wisdom. I don't want to make this decision on my own.*

"We'll vote," he said. "Raise your hand if you want to go through." He raised his hand.

Taryn stared at the desert like it was going to bite him. "There's no stones down there. Eladar said to find a stone that gives life, but all that's down there is burnt to a crisp." He took a deep breath and raised his hand. "Why not us, too?"

Lizzy glanced up from the dirt. "I don't want to go around or through it. We're going to die either way. All I want to do is go back to Buckwheat Inn and sleep on that soft bed. I guess I vote to go through, because it's the quickest way to get this all over with."

Kai leaned against a rock, agreeing with everything Lizzy said. *This is the first time we've agreed about anything. Too bad it's about how we're going to die.*

"The desert it is."

CHAPTER THIRTY-EIGHT

Shimmering Rocks

Lizzy stood under the statue that was pointing out to the desert. A dull ache filled her heart as she gazed across the black sand. There was nothing out there. *I wonder what Mother's doing right now. Maybe she's searching for me.* Lizzy blinked back tears. *Or maybe she rescued Rica, and they aren't looking for me at all.*

The dirt beneath her feet was freshly dug. Her guitar was under there, carefully wrapped with blankets and burlap from the packs to keep it dry. *Directly under the hand.* She memorized the site. She was coming back for it as soon as she could. She could still remember Dad giving it to her before he left for good. It was all she had of him.

She wiped away the tears that streamed down her cheeks. *It's just a guitar. A thing. It isn't Dad. Quit being so dumb.* But she didn't want to leave it. She didn't want to walk across that dead, black desert. She didn't want to do anything but bathe and sleep. And see Dad.

Kai and Taryn were putting on their packs. They'd decided they couldn't take Minnie with them, so they organized the food and water into three packs. They'd wear their cloaks to protect from the sun and carry their weapons. Everything else was staying behind. When they were ready, Kai let her go. She trotted away when he chased her, pausing only once for a last look, and then slipped down the hill and made her way north.

"She'll be fine," he reassured them. "She'll remember Buckwheat Inn. They'll take care of her until we can go back."

He should know. He knew everything about horses, but Lizzy found it hard to believe him. She couldn't stop the tears as they began the descent down the rocky hill onto the ash and black sand.

Adoyni, help us. We can't do this alone. The word *alone* echoed in her head. *Mother doesn't love me. Dad cared so much that he left. All Rica can think about is that girl. No one wants to hear about me or what I'm feeling. Eladar cared, but he left, too.* She fought back the tears but couldn't stop them as anguish consumed her heart. *Why do people always leave me?* She stumbled and felt arms encircling her as she put her head on the shoulder and wept. She didn't want to be alone. She didn't want to be unloved. The shoulder grew wet as the tears continued to fall.

"We'll make it," Kai said, hugging her tighter. "With Adoyni, we're not alone. He loves us too much to leave us alone for even a second."

Lizzy gulped. *How did he know what I was thinking?* "H…how do you know? He's not even here."

"Yes, He is. I know His love because I've felt it," Kai replied. "And you have us."

Lizzy pulled back. Taryn was standing with his pack on, awkwardly torn between comforting her and running away. She wiped the tears away and took a deep breath.

"It's that stinking desert," Taryn said. "It's trying to take every good thing away. Can't you feel it? It's evil."

The words reverberated over the blackness. Lizzy watched the air ripple in the heat. It made the rocks in the distance shimmer and quake. *If it does that to rocks, what's it going to do to me?*

Taryn continued, "I was taught that there's no higher power from my dad. All he values is thought and self-control. But I never agreed. I always felt like there had to be someone or something more to explain this life. Then one day, when I was young, I was walking through the market, and I saw this book that claimed to know the way to talk to the dead. There was a boy about my age right in front of me with his mother. They were holding hands and laughing. You could tell she loved him very much." Taryn's voice cracked.

As Lizzy listened, she couldn't take her eyes off the desert. There was some strange fascination to it that consumed her whole being.

"As I stood there with the book of spells in my hand, it all clicked. I could use Zoria to get what I wanted." Taryn cleared his throat. "All I wanted was to talk to Mom. To know her. Just for one day. So I bought the book. I swore that when the time was right, when she could be really proud of me,

I'd use it. That book led me to the Goddess and into more books of spells."

"Have you used it?" Kai asked quietly.

"It's still at home waiting. But my point is this. All the books of spells and the Goddess are nothing like Adoyni. When I saw Belial for who he really is, and when I prayed to Adoyni, I felt peace. Maybe love. I've never gotten that from a book. And if He says to go through that desert, I'll go through it. If I die, Adoyni will take care of me." Taryn took a deep breath.

"Let's go. It's only going to get hotter," Kai said. He started walking. "You do know why this desert is evil, don't you? This is where Lesu was killed. This whole area was filled with Unwanteds and all sorts of evil creatures. Somewhere in the middle Lesu fought them and then gave his life to save the world. The Slayers must've been watching in these hills."

The sand was black and hot under Lizzy's foot. Maybe the evil ones were burned to death. Maybe it was their wickedness that colored the sand. She shivered in spite of the burning sun. She knew there was no hope. Lesu wasn't coming to save them. The heat or the Unwanteds would kill them. She took another step deeper into the heat.

CHAPTER THIRTY-NINE

Pies in an Oven

Taryn adjusted the strap digging into his shoulders. He wasn't going to complain about the weight of the water, though. It was more precious than gold. He sank up to his ankles in the sand, making every step harder. It was only midmorning, but he felt like he'd run all day.

He regretted his brave words about the desert. He wasn't sure if they'd even make it to the next morning. The sun was making him feel like a pie in a baker's oven. Lizzy panted beside him, her brown shirt soaked with sweat. Kai plowed ahead, but he stumbled and fell as much as the rest of them. They stopped when the sun was directly above for a small swallow of water. Lizzy mentioned food, but it was too hot to eat.

What will Zoria do now that I prayed to Adoyni? She's probably very angry at me. He didn't like the idea of making Her angry. Adoyni was strictly prohibited, and rumors circulated about some who had chosen Adoyni over Her. The gossips said they didn't live long. *I wonder if there's any way to break my oath with Zoria without making her angry. Maybe Nighthawk, I mean, Mom, will know.* Taryn trudged behind Kai and Lizzy through the sand until the sun was setting in the west.

Kai made his way to a hollow in the dunes and stopped. He peeled the pack off his back and dropped to the ground. "Wanna rest for awhile?"

Taryn didn't say anything as he dropped his pack and crumpled onto the sand, panting. His shirt was soaked with sweat.

Lizzy nodded and sank down, stretching out on the sand. "Hot. And thirsty."

"We should eat," Kai pulled out some bread. Lizzy pulled out some of the beef they had brought. "Don't drink too much."

Taryn thought he could drink the whole flask of water. "At least it's not squirrel."

"I thought you were going to hurl that night," Lizzy giggled from under her cloak.

They were surrounded by black sand. Not a blade of grass sprouted anywhere. The hills still dotted the sand, but they looked small in the distance. Rocks and boulders lay scattered on the sand, as if they had been thrown off the hills into the desert.

"We'll rest for a while, and then keep going," Kai said. "We can stop in the heat of the day and huddle under our cloaks until the sun passes."

"Who died and made you king?" Taryn asked in a weak attempt at humor. No one laughed.

"What's that?" Lizzy asked. From the north, it looked like a wall of sand stretching up to the sky. It was coming straight at them. They stared as the wind began to pick up. "It looks like a …"

"A sandstorm!" Kai yelled. The wind whipped over the dunes and into the hollow. "Get under your cloaks."

The wind grew stronger. Small grains of sand pierced Taryn's skin, leaving red welts. He pulled his cloak over his head and knapsack. The thick cloak protected him from the sand. *Sure glad we brought these!* He peeked under his cloak.

Kai chased after two of the bags as Lizzy ran after the last one. She leaped after it, but her fingers missed. It flew up and over the dune. She followed as the wind gusted harder. She stumbled against the force of the gust and fought for balance as it blew even harder. Then, teetering against the gale, she struggled to stay upright as the wind yanked her hair. She fell backwards, landed on her back, and didn't move.

"Lizzy!" Taryn yelled. He ran to her. "Lizzy! Get up!"

Kai joined him and cradled her head in his hands. He quickly pulled back a hand and gasped when he saw it was red with her blood.

"Oh, no," Taryn whimpered. *This is my punishment for praying to Adoyni. Zoria knows, and now she's taking it out on Lizzy.* "Don't let her be dead."

Taryn felt a rage sweep through him as he sat beside Lizzy and blocked the sand from her face with his cloak, ignoring the sharp stings from the flying sand. In the heat, he shivered with fear. If Zoria was hurting Lizzy to punish him, then he would rather worship Adoyni. He was sick of living in fear. He thought of the peace in the meadow and shoved his terror deep within him.

"Adoyni, I believe in You! Please make the storm stop!" He realized that this wasn't the politest way to talk to someone who could control everything, but he didn't have time for niceties. "Make it stop!"

He was still screaming for it to stop when he realized that the wind had gone away. Kai still held her hand, but there was blood everywhere, soaking into the sand.

Lizzy lay as if she was dead.

CHAPTER FORTY

It Takes Two

Kai held Lizzy's head in his hands. *Of all the places to fall, why did she land on the only rock around here?* The blood seeped through his fingers. "Wake up, Lizard-breath. Open your eyes." Lizzy never stirred. Kai looked at Taryn holding Lizzy's hands and saw his fear reflected in Taryn's eyes.

She took a small breath and opened her eyes.

"Did you see that?" Taryn pointed. "I think she breathed!"

Kai knew he had to stop the blood loss as soon as possible. "Taryn, get some clean cloth from somewhere to bandage her head."

Taryn took off like a shot. He rustled through the bags and finally took the bag from his books. Kai watched him with shock as he threw the books in the dust abruptly and tore the bag into strips.

Kai inspected the wound on the back of Lizzy's head. A gash as long as his hand streaked across the back of her head. It was as wide as his finger, and blood poured out of it. He knew that it would quickly become infected from the sand.

"Taryn, get my flask of water," he said. "I'm going to clean this first."

"No." Lizzy stopped Taryn. "Don't waste water. Drinking. More important."

"Yeah, and we'll enjoy watching you die of infection," Kai said sarcastically. He splashed a little water on the wound and then wrapped the cloth around her head. She groaned as the cloth touched the wound. He picked her up and took her back to where their bags were, laying her down on the sand. "Try to get some sleep."

She obediently closed her eyes, and they crept away where they could talk without disturbing her.

"What do we do? Go back?" Taryn asked. "We can't keep going, not with her like this. She'll never make it."

"We can't go back," Kai snapped. His hands were covered with blood, but there was no way to wash it off without using up their water. He grabbed some sand and rubbed his hands with it. There was a long pause as he scrubbed his hands with the sand. It made a horrible mess. "I don't know what to do. Nothing's working."

Taryn started to say something and then stopped. Kai raised an eyebrow.

Finally, Taryn continued. "I prayed to Adoyni during the sandstorm, and then it stopped. I don't know what Zoria will do, and I don't know what it all means, but we're not alone."

Lizzy was barely able to stand in the morning, but when they mentioned returning to the hills, she took wobbly steps east. Taryn's words continued to echo through Kai's head the next two days. *We're not alone.* But he so desperately wanted to give up. They let Lizzy set the pace and rested when she

needed it. They didn't make it too far. They hid the
fact that one of the flasks was empty and gave her
water whenever she wanted it.

Two days later, Kai huddled under his cloak
when the sun was directly over them, waiting for it
to pass. The heat surrounded them, rising from the
sand to meet the sun rays in the air. Hiding under
the cloaks protected them from the direct sun rays,
but Kai never felt like he could catch his breath.
He sweated and panted until he felt the sun move
down to the west, feeling trapped and hopeless. He
pounded the sand with his fist, wanting to scream.
*How could I be so stupid to leave! What's happening with
Rhiana?*

He calmed down some when he pulled back his
cloak and looked at Taryn and Lizzy. Their faces
were burnt dark red like baked apples. Lizzy's hair
looked as black as the people in the south with
the sand matted with blood. Streaks of blood ran
down from her head to her neck, and the cloth
they used as a bandage was soaked with it. She
never mentioned the pain, but he saw it in the way
she walked and the way she put her hand on her
forehead, and her eyes didn't sparkle with laughter
anymore.

They had to do something, or she was going
to die. They took turns supporting her through
the dunes, but they got worn out even faster. They
stopped for the night, too exhausted to go on. The
moon was like sunlight when it sparkled off the
sand. It would have been beautiful if they weren't

so thirsty. Lizzy lay on the ground, shivering, even with their cloaks on her.

Kai felt her forehead. "She's burning up." He paced while Taryn stared at the stars.

Taryn turned to his books and then picked up the wordless one. "Your book has nothing in it." He flipped through it aimlessly. "Look, still no words." It makes no sense. Remember at the inn? We both touched it and words appeared. Come here and try."

Kai obeyed, kneeling in the cooling sand, and words slowly appeared in the dim moonlight He moved closer to read them. "*And the prayer offered in faith will make the sick person well; the Lord will raise him up.*" He stared at Taryn. "Do you think it would work?"

"I believe in Adoyni," Taryn admitted. "But if Zoria ever finds out that I've been praying to Adoyni, She'll get angry. It could mean my life."

"Well, I won't tell her." Kai grinned for the first time in days. He wished he hadn't. The grin made his lips tear. He sobered. "If we don't do something, she'll die. You know that."

Taryn flopped back in the sand. "I just wanted to go to the Temple. I didn't want this." He stomped over to Lizzy.

Kai followed him and sat down on the other side of Lizzy. She was moaning and twitching. He didn't think she was even aware of them anymore. *Please let this work, Adoyni. We have no other hope but*

You. He took her hand while Taryn took her other hand. Her skin felt like it was going to burn his.

He closed his eyes. "Adoyni, we don't have any other help. Lizzy is hurt badly, and we need her to get better. Can you please heal her?" He peeked out of one eye. Taryn had his eyes squeezed shut. "Please, Adoyni." He felt the heat draining out of her hand. *Is she dying?* He felt for a pulse.

Lizzy groaned when he pressed on her throat. She opened her eyes slowly, blinking furiously, and took a deep breath. "What are you doing?" Her voice cracked.

Kai jumped and pulled his hand back. He refused to get his hopes up about their prayer and ignored her question. "Let's check your head since you're awake." He untied the cloth. It stuck on her hair, soaked with blood, and Taryn gently pulled it free. The soft moonlight fell on pink, healthy skin.

Lizzy turned her head. "What's wrong?"

"Nothing's wrong!" Taryn laughed. "You're healed. That gash is gone! Nothing's there anymore. Adoyni healed you, Lizzy. We prayed, and He did it."

Kai didn't really know what he expected Lizzy to do, but he certainly wasn't prepared for her reaction. She put her head between her hands and sobbed.

CHAPTER FORTY-ONE

Reasons for Tears

Lizzy didn't know why she cried when she found out the wound was gone. Maybe it was relief that she wasn't going to die. She had no idea, but she blubbered like a little girl until the tears no longer came. Then she cried more, her shoulders shaking with tearless sobs.

Kai and Taryn had no idea what to do. They wrapped her shoulders with their cloaks. They offered her water and food. They tried to talk to her. But all their kindness only made her bawl more. When she was done, she was thirstier than she'd ever been and was too embarrassed about crying to look at them.

The next morning Lizzy was amused when Taryn got very excited over prayer and experimented on all sorts of things. He started by asking for new shoes. "Look! These have holes everywhere," Taryn said. "I'm going to pray for new shoes."

So he did. But nothing appeared. He didn't give up, though. He prayed his old shoes would be repaired. After nothing happened, he thought that the correct word was *healed*, so he tried again. The shoes never changed. He pulled them on with a look that reminded Lizzy of a lost puppy. She was surprised that his lack of results didn't bother

her. Adoyni healed her. She knew this without any doubt in her heart.

They shouldered their packs and started walking. When the sun was hottest, Kai stopped and offered her a sip of water. She saw the flask hanging empty at his side.

"Where'd all the water go?" she asked. "Aren't there more flasks?"

"This is the last one," he said, not meeting her eyes. "Here, take your sip. We walked several days before you were healed. Take the water."

"No."

Kai stared at her like she had sprouted wings. "No?"

"No, you drink it. Or Taryn. I don't want it." She pulled her hood over her head. "I know what you did. You let me drink as much as I wanted while I was sick. I won't take another sip."

Taryn stared at the water. She knew he wanted it. "Well, you had a fever," he said.

She sat in the sand and tried not to yelp when the sand burned her. "I'm not drinking it."

She passed the water to Taryn and wrapped up in her cloak to block the sun before she gave in to the urge to snatch the water back. Thinking that sleep would take her mind off her thirst, she closed her eyes, but the heat kept her awake. She didn't remember drifting off to sleep, but she saw pure water sparkling in a small pond surrounded by the strangest trees she'd ever seen. They were tall, but the branches only grew at the top of the trees. It was so real she could hear the wind in the trees and taste the water. She jerked awake. She peeked under her cloak and saw Kai and Taryn stretching.

"Let's go." Kai didn't bother shaking off the sand.

They groaned and followed him. She tried to dust the sand off her, but it was everywhere. She was sick of it. It was in her eyes, her ears, her nose. She felt it on her burned cheeks. The guys were no better. They were covered with black grit. *How long until the sand sinks into our bodies and clogs our hearts and fills our lungs?* She plodded after Kai, dark thoughts seeping into her soul. Several hours later, Lizzy didn't think her legs could walk any farther. She fell to the sand and panted.

Kai handed out the water carefully. "Drink it slowly. It's the last that we have."

Lizzy stared at the liquid in her cup. It was barely enough for a swallow, and yet it was so precious. *The last of the water. We'll last one day, maybe, without it. Oh, Adoyni, help us.*

After some time, Kai pointed ahead. "What's that?" His voice sounded like a squeak.

Lizzy saw something long and straight sticking out of the dunes ahead of them. She tilted her head. *That looks familiar.* As they came closer, they saw that the sticks were quite tall, and they had things growing from the tops of them. She knew where she'd seen them before.

"There's water down there." Her voice broke.

She surged ahead, but Taryn overtook her with his long legs. She struggled up the last dune and slid down the other side. The trees spread out in front of them, sprouting out of dirt. *We've made it to the other side of the desert!* She led the way through the circle of trees, already tasting the water. It was just like her dream. *I'm going to dive in and drink all I can!* The trees opened up to reveal an open space. On her right was a large rock. Ahead of her was nothing but dirt so dry it was lined with cracks. She stumbled and fell to her knees.

"Where's the water?" Kai asked. "You said there was water here."

"I don't know," she said. Tears fell down her cheeks again. "There was water. Lots and lots of water."

She sat there in the dirt. *Why did this happen? Why has He brought us so far, to suffer so much, only to die?* She fingered her darts. She drew one out of the quiver. If she died, then no one would save Rica, and she'd never see Dad again. She pictured Belial lying on the ground in front of her. *If he were here, I'd stab him in the heart for causing all these problems.* She took a dart out of its quiver and stabbed it into the ground.

The ground rumbled. She looked up to see if there were storm clouds, but the sky was clear. The rumble came again, louder, like thunder, but it was under the ground. It continued, growing louder each time. Then the ground shook. It was a little tremor, but the third time it shook so hard Kai and

Taryn were knocked off their feet. Taryn landed next to Lizzy.

"Don't tell me it's an earthquake," he said. His face was white as he tried to find something to hold onto. "Haven't we been through enough already?"

* * *

Rhiana stared at the picture of one red pansy in a glass of water above Mom's chair. But it wasn't the pansy that caught her eye. It was the water. She was so thirsty.

Before Mom left with Dad, she had carried Rhiana to the couch to give her something new to look at. Mom said that restlessness was a good sign of improvement. Then she got her some blankets and books. That was when she saw that Rhiana didn't have the crystal around her neck anymore and asked if she had lost it.

"No." She shifted to sit up. "I just got tired of wearing it. It didn't seem to help."

Mom walked away. She came back and placed the crystal around Rhiana's neck. Then Mom kissed her cheek. "We need to do everything we can to get you better. Now I don't want you to worry while we are gone. It will be a long time. We're going to the Temple of All to pray to Zoria for Her blessing. After that, we'll be waiting for the judgment. It may take a while, but I know the Goddess will bless us. You rest here and focus on getting better."

She swallowed hard. "Do you think Kai will come back?"

"I don't know." Mom adjusted the blankets.

Rhiana felt tears rise in her eyes. "But I miss him."

"So do I," Mom said. "Don't worry. We'll hear from him soon."

Rhiana heard the words die off. *Mom's just telling me what she thinks I want to hear. She's scared for Kai.* "If they say you have to go work for that man, will I see you again?"

Mom pushed back her hair behind her ears. "If I have to go, I'll still come back here to get my things. After that, I don't know. But don't worry. Zoria will protect us. It will be okay."

Mom and Dad said goodbye, and the house fell quiet. Rhiana didn't want to think about what might happen. She couldn't imagine a life without Mom and Kai. She fingered the crystal while she thought of Kai, her thirst growing every moment. She hoped Mom was right when she said Zoria would protect them because they needed help from someone.

CHAPTER FORTY-TWO

Dreams Come True

Taryn made a list in his head of everything they had been through: windstorms, thunderstorms, unreal rainstorms, mountains, deserts, and now an earthquake. He clung to the earth as the trees bent above him. Lizzy was screaming, but he couldn't hear anything other than the groans of the earth and the trees breaking above him. *Will I be swallowed by the deep or stabbed by a tree?*

Kai was in front of him, flat on his stomach, yelling, but Taryn couldn't hear him over the noise. Kai crawled to them, making his way over a small hill of dirt that wasn't there a few seconds ago.

"Look!" Kai roared with a huge grin on his face. He crawled toward them, ignoring the branch that dropped five feet away from him. He reached them. "Look!"

Taryn shook his head. *He's lost it. He's completely nuts.* He looked down at Kai's hands covered with dirt. *Only a child or a crazy person would be so excited about dirt.*

Lizzy started laughing. "It's my dream! I told you I dreamed this!"

Kai was still holding his hands out to Taryn. And that's when he saw it. Kai was holding mud! There hadn't been mud a few minutes ago. And for there to be mud, there had to be water. If there was water, they could drink. They huddled on the ground, while it shook and quaked, laughing and shouting like they had lost their minds.

The trees stopped swaying, and the noise died down. The dirt in front of them a few minutes ago was replaced with a beautiful crystal clear pond. The water sparkled and shimmered in the sun as it filled the pool deeper.

They paused only long enough to take off their swords and shoes. Then they ran straight into the water. Taryn ran as deep as his neck and used his hands to pour the water into his mouth. He drank until he started coughing, water spilling over his parched lips. Lizzy dove in the pool beside him, the water washing away the black sand and blood. Kai splashed around, drinking and laughing.

After a few minutes, Taryn stopped drinking to look around. "What do you think happened? Where'd this water come from?"

Kai splashed Taryn. "Who knows? Honestly, I don't really care. We would've died here if it hadn't come. That's all I care about."

"I've been thinking," Lizzy said. "I got really mad that we were going to die after everything we've been through. I took one of my darts and stabbed the earth. That's when the tremors started. Remember Alyn said that it could cut through the vilest evil."

"Are you saying that the dart did this?" Taryn washed his face.

Lizzy nodded. "Maybe there's something special about the darts, like they set things right or renew life. Maybe each of our gifts does something."

Kai stopped smiling. "I don't think I'm going to be using that sword."

"Why not?" Taryn asked, surprised.

Kai didn't answer right away. "Well, because that word on it ruins the sword. I can't imagine standing in front of a Seeker and pulling out a sword that says *Surrender* on it. The Seeker would probably laugh me to death."

"Maybe it means for your enemy to surrender, not you." Taryn tried to help.

"Well, I personally hope that you never have to use it," Lizzy said. "Maybe we've beaten that army across the desert, and we'll be able to find that canyon without seeing them."

"Don't get your hopes up," Kai warned. "It's possible they'll be waiting for us at the canyon. This may get harder as we go farther."

Harder? This couldn't get any harder than it already is. Taryn felt thirsty again and took a deep drink. The water felt so good sliding down his throat.

Lizzy glared at Kai. "Joy-killer."

"Don't start fighting again," Taryn pleaded. "Can't we just enjoy something for once?"

"Lizard-breath," he shot back.

She stuck out her tongue and splashed him. He dove under the water, and she screamed as he dunked her. Taryn glanced at Lizzy when she resurfaced, and she winked. *Kai's turn.* He grinned as they attacked. Kai yelled and fought them the whole time. By the time he was under, they all swallowed more water.

Lizzy swam for the edge of the water. "I never thought I'd want to get out, but I feel so tired. I think I'm going to go sleep for a minute."

A nap sounded real good, so they climbed out and let the sun dry them. Taryn shifted the sand around until he had a pile that was shaped like a pillow. It almost felt like a bed. He put his head down and sighed deeply. *This is perfect. I could sleep for a week!*

The ripples of the water matched the swaying trees in the slight breeze, making the perfect lullaby. As his eyes began to close, he had the feeling that he shouldn't sleep. They had to do something, go somewhere quickly, but he couldn't remember what in his tiredness. He stopped trying to remember and drifted off to sleep.

* * *

Kai yawned. *We need to get going to the canyon.* But he felt so tired that he didn't care about it anymore. They had suffered so much that they deserved a little rest. He closed his eyes and let sleep take him away.

In his dreams, he heard a voice. It jerked him awake. *Kai, wake up now!*

He sat and yawned. *What a dream.* He stretched
and closed his eyes.

Kaison Teschner! Wake up and get moving!

The words resounded in his head. He shook
his head. The voice sounded familiar. It was a little
deeper than Dad's and less gravelly than Timo's.
Eladar! He scanned the skies, but there was no sign
of the white horse. He rubbed his eyes, instantly
regretting it as the sand burned his eyes. *Eladar, is
that you? Can you hear me?*

*I can hear you. You need to stop sleeping and get
moving.* Eladar sound faint, like he was speaking
from a long way off.

Kai smiled. *Where are you?*

*Around Northbridge. I'm coming your way, though.
You've got to get moving. The army is almost to the
canyon.*

Kai blinked. *How do you know that? How did you
know I was sleeping?*

Eladar chuckled. *I can tell when you are sleeping
because your thoughts quiet down. As for the army,
we have our ways in Merrihaven. I can't keep this
conversation going for long. Have you found the
stone?*

Kai groaned. He'd forgotten all about looking
for a rock that gives life. *No. Have you found out what
that means?* He blinked. For the first time since they
entered the desert, there were rocks around. *We're
surrounded by rocks.*

*Find that stone and then run. You've wasted too
much time. I must go. Stand firm.*

Kai swallowed hard. *Stand firm.* He shook his head as Eladar's presence faded away. He stood up and groaned from the aches in his legs. He shook Lizzy and Taryn awake. Lizzy sat up quickly, her red hair wild from sleep, groaned, and laid back down. Taryn refused to move.

"I'll kick you if you don't get going," Kai warned. "Eladar said the army was near. We have to hurry."

Taryn rubbed sand into his eyes accidently and yelled with pain. Lizzy rolled her eyes as she got her hair wet and braided it quickly.

"There were no rocks all through the desert, and we're running out of chances to find that stone that Eladar told us about. Let's look here for something that might give life," Kai said.

He walked through the trees. Lizzy and Taryn followed, yawning. One rock, taller than him, stood alone, propped up by a smaller boulder underneath it. Deep gouges cut into the rock. He traced the grooves on the rock with a finger. It must have been a sharp knife to make so many cuts in the thick rock. The marks stretched from the top of the stone to the bottom. *It's like someone was executed here.*

The stories said that Lesu was cut into pieces in this very desert. *Could this be the very stone where they cut Lesu into so many pieces?* Kai stared in morbid fascination. There were hundreds of cuts. *Who could have stood such pain? I'm sorry, Adoyni. I'm sorry*

I didn't believe. I've been so lost. I don't deserve a second chance, but I'll do what You ask.

Lizzy stared at the stone. "There's something under it."

"Yeah, sand," Taryn snapped. He was tracing one of the scored lines in the rock with a finger. "Do you think this is where they killed Lesu?"

"I think so," Kai started to say. "I think…"

"Listen to me," Lizzy said louder. "There is something under the rock. I can see it. It's like a bag or something. We need to dig it up."

"Lizard-breath, I'm sure there's something under there," Kai said. "But I don't think we have time to dig it up."

"I'm not leaving until we do." Lizzy put her hands on her hips. "I knew that we shouldn't go into that town, but no one listened to me. This time you're going to listen to what I'm telling you." Her green eyes flashed with anger and determination that matched her red hair.

Kai sighed and started digging up the sand. "This is a waste of time. The sun is starting to set. We only have a few hours of light left."

"You've got to be kidding," Taryn groaned as he copied Kai.

Lizzy didn't acknowledge their comments. She frantically dug beside him. After a few minutes, she told them to adjust their digging to the south a little. The hole grew bigger and deeper. Kai was about to stop and drag her away from the hole when she gasped.

"There it is!"

The next few scoops of sand revealed burlap. He scraped out the sand. There were three burlap bags at the bottom of the hole. He lugged them out, barely able to lift them. They were filled to the brim and tied tightly shut. A small emblem was on the front of each bag - one norsaq, one sword, one shield.

Kai gasped. The emblems matched the gifts Alyn had given them. *Someone is watching out for us. The stone that gives life! Of course!* Life was given to Lesu after he was killed.

"How in the world did you know that it was there, Lizzy?" Taryn dropped down beside his bag with the shield.

"I don't know," she admitted. "Remember that tower at Heniah with Eladar? I could see that too before he lowered the shield. It's like I'm beginning to see things that no one can."

Taryn started to open the bag. "That's a handy trick! Do you think this has something in it to fix the river? Some mysterious ingredient no one has thought of?" He pulled the strings open to reveal white granules. He scooped some out, tasted it, and spit it out. "Salt!"

"Salt?" Kai echoed. "Why salt?"

"How should I know? It's *not* going to work!" Taryn kicked the bag. "What's it going to do? We could've thrown salt in at Albia. Mischa would still be alive!"

"Maybe it doesn't matter what it is," Lizzy said.
"Maybe it matters what we believe."

Taryn yelled. "How can salt do anything? What
am I supposed to believe in? Salt?"

"I don't know how," Kai joined in. "But I know
it's going to work. We'll take them with us. Eladar
talked to me and said the canyon is close, and so is
the army. We need to go. Now."

Taryn groaned as he lifted his bag. "This is
stupid. It's just going to waste our energy and slow
us down. What idiot put salt in these bags?"

Kai didn't bother answer him as they filled their
flasks with water. They hefted their bags on their
shoulders, feeling the weight as they started east.
He led the way up the hill, climbing to the crest
of the hill. Rocks littered the sand and gradually
replaced it. He reached the top and stood there
panting as the others joined him. They were
standing on the highest hill, giving them a bird's
eye view. A small valley stretched out in front of
them. On the other side of the valley, the ground
was broken into deep canyons that led into steep
mountains. The canyon in front of them was
shaped like a crescent with a river flowing out of
it. Nestled at the mouth of it was a massive castle
surrounded by a large stone wall. Soldiers with
long bows, garbed in armor, patrolled the walls and
guarded the heavy wooden gate.

The crescent canyon! We found it! Kai almost let out
a cry of triumph until he looked closer. His heart
dropped as he surveyed the scene. It would've been

easy to sneak around the castle to enter the canyon. But the walls were built over the river. The only way into the canyon was through the fortress. He groaned. *Why isn't something easy for once?*

He looked closer at the river. Behind the stronghold, the river flowed down a waterfall. Kai shook his head in disbelief. The river was crystal clear as it tumbled down the canyon and entered a tower that was straddling it. When it left, it was brown and contaminated. Whatever was poisoning the river was *inside* the walls. The castle was surrounded by a wide pit. The only way in was over the guarded drawbridge and through the gates.

"That's nice," Taryn said sarcastically. "Cleansing the river would be easy, but now that the poison is surrounded by a castle, it's no problem. In fact, I wish it would've been more of a challenge. This is too easy."

Kai stared at Taryn like he had lost his mind. Lizzy ignored them, staring at the fortress with despair in her eyes. A movement caught Kai's eyes.

"Get down!" He grabbed Lizzy's arm and pulled her to the ground. "It's the army. They're coming!"

DEFEATS

"A wise man fights to win,
But he is twice a fool who has no plan for possible defeat."
~Louis L'Amour

Foehn watched from high in the sky, horrified that the storm he brought had injured the girl. He didn't mean it to. He liked the way her laughter flew up to him. If she died, he would never forgive himself. He lingered over the boys as they watched over her. He saw them give her water when they so desperately needed it for themselves.

He never had a friend like that. Never had someone who cared about him that much. Refkell and the Master would not care, not unless they needed him to do something. He wondered what it felt like to be with someone who loved you like that.

Foehn checked on the three friends making their way across the desert. He found himself laughing when they jumped in the water and came in closer as they examined a stone and talked of Lesu. He found it hard to believe. Who would willingly die for someone else? Was this love? He decided to talk to this Lesu. If He had conquered death, maybe Lesu would know a way to escape from the Master. He kept his plans secret, deep where the Master would never know, and watched the three closely.

CHAPTER FORTY-THREE

One with the Unwanteds

Taryn listened to Kai as the army came closer. It looked like a black shadow crawling over the barren land. The sound of their footsteps drummed in his head, beating out every thought but their failure. He threw the bag of salt on the ground. *It just isn't fair.* With the army, there was no way they could get in the castle. And there was no way to cleanse the river without going into the castle.

Kai never took his eyes off the castle like he didn't even know the army was coming. "I bet that tower on the left has the poison because the water looks fine when it flows underneath the tower. But look on our side where it comes out. It's all brown and toxic. See? We need to get in there."

"Are you forgetting about the giant stone walls and huge gates with all the soldiers around?" Lizzy pointed out. "And a whole bunch of them back there?"

Kai looked at the mass of soldiers coming at them for the first time with a serious expression. Then he grinned as inspiration struck him. "They are going to help us. We'll blend in with them until we're in the courtyard and then we'll sneak into the tower. Bring your weapons and the bags of salt."

Taryn studied the castle. Two tall towers were on each side of the courtyard. Halfway up the towers, a bridge high above the ground connected them. As far as he could see, using the bridge was the only way to get into the tower over the river, unless someone climbed up, but he didn't think even Kai could. He glanced to the tower on the left and felt goose bumps rising on his arms even in the heat of the desert. It was made out of white stone with green vines crawling to the top, creating a picture of life. At the very top was a giant flame.

"I can't," he whispered. "I can't go with you. That's a temple for Zoria. If I go in there and help you, She'll know. The night before we got on the coach, I swore an oath. The one the priests say. I bound my soul to Her. If She finds out I've been helping you, or that I've been praying to Adoyni, She'll….She'll kill me."

"What are you talking about?" Kai snapped. "You act like She's in there, waiting for you. We don't even have to go close to that temple. We're not turning back now!"

"Sh!" Lizzy hissed. "They'll hear you." She gestured to the army.

"Look! There's people down there!" Kai said, argument forgotten.

In the midst of the Unwanteds was a large group of people being pushed and pulled along. Three Seekers followed with long whips, their large weapons hanging off their belts.

"Who do you think they are?" Taryn dropped his voice to a whisper.

Lizzy spoke softly. "Haven't you heard of those people disappearing? I thought it was just rumors, but I guess it was really happening. What do you think they are doing with them?"

"What makes you think we know?" Kai replied. "Listen. Once we're in, we'll get into the tower and take out the poison. We'll go when the army's hidden from view by that hill and then take that path to the bottom."

Taryn saw a small trail curling down the cliff wall like a snake. It was covered with small boulders and loose gravel, sometimes disappearing completely from view. His heart sank. It was maybe a foot wide.

"Go as fast as you can," Kai commanded as he watched the army disappear from sight. "Be very careful. If you slip, you'll take us down with you."

Taryn's stomach started doing flips. He was never any good with heights, and the trail was as wide as a sheet of paper. *One stumble and I'm dead.*

* * *

Lizzy looked at the path and breathed a prayer as she started down. *Adoyni, please help us down. But not too quickly!* Kai was waiting for her at the first bend, watching her descend. He waited for a minute before continuing down the next stretch. She made it to the bend and glanced back to Taryn. He was as white as the sheets on her bed at home.

They were about halfway down when they heard
noises of armor banging and the sound of voices.
She hurried faster, but her legs were shaking so
badly it was hard to walk. She made it to the next
corner and paused for a breath. When she took her
next step, the rocks slid under her foot, and she
slipped. She grabbed the closest rock and clung
to it, her legs shaking. She picked her next step
carefully, but she slipped and fell to her knees. She
stood up cautiously, blood seeping through her
pants. Kai waited for her to catch up with him.

Taryn came up from behind, breathing heavily.
"I liked the desert better."

"You could go back," Kai smiled suddenly. "Lead
the way."

"Be my guest." Taryn stepped up onto a boulder
as he spoke. The rock shifted as Taryn put his
weight on it. "Oh, nuts!"

The rock rolled off the side, and Taryn was
thrown up in the air. He grabbed her arm, pulling
her over with him. Kai yelled and caught her foot.
They jerked to a stop, dangling in the air. She
looked back. Kai was hanging off the cliff and was
holding them with one hand.

Kai's hand began to slip and then it lost its grip,
and they dropped. She yelled as they fell through
the air, crashing into the cliff and tumbling with
rocks knocked free. Through the dust, she saw Kai's
arms flailing and Taryn's cloak as they plunged to
the bottom. She rolled to a stop at the bottom and
groaned as Kai landed on top of her. She pushed

him off as she got to her hands and knees. They were at the bottom of the cliff, almost on the path that led to the castle.

Kai moaned. "Thanks, Taryn. Nothing better than a tumble down a cliff."

Taryn cautiously rubbed his shoulder and glared at Kai. "Like I planned it."

"Come on, guys," Lizzy piped up, afraid they would start fighting again. "We're all okay. Just some bumps and bruises." She regretted the words as soon as she stood up. *There's more bumps and bruises than I thought.* The guys stayed in the dirt. "Let's go! The army's about to come around the corner."

They hobbled to a large boulder as fast as they could and hid behind it, pulling their cloaks over their faces, and waited for the first of the Unwanteds to pass by. Lizzy thought her heart was going to beat out of her chest as the army approached.

Kai waited for a few minutes and then mouthed, "Stand firm." He pulled his cloak tight around him, hiding his sword, and shuffled around the rock. She glanced back at Taryn. His face was white, and his brown eyes seemed to plead for her not to go. She took a deep breath and followed Kai into the army.

CHAPTER FORTY-FOUR

Saving the Day

The stink from the Unwanteds made Lizzy want to gag. She shuffled along with them and dragged her left leg like it was dead. Bright copper hair caught her eye as she searched the crowd. *Nighthawk Nephesus!* She pushed closer. The priestess didn't seem to notice Lizzy as she gave orders to a Seeker. Lizzy shrank from being discovered, but she strained to hear what Nighthawk was saying.

"When we get there, get the prisoners ready for the sacrifice," Nighthawk ordered. "We'll kill them all since today's the first day of spring. And bring Rica to me. I have a job for him."

Lizzy missed the reply as they became bottled up at the drawbridge of the castle. *Rica's alive!* She stood on her toes to search for him when someone gripped her arm and pulled her down. She whirled around to see Kai and Taryn behind her.

"What are you doing? Trying to get killed?" Kai said, his blue eyes sparkling with anger.

"I saw Nighthawk." She rubbed her arm where Kai had grabbed her. "They're going to kill the prisoners, and Rica's here somewhere. I've gotta find him."

One of the Unwanteds slammed into them and snarled. The desert fell behind as they walked across the bridge into the castle.

"Nighthawk?" Taryn asked. "I've got to talk to her."

"No," Kai protested. "If she sees you, it'll be all over. We've got to stop that poison. Then we can worry about the prisoners and Nighthawk."

"There may not be time," Lizzy argued. "She wants Rica for some reason. She said he could be useful. I've got to get him out of here before she does anything to him."

"Yeah, and if I talk to Nighthawk, she can sort this all out," Taryn joined in. "Maybe she'll even help us when she knows who I am."

The crowd pushed into the courtyard. At their destination, the Unwanteds wandered, as if unsure of where to go. Two Seekers strolled through the press of people with long whips. Approaching the prisoners, they herded them deeper into the castle. Lizzy peered after them, but she didn't see Rica. The sounds of whips cracking filled in the air as the prisoners, weary from the long trek, moved slowly. The Unwanteds surged back toward the gates, but the iron bars rolled shut, trapping them.

Taryn glanced around at the thinning crowd. "It's not going to be long until they notice us. It shouldn't take all three of us to stop the poison."

Lizzy seized on what Taryn was saying. "I'll meet you in the tower with Rica. They don't even know that we're here. A few minutes won't hurt."

Kai glanced around, doubt filling his blue eyes.
"I don't think it feels right, but go on. Just don't get
caught. If one of you gets discovered, our element
of surprise is gone. Meet me at the tower as soon as
you can. Stand firm."

Lizzy mumbled *Stand firm* back and dimly heard
Taryn saying it. She followed the Seekers and
gripped her norsaq under her cloak. She could
already see Mother's pleased smile as she wrapped
her arms around Lizzy in a giant hug. Dad would
come home, and they'd be a family again.

She tiptoed after the Seekers into a dank
hallway that sloped under the castle. It grew darker
as they descended underground into the dungeon.
She followed silently in the shadows until she heard
the bang and clank of metal. Cowering in the dark,
she cringed in a hollow in the wall, as the Seekers
forced the prisoners through large gates and
fastened it shut with a heavy chain and padlock.
They pulled on the chain a few times to make sure
it was secure and headed straight toward her.

* * *

Taryn didn't wait around for Kai to change
his mind. He dashed across the courtyard after
Nighthawk. She walked gracefully up the winding
stairs to the Temple. As he made his way up the
stairs, he traced figures of ivy and flowers carved
into the wall. All temples were adorned with plants

and flowers. *I guess it's hard to have real plants in the desert.* His shield hung heavily on his arm, and he shifted it to hold the crystal closer.

He lurched to a stop when he saw Nighthawk standing five feet away as she pulled open a door. The words he'd been planning to say disappeared. She slipped through the tall door decorated with gold vines with silver leaves before he could get anything out. He caught the sweet smell of incense.

At the door, he had a good vantage point of the courtyard and the other tower. He glanced down at Kai making his way toward the tower over the river. Taryn slipped through the temple door and grinned at the Preparation Room. Benches lined the room with baskets underneath for storing street clothes. Water streamed down the far wall, providing a place to wash. White silk garments were laid out next to the towels. Taryn grinned. Surely with these fine items, he'd find the forgiveness he needed.

His shield was too large for the baskets, so he hid it with the salt behind the door and covered them with his cloak. As the water washed away the dirt, he couldn't hold back the anticipation growing inside him. He dried off with the coarse towel and slid into a white silk robe. He chuckled as he chose a gold belt from the variety of colors. A quote from his books flashed in his mind. "Gold symbolizes the sun. Just as the sun blazes hot, this color represents masculine energy and magical power."

He caught a glimpse of himself in the mirror.
Even with his red face, he looked like a priest. He
adjusted the robe, but doubts remained. *What if
Zoria knows I prayed to Adoyni? Could I convince Her
that I was misled by the others?* But he wasn't so sure
what he believed of Adoyni anymore. He tugged at
the belt, placing the knot on his hip, and shoved
down the worries. Picking up the crystal sphere,
he smiled, feeling the power prickle his fingers.
He strolled to the door and entered the main
sanctuary of the temple.

CHAPTER FORTY-FIVE

Hopes Fall

Kai watched Lizzy and Taryn race away. *Should I have told them to stay?* But he'd seen the desperation in Lizzy's eyes and the lust of power in Taryn's. He gripped the hilt of his sword under his cloak.

The courtyard quieted as the Unwanteds left. Now he could hear the rushing water of the river. He ran his hand along the wall as he explored. The sun began to set, casting eerie shadows. A long arched bridge ran from the temple to the tower. By the temple, a door opened and two people walked out onto the bridge. Kai jumped back deeper in the shadows when he saw Belial.

"Kill all the prisoners and bring me their ashes." Belial's voice drifted down. "I want to poison the river so badly tonight, that when I save the world, none will question my power."

Kai leaned forward to hear the reply, but the noise of the river drowned the words. He caught a flash of red hair in the torches on the bridge. Then Belial's voice rumbled down. *It's Nighthawk. Taryn better not come stumbling out and get caught by Belial.*

"Yes, and tell Refkell to bring her to me. I shall have need of her soon. As for you, once your tasks are completed, leave for the capital. You will proclaim my success to the king and the court."

Nighthawk hustled back into the temple. Incense drifted down to Kai from the temple as she opened the door, and he remembered Shona dying at the temple of Northbridge. He fought back a searing flash of rage, recalling Alyn's words of caution to control his anger. As he watched Belial stride to the tower like a lion stalking his prey, Kai gritted his teeth. *You're not going to kill anyone anymore.* He was suddenly glad he let Lizzy go. Hopefully, she could free the prisoners before the Seekers followed Belial's orders. *Belial ordered some woman brought to him. Who would that be? Did they already catch Lizzy?* Maybe splitting up was a bad idea.

Belial disappeared into the shadows of the keep. Kai watched to make sure he didn't come back. *If I can get to that bridge, I can find a way in to where they are poisoning the river.* He tried not to think about what he would do when he found the poison. *Just get there first.*

He backed up against the wall surrounding the courtyard to gain a better view of the bridge. The white tower gleamed in the setting sun across from him. His fingers scraped against the large stones set in mortar. He tested the cracks between the rocks and grinned as he swung the salt over his back.

It was easy climbing up the wall even though his fingers stung. He was halfway up when a pebble bounced to the ground. It hit the wall twice and clattered to the ground. If any of the soldiers heard that, they'd see him. He inched closer to the bridge, hoping to get into its shadows when he heard footsteps. And they were coming closer.

* * *

Lizzy pressed against the wall of the tunnel and pulled the cloak around her. The Seekers strode toward her, laughing about the fear of the prisoners. She let out her breath as their voices faded away down the hallway. Gathering the bag of salt and her norsaq, she slipped out the shadows and approached the doorway to a large room. To her left was a large fireplace with a fire blazing. Straight ahead of her were large iron gates with bars. The prisoners were collapsed behind them on the stone floor. Some of the women were clutching small children while the men rested with their hands on their knees.

"Rica?" Lizzy raced to the bars. "Rica? Are you there? Does anyone know where Rica is?"

"Quiet, girl! You'll bring the Seekers back! They'll be in an unpleasant mood, and we'll bear the brunt of it." The woman who spoke looked slightly older than Lizzy.

"I just need to find my brother," she whispered. "Do you know of him? He's tall and has dark hair and dark eyes."

A woman frowned. "One of the Seekers took him away a couple days ago. They said something about Nighthawk. Now can you find a key?"

Lizzy groaned. She was too late. Nighthawk had already taken Rica. There was no way she could rescue him with the priestess around. *How am I going to tell Mother? Why couldn't I have died? That would be better than facing Mother.*

"Miss?" The woman's voice broke her thoughts. "I'm sorry for your loss. I am. But lots have died, and more are going to if we don't get out of here. Can you help us?"

All she wanted was to lie down and cry until the tears stopped coming. The woman shifted, and Lizzy saw a small baby wrapped in a dirty pink blanket in her arms. The baby waved her arms and cooed.

"No one else is dying tonight." She stood up, her grief giving way to anger. "I'm getting you out of here."

"That's not going to happen, Lizzy." A man's voice came from behind her. The people behind the bars drew back with surprised looks on their faces. She turned around, wondering where she'd heard that voice before, and gasped as the light fell on the man's face.

Rica was standing in the hallway holding a torch with one hand. His dark hair was slicked back, contrasting with the white clothes he wore. A large key hung on his red belt.

"You're not taking these prisoners anywhere." Rica said. His face was grim and his eyes were empty. "Their lives will bring the Master his new kingdom."

CHAPTER FORTY-SIX

Through Doors

Taryn left the Preparation Room and walked deeper into the temple. His heart raced as he knew he was about to seize his destiny. The bright lights from the torches and candles blinded him. The scent of incense was so thick that he could taste it. Through the haze, he saw the room had four doors leading in four directions. *Where did Nighthawk go?*

"Oh, good, you're here." A voice drifted through the blinding light and incense.

Taryn stood straighter. *They've been waiting for me.* A priest slightly older than Taryn entered the room. He wore the same white silk robes which made his pale hair look even more bleached. On his left cheek were two spiral tattoos. Taryn fought back a wave of jealousy. Unable to find his true name, he was denied even the first symbolic tattoo of complete devotion to the Goddess.

"Nighthawk said you would be coming," he continued.

"N...Nighthawk said I was coming?" Taryn asked. "I need to talk to her."

The apprentice looked at him with disgust. "The Priestess is too busy to chat with people like you. Anything you have to say will first be told to me, her chosen apprentice. If I think it's vital, I'll take it to her. Your place is to serve as you have been told and not question orders."

Taryn swallowed. He knew initiation was difficult, but he had expected a warmer welcome. "What am I to do, Priest?"

"You may address me as Moran." The priest turned toward the door he'd come through. "I will show you what your task is."

Taryn shifted the heavy crystal sphere to his other hand and followed. *We must be over the dungeons. I bet Lizzy's under this floor.* A dark hallway led to a larger room made out of solid stone. Stars glittered through the windows. His footsteps echoed as he made his way to Moran, who was standing at the large altar in the center of the room. The tall altar was made out of white stone. Ladders were placed on each side. On the altar was a giant pile of wood. Torches were placed beside the ladders.

"This is where we sacrifice to the Goddess," Moran explained. "They come through the door on the left and are led to the altar. After the fire has died, the ashes are collected and taken through that door." Moran pointed to the right. "Mark that door well."

Sacrifice? I've never heard of anything like that. "Why?" Taryn asked.

"Don't you remember what Nighthawk told you? Tonight your job is to gather the ashes and take them to Belial so that he can poison the river with them." Moran gave him an icy frown and started back the way they came. "Now, come. It's time to get started."

Taryn hesitated, questions spinning through his head. *Ashes? Sacrifices?* Dread filled his heart. He wanted to join Nighthawk in her labors, but not like this. "What is sacrificed?"

Moran spun on his heel and glared at him. "You are denser than I thought. The prisoners you came with. Remember? You walked with them for days until you pledged your allegiance to Nighthawk."

"But...I...I..." Taryn's words died as Moran's words sank in. "I mean, I'm not..."

"Rica!" Moran's voice cracked like a whip. "You are not here to question or understand, and no one cares what you think. You've been given a job. Now do it! There are at least sixty prisoners down there waiting, and we don't have all night."

Taryn followed Moran. *He thinks I'm Rica! Do I tell him who I am? Are they really planning to kill everyone?* "How did Belial find out that the sacrifice cleanses the river?"

Moran smirked. "Cleanse? That's for tomorrow night. Tonight we're going to poison it until someone just taking a sip dies. Then Belial shall appear even greater than before."

Taryn stopped in his tracks. The death of sixty people was repulsing even if it meant the world would be saved. *But to poison the water?* Taryn stared at the symbols of the Goddess lining the hallway and the mark of dedication on Moran's face. He knew with a sinking heart that Eladar was right. He groaned.

The door on the left opened as they entered the room, and Nighthawk swept into the room. Her red hair was pulled back into bun, but strands fell into her face. She slammed the door, her face as hard as death itself.

"What are you doing, Moran?" she snapped. "The sacrifices should have started by now. The Master awaits."

"My humblest apologies, Mistress." Moran bowed low. "Rica just got here, and I have showed him what to do as you requested. We're starting in a few minutes."

"Rica?" Nighthawk glanced at Taryn for the first time, her brown eyes confused and then startled. "This isn't Rica." She paused. "This is someone I didn't expect to see."

Moran's face went white as he bowed even lower. "My sincerest apologies."

"I'll deal with you later," Nighthawk's voice was sharp. "For now, get the prisoners into place. I'll be there shortly once I deal with this."

Moran walked backwards to the door behind him, holding his bow until he was through. Nighthawk moved closer to Taryn, a strange cold light in her eyes.

"Now, just what am I going to do with you, Taryn?"

* * *

Kai stared in horror as the rock clattered to the ground. The setting sun cast long shadows across the courtyard, but it wasn't dark enough to hide him. He clung to the wall, his fingers and toes burning from the strain, and held his breath.

Footsteps above him shuffled closer and paused. Kai pressed against the wall, hoping the cloak would camouflage him. A long silence followed. The seconds seemed like minutes as sweat dripped down his face.

The footsteps moved away. Kai waited until he couldn't hear anything and climbed the rest of the way up the wall. He glanced at the Temple on the left to see if anyone was coming and then scrambled over the railing of the bridge and grinned. *No problem.* He moved silently toward the large wooden door of the tower above the river. He eased it open, listening for the slightest creak or moan, but the door was silent.

The room he entered was empty except for a spiral staircase. Kai shifted his bag of salt and crept up the stairs. His steps made a hollow clank that echoed through the stairs. He cringed at every sound. As he approached the top, he began to crawl, keeping his head low. He peered over the last stair.

At the top of the stairs was a narrow hall that ended at a large wooden door. As he watched, the door flew open, and two Unwanteds came out. Belial followed them. They stood by the door with swords ready.

"I want complete privacy," Belial snapped. "No one is to come through this door, other than the servant with the ashes. Do you understand?"

They nodded. With a grunt, Belial spun on his heel and slammed the door behind him. Both of the Unwanteds looked young and strong, and Kai had a feeling they knew how to use the swords they were holding. The ease and familiarity they had when they took their posts reminded him of Alyn's graceful movements.

He eased down a step and rested his head on the stairs. The strap of the bag of salt cut into his shoulder. He was the only one to stop Belial. *Where are you, Eladar?* He called in his mind, but there was no answer. He couldn't wait for Taryn and Lizzy.

He slid the sword out of its scabbard and ran his finger over the word *Surrender.* He shook his head. *What kind of warrior surrenders?* He shifted the bag of salt one more time and stood up, his heart pounding heavily. He swallowed, barely believing what he was about to do. As he walked up the last steps, the Unwanted snapped their swords in front of them, ready to strike.

CHAPTER FORTY-SEVEN

Wishes Come True

Lizzy stared at Rica with horror. He showed no inclination that he was happy to see her. "You're alive! But...I thought you were dead."

"Obviously I'm alive," Rica snapped. "Now move out of my way." He stepped toward her, fingering the key on his belt. His dark eyes had a strange light in them.

She backed against the gates, the force of his words frightening her. He had lost his temper with her many times, but he'd never spoken like that before. His words were cold and harsh, his eyes held no warmth. She felt the lock against her back. "What are you going to do?"

"I'm taking these prisoners to the Sacrifice Room." Rica took the key off his belt.

"What room?" Lizzy questioned. "What are you talking about?"

"You're wasting my time, Lizzy. Tomorrow's the first day of spring." Rica lost his patience. "Their ashes are taken to Belial and he uses them to poison the river."

"Ashes? Belial's burning them to death?" Lizzy cried. "And you're *helping*?"

"Of course I am," Rica scoffed. "And so will you when you see the light. The poison's exterminating the weak, leaving only the ones who believe in Belial. Once the deluded are dead, Belial will take his place as king. Then we'll see what a king, a god, is supposed to be like. He will bestow many blessings on me when this is over."

"Who told you this crap? Nighthawk? Belial?" Lizzy tried to reason with him. "It's lies. Look, Rica! They're murdering little babies."

"It's far better for that baby to die than to live with the foolish notion that Adoyni is real." Rica moved closer to her, his dark eyes like hard lumps of coal.

Lizzy couldn't believe what she was hearing. "What did they do to you after they took you from the coach?"

"Nothing," Rica snapped. "Nighthawk showed me all I could have if only I served Belial. You can, too. You only have to swear allegiance to him. I can tell you the words."

Lizzy hesitated. Maybe this was the way to make Mother love her.

"Please, miss," the woman behind her called out. "Don't let them kill my baby. Take me if you have to, but please save her. She never hurt anyone. Don't let her burn." The small baby in her hands began to cry as if she knew was happening.

The words jolted Lizzy. She glared at Rica. "I serve Adoyni. He'd never command His worshippers to burn a tiny baby. And I'm not going to let you kill anyone."

"What are you going to do?" Rica sneered, hate clouding his face. "You know I'm better than you.

Mother loves me more than you. She has to put up with you, but it'd make us all happier if you were gone."

Lizzy gasped, feeling like she'd been punched. Rica fiddled with the key. She waited for tears to come, but they didn't. *I'm not listening to anything he says.* The key glinted in the light of the torches. If she could get it, she could set the people free.

She launched herself at Rica. He saw her coming and twisted, the key held out behind him. She collided into him. He stepped back to keep his balance. She grabbed his arm and pulled, but he was too strong. *Just a little more.* She strained for it. She felt his hand on her neck squeezing tight as she focused on the key. His hand pressed harder. She saw black spots on the silver key. Then everything went dark.

Nighthawk's words echoed through Taryn's head. *Just what am I going to do with you?* Those weren't the words he'd expected from his mother. *Maybe she doesn't know I'm her son.*

"I couldn't find you." Nighthawk didn't seem to notice his confusion. "Belial charged me to find all of you. Kai and Lizzy were easy. So I set a spell on that pamphlet to go to the child of the Slayers. I had almost given up that day in Albia when you ran up with the pamphlet in your hands. And you were gullible enough to believe that you were going to help us cleanse the river." She laughed, but it sounded harsh.

Taryn found himself speechless. The incense filled the air. He could smell it when he breathed. It soaked into every pore, muddling his thoughts. Nighthawk's words seemed to come out of nowhere and everywhere at the same time. He blinked as his eyes stung from the smoke.

"Everything was perfect," she said. "Then you met up with that meddling Archippos." She spat out the word. "After that, you forgot the Temple. You turned your back on the Goddess. But now you are here. What am I to do? I could take you to Belial, but he's already angry with me. I could take you with me, but to what end? Perhaps it's best to kill you here."

Her words sent chills down his back. "But you're...going to kill those people." He wanted to ask if she was his mother, but he stopped. *How could she want to kill me?*

"Yes, I am," she sneered, her beauty marred by evil. "And I'll do anything to get what I want."

"Zoria isn't like this," Taryn protested.

Nighthawk's laughter rang out through the room, harsh and jarring. "You believe that? You *are* gullible. You think the Goddess is kind and loving. That's just a way to get more to worship Her. But, enough of all that. It's time for you to join us." Her words suddenly became smooth and silky.

Taryn relaxed a bit, the weight of the crystal sphere in his hands growing heavy. "You still want me to join you?"

"Of course, my boy," she said. "There's much for you to do. You don't know what you could accomplish with your full power."

The hazy room made it hard for him to see Nighthawk's face. *Did I imagine that evil look on her face?* Her voice was soothing. He didn't know what to believe or do anymore.

"Repeat these words after me, Taryn." Nighthawk said through the smoke. "Just a few simple words, and then it will all be over. *I, Taryn Wallick…* "

Taryn started to obey, but he felt a breeze on his face. It brought the scent of the desert. The wind whipped around him, blowing his hair. The incense disappeared. He took a deep breath of fresh air and remembered the stone where Lesu was killed, crisscrossed with scars from the knives that pierced his body.

Taryn took a deep breath of fresh air. "All your vows and spells do not hold the power of love like Lesu does. I will not worship a goddess that requires hundreds of people to die so that one person can reap the power they crave. I will worship a God that gives His life so that all may live. I will worship a God who loves me!"

Nighthawk's face drained of color as she stepped back from the power of his words. She pulled a wand out from her cloak. He lifted the sphere. With the crystal, he had the power to do whatever he wanted. The light sparkled off it, causing dots of light to reflect around the room.

He gazed at the crystal one last time and then threw the sphere at Nighthawk as hard as he could. The crystal flew through the air, light bouncing off it and around the room. Nighthawk never saw it coming. It smacked her on the forehead. A loud crack sounded through the room, and she dropped without a sound. Her wand dropped from her hand as the crystal rolled away from her lifeless body.

Taryn stared at what he had done. He'd killed his mother. He started toward her when he heard screams from the Cleansing Room. He hesitated. The shrieks intensified. Taryn winced, and ran out of the room, away from Nighthawk's body.

CHAPTER FORTY-EIGHT

One Bloody Sword

Kai approached the two Unwanteds slowly. They snapped to fighting positions as he came closer. He raised his sword, the word *Surrender* flashing in the light. He choked back his anger. He was *not* going to surrender. He was not going to give up until Rhiana was saved. Through his rage, he swung as hard as he could at the closest Unwanted.

His opponent blocked the attack easily. The swords clang loudly from the force. The Unwanted snarled as it smoothly pulled its weapon clear and swung at Kai. The speed of the creature forced Kai to stumble backwards. He collided into the railing of the stairs and barely blocked the descending blade before it struck him. Kai pushed off the railing, fury sweeping through his body. He danced away from the Unwanted, more cautious of its ability.

Seeing an opening, Kai pressed the attack. The Unwanted evaded him easily. Kai lunged forward, not bothering to keep his guard up. The creature ducked under Kai's thrust, its sword flashing in the light, and then it stabbed and connected with Kai's leg. Kai wanted to scream from the pain, but he leapt backwards to avoid the blade.

He groaned as he dodged the attack. The creature's sword, now red with blood, continued to rain blows on him. He blocked them with his sword, barely able to respond. His arm grew weary from the strain. His injured leg grew weak, and he fell to his knees.

The Unwanted snarled, victory in his eyes. He thrust but misjudged the distance and overreached. Kai pushed the sword away and stabbed upward under the Unwanted's arm. The sword went deep into the Unwanted's chest. It took a ragged breath and was still. He kicked the body away, disgusted with what he had done. He ignored the blood gushing down his leg and turned to the other Unwanted.

"I don't want to kill you," he said quietly, trying to catch his breath. "Let me go through, and you'll be free to go."

The Unwanted showed no sign of comprehension. It didn't even seem to notice that its partner was dead on the floor. As Kai drew nearer, it raised its sword as a warning.

Kai tried again. "We don't have to do this. Just let me through."

The creature growled, sounding like a wild animal trapped. It swung at him, but Kai dodged easily and feinted. The Unwanted fell for the trick as Kai quickly changed directions and slashed it across the neck. It crumbled to the floor, blood pouring out of its throat. Kai fought waves of nausea as he watched. This was a person once. And he had killed him.

He pushed the thought away quickly. The pounding in his leg increased. The blood was oozing out of a wide gash. He cut a portion of the Unwanted's shirt off and tied it around the wound, gasping as he tightened it over the cut. It slowed the blood, but the throbbing grew worse. He took a deep breath, gripped his sword harder, and eased the door open.

The room was large. The torches cast an eerie light on the stones. On the far wall, red drapes covered the wall from top to bottom. In the center of the room was a large hole where the sound of the river came up. Over the opening in the floor was a large silver cauldron fastened to a strong iron framework with bars that angled in different directions. The pot was tipped so that a little of the liquid inside spilled into the river. Beside the hole was a wooden table without any chairs. On the table was an array of bottles filled with various liquids. Belial stood beside the table with his back to Kai.

"I was hoping you'd make it past the Unwanteds," he said without turning. "It will be good for you to see this before you die."

Kai kept his sword up as he approached.

Belial didn't seem to care that he was there. "After I add the poison to the ashes, it goes into the river. Once the poison is in the water, it continues to grow, so just taking away the cauldron won't do a thing." Belial turned to face Kai.

Kai stopped. He was still too far away to attack Belial, and something held him back. Belial was dressed in black robes and at his side was a sword, but he didn't bother to draw it. His dark hair was slicked back. Kai shook his head. He looked exactly like he had when Kai met him that day in the barn. When Kedar was still alive.

"I'm here to stop you," Kai said. "And to stop you from becoming king."

Belial laughed. It echoed through the empty room. "That's almost as funny as your sad little look when I fired you, stable boy. You would've thought I'd ruined your whole life that day. King? Nothing survives without water, boy. Everything needs it. When I control it all, I shall give life and take it away as I see fit." His voice bounced off the walls. "I'm going to be the god of this world."

Kai gripped the hilt tighter. "A man can't be a god. That's impossible."

"What do you think I am?" Belial's voice cracked like a whip. "I say who lives and dies. I poison the river tonight to give life tomorrow. How much more godlike can you get? Any man can seize the world from Adoyni. With the power of Seiten, I already have snatched control of two of the elements that make up this world. Air and Water obey my every command. Soon Earth and Fire will be mine. Then the whole world and all who reside here will be my slave."

"You don't have any authority over the water," Kai protested. "You only poison it."

"Show some respect, boy." Belial stopped laughing, and his face grew evil. "Your family has been in my hands ever since you killed Kedar. One word from me and their pathetic little lives will be snuffed out."

Kai roared with anger and charged Belial. Belial calmly drew his sword and blocked Kai's swing. The impact jarred Kai's teeth as the swords met in the air. He crouched, sword ready, and swung again. Belial moved quickly, circling before he attacked, tearing Kai's sleeve. Kai danced back, wary now of the speed and strength of his opponent. Belial lunged again. Kai blocked as he stumbled back. The bottles rattled and fell as he crashed into the table, pain ricocheted across his back. He jumped sideways, out of range of Belial's blade, and landed next to the cauldron.

Belial glanced at the blade in Kai's hand. "You want to surrender? Fine. I accept."

Anger swept through Kai. He wasn't going to be mocked again. He wasn't going to stand there and let someone else think they were better than him. "You will surrender to me."

Belial laughed again. The sound added fuel to Kai's rage. He ignored all caution and lunged. Belial blocked his thrust and slashed at him. Kai whirled away, but as he circled around, Belial moved in closer and punched him in the jaw. His head jerked back as he stumbled. Belial gave a roar of triumph and jumped toward him, missing Kai by inches.

Kai staggered away, closer to the pit, his head pounding from the force of the blow. His legs were shaky, and he couldn't catch his breath. He waited for an opening.

Belial lunged. Kai ducked and brought his blade up to strike Belial in the chest. Belial whacked Kai's sword. He felt the sting as the weapon flew from his hand, spinning and clattering to the ground. Kai watched in horror as it slid away. Before he could do anything, Belial plunged his sword into Kai's side. Kai heard himself scream in agony as the sword pulled clear.

He pressed his hand on the wound, fighting waves of pain. He stumbled back against the frame of the cauldron. The bag of salt thumped against his thigh, causing him to stumble off balance. He grabbed the frame to stay upright, fighting back fear. *He's going to kill me.*

"Running again?" Belial closed in. "You don't need to. If you swear allegiance to me, I'll forgive you and your debt."

Kai watched Belial's sword, dripping with his own blood, come closer. The blood trickled off, leaving little puddles behind. "Never. I'm never surrendering to anyone."

"I'll even free your family. Turn it down, and you all will die," Belial lifted his sword for the killing blow.

Kai longed for his sword, but it was too far away. He was trapped between Belial and the pit.

The frame for the cauldron dug into his back. He grabbed it, ignoring the pain, and swung out over the abyss. He pulled himself out to the cauldron, using the lip of the pot to support his weight. His side burned as his shirt grew wet with blood. His leg pounded furiously as he was forced to put weight on it. The salt pulled him down to the river.

Belial stood quietly, watching Kai move out of reach. "Is that how it's going to be? Well, you brought it on yourself." He looked at the red drapes on the far wall. "Come to me now."

Kai twisted, his wound opening further, to look behind him. The curtains moved. A girl stepped out from behind. Her dark red hair covered her face, but there was something about the way she moved that seemed familiar to Kai.

"It can't be," he whispered, but he knew it was Shona. He leaned closer as she crossed the room and bowed. Belial flicked back her hair and put the sword to her throat. Kai gasped, pain deeper and stronger than any physical hurt flooding his entire body. Shona wasn't dead as he thought. She was an Unwanted. He groaned in agony. His dream, so long ago, had come true, and he was going to have to watch her die again.

"Shona," Kai called, ignoring Belial's delighted smile. "What happened? Can you hear me? Do you know it's me?"

"Answer him, slave," Belial commanded, pushing the sword, still red with Kai's blood, into Shona's throat.

A small trickle of blood dripped down her throat. Her words were as soft as a whisper. "Help me."

The words pierced his heart. There was something of her left. As joy swept over him, he felt despair overwhelming him. *What can I do? Even if I survive, is there a way to change her back?*

He watched as her eyes filled with tears. Then whatever human was left of her disappeared, and a coldness like death swept over her face. She snarled at him more like a wild animal than a person.

"It's not the crystals killing your family," Belial said softly, watching Kai. "It's not the Temple. It's not even your deluded belief in Adoyni. You are the one killing your family."

The blood on Shona's throat flowed faster as Kai watched Belial pressed the sword deeper into her neck.

CHAPTER FORTY-NINE

A Few Inches Too Short

Taryn dashed down the long hallway as the screams grew louder. He paused. He had no weapon. *My axe and shield!* He rushed back to the room where he'd left them. The white robes tripped him as he ran, but he ignored them. He snatched up the shield and axe. *I should take the salt.* He paused. He was sick of carrying things. He'd been a packhorse since they left the coach. *Why should I keep carrying things I'm never going to use?*

He sighed and threw the bag of salt on his back, feeling the weight pull him down. He broke into a run past Nighthawk's body. Waves of guilt swept over him as he thought about what he'd done. If she was his mother, he'd never forgive himself. *I'll come back for her after I save these people.* He sprinted down the hallway and hesitated at the door. *What am I going to do?* Kai would get all angry and go charging in. He'd probably come out the victor, too. *I'm not like that. I'm not a fighter. Maybe I should go get him.* A baby shrieked. He didn't have time to get anyone. He gripped the shield tighter and flung open the door.

Twenty of the prisoners stood on the altar. Their hands were shackled to a long chain that ran above their heads and was padlocked on each side of the altar. The wood shifted under their feet as they fought against the bonds. One woman with only one hand chained held a wailing baby close to her chest. Her shoulders shook as she wept.

Rica was climbing down the far ladder. He walked around the altar and stopped when he saw Taryn. "Moran?" He called without turning from Taryn. "Someone's here."

Moran put down the torch and strolled toward him. "What are you doing here? Did Nighthawk send you?"

Taryn approached the altar. "Let them go. Now."

Moran burst out laughing. "You think you could stop me? With a shield?" He sobered. "Do you see this?" He pointed to the tattoo of his two spirals. "You know what this means. I passed the first two tests. Once this task is done, Belial promised me the title of Eldest Priest and all of the blessings that come with it. So you see, there's nothing you can do. Your magic won't stop me." He looked Taryn up and down. "Rica, go get the others. We've got a lot to do tonight."

Rica hesitated. "What about him?"

"If I can't handle this," Moran scoffed. "I'm not worthy of the title of Eldest."

"Where's Lizzy?" Taryn asked Rica.

Rica refused to meet Taryn's eyes. "You'll see her soon enough." Sadness seemed to pass over his face before he shook himself and strode out of the room.

Taryn swallowed. *What did that mean?* He winced. *Has she been caught?* Moran ignored Taryn as he marched to the altar, his white robes swirling around his feet. Taryn shifted on his feet, unsure of what to do. Moran picked up a torch. Taryn looked up at the altar. A small boy around seven stared down at him. His sandy hair was messy and his face was dirty, but his hazel eyes showed only confusion. The bald man to the boy's right stood with his hands chained. His head was hung low as he sobbed.

"Are you going to save us?" the boy asked. "I know you can. Look, Da, don't cry." The boy tried to move closer to his Da, but the chains pulled him back.

"I...I can't stop him," Taryn stammered. "He's almost an Eldest. That makes him very, very powerful. I'm sorry. I can't."

"He's...he's going to kill us!" The man gulped out through his tears to the boy. "No one can save us now."

The little boy's face fell and tears began to form in his eyes. "That's not true, is it?" He looked back at Taryn, his face full of misery. "I thought you were going to save me. I don't want to die."

Taryn glared at the boy's father. He was sick of fathers who made their kids cry. *How many nights did I cry, missing Mom and Dad? How many times did Pater get that look of disappointment on his face and walk away leaving me feeling empty?*

"I'll stop him," Taryn promised. "Just don't cry."

The little boy choked back his tears. *Rica said to swing and hit.* He took his axe and rushed Moran. He was close when he swung. As the axe arched, it grew heavy. Taryn lurched to a stop. It continued to get heavier as he strained. His wrist burned until he dropped the axe. It fell to the floor and crashed.

Moran laughed as Taryn glared at him. *What can I do against magic?* The people chained on top of the altar began to scream again as Moran lit the wood with the first torch. The fire spluttered as it grew. Taryn left the axe on the floor and charged. He was inches away from Moran when the priest flicked his hand. Taryn felt a punch in his stomach from an invisible giant fist. He fell to the floor, gasping and clutching his stomach. Moran picked up the second torch, regarded Taryn, and threw it casually onto the wood. Taryn heard the little boy screaming.

I can't attack him, but I can put out the fire! He ran to the torch and pulled it free from the wood. The torch clattered as it flew across the room. The fire was eating at the wood in the pile. The smoke made him cough as he burned his hands on one log, but he managed to pull it free. *It's working!*

The people were watching him. Da even stopped his sobbing. He flung the kindling away from the altar. His chest tightened. He rubbed it, but the feeling intensified. The wood fell from his hands as he gasped for a breath. The pressure squeezed the breath out of his lungs. He looked up, black spots appearing in front of his eyes, to see Moran staring at him coolly. Moran pointed at Taryn and then waved his hand to the wall across the room. Taryn's body was picked up off the floor. He flew across the fire, seeing the boy's scared eyes, and slammed into the wall with his left shoulder. He heard a crack in his shoulder as pain swept over his body.

He slid to the floor. The bag of salt fell onto his back, knocking the wind out of him. He got to his knees, unable to put any weight on his left arm. Pain shot through his wrist to his stomach, leaving a sick feeling every time he tried to move his arm. The room was filling with smoke as the fire grew larger. Moran threw the last torch onto the wood. The sound of his laughter covered the screams as the fire licked at the toes of the people on the altar.

* * *

Lizzy groaned as a piercing headache shot through her brain. She couldn't even remember where she was. She sat up and held her head. It felt like an army of tiny soldiers stabbing her with sharp swords. She rubbed her forehead and moaned again. *What happened? Where am I?* She squinted through iron bars.

She was *inside* the iron bars! The memory of Rica flooded back. He had knocked her out and thrown her in the prison. *Is he planning to sacrifice me, too?* She knew from the look in his eyes he was capable of it.

She got to her knees and grabbed the bars for support. Her whole body ached as she moved. She limped to the gate and shook it as if it would magically open. The chain rattled, but the gates stayed locked. Disgusted, she spun around and leaned against it, surveying her fellow prisoners. They were watching her silently with eyes filled with despair.

"Where is she?" Lizzy asked. "Where's the woman with the baby?"

Silence. A few people shifted. Others wouldn't look at her.

"What happened?" Her voice rose, but she didn't care. "What did Rica do?"

"He took them," an older man answered slowly. "He threw you in and grabbed maybe twenty people, fastened them to a big long chain, and left. He said he'd be back for more."

Lizzy bit her lip as panic and helplessness swept through her. She felt the bars against her back. She wanted to shake them and scream, but she knew that wouldn't help. She was alone. Taryn and Kai were gone. She was trapped. And alone.

A scream of fear and pain echoed through the hallway. Lizzy had heard a pig shriek like that when it was butchered. She felt goose bumps rise on her arms as she clung to the bars.

"They're being burned," the man whispered as the scream died off. "You've got to save us before it's too late."

"What can I do?" Lizzy asked, frantic to get out. "I don't have any way to stop this."

The shrieks grew louder. It was all her fault. She'd failed again. She wiped the tears on her cheeks away with the rough sleeve of her cloak as she remembered the little baby. The sounds of wailing increased as Rica pushed open a door. Behind him, she saw the hallway slope up to another room. The prisoners pressed against the back wall as he approached, leaving Lizzy alone by the gates.

"You're awake," Rica said with no emotion. "Have you come to your senses yet?"

Lizzy blinked back the tears and faced him. "You're a murderer."

"Grow up, will you?" Rica stopped in front of her and jiggled the key. "Yes, a few will die, but their deaths will save the world. If you can be calm, I can help you. We'll be a family again."

Pictures sprang to mind of returning to Mother and being greeted with hugs. Lizzy could feel Mother's arms around her. She could hear the words *I love you*. And all she had to do was go along with Rica. Tears began to fall again. She wiped them away angrily and adjusted her pack on her back. Under her cloak, her hand brushed one of the darts for the norsaq. Her fingers wrapped around it and squeezed it tight.

"Please," the man said behind her. "Please don't let him burn us like he did those others."

"Enjoy talking," Rica's dark eyes flashed with hate. "You're next."

Lizzy gasped, jolted out of her dreams. His face, through the bars, was full of loathing as he glared at the other prisoners. *How could we be a family again when he's like that?* He used to make them laugh. Now she couldn't see any laughter in his eyes. The key sparkled in the light. *If I could get that key, I could get us out of here.*

She whipped the dart out, her cloak flying around her. Before she could think or tell herself to stop, she thrust it through the bars of the cell and plunged it deep into Rica's stomach. Rica's eyes grew wide as the dart plunged into him. She screamed as she watched blood pour from the wound.

Rica stumbled back. She let the dart slip through her fingers. He swayed. Blood leaked between his fingers, soaking his stomach. His face grew white, making his dark eyes stand out. He had a confused look on his face as he looked up at her.

"W…why did y…you..?" He crumpled to the ground.

She fell to her knees and reached to him, but he was out of her grasp. "No, no, no!" The words poured out of her. "I didn't mean to do that. I just couldn't let you kill these people." She pushed against the bars, but they didn't move. "What have I done?"

Screams echoed down the hallway again. *Someone's still alive in that room!* She jumped to her feet. Someone would be coming soon, and she had to help Rica. *Where'd the key go?* She peered through the bars and saw a flash of metal. The key was lying on the ground past Rica. *He must've thrown it when he fell.* She took out another dart, and tried to pull the key toward her. She stretched as far as she could, but no matter how hard she pushed, the dart was too short.

She had killed her own brother for nothing. There was no way out. The key was out of her reach. She fell to her knees and sobbed.

CHAPTER FIFTY

The Way Out

Kai watched the red blood on Shona's white skin trickle down her throat, mesmerized at the sight of her life draining away. The salt pulled him down. He strained, feeling the burn of the metal frame of the cauldron on his hands, as he struggled to stay out of Belial's reach. Warm blood trickled down his side. He didn't have long before he passed out and fell.

"So, what's it going to be, Kai?" Belial asked, his voice icy. "You can continue in your own stubborn way and refuse to swear allegiance to me. If you do, I'll kill Shona right in front of your eyes. Then I'll rip Northbridge in two, killing the rest of your miserable little family."

Kai glared at Belial through a haze of pain. "I won't let you touch any of my family."

Belial laughed loudly, his cruelty echoing in the sound. "Let me?" He chuckled again. "Wake up, boy. With one word, your dear little Shona will throw herself onto my sword. I am *letting* you choose whether you want to save your family."

Shona shuddered violently. "Kai, only you can save us."

"What about Taryn and Lizzy?" Kai asked. *Maybe Belial is right. Maybe I should just do what he says.*

Belial laughed again. "Of course I won't hurt them. I only wanted to talk to them. It was that meddling Archippos that set you three into a panic."

Kai shifted. He hurt so bad he wondered if he'd be able to climb off the cauldron. *It's so hard to think.* "I'll do what you say if no one gets hurt," Kai agreed.

"Come off the cauldron," Belial commanded.

Kai crawled toward the stone floor. The bag of salt caught on the frame. He jerked it angrily until it pulled free. He slipped and caught himself on the frame between the cauldron and the room. In front of him was a small stone. He picked it up. *An uncut gem. Eladar said Adoyni chose me out of a field of thousands.* He straightened up, fighting tremors of pain, balanced on the lip of the cauldron. Eladar's words echoed in his head.

Wind tousled his hair as he fingered the pebble. He smelled the sweet aroma of the pond where they'd found the salt. He remembered the stone where Lesu was killed. Strength drifted on the wind with the aroma. Something flashed in his eyes, and he saw his sword lying past Belial.

It wasn't about doing what he wanted. He suddenly knew he had to surrender to Adoyni's will, to His great love, and let Adoyni protect everyone he loved. Surrendering wasn't shameful. It took a strong man to allow Adoyni to do His will. And that strong man would do great things. *Do what You want with my sword, Adoyni. It's no longer mine. It's Yours.*

The sight of Belial poised to take Shona's life no longer made Kai hot with rage. A strange peace settled on him.

"You can't give life. You can only corrupt it, taint it, and twist it to be a living death. You'll never be a god." He straightened up, the rock still in his hand. "I know Adoyni will take care of my family. And I've had enough of you hunting me down and hurting my friends. It stops here!"

He dove for Belial, planning to use his hands to tear Belial apart, but the sack of salt caught again on the frame. Kai twisted and pulled the bag from his back. He hurled it at Belial, determined to knock his head off. The wound in his side sent searing pain across his chest as the bag swung. It flew out of his hand. Kai roared as the bag fell short. Belial pulled his arm back to kill Shona. The bag dropped into the gap to the river. The sword flashed at Shona's neck. Kai struggled to reach her. He heard a splash as the salt hit the water as he scrambled off the cauldron.

Belial's sword barely moved, as if time flowed slower. *Like when I beat Alyn!* Kai's sword lay ten feet away. He gauged Belial's movements with satisfaction. Diving for his blade, he somersaulted as he grabbed it and sprang to his feet. Belial's sword was only a fraction of an inch from Shona's neck.

Kai leaped to Belial. With a swift stroke, he blocked the cold steel and swung his blade for the kill. Belial responded sluggishly to his attack and twisted away. Kai lunged at him but missed Belial's neck, connecting with his arm instead. The limb fell to the ground. Kai ignored the nausea that rose as Belial held his right shoulder and screamed with pain.

Kai swung again as frothy water shot out of the hole, drenching the cauldron. Brown filth rushed to his feet, churning angrily, soaking Kai as it gained momentum and filled the room. It smelled so rank that Kai wanted to throw up. He ran to Shona, but the water pushed him away as it grew deeper, filling the room with the taint. He gagged as he accidently swallowed some of the filth. He spat quickly as his stomach rolled. *I can't get sick from one swallow, can I?* He wanted to throw up, but he caught a glimpse of Belial running to the door. Kai thrashed through the water after him but was knocked back by a large wave.

A blast sounded under his feet, and the stones of the floor began to rock. Water pushed through the floor. Kai saw a geyser erupting from the hole in the floor. It hit the ceiling and knocked the stones free. He held his hands over his head as he felt the floor disappear from his feet. A stone landed on his head, and he blacked out.

Lizzy knelt on the hard stone floor, ignoring the pain in her knees. She stayed there, as close to Rica as she could get, and stared at the key through a haze of tears. *I killed him, and I didn't get the key.*

"Miss," the man behind her whispered. "You've got to do something."

"Why don't you do something?" Lizzy snapped without turning. "Why does it have to be me? In case you haven't noticed, I'm locked up like you. There's nothing special about me."

The words hung in the air. That summed up her life. Nothing special. No one ever noticed if she was around. No great talent. No great beauty. The tears flowed faster as she watched Rica. He hadn't moved. The pool of blood grew larger around him. *Why was I so stupid?* She put her face in her hands and sobbed.

Suddenly a fresh wind blew her hair back from her face. She stopped crying to look up, expecting to see a door open, but the room was unchanged. The wind dried her tears and brought the scent of flowers. She closed her eyes. She hadn't seen flowers since that meadow where they had found the shrine for Adoyni. The aroma swept away her aches, her tears. It replaced them with the wonderful feeling of peace. Of love.

She remembered what Eladar had said. *You are wanted by One who loves you more than you can ever imagine. Created by One who brought you into existence only to talk to you. And you can do more than you ever dreamed.*

She smiled, breathing in the sweet smell. She knew now that she couldn't make Mother love her. But that didn't make her unworthy of love. That didn't mean no one else loved her. She remembered the stone where Lesu was killed. *Adoyni's love is far greater than Mother's, and I've ignored Him, just as Mother ignored me. I will not spend the rest of my life chasing after Mother's love.*

She wiped away all of her tears and, using the bars, got to her feet. *Now, Adoyni, please help me save these people. And me.* The weight of the salt dug the straps of the bag into her shoulders. *Well, however I'm getting out of here, I'm not carrying this stupid salt anymore!* She dropped the bag to the floor.

She walked down the row of metal bars, shaking each one. Nothing gave. She examined the walls around her, but they were carved out of the stone the castle was built on. She sighed in frustration. *There has to be a way out.* She walked back. *Or some way to open that lock.*

She tripped over the bag of salt. She caught herself with the bars and glared at it. *What a waste of energy to cart the dumb thing around!* She kicked it and hopped on one foot while her toes stung. The lock flashed in the light, teasing her.

Then a thought hit her. *That's just dumb, but it's worth a shot.* She tore open the bag of salt and pulled out a handful. Stretching through the bars, she dribbled it on the lock. It trickled out of her hand, over the lock, and to the ground. Nothing happened. She wiped her hand off on her pants, angry at such a stupid idea, and turned her back to the lock. *What else is there, Adoyni?*

The man who had been talking to her stood up and joined her at the gates. "Do that again," he ordered.

The metal where the salt had touched was a darker color, and it looked like it was flaking a bit. She yelped with excitement and poured on more salt. After a few seconds, the metal began to rust away. She shrieked for joy. The man started pouring salt on the bars around the gate.

She reached through the bars and tugged on the lock. It held for a second and then crumbled to the ground. She pulled the chain free, her hands shaking with urgency to get to Rica. Pushing the door open, she ran to her brother's side. She carefully turned him over to see that the dart was still impaling him. She gritted her teeth and pulled it free. His face was whiter than normal. As she pushed back his dark hair from his eyes, he took a shuddering breath and lay still.

"Rica!" she cried. "You're alive."

He took another breath. "Maybe."

She laughed, tears coming from relief. She dashed them away quickly. *I've never cried this much before!* "Are you okay?"

"First you stab me to death and then you nurse me back to health." His voice was weak, but his complexion didn't seem so white. "Sisters are the death of their older brothers."

"If you can joke, you're fine!" Lizzy grinned. "I'm sorry, but it's just that…" She didn't know how to finish that sentence. "Are you not weird anymore?"

"I'm not sure how to answer that," Rica grinned feebly. "If I say I'm weird, are you going to stab me again?"

"You *are* back to normal!" Lizzy ignored his joke. *Alyn said the darts could cut through the vilest evil to bring new life. The dart must have killed the evil in Rica.* "The dart fixed you!"

"Yes, it almost did," Rica said dryly. He was warily examining the wound in his stomach. "A few inches lower, and no grandchildren for Mother and Dad."

She blushed. "Well, you weren't really giving me much time to aim."

Rica sobered. "I'm sorry. I did some terrible stuff and said horrible things to you. I wasn't myself, but that doesn't excuse my actions. Will you forgive me?"

Lizzy started to accept his apology, but the screams from the other room began again with a fury. They echoed through the room and cut off her words. Rica's face grew white again.

"I killed them, didn't I?" he whispered. "I took them into that room… oh, no." He groaned. "I've got to get out of here. By the gates, there's a turn in the river. I'll meet you there."

He struggled to his feet and hung on to her for support. He held a hand over his wound.

Lizzy clung to him. "I need you to help me get these people away. There's Unwanteds and Seekers here, and they're not going just let us walk out of here. Don't go."

Rica faced her. "I can't do it, Lizzy. I'm sorry. I can't risk facing Nighthawk or Belial. I feel like they could take me back with one snap of their fingers. I'm not the hero you think I am. You're that hero." He gave her a strong hug. "I love you."

"I love you, too," she whispered, fighting tears again.

Rica shuffled to a door on the opposite side of the room. He opened it, and with a long look, disappeared.

She gulped back the tears and smiled. She turned to the other prisoners. "Come on." She picked up her norsaq. "I know the way out of here."

CHAPTER FIFTY-ONE

Out of the Frying Pan

Taryn struggled to his feet while trying to catch his breath. Through the flames and smoke, he saw the prisoners trying to stomp out the fire. The wood shifted under their feet, and they hung by their wrists until they found stable ground. The fire grew stronger as it reached the bigger logs. The little boy was crying now, but his Da didn't seem to notice.

Moran ignored Taryn as he tended to the fire. Taryn was fascinated by Moran. The ease in which he had flung Taryn around awed him. *To have power like that.* He wished he had brought his crystal sphere instead of the stupid salt and shield. *It's all Father's fault for not letting me study at the Temple like I wanted. I could've been just like Moran.* He swallowed.

But Moran was evil. Willing to murder for more power. *And I want that?* He saw the flames leap up higher on the altar. *What can I do? Any attack on Moran, and he'll knock me back without a thought.* He picked up his shield and gasped as the pain shot up his arm and into his back. *Adoyni, help me know what to do.* He heaved the salt onto his back. "You've got it all wrong," he shouted.

Moran stopped what he was doing. "Go away before you get seriously hurt."

"You think you want power, but it's toxic. One small taste of it will poison your soul, and you won't even know it." Taryn moved closer to the fire, feeling the heat from the flames. "You think it will fill that void in your life. But it won't." *Who am I talking to, Moran or me?* "All the magic in Eltiria will never give you what you want. I wanted to be just like you, but now I see what you are."

"What am I?" Moran forgot about the fire, his brown eyes flashed with anger.

"You're a slave filled with cravings for power. You'll never get enough, and you'll end up bitter and empty. I'll take whatever Adoyni gives. If He wants to use me to do something great, I'll be here for Him to use." Taryn saw the little boy staring at him. His cheeks were wet from tears. His Da was ignoring him as he wallowed in his grief. *I'm not going to let that boy die alone.* "And I'll die if that's what He wants."

Taryn broke into a run and leaped up onto the altar. The flames singed his robe as he scrambled over the burning logs and flames. He smothered the sparks on his clothes, coughing. His eyes stung from the smoke surrounding him.

"Are you insane?" Moran yelled. "You want to burn with them. Fry yourself up!" Moran raised both his hands.

Fire shot up over Taryn's head, and he dove to the center of the altar where the fire hadn't reached yet. He grabbed the chain and felt his hands burn.

"What are you doing up here?" the little boy asked. "Go fight him!"

"I'm getting you out of here," Taryn messed the boy's hair up. He started coughing as the smoke suffocated him.

There had to be a way to put out the fire, but everything around him was flammable. Wood. *Clothes?* Maybe he could smother the flames with their clothes. He gave up on that idea. The flames were higher than his head now. He shifted his pack. *Salt!* He shook his head. *That's got to be the dumbest idea I've ever had.*

The fire popped in front of him, and the log he was standing on shifted. He was thrown off balance and caught the chain to stay on his feet. *It's all I've got.* A woman began shrieking as the flames lit her skirt on fire. An older man on the other end was twisting frantically trying to put out the fire that was crawling up his legs.

Taryn threw the salt into the fire. He scattered it around as far as he could reach until the bag was empty. The fire raged around him. He threw the bag into the blaze with fury. The flames were brighter than any fire he'd seen before. It was so intense that it was glowing orange. *It's all going to blow, and we're in the center of it all!* He grabbed the chain. "Adoyni, protect us!" He shouted as he held the shield above his head.

The fire soared above him, but the heat faded away. Close to him, the flames popped and emitted little puffs of smoke as they died out. The flames were so bright Taryn had to shade his eyes. The blaze grew until he was inside a ball of orange flames, the shield creating a shelter around everyone on the altar.

A distant rumbling around them grew louder. Taryn squeezed his eyes shut as the brilliance overtook him. There was a large explosion and a sudden force of wind. Taryn opened his eyes to see the logs falling to the ground as the flames were extinguished. The fire was gone. The people on the altar cheered as they saw the chains had melted away, and they were free.

Taryn laughed, not believing what he saw. "It was Adoyni's shield. It protected us. Did you see that?"

The little boy grinned at him. "I knew you could do it."

Taryn grinned and scrambled off the altar. There was no sight of Moran. Only a pile of ashes and a melted crystal sphere was lying on the ground. *So his magic wasn't strong enough to conquer Adoyni!* He laughed as he helped each person off the altar. The woman with a baby gave him a giant kiss on his cheek, which made him blush as red as the fire. She chuckled and shifted her baby to her other arm. The little boy placed his hand firmly in Taryn's good hand.

"Let's go." Taryn squeezed the boy's hand and led the way off the ruined altar. "I know the way out."

* * *

Kai opened his eyes and saw stars above him. He jumped to his feet, feeling his side throb. Rocks and rubble fell off him as he stood. All that was left of the tower was a large pile of stone and rocks. He heard the roar of the river far below his feet. He crawled over the piles and looked down the deep hole. The river was flowing cleanly and freely. The poison was gone.

He grinned. It was done. It was time to return to Rhiana now. *Shona!* He leaped to his feet and bounded over the piles to the courtyard. *Where'd she go?* He gasped, trying to ignore the waves of sharp pain from his side, but he couldn't. Pausing, he ripped his cloak and wrapped it around his chest, pulling it as tight as he could. *That should work for awhile. Where'd Shona go?* Something glinted off to his right. It was the hilt of his sword. He pulled it out from the rocks. It was undamaged. He ran a finger over the word.

"Okay, Adoyni, I get the message," Kai whispered. "I surrender. Now what?"

He heard a scream from the courtyard and ran out of the destroyed tower. Taryn enter the courtyard, holding the hand of a little boy. Taryn moved funny, like his arm was hurt, and he looked like he'd been through a fire. He stumbled once and came to a stop. Lizzy emerged from a doorway across from Kai with a large crowd of people behind her. Kai turned to see what she was pointing at frantically.

As he moved into the courtyard, he saw Belial. He was dripping wet and holding a long sword. Blood streaked down his right side and his sleeve hung empty. Kai had never seen such raw hatred before, and it chilled him to the bone. He realized that Belial was only playing with him before. Now Belial was truly angry.

Kai gripped his sword and strode toward Belial, determined to cut him down where he stood. A flash of light caught his eye. Eladar was inside the courtyard facing Belial. Eladar stood with wings extended. He pawed the ground and shook his head, the long white mane flowing like a waterfall.

Well done! All three of you have exceeded my expectations. I'm so proud of you! I'm sorry I wasn't here sooner. Some unexpected things came up that I had to take care of, but I see you didn't need me. His voice was filled with warmth and humor.

"Eladar!" Lizzy shrieked with joy. She sprinted toward him.

Back, daughter! I don't want any of you around Belial. Even wounded like that, he's too much for you right now. Wait until I have distracted him and then slip out the gates. Get these people to safety.

Lizzy stopped, confusion in her eyes. "But I thought we won."

Not until you are out of here and Belial is taken care of. Go now.

"But what about you?" Kai asked. "We can help fight." He lifted his sword and fought back the pain as it swept through his body.

No! Get to safety. I'll be fine, and I'll find you when this is over. As to reinforce his words, Eladar reared, pawing the air, and charged Belial.

Belial waited calmly as Eladar approached. As the Archippos thundered closer, Belial swung with his sword clumsily with his left hand. Eladar dodged and struck out with his teeth. Belial jumped back quickly and tripped over a rock. He fell as Eladar circled him. Kai cheered. *Eladar will be fine. I don't know what I was worried about.*

Belial got to his feet, his face white with rage. He watched Eladar for a minute and then flung out his hand like he was wiping something off a table. The doors around the courtyard creaked open. Unwanteds spilled from the rooms, filling the courtyard. Three Seekers followed them. Kai gripped his sword.

"Kill them all," Belial screamed. "I'll take care of the Archippos."

Kai watched as the surge of Unwanteds raced toward Lizzy and Taryn. *How are we going to fight so many?* As he stared at the Unwanteds, the people behind Taryn and Lizzy pressed forward. With a great cry, they grabbed rocks and rushed to meet Belial's army.

Kai grinned. *That should even the scale a little.* He bounded toward Lizzy and Taryn. *In a few minutes, this should all be over!*

* * *

Lizzy yelped as Kai swept her up in a big hug, squeezing the air out of her. "Get away from me," she gasped out. "You're soaking wet."

"Were you taking a bath while we did all the work?" Taryn asked as he pounded Kai on the shoulder. He grinned as Kai yelled in pain.

"Yeah, and fixing the river!" Kai rubbed his shoulder. "The water's clean again. What were you doing? Playing with fire?"

Taryn grinned, his teeth brilliant white against his dirty face. "Something like that."

The Unwanteds slowed as the prisoners met them. There was a clash and roar of fighting. Eladar stood his ground, but the three Seekers circled behind him.

"Chickens," Lizzy yelled at the Seekers. "Come here and fight if you're brave enough."

Taryn looked at her like she had lost her mind. The Seekers roared and raced toward them, dodging through the crowd.

"You got your wish," Taryn groaned. "They're coming for us."

She took her sling out and swung at an Unwanted in front of them. The stone soared gracefully past the Unwanted and fell.

Kai shook his head. "I don't know why you keep trying to use that thing. You have the worst aim."

She glared at him. "Just do something useful for once."

Kai grinned, but she noticed the pain in his eyes and saw blood streaking down his side. Taryn held his arm in a funny way. *Even with the prisoners and Eladar, we may not get out of here alive. Adoyni, I don't want to die.* She had a sick feeling in her stomach.

Do not give up hope, daughter. Eladar spoke in her mind. *Adoyni is with us.* The thought swept through her mind like a cool breeze.

Kai yelled, scaring her, and ran at an Unwanted. Taryn followed, swinging his axe and holding his shield awkwardly with his bad arm. Lizzy leaped to join them. The Unwanteds surrounded them in their fury. Lizzy blocked one attack with her sword. Remembering what Alyn had taught them, she twisted and brought the blade down quickly. It worked. She felt a jolt. The Unwanted froze and fell to the ground as she pulled her sword free. Her stomach lurched as she watched it die, but another Unwanted grabbed her hair and pulled her backwards. She screamed as she was dragged off balance. She stabbed behind her. The sword found its mark. She tripped and fell on the Unwanted, slashing as she fell. It never got up again.

She got to her feet and saw Kai. Unwanteds lay scattered at his feet. She held her breath as more grabbed at him. He hacked at one holding a dagger. He missed. The dagger slipped past his guard and stabbed him. He crumpled to the ground, holding his stomach. The Unwanted stood over him, dagger raised for the killing blow.

Lizzy grabbed her sling. Kai's words echoed in her head. *You have the worst aim.* She remembered what Alyn said. *Clear your mind. Think of nothing else but what your target is. Your aim will be true.*

She focused on the Unwanted. She swung and aimed. The stone flew out of her sling. For a moment, she thought she had let go too soon, but the rock arced at the last minute and slammed into the Unwanted's forehead, jerking its head back as it fell.

"Well, what do you know?" Kai grinned weakly as he got to his feet. "That thing really works!" His smile faded. "Behind you, Lizzy!"

She spun to see a Seeker pushing through the crowd toward her. The Unwanteds pulled back to let him pass. Her heart seemed to stop pounding as it drew closer. She looked at the sling in her hands. It was a little weapon against a giant warrior. It wasn't enough.

"I'm going to rip your throat out," Lizzy growled. Her words trembled a bit.

The monster grinned, his yellow teeth sharp and rotten. He ran at Lizzy and swung his axe. She stared at the axe as it whistled through the air toward her face.

CHAPTER FIFTY-TWO

This Is For...

Taryn heard Lizzy screaming, but he couldn't help her. He swung wildly at an Unwanted rushing at him. The axe hit the creature's sword. He pulled back and blocked the attack with his shield. His breath came in gasps, but he wasn't backing down. He spun on his heel, his axe outstretched. As he turned, the Unwanted moved to block his advance. *Got you!* He twisted his axe, and it slipped under the sword and into the beast's chest. The Unwanted fell to the ground.

He turned to see a Seeker heading for him and gripped his axe tightly. Taryn knew that he'd done better than he expected fighting the Unwanteds, but this was a trained warrior. He couldn't face it alone. Then he realized that he didn't have to. He had Adoyni to fight for him. He shifted his shield, ignoring the nausea that swept through him.

The Seeker swung at him with the axe. He dodged and felt a sting in his cheek where the axe grazed it. He tripped over a rock as he retreated. The Seeker smirked and jumped closer.

Taryn regained his balance and poised. The Seeker chuckled without any humor. It swung quicker than lightning. The axe deflected off Taryn's shield and bit into his leg. He cried with pain as warm blood ran down. He tried to take a step, but his leg crumbled underneath his weight. He caught himself before falling and stood on one leg. The Seeker closed in again.

This time Taryn waited, standing firm like Eladar always said to do. His fear calmed. His breathing was steady. The Seeker attacked again, but this time Taryn whispered a prayer and raised his shield as his arm shrieked in pain.

Nothing magical happened. The axe was heading straight for his unprotected head. He almost panicked but gritted his teeth, trusting Adoyni to protect him. There was a bang. The axe stopped in midair, blocked by nothing that Taryn could see. The amber eyes of the Seeker grew wide with fright as Taryn laughed. Adoyni proved once again to be stronger than any magic.

"This is for Mischa," Taryn yelled. He swung the axe at the creature's head. It raised its arms to protect itself, but the axe cut through them and hit it in the forehead. The Seeker roared as Taryn pulled it free. "And this is for scaring the wits out of me." Taryn pivoted on his good leg and hit the monster in the chest. It gasped and fell to the ground. He stood over it, his body pulsating with pain and drenched in blood, but he'd never felt better.

Until he saw Lizzy. She was facing a Seeker with just the sling. The sling that she never hit anything with. He yelled at Kai to help her, but he was circling another Seeker. Glancing over to Eladar, Taryn knew he couldn't help as he was locked in battle with Belial. Belial threw a stone from the demolished tower at Eladar. It spun through the air and hit him in the chest, leaving a large red spot. Eladar screamed in pain.

He's going to die. And then we're all going to die.

* * *

Kai raised his sword. *Surrender* gleamed in the setting sun. *Adoyni, work your will. But, I'd really like us to live!*

The Unwanteds charged. The first one to reach him didn't even have a weapon. Kai evaded the attack and slashed its head off. The blow sent radiating streams of pain through his body. He gasped and tried to breathe normally, trying not to look at the headless body, trying not to throw up, trying not to think of them as people. They came in an endless sea. Everything became a blur as he struggled to stop their attacks, to survive. The sea parted, giving him a chance to catch his breath. He panted, his body aching with each movement. *Are we winning? Why did they stop?*

He groaned as he saw a Seeker come through the crowd. It roared a challenge as it drew near. Kai let rage sweep over him. *It's time for it to start feeling some of the pain I'm feeling!* He waited for it to come closer.

The Seeker stopped just out of his reach and chuckled. Its rotting skin shook with the movement. "Surrender? If that's what you wish, then I accept."

Kai's anger grew at the taunting. "You can surrender if you wish. My Lord might have mercy on you."

"Mine won't," the Seeker said. He removed his cloak and threw it to the ground. His chest plate glinted in the sun, blinding Kai. "He's ready to tear your guts out."

He swung his axe, and Kai jumped back. One hit could knock his teeth out. He waited for an opportunity to strike.

"Are you scared?" The Seeker jeered.

Kai gritted his teeth and circled the Seeker. It swung its axe. Kai blocked it. It swatted his sword aside and hit his arm. Kai tumbled and landed on a boulder. He yelled with pain.

The Seeker swaggered to Kai. An evil chuckle filled the air. "I was hoping for more of a fight. This was too easy."

Kai fought back the pain. *It's toying with me.* Kai stood up and glanced over to Lizzy. She was facing a Seeker with the sling in her hands. Her face was white and her hands trembled, but she wasn't backing down. Taryn was fighting a Seeker, but he held the shield up waveringly with his wounded arm. Eladar was battling with Belial, retaliating with lightning and his hooves, but he was covered with blood. *I've got to help them.* He looked back at the amber eyes of the Seeker. They no longer scared him. He knew what he had to do.

He took a deep breath and let it go, picturing anger draining out of his body. "I've had enough of this!"

It leaped back at his words and held the axe in a defensive stance. Kai ignored all caution and lunged at the beast. It blocked his first thrust and flung its axe at him. Kai whirled away from the axe, but as he circled around, the beast punched him in the jaw. His head jerked back as he stumbled over the rocks. The monster gave a roar of triumph and jumped toward him, grabbing up his axe and attacking. The blow missed, but only by an inch.

He rolled away from the Seeker, his head pounding from the force of the blow, and got to his feet. His legs were shaky, and he couldn't catch his breath. *What happened? I thought if I got rid of my anger, my opponent would slow down.* He waited for an opening, praying that Adoyni to slow the Seeker down, and fought back his impatience. *It will happen when Adoyni wants it to.*

The Seeker, seeing a killing blow, lunged, his axe arcing out to Kai's head. Kai blinked. Incredibly, the speed of the weapon slowed to a crawl. Kai grinned. *Now!* He ducked under the axe, brought his sword up, and pierced the chest of the beast. It slid through the armor smoothly.

"This is for Shona," he hissed. He pushed with all his strength and twisted. The Seeker cried out in

agony, dropping the axe. He pulled the sword out
and prepared to strike again. But the Seeker fell to
its knees, clutching its chest. It gasped for one last
breath and fell to the ground.

Kai waited for it to rise, but the beast was dead.
He started to yell with triumph, but Eladar's shriek
filled the courtyard.

Lizzy screamed. The Seeker swung as she
ducked and ran closer to the shelter of the wall
surrounding the courtyard. Spinning on her heel,
she let a stone fly. It flew true and crashed into
the monster's chest. It roared with anger. *That's
not enough to hurt it!* Panic overcame her, making it
hard to think or move.

"Ready to join your dead friends?" The Seeker
raised its axe.

Lizzy swallowed. She didn't have any more
stones. Looking at her feet, the ground was covered
with smooth sand. No stones to throw. The Seeker
closed the distance and attacked with so much
speed she didn't even see the axe coming. She only
felt the blinding pain as the axe sliced her leg. She
shrieked in agony.

It watched her hobble closer to the wall with a
smirk. "It's a good thing I'm going to kill you. How
could you ever tell your Mother that you failed
again? She'll never love you after all of this."

Stumbling back until she felt the cool stone wall on her back, she pulled her norsaq free and loaded a dart on it. The monster growled. She shook with fear. *Adoyni, I need you. I don't want to die now.*

She took her time to aim. The Seeker wore a dark shirt under his cloak. As Lizzy pulled her arm to throw her dart, the shirt shimmered and then disappeared. She blinked and saw armor under the shirt. She winced. *Can this dart pierce armor? Probably not.* But there was a small chink in the iron rings where its heart was. *That's the spot! Adoyni, help me hit that hole!*

The creature rushed her, closing the distance quickly. A few seconds and she could no longer throw a dart at it. She let the dart fly. The monster batted it aside like a toy. She loaded the norsaq again, her hands trembling. She didn't have much time, and that was her last dart. If she missed this time, she was dead. She watched the monster warily and feigned a thrust. As the Seeker brought its axe up to block, she threw the dart with all the strength she had. It flew toward the monster, quicker than lightning, and lodged deep in its chest. The Seeker roared as it fell to the ground. But her victory was short lived when she looked up.

CHAPTER FIFTY-THREE

Chosen

Kai stared in horror as Belial and Eladar dueled. Belial was using magic to lift boulders and hurl them at Eladar. Eladar rose up in the air with his giant wings and dodged them. He streaked through the sky at Belial, but Belial effortlessly tossed another rock. Lightning blasted the stone and shot to Belial, who leaped to the side. His robes were singed.

"Eladar needs our help," Kai yelled to Lizzy and Taryn. "Come on!"

They hobbled through the empty courtyard. The prisoners were streaming out of the gates to follow the river to safety. Belial noticed them coming and alternated throwing the rocks at them and Eladar. Kai dodged the rocks while tripping through the bodies of Unwanteds. Lizzy screamed as a flying rock hurtled toward her. She stared at in horror, like a paralyzed animal in a trap, unable to run. Lightning blazed down from Eladar and hit the rock. Lizzy cowered as small stones pelted her.

Get out of here while I hold him off. Eladar commanded. His voice was weak and weary.

No! Kai argued. *We're not leaving here without you. We can beat him together.*

Eladar faintly chucked. *Always stubborn.*

"Look out!" Taryn yelled.

A beam of wood from the tower soared through the air at Eladar and slammed into his chest. Eladar squealed in pain as he spun through the air, tumbling down in a slow spiral. At the last moment, he spread his wings, slowing his descent. He crashed into the ground and lay still.

Kai roared in anger and sprinted across the courtyard. The rocks were falling like giant deadly raindrops. They landed with a crash and bang. Eladar raised his head. Kai couldn't see what he did, but the rocks stopped without warning. Belial stood with his left arm outstretched like he was frozen.

They raced past Belial and fell to their knees next to Eladar. Kai had a sick feeling in his gut. The way that Eladar laid reminded him of when Kedar died. Eladar's wings were stretched out along the ground, and his head was in the dirt. One front leg was twisted in a funny way, and the ground around him was red with blood.

You must go now. Find a way to cleanse the river and then leave. Because of your work, Kai, Belial was too weak to resist the prison I put him in. I did all I could, but it won't hold for long. I can fight no longer.

Kai tried to stop the flow of Eladar's blood with his cloak. "It's done already. We found salt in the desert where Lesu was killed, and it cleansed the river." He looked at his cloak, soaked with blood. "How can we help you?" His voice shook.

"It did?" Taryn interrupted, curiosity filling his tone. He used his cloak for the wounds on Eladar's side. "Why in the world would plain old salt do anything?"

Eladar snorted weakly. *It wasn't plain salt. Those were tears. Each bag was filled with salt from Lesu's tears that He shed for you.*

Kai moved Eladar's head into his lap, hoping to ease the pain. "Cried for us? Why would he do that?"

Because He feels your pain. He sees your grief over your family, Kai. He sees how you long for love, Lizzy. And, Taryn, He knows your loneliness and suffering. But He not only sees it, He feels it too, for He is there with you when you cry. And yet grief has come to good. Grief provided a way to purify the water.

Lizzy smoothed down his white mane, her tears mixing with the blood on her face. "Don't leave us again."

I'm afraid I have no choice, daughter. My time has come. Knowing you was one of the greatest joys of my life. Always remember Adoyni's love and stand firm.

Kai brushed the white forelock out of Eladar's eyes. *He's saying goodbye.* He blinked back the sudden tears, but they spilled down his cheeks.

"But you can't die," Taryn protested. His voice shook. "We need you."

You no longer need me. You have found your power, Taryn. It's in Adoyni. And your true name, the one you have been searching for, is Son of Adoyni.

Tears streamed down Taryn's cheeks, but he didn't say a word.

"Thank you, Eladar," Kai said. His voice broke when he spoke. "Thank you for kidnapping me."

You have allowed Adoyni to polish you into a beautiful gem. One to outshine all the others. I am proud of all of you. Don't trust the other Archippi.

"Why not, Eladar?" Kai asked urgently. He blinked back his tears.

Eladar's eyes flickered once. *The beautiful singing...* His eyes grew blank, and Kai knew he was gone. He closed Eladar's eyes. Lizzy buried her head in his mane and bawled. Taryn put his head in his hands. His shoulders shook as he cried. Kai left his hand on Eladar's head and felt tears race down his cheeks. *What will we do without him?* In the midst of his raw grief, a slow burn of anger grew. *I'm going to rip Belial apart limb by limb.*

He struggled to stand up and limped to Belial. The man was still frozen with his arm outstretched. Kai yelled and swung his sword at him. But the sword hit an invisible wall a foot away from Belial. The force of the blow reverberated through Kai, sending waves of pain through him. He thought he saw Belial's eyes twinkle with malice. He growled and pulled back to strike again.

Taryn stopped him with a hand on his arm. "It's no good. No sword will pierce that wall. Look. He's able to move his hand a little. We'd better get out of here before it wears off."

Kai snarled. "I'm not leaving here until he's dead." But even as he said it, he knew running was the only option. He pointed his sword at Belial. "I'm coming back for you, and I'll make you pay for what you have done." He stumbled to the gate and dropped to the ground, too tired and weak to stand anymore. "I don't think I'll make it through that blasted desert again."

Lizzy wiped her tears away. "Just what do you suggest we do? Fly out of here?"

Kai heard the distant pounding of wings. "Eladar!" He turned, but the white body lay in the middle of the courtyard. He scanned the skies. There on the horizon came three Archippi.

* * *

Lizzy watched the Archippi fly toward them. Angry thoughts swirled through her. *If they had come earlier, maybe Eladar would be alive.* A black Archippi landed beside Eladar followed by a dark bay and a sorrel with white feet. They dipped their heads and sniffed his body. Lizzy sensed their grief as it filled the air. Then rocks began to tremble. They rose from the ground and covered Eladar. Tears streamed down Lizzy's face as Eladar was slowly buried. When it was finished, the Archippi walked to them.

Lizzy stared at Eladar's rock grave. "Why didn't you come sooner?"

The black Archippos shook his head. *It's against the law to enter your world until the king calls us. Eladar was one of the few who dared to break this law.*

"But you came! You just came late!" Lizzy's angry words poured out like her tears.

We overcame our fear too late. We'll never forget what our indecision cost us. Eladar was a true friend. Grief and regret flowed through his words. *You are injured beyond our skill to heal you, but we can take you to Northbridge.*

The black Archippos knelt down beside Lizzy. She slid onto his back, her heart pounding nervously. She held onto the silky mane as he stood up. She heard a chuckle in her mind. *I won't let you fall.*

His wings began to beat, and they left the ground before she knew it. Her heart ached as they rose up to the clouds and Eladar's grave disappeared. His final words echoed in her mind. *Always remember Adoyni's love.* She felt the wind in her face and closed her eyes, lulled into sleep by the steady beat of the wings.

Taryn decided that of all the things they'd done, flying had to be the most terrifying. And the most sickening. His stomach lurched as they flew higher. He clung to the sorrel Archippos and hoped he wouldn't fall off. He watched the countryside slip past as they sped through the clouds. Somewhere

down there was Nighthawk. *What happened to Mom?
Is she okay? What will she say when I tell her that I'm her
son?*

Eladar's words rang in his ears. *Son of Adoyni.
What does that mean?* He was going to find out as
soon as he could. The Archippos turned north, and
Taryn choked back a yell as he almost slipped off.
He grasped the mane tightly and concentrated on
keeping his stomach under control.

* * *

As the bay Archippos lifted from the ground, Kai
looked back at Eladar's grave, fighting tears, as they
circled into the clouds. It was a humble memorial
for one so brave. He saw the Unwanteds scurrying
across the plains. Shona might be down there
somewhere. *Did she recognize me?* He was going to
find her and change her back somehow. He thought
of the rest of his family. *Are they okay? Did Rhiana die?*
Black spots appeared before his eyes as he searched
for Shona. He closed them and fell into darkness.

We're here. Hang on just a while longer. The words
jolted Kai. He tried to sit up but cried out as his
muscles shrieked in agony. Through a haze of pain,
he saw that there was no land, not even a cloud,
under him. Ahead of him was a floating island in
the sky. He could see the layers of dirt as they went
higher. The dirt gave way to thick lush grass.

The pain swept over him, so he put his head down in the bay's mane. He was jerked awake when they landed in a meadow where a crowd of Archippi was waiting. *Archippi in Northbridge?* He blinked, trying to make sense of what he was seeing.

My lord, we found Eladar. The bay Kai was sitting on was talking. His words were filled with grief. *Unfortunately, we were too late. He was killed by the traitor Belial.*

Through the fog of pain, Kai saw Lizzy and Taryn slide off the Archippi and run to him. Lizzy limped, and Taryn was cradling his arm. Kai couldn't figure out why Lizzy was crying. *Is she sad about Eladar?* He tried to ask her, he couldn't get the words out. *What's wrong with me?*

He laid his head back on the Archippos' neck, noticing the blood that streaked down the side and leg of the horse. *He wasn't at the fight. That must be my blood.* He stared at the red, shocked by the amount of it. *Am I going to die?* He felt Lizzy's hand squeeze his.

A tall gray Archippos stepped forward. *You did well to bring them to Merrihaven. They may have been killed in the earthquake at Northbridge. We have just learned that most of the city is gone. Welcome, humans. We know that you are weary, hurt, and filled with grief. Come and enter our halls of healing.*

Kai stopped breathing. *Northbridge! Earthquake!* Like a sharp blow, he remembered Belial had said that he'd rip Northbridge apart. *My family!* He groaned.

Lizzy turned from Kai. "Northbridge! My Dad's there. You have to take us back!"

That's not possible. The gray lowered his head. *We are bound by law not to return until the king commands. You will have to wait here until he calls us back.*

Kai felt a cold horror grip him. Merrihaven was a prison. Eladar said not to trust the Archippi, and they had. The black spots started to take over again, and his hand loosened in Lizzy's.

"We're losing him!" Lizzy yelled.

Kai fought back the darkness and saw a person his age step out from the crowd. He lifted Kai off the bay and onto a litter. Kai tried not to groan, but he couldn't stop himself as the pain became almost unbearable now that he was conscious. He just wanted them to lay him down and leave him alone.

The young man bent over him, his blue eyes reassuring. "You'll be fine. You're in good hands."

"That's because he's in my hands, not yours." A girl with dark hair smiled down at him. "Don't forget that I taught you all you know."

"You're…you're Aric, aren't you?" Lizzy gasped.

"I am. Well, I was." The guy grinned. "It's a long story. I promise to tell it to you later."

Lizzy nodded and blushed. He laughed quietly as they moved to carry the litter. Kai fought back waves of nausea as it rocked back and forth. Lizzy and Taryn walked slowly on each side, their hand on the litter. He took their hands and squeezed. They were still together. They had survived. Their presence smoothed the raw grief and pain he felt.

He'd find a way back to Northbridge, and he'd find his family. And he wasn't going to wait until the king called him back. There was a way. He knew in the deepest part of him that he was chosen. Chosen by Adoyni to do great things. He smiled through the pain. Adoyni would use him to make everything right.

REUNIONS

"Let us draw near to God with a sincere heart
in full assurance of faith,
having our hearts sprinkled to cleanse us from a guilty
conscience and having our bodies washed
with pure water."
~HEBREWS 10:22

Foehn circled above the castle and waited for Belial to move. The courtyard was empty, leaving only the fallen and Eladar's grave behind.

Nighthawk raced down the long stairs that led from Zoria's temple. There was a large red welt on her forehead. Foehn grinned. That boy had a good arm when he wanted it. She gasped when she saw Belial. As she approached, the invisible prison that held him dissipated, and he sank to the ground, weakened by his many wounds. She caught him and carefully laid him in the dirt. She used her dagger to rip her cloak into strips and began to stop the blood.

"You need a doctor," Nighthawk said, her face white.

"I need them killed," Belial groaned. He yelled as Nighthawk pulled the cloth tight around the wound. "They'll be far more dangerous now that they know their true power."

He struggled to sit up. "Foehn, catch up with them. I don't care if you kill those vermin Archippi, but make the three fall to their death. Go now." Belial leaned back against Nighthawk wearily.

Foehn hesitated. He didn't want to obey. He remembered Lesu's love and prayed to Adoyni for help. If those three could fight Belial, he would too.

"What are you waiting for, slave?" Belial was screaming. "Obey, now!"

The last time Foehn had tried to disobey, he didn't have the strength to resist. This time was different. Adoyni's love and power flowed through him. The chains that Belial put on slipped off. Adoyni freed him. He laughed with joy as he spun into the sky.

Belial roared with anger. "Go then! I don't need you! Earth will come to me, and it's stronger than Air." He struggled to his feet, raising his left arm, and uttered a spell. "Take the magic from my heart. Tear Northbridge apart." With a cry, he fell to his knees as Nighthawk supported him.

Foehn ignored them as he whipped away. He was free! The words echoed as he laughed with the birds surrounding him. He had found the only One who could rescue him from his chains, and he was full of joy and peace now. He knew nothing could hold any power over him like Belial had.

He caught up with the Archippi as they flew down River Shammah. The pure water cleaned the toxic water away as it raced to the sea. People in towns and cities cried with delight as the taint was erased.

The Archippi flew through the Razors and up to the sky. Foehn hesitated in the foothills. Home was within his grasp. He was finally free to return, but now he was uncertain. He had dreamt of returning, but now he didn't know what he would find if he dared go back. What would the Ancients say at home? Would they mock him or be ashamed to know him? Would they shun him the way he had shunned them? Questions whirled in his mind as he considered whether he should return. He inched toward home, deciding to take a quick glance before leaving for the final time.

As the trees and streams grew more familiar, he wanted to stay. This was where he belonged. A great sadness grew over him as he thought of how he had turned his back on everything he truly loved and lost it forever. The others would never forget what he had done.

He crept close, but his heart dropped when he saw them hurry to meet him. Foehn stopped, unsure of what to do. But they flew to him, laughing with joy, and caught him up in a strong embrace.

And so he went home, surrounded by the jubilant Ancients, and knew that the past was forgiven, the present was joyful, and the future was filled with hope.

Made in the USA
Charleston, SC
27 February 2013